The Reset

PEONY BROWN

Exit 26 Publishing

About the author

Dear Readers,

Life is a collection of stories—some whispered in quiet moments, others unfolding in the rhythm of our daily lives. We are given glimpses into the human heart through every encounter, shared experience, and unexpected turn. In these moments, stories are born, waiting to be told by those who see the world through the belief that love is the answer.

For years, I worked alongside an extraordinary individual whose quiet strength and unwavering love for her family illuminated my understanding of what love truly means. Her life was not filled with grand gestures or romanticized ideals but with the kind of love that endures—patient, selfless, and deeply rooted in the everyday. She became a testament to the power of love in its purest form, teaching me that the most profound stories are often the ones we live without even realizing.

Her influence became the foundation of my writing, shaping not just this novel but my entire approach to storytelling. Every person we meet carries a story, and every moment holds the potential to reveal something extraordinary. Through these pages, I hope you will find a reflection of your own experiences and be reminded that love—in all its forms—has the power to heal, connect, and transform.

As you journey through this book, I invite you to see the world through this lens. May you recognize the beauty in the everyday, embrace the lessons found in unexpected places, and, most importantly, never forget that love is the thread that binds us all together.

With heartfelt gratitude,

Peony Brown

P.S.

Life is filled with moments of decision—crossroads where we must choose a path, sometimes without knowing where it will lead. These choices become our reset moments, opportunities to change our trajectory and step into something new. Some decisions may seem small initially, but their impact lingers in ways we never expected. Others may feel impossibly heavy, but they reveal themselves as what leads us toward a greater purpose in time.

No one is exempt from these moments. They come to us all, asking us to look within and trust what we find. So when the time comes, listen to your heart—your choice, your reset, will be waiting for you. And through it all, may you walk with grace, knowing that every decision, whether painful or joyful, carries the potential for growth, healing, and love.

To the many families who have touched my heart and demonstrated love in its purest form—to you, I dedicate this book. Your acts of kindness, your unwavering support, and the boundless love you share with those around you have been a beacon of hope and inspiration.

Love begins with a single gesture in its most contagious and rewarding state: loving just one person and extending them grace. This grace binds us together in a world where none of us are perfect, and our perspectives often diverge. It allows us to embrace our differences and find common ground in our humanity.

This story is for everyone on their journey to discover the profound impact of loving their neighbor. May we all find the courage to give love a chance, to forgive generously, and to cherish the connections that make our lives richer.

With deepest gratitude and hope,

Peony Brown

Contents

Chapter 1: Streets of Chicago

The afternoon sun was casting a warm glow across the west side of Chicago, its sunrays dancing on the faces of the neighborhood's residents. Girls in colorful dresses were jumping rope on the sidewalk, their laughter rising and falling with each turn. Even though it was not the right thing to do, some boys started looking at the girls as the dresses began to fly up on the backside of the girls. It was playful and peaceful because the girls around this neighborhood knew this would draw particular attention from the boys. Then, in a nearby park, you can hear the sounds of some young boys playing a spirited basketball game with their sneakers squeaking against the weathered concrete and talking at each other. Through all that, you could still hear the rhythmic thuds of baseballs hitting mitts echoing from the corner of another park.

Amidst this symphony of everyday life, here I am, a teenage black man named Turland Deville, some around the neighborhood sometimes call me "Caddy," sitting on the stoop of our apartment building, with a small pebble twirling between my fingers, with my gaze drifting toward the horizon, and the distant Chicago skyline a hazy promise of something more. This pebble rolls smoothly across my palm, its calm surface in contrast to the warmth of my skin. So, I turned it over, studying its contours as if it held the answers to the questions that lingered in my mind.

The creak of the door behind me breaks my reverie. Jerry emerges, his restless energy palpable as he paces back and forth on the stoop. Dame follows, leaning against the railing with effortless grace, while Russell sprawls out on the steps below, his eyes tracking the pretty black girls who pass by.

"Yo, Turland," Jerry calls out, his voice cutting through my thoughts. "You have been out here all day or what?"

I shrug, a faint smile playing on my lips. "Just thinking, man. Just thinking."

Dame chuckles, shaking his head. "You always thinking, T. What's on your mind this time?"

My fingers close around the pebble, its edges pressing into my palm. "The future, I guess. What's out there beyond all this."

Russell laughs, his voice carrying a hint of joy. "Beyond all this? Man, you dreaming again."

I meet his gaze, my own unwavering. "Maybe. But sometimes, dreams are all we got."

The words hang between us, a shared understanding of the hopes and fears that bind us together. On this stoop, we realized we are more than just four friends—we are brothers, united by the challenges and possibilities of the world we inhabit.

I look down at the pebble in my hand, its surface warmed by my touch. It is a small thing, insignificant to most. But to me, it holds a glimmer of promise – a reminder that even the most ordinary object can have the potential for change.

The sun continues its slow descent, casting long shadows across the street. As we sit together, the sounds of the neighborhood washing over us, I can't help but feel a flicker of hope—hope for a future that is ours to shape, a future that lies just beyond the horizon.

Jerry's voice breaks through my thoughts, his words tinged with a familiar frustration. "It's all good to dream, Turland, but what about now? What about the fact that we're stuck here with no money, prospects, or way out?"

I turn to face him, my expression thoughtful. "I hear you, Jerry. But just because we're here now doesn't mean we'll be here forever. We gotta keep believing there's something better out there for us."

Dame snorts, his tone sarcastic. "Yeah, right. Like what? A fancy job? A big house? That stuff's not for people like us, man."

I shook my head, my voice calm but firm. "No, not like that. I'm talking about something deeper. Something that gives our lives meaning, you know? Something that makes us feel like we matter."

Russell sits up, his eyes narrowing. "And what's that supposed to be?"

I pause, searching for the right words. "I don't know exactly. But I feel it deep down. It's like there's this light waiting to be let out. And maybe, if we keep pushing, keep believing, we'll find a way to make it shine."

Jerry stops pacing. His gaze locked on mine. "That's some poetic shit, Turland. But how's that going to help us pay that light bill? How will that keep us from ending up like our families and others out here, working ourselves to death for nothing?"

I lean forward, my elbows resting on my knees. "It's not about the money, Jerry. It's about finding our purpose. It's about making a difference, even if it's just in our little corner of the world."

Dame laughs, but there's no money in it. "Make a difference? In this place? Good luck with that."

I look at each of them in turn, my voice steady. "I know it seems impossible. But we have to try. We have to believe that there's more to life than just surviving. That we can be a part of something bigger than ourselves."

Russell nods slowly, his expression thoughtful. "I feel you, Turland. But how do we even start? Where do we go from here?"

I stand up, the pebble still clutched in my hand. "I don't know. But I know this — we can't wait for something to happen. We gotta make it happen, one step at a time."

As I look out over the neighborhood, the setting sun painting the sky in shades of orange and pink, I feel a sense of determination rising within me. The road ahead may be uncertain, and the challenges daunting. But now, surrounded by my friends, I know anything is possible.

We are the dreamers, the believers who refuse to be defined by our circumstances. Together, we will find our way to a brighter future than we can imagine.

The distant wail of a siren pierces the evening air, a familiar sound of the nightlife in our neighborhood. It's followed by the rhythmic clatter of a passing train, its metal wheels grinding against the tracks. These noises are the constant backdrop of our lives, a reminder of our gritty reality.

The streetlights flicker to life, casting a dim glow over the cracked sidewalks and weathered buildings. The laughter of children playing in the nearby park mingles with the muffled bass of hip-hop music emanating from a passing car.

Dame leans back against the stoop, his eyes scanning the street. "You know, sometimes I wonder what it would be like to wake up someplace else. Someplace where the sirens don't keep you up at night, and the air doesn't smell like a mix of exhaust and desperation."

Jerry chuckles, but there's an edge to his voice. "Keep dreaming, Dame. We're stuck here, just like everyone else."

I shake my head, the pebble still clutched in my hand. "We don't have to be stuck. We can change things, even if it's just a bit at a time."

Russell raises an eyebrow. "And how do you propose we do that, Turland? Are we going to start a neighborhood watch or something?"

"Nah, man," I reply, a smile tugging at the corner of my mouth. "We start by believing in ourselves. By not letting this place define us or what we can become."

Dame scoffs, but there's a glimmer of something in his eyes – a flicker of hope, perhaps. "Easier said than done, my friend."

I nod, acknowledging the truth in his words. But I refuse to let it dampen my resolve. "I know it won't be easy. But we owe it to ourselves to try. To dream big, even if everyone around us tells us it's impossible."

The conversation lulls as we each drift into our thoughts, the weight of our shared reality settling over us like a familiar blanket. The street is quieter now; the children have retreated to their homes for dinner, and the music is fading into the distance.

I felt this sense of unity with my friends – a bond forged by our struggles and dreams we cling to. And I knew, deep in my heart, that together, one day, we could make a difference. We can rise above our expectations and create an entirely new future.

The pebble in my hand feels smooth and calm, a tangible reminder of our potential. I closed my fingers around it, holding tight to its promise.

It felt a little crazy to think we were the dreamers of the West Side, the ones who dared imagine a world beyond these streets. Though the path ahead may be uncertain, we will walk it together—one step at a time.

But as quickly as the vision comes, it fades, replaced by the harsh truth of our present. The weight of responsibility, the fear of failure, and the endless obstacles that stand in our way threaten to crush my spirit, leaving me feeling small and insignificant in the face of such overwhelming odds.

Russell's voice cuts through the silence as I sink into despair, injecting much-needed levity into the moment.

"Hey, did y'all hear about Miss Johnson's new boyfriend?" he asks, a mischievous grin spreading across his face. "Word on the street is he's got a record longer than my arm!"

We all can't help but chuckle at Russell's comment, the tension in the air dissipating as we allow ourselves to be swept up in the latest neighborhood gossip. It's a welcome reprieve from the heaviness of our thoughts, a reminder that even amid our struggles, there is still room for laughter and lightheartedness.

As we trade jokes and playful jabs, I feel a sense of gratitude wash over me—gratitude for the friends who stand beside me and together. The laughter fades as a figure emerges from the shadows, his presence commanding our attention. He moves with a confident swagger, his head held high, and his eyes scan the group with a calculating intensity. The gang member's appearance is striking—he's dressed in a crisp white T-shirt, his muscular arms adorned with intricate tattoos that hint at a life lived on the edge. A gold chain glints around his neck, catching the moonlight as he approaches us.

I feel a sense of unease wash over me, my instincts telling me that this man brings with him a world of trouble. Yet, there's something magnetic about his demeanor, a charisma that draws us in despite our better judgment.

"Well, well, well," he drawls, his voice smooth as silk. "What do we have here? A bunch of young bucks looking for a way to make some quick cash?"

His words hung in the air, a temptation that was hard to resist. I glanced at my friends, seeing a mix of curiosity and apprehension in their eyes. We all know the dangers of getting involved with the wrong crowd, but the promise of easy money is a siren's call that is hard to ignore.

The gang member senses our hesitation and leans closer, his voice dropping to a conspiratorial whisper. "Listen up, fellas. I've got a proposition for you. More than you've ever seen, a chance to make some real dough."

My heart races as I consider the possibilities, the dreams that could be within reach if we take him up on his offer. But a nagging voice warns me that nothing comes without a price.

Everyone looked to Turland, seeking guidance in his steady gaze. He's always been the one to keep the friends grounded, to remind everyone of what's truly important. As everyone's eyes met, the conflict on Turland's face, the battle between his desire for a better life and the knowledge that some risks are too significant to take.

The gang member's words continued to flow, painting a picture of wealth and power that was hard to resist. But as we listened, I couldn't shake the feeling that we were standing on the edge of a precipice, one wrong move away from falling into a world of darkness from which there may be no escape.

Turland's brow furrows as he weighs the gang member's proposition, his fingers absentmindedly twirling the small pebble he'd been holding. The smooth surface of the stone seems to anchor him amidst the swirling chaos of his thoughts. He knows that the offer could change their lives, providing a way out of the suffocating confines of their neighborhood. But at what cost?

Jerry shifts his weight from foot to foot, his restless energy palpable as he considers the potential for quick cash. His eyes dart between the gang member and his friends, seeking validation for the temptation that gnaws at him. On the other hand, Dame leans back against the railing, his arms crossed and his expression guarded. He's seen too much and knows too well the price of easy money.

Russell, ever the charmer, flashes a grin at the gang member. "Sounds like a sweet deal, my man. But you know, we've got to think about it. Can't just jump into something without knowing the details, right?" His words are smooth, but his tone's an undercurrent of caution.

As the gang member begins to lay out the specifics of the proposition, Turland's mind races with the possibilities and the consequences. He pictures his mother's face, etched with worry and disappointment if he were to get involved with the wrong crowd. He thinks of the dreams he's harbored, the hopes of making something of himself, of breaking free from the cycle of poverty and violence that has claimed so many of his peers.

The weight of the decision settles heavily on Turland's shoulders, and he takes a deep breath, trying to clear his mind. He knows that this choice could define the course of his life at this moment. As he looks at his friends, each grappling with their internal struggles, he realizes they're all standing on the same precipice, teetering between the promise of a better future and the threat of being swallowed by the darkness lurking in their community's shadows.

Turland's voice is quiet but firm as he speaks, cutting through the thick tension in the air. "We appreciate the offer, but we need time to consider it. This isn't a decision we can make lightly."

The gang member nods, his eyes narrowing slightly as he assesses Turland's resolve. "I feel you, man. But don't take too long. Opportunities like this don't come around daily, and plenty of hungry young ones would jump at the chance."

With those parting words, the gang member turns and saunters away, leaving the four friends alone with their thoughts and the weight of the future bearing down upon them. Turland's gaze returns to the distant horizon, his mind churning with the impossible choice that lies ahead. He knows their lives will never be the same regardless of their decision.

As the gang member's footsteps fade into the distance, a heavy silence descends upon the group. Turland can feel his friends' eyes on him, searching for guidance, for a glimmer of hope in the face of this daunting decision. He takes a deep breath, the air thick with the scent of cigarette smoke and the faint aroma of home-cooked meals wafting from nearby apartments.

Jerry is the first to break the silence, his voice tight with excitement and apprehension. "Man, this could be our ticket out of here. No more scraping by and watching the world pass us by while we're stuck in this same old grind."

Dame shakes his head, his eyes fixed on the cracked concrete beneath their feet. "But at what cost? We all know how these things go down. One wrong move, and we could end up like so many other brothers out here - dead or in prison."

Russell leans forward, his elbows resting on his knees as he looks at each of his friends. "We've always talked about making something of ourselves, about being more than just another statistic. Maybe this is our chance to make that happen."

Turland listens to their words, feeling the weight of each syllable as it settles upon his shoulders. He knows that they're all looking to him for an answer, for a way forward in a world that seems determined to hold them back. And yet, even as his heart yearns for the promise of a better life, his mind is filled with the echoes of countless cautionary tales of lives destroyed by the allure of easy money and the price of power.

As night has taken over and the moon casts long shadows across the stoop, Turland finds his voice. "We've been through a lot together, and I know we all want something better for ourselves and our families. But this... this is bigger than us. We need to think long and hard about what we're willing to risk, about what kind of future we want to build."

He looks at each of his friends, seeing the hope and the fear of war within their eyes, a reflection of his inner turmoil. "Whatever we decide, we do it together. We've always had each other's backs, and that won't change now. But let's take some time to think this through and weigh the consequences and possibilities. Because once we step through this door, there's no going back."

The four friends sit silently under the moonlight. Each lost in their thoughts, dreams, and fears. The night stretches before them, a vast and uncertain landscape that holds both the promise of redemption and the threat of ruin. And as they sit there, bound by the ties of friendship and the weight of the choice that lies ahead, they know that the path they choose in the coming days will shape not only their own lives but the lives of all those who look to them for hope and guidance in a world that so often seems devoid of both.

Chapter 2: The Proposition

The basement air hung thick with anticipation of the gang leader we now know as Slick as he emerged from the shadows, his confident stride commanding the room. Turland's eyes followed the gang leader's every move, a mix of unease and intrigue swirling in his gut.

Slick's voice cut through the silence, smooth as silk. "Gentlemen, the time has come. The bank on East 47th Street - that's our target."

Jerry leaned forward, his eyes gleaming with excitement. "How much are we talking, Slick? Enough to finally get out of this hellhole?"

Slick smiled, a flash of gold tooth. "More than enough, my man. But this ain't no smash and grab. We gotta do this right."

As Slick laid out the details, Turland's mind raced. The promise of a big score and a chance to change their lives was almost too good to be true. But the risks...

Dame and Russell exchanged wary glances and arms crossed defensively. Turland could see the hesitation etched on their faces, the unspoken fears hanging between them.

"Look, I know it's a lot to take in," Slick continued, his tone persuasive. "But this is our shot. Our ticket out of this life. No more scraping by and wondering where our next meal's coming from."

Turland felt the weight of Slick's words settling in his chest. It was a chance to break free, to build something better. But at what cost? His conscience nagged at the edges of his thoughts. A quiet voice drowned out by the allure of the plan.

Jerry was practically vibrating with energy, his eagerness palpable. "I'm in, Slick. Just tell me what I gotta do."

Slick nodded approvingly. "That's what I like to hear. Dame, Russell - what about you?"

Turland watched as his friends shifted uncomfortably, the gravity of the decision pressing down on them. In this neighborhood, opportunity was scarce. But they'd all have to live with the price of taking it.

As Slick's gaze swept over the group, I found my voice. "What about the risks?" I asked, my words measured and cautious. "This ain't no small job. We're talking about a bank, man."

Slick's eyes locked onto mine, his stare unwavering. "Turland, my man, you gotta think big picture here. Sure, there are risks. But the payoff? It's worth it."

I nodded slowly, my mind churning with the weight of the decision. The promise of a better life, of leaving the struggles of the West Side behind...it was intoxicating. But the nagging voice of my conscience wouldn't let up, reminding me of the line we'd be crossing.

Jerry, unable to contain himself any longer, leaped to his feet. "I got questions, Slick. How are we going to do this? What's the plan?" His words tumbled out in a rapid-fire barrage, his hands gesturing wildly.

Slick held up a hand, a smile playing at the corners of his mouth. "Easy, Jerry. I got it all figured out. We're gonna hit the bank right when they open. In and out, quick and clean."

I watched as Jerry nodded eagerly, his eyes alight with excitement. "What about security? Cameras?"

"Taken care of," Slick assured him. "I got a guy on the inside. He'll make sure we got a clear path."

As they delved into the details, I sat back, my thoughts a tangled web of hope and apprehension. The abandoned factories, the shuttered schools, and the vacant lots all stood as reminders of the broken promises that littered our community. This plan, dangerous as it was, felt like a lifeline—a chance to rewrite our stories.

But the weight of the decision settled heavily on my shoulders. The church bells that once rang out with hope now seemed to toll a warning, a reminder of the lives that hung in the balance. I glanced at Dame and Russell, seeing my own conflicted emotions mirrored in their eyes.

Jerry's voice broke through my reverie, his tone insistent. "We gotta do this, y'all. This is our chance. Our shot at something better."

I felt the pull of his words, the seductive promise of a brighter future. The West Side had taken so much from us and ground us down until hope was a distant memory. But this plan was a glimmer of light in the darkness, a chance to break free from the cycle of poverty and despair.

As Slick leaned forward, his eyes gleaming with anticipation, I knew the moment of truth had arrived. The decision that would shape our lives for better or worse. I took a deep breath, feeling the weight of my friends' gazes upon me.

In that dimly lit basement, with the ghosts of our past and the uncertainty of our future swirling around us, I met Slick's stare head-on. The words that would seal our fate danced on the tip of my tongue, a promise and a prayer rolled into one.

I let my mind wander, the possibilities of a life transformed by this heist playing like a movie reel. I saw myself walking down a bustling city street, the weight of the West Side lifted from my shoulders. A crisp suit, a briefcase in hand, a man with a purpose and a future. I imagined the looks on my family's faces when I handed them the keys to a new home, far from the decay and violence that had defined our lives for so long.

The dream shifted, and I stood before a small storefront, the sign above the door bearing my name. Turland's Corner Store. It was a place where the community could gather, where I could give back and make a difference. I saw the smiles on the faces of the neighborhood kids as I handed out free school supplies and the gratitude in the eyes of the elderly as I helped them with their groceries.

It was a beautiful dream, a tapestry woven from the threads of hope and longing that had sustained me through the darkest times. But even as I lost myself in the fantasy, a small voice whispered in the back of my mind. The price of that dream, the risks we would have to take, and the lines we would have to cross.

I blinked, the vision fading as the damp basement walls came back into focus. Slick was still talking, his voice a low, urgent murmur. Dame and Russell were nodding along, their expressions a mix of fear and determination.

I swallowed hard, my heart hammering in my chest. This was it. The moment that would define the rest of our lives. I thought of the scholarship, the glimmer of hope that had sustained me for so long. But even that seemed distant now, a fading dream in the face of the stark reality before us.

I looked at Jerry, his eyes shining with a fierce intensity. "We're in this together," he said, his voice barely above a whisper. "All for one, and one for all."

The words echoed in my mind, a rallying cry from our childhood. A promise that had seen us through the darkest of times. I felt the weight of that bond, the unbreakable ties that had brought us to this moment.

I nodded slowly, my decision made. "Let's do this," I said, my voice steady despite the fear in my gut. "For the West Side. For our future."

Slick grinned, his teeth flashing white in the dim light. "Wise choice, my brothers. Wise choice indeed."

As we clasped hands, sealing our fate with that simple gesture, I felt a surge of adrenaline coursing through my veins.

The dye was cast, and the path was chosen. And though the road ahead was uncertain, one thing was clear.

We would face it together, come what may. For better or worse, we were in this now—four brothers united by a dream and a desperate hope for something more.

The scene fades to black, the weight of their decision hanging heavy in the air.

Slick's words still hung in the air, the gravity of the proposed split settling over us like a heavy fog. The room fell silent, save for the soft creaking of chairs as we shifted in our seats, the weight of the decision bearing on our shoulders. I could feel the thick and palpable tension as we grappled with the implications of what lay before us.

My mind raced, a whirlwind of thoughts and emotions. It was a 50/50 split, with Slick taking half and the rest divided among us. It seemed like a small price to pay for the chance at a better life, a way out of the endless cycle of poverty and struggle that had defined our existence. And yet, the doubts lingered, the unspoken fears whispering in the back of my mind.

Unable to contain his excitement, Jerry leaped to his feet, his eyes blazing with an enthusiasm I hadn't seen in years. He paced the room, his words tumbling out in a rush of confidence. "Don't you see?" he exclaimed, his voice rising with each step. "This is our chance, our ticket to freedom. We can't let this opportunity pass us by."

I watched as Dame and Russell exchanged glances, their initial reluctance slowly crumbling beneath the weight of Jerry's persuasive arguments. They nodded, almost imperceptibly at first, then with growing conviction. I could see the flicker of hope in their eyes, the same desperate yearning for something more that burned within my heart.

"Think about it," Jerry continued, his voice dropping to a conspiratorial whisper. "With the money from this job, we could finally break free from the West Side and start fresh somewhere new. No more scraping by, no more living in fear. We could build something real, something that's ours."

His words painted a picture of a future I had scarcely dared to imagine, a life beyond the confines of our gritty reality. I could see the pieces falling into place like a long-forgotten puzzle in my mind's eye—a chance to make a difference, to create something that mattered.

And yet, even as the allure of the plan took hold, I couldn't shake the nagging sense of unease that lurked beneath the surface. The risks were high, and the stakes immeasurable. One wrong move, one misstep, and everything we had worked for could crash around us.

But as I looked around the room, at the faces of my brothers, the men who had stood by my side through thick and thin, I knew we were in this together. Whatever the outcome, whatever the cost, we would face it as one. For better or worse, our fates were intertwined, our destinies forever bound by the choices we made at this moment.

My mind raced, fragments of thoughts colliding like shards of broken glass. The promise of a better life, the chance to make something of ourselves, warring with the fear of what could go wrong. Prison. Death. Losing everything we had fought so hard to hold onto.

But even as the doubts swirled within me, I couldn't deny the pull of Slick's vision. A world where we called the shots and where we were the masters of our destiny. It was a siren song, luring me closer to the rocks, and I knew I was powerless to resist.

"We do this together," Slick murmured, his eyes locking with each of ours. "Brothers, united by a common purpose. Bound by the ties that run deeper than blood." His voice was a whisper, but it carried the weight of a thousand promises.

At that moment, with the decision made. I could feel it in the air, the way the room seemed to hold its breath, waiting for the final piece to fall into place. We were in this now, for better or worse, and our choices forever changed our lives.

As the conversation reached its crescendo, Slick leaned in, his face mere inches from mine. "This is our time, Turland. Our moment to seize everything we've ever wanted." His breath was hot against my skin, and his words were branded upon my soul.

The room fell silent, the weight of the decision hanging like a tangible thing. I could feel my brothers' eyes upon me, waiting for my response. At that moment, I knew that there was no turning back. We were in this together, come what may.

My voice was steady as I spoke, the words spilling from my lips like a sacred oath. "Let's do this. Together, as brothers. No matter what happens, we stand as one." And with those words, our fate was sealed, our destiny written in the stars.

I rose to my feet, the wooden chair scraping against the concrete floor. The sound echoed through the room, a final punctuation mark on our decision. I could feel the resolve coursing through my veins, a fire that burned away the last vestiges of doubt and uncertainty.

My eyes locked with Slick's, and in that moment, I saw a flicker of surprise, quickly replaced by a look of respect. He knew, as I did, that this was a pivotal moment, a turning point in our lives that would define us for years to come.

I extended my hand, my palm rough and calloused from years of hard labor. Slick's hand was smooth, his grip firm as he clasped my hand. The gesture was simple, but it carried the weight of a thousand unspoken words.

My brothers followed suit one by one: Jerry, his face split into a wide grin, his eyes sparkling with excitement; Dame, his jaw set, his eyes narrowed with determination; Russell, his hand trembling slightly as he reached out, his face a mask of barely contained emotion.

As each of them shook Slick's hand, I could feel the energy in the room shift, the air crackling with a new sense of purpose. We were no longer just four friends bound by circumstance and shared history. We were something more significant than the sum of our parts.

The pact was sealed, and our bond solidified at that moment. We were in this together, for better or worse, our lives forever intertwined by our choices. As we stood there, our hands clasped together, I could feel the weight of our decision settling upon my shoulders.

There was no going back now, no turning away from our chosen path. We were the masters of our fate, the architects of our destiny. And as I looked into the eyes of my brothers, I knew that whatever lay ahead, we would face it together, united in our resolve and our unbreakable bond.

The future was uncertain, but one thing was clear: we were in this until the end, no matter the cost. As we stood there, our hands still clasped together, I couldn't help but feel a sense of hope, a glimmer of possibility in the darkness surrounding us.

Perhaps this was our chance to break free from the chains that had bound us for so long. Maybe this was the moment that would define the rest of our lives, the turning point that would lead us to a better future.

The moment passed as we released our hands, but the feeling remained. Our decisions have changed and transformed us. As we looked at each other, I could see the same determination and fierce resolve reflected in each of their eyes.

We were ready, prepared to face whatever challenges lay ahead. And as we stepped out into the night, the cool air washing over our skin, I knew that nothing would ever be the same again.

The weight of our decision hung heavy in the air as we stepped out into the dimly lit alley. The faint glow of a distant streetlight cast long shadows across the pavement, and the silence was broken only by the sound of our footsteps echoing off the walls. I glanced at Jerry, his face a mix of excitement and apprehension, and I knew he was feeling the same adrenaline rush coursing through my veins.

Dame and Russell walked a few paces ahead, their heads bent together in quiet conversation. I couldn't make out their words but could sense the tension in their hushed tones. We were all grappling with the gravity of what we had just agreed to, the risks we were willing to take for a chance at a better life.

As we emerged from the alley, our neighborhood's familiar sights and sounds greeted us: the distant wail of a siren, the laughter of children playing in the streets, the bass thump of music spilling out from an open window. These were the rhythms of our lives, the backdrop against which we had grown up and struggled to survive.

But tonight, everything felt different. The air was charged with a new energy, a sense of possibility that we had never allowed ourselves to feel before. We were no longer just four friends from the West Side, bound by our shared history and the weight of our circumstances. We were something more, something greater than the sum of our parts.

I felt a hand on my shoulder and turned to see Jerry, his eyes shining with fierce determination. "We're doing this," he said, his voice low and steady. "We're going to change our lives, change everything."

I nodded, my throat tight with emotion. "Together," I managed to say, my voice barely above a whisper. "No matter what happens, we're in this together."

As we walked on, the city sprawling out before us like a map of our destiny, I knew there was no turning back. We had made our choice, and now we would have to see it through, no matter the cost. The future was uncertain, but one thing was clear: we were brothers, bound by a love that ran deeper than blood. Together, we would face whatever lay ahead, united in our resolve and our unbreakable bond.

Chapter 3: Preparing for the Heist

The flickering light of a single bulb illuminated our faces as we again gathered around the table in the damp basement. The air felt even heavier with all the weight of our plans. Jerry stood tall at the head, like a general ready to lead his troops into battle.

"Listen up, y'all," he says, his voice steady and strong. "Slick gave us the lowdown. This bank job's gonna set us up for life if we do it right."

He taps the blueprints before us, his finger tracing the path to our future. I lean in, my heart pounding as I absorb every detail. This is it—our ticket out of this place and this life that is slowly suffocating us.

Russell leans back in his chair, a smirk playing on his lips. "Y'all won't believe what I got off that bank teller I know," he says, his eyes gleaming with mischief. "Took her out for a hot dog and fries on her lunch break, turned on the charm, and she sang like a canary."

He chuckles, clearly pleased with himself. "Got the whole security setup now, just in case Slick left something out on purpose. Cameras, guard rotations, the works. We're golden."

I can't help but smile at Russell's antics, even as a pang of envy hits me. I've always admired and wished I could emulate his easy confidence and how he navigates this world we're trapped in.

But beneath the bravado, I know he's just as desperate as the rest of us. Just as hungry for a way out, a chance at something better. We all are. It's what's brought us here, huddled in this basement, plotting a heist that could change everything.

My gaze drifts to the grimy window, to the sliver of night sky visible through the cracked glass. Beyond these walls, there's a world waiting—where we could be more than just kids from the West Side scrambling to survive.

A world where our dreams could be more than just distant fantasies.

Jerry's voice snaps me back to the present. "This is our shot," he says, his eyes boring into each of us. "Our chance to break free. We gotta make it count."

I nod, my resolve hardening. He's right. This is our moment. Our opportunity to seize a different kind of future, one where the chains of our past do not shackle us.

One where hope isn't just a fleeting whisper but a tangible reality we can grasp with both hands.

Dame's fingers retrace the map's lines. His brow furrows in concentration. "What about the security cameras?" he asks, looking up at Jerry. We need to make sure we're not caught on tape."

Jerry nods, his expression serious. "Russell's intel should help with that. He said the cameras have a blind spot near the back entrance."

"And the getaway route?" Dame presses, his tone urgent. "We can't afford any mistakes there."

As they speak, I feel a sense of unease churning in my gut. The gravity of what we're planning hits me like a punch to the stomach. It's not just about the money anymore—it's about our lives and our futures. If we make one wrong move, we could lose everything.

I take a deep breath, trying to steady myself. "Guys," I say, my voice quiet but insistent. "Are we sure about this? I mean, sure?"

The room falls silent, and all eyes turn to me. Surprise flickers across their faces, followed by a hint of uncertainty. They know me as a dreamer always looking for a way out. But this—this is different.

"I know we're all desperate," I continue, choosing my words carefully. "But this - this could change everything. And not just for us. For our families and our community. We have to be sure it's worth the risk."

Jerry studies me for a long moment, his gaze intense. "Turland," he says, his voice low and serious. "This is our chance. Our one shot at a better life. We can't let fear hold us back."

I nod slowly, understanding the weight of his words. But the doubt still lingers, a persistent whisper in my mind. Is this the only way? Or are we just trading one set of chains for another?

Dame clears his throat, breaking the tension. "Let's go over the plan one more time," he suggests, his focus returning to the map. "We need to make sure we've got every detail covered."

As they launch into the specifics, I push my doubts aside to focus on the task at hand, on the glimmer of hope that this heist represents. But even as I nod along, force a smile, and join in the planning, I can't shake the feeling that we're standing on the edge of something bigger than ourselves.

Something that could either set us free - or destroy us completely.

The meeting winds down, and the basement falls silent, save for the soft rustling of papers and the creaking of old chairs. I look around at my friends, at the faces I've known for as long as I can remember. Jerry stands, stretching his arms above his head. "Alright, boys," he says, a grin spreading across his face. "One more day, and then we're in the clear. Time to get some rest."

Russell chuckles, the sound cutting through the heaviness in the air. "Rest? Who needs rest when we've got a fortune waiting for us?"

Dame rolls his eyes, but there's a hint of a smile playing at the corners of his mouth. "Don't count your chickens before they hatch, Russ. We've still got a job to do."

The banter continues as we gather our things, the tension slowly easing from our shoulders. For a moment, it's almost like old times - just four friends, laughing and dreaming of a brighter future.

But as we make our way up the creaky stairs and out into the night, the reality of our situation settles over us once more.

The streets are quiet, the only sound the distant wail of a siren and the soft thud of our footsteps against the pavement.

I linger behind, watching the others disappear into the shadows: Jerry, with his confident stride and unwavering determination; Russell, his laughter still echoing in the darkness; and Dame, his mind no doubt still whirring with plans and contingencies.

And then there's me. Turland Deville, the dreamer. The one who's always wondered if there's something more to life than the hand we've been dealt.

I glance back at the basement door, blueprints and notes still scattered across the table. The weight of our choices seems to press down on me, a physical burden that I can't quite shake.

But even as the doubts swirl, I know there's no turning back now. We've chosen our path, for better or worse.

And as I turn to follow my friends into the night, I can't help but wonder where that path will lead us - and what kind of men we'll be when we reach the end.

As I walk through the gritty streets of Chicago, the city's vibrant yet harsh reality serves as a backdrop to my introspection. The familiar sights and sounds wash over me—the distant laughter of children playing in a rundown park, the pulsating beat of hip-hop music spilling from a passing car, and the enticing aroma of soul food wafting from a nearby restaurant.

My mind drifts, the weight of our impending heist momentarily forgotten as I catch sight of a lovely couple walking hand in hand down the street. Their eyes sparkle with a love that seems untouched by the hardships surrounding them, and I can't help but imagine a future where I might find that same connection.

"Maybe one day," I whisper to myself, a wistful smile on my lips. "Maybe one day, I'll have someone to walk beside me, to dream with me."

It's a fleeting thought, a beacon of hope amidst the uncertainty, but it's enough to remind me that there's more to life than our desperate choices.

This night felt like a groundhog night into the morning because, before I knew it, the day of the heist would be here, and I couldn't stop reliving the night we kept going over the plans. Maybe I missed something, or perhaps if I remember the night differently, it would change the whole plan. The air in the basement is thick with tension as we gather for a final run-through of the plan. Jerry, Dame, and Russell are already there when I arrive, their faces a mix of determination and apprehension.

"Alright, let's go over this one last time," Jerry says, his voice steady despite the moment's weight. "We all know our roles, right?"

We nod in unison, the gravity of our decision settling over us like a shroud. Dame's fingers drum a nervous beat on the table while Russell's usually playful eyes are hardened with resolve.

"We've got this," Russell says, his words a mix of bravado and reassurance. "We've been through tough times and always had each other's backs."

I feel gratitude for my friends and the bond that has held us together through the years. But even as I draw strength from their presence, I can't shake the nagging sense of unease that coils in my gut.

"Guys," I begin, my voice barely above a whisper. "Are we sure about this? I mean, sure?"

The question hangs in the air, fragile and threatening to shatter the illusion of certainty we've built around ourselves. For a moment, no one speaks; we are lost in our thoughts and doubts.

But then Jerry clears his throat, his gaze unwavering as he looks at each of us. "We're sure," he says, his words a solemn vow. "We're doing this for each other, for the chance at a better life. We've come too far to turn back now."

And with those words, the last vestiges of hesitation fall away, replaced by a steely resolve that binds us together. We are brothers, united by our shared struggles and our unwavering loyalty to one another.

As we make our final preparations, I feel a sense of calm settle over me, a quiet acceptance of our chosen path. Come what may, we will face it together, just as we always have.

As we step out into the unforgiving streets of Chicago, I know that whatever the future holds, I will carry the memory of this moment with me—a reminder of the unbreakable bonds that have shaped my life and the dreams that still flicker in my heart.

Jerry's words echo in my mind as we make our way through the dimly lit streets, the weight of our decision pressing upon us like a physical force. The city's pulse thrums around us, a cacophony of distant sirens and the low rumble of passing cars, but we move as if in a bubble, isolated from the chaos surrounding us.

Russell falls into step beside me, his usual swagger replaced by a pensive frown. "Do you think we're doing the right thing?" he asks, his voice barely above a whisper. "I mean, what if something goes wrong? What if..."

He trails off, but I can see the fear in his eyes, the unspoken doubts that haunt us all. Instinctively, I squeeze his shoulder, a silent gesture of support. "We've got this," I say, injecting my voice with a confidence I'm not entirely sure I feel. "We've planned for every contingency. And besides, we've got each other's backs, no matter what."

Russell nods, a flicker of his old grin resurfacing. "Yeah, you're right. We're in this together, come hell or high water."

As we round the corner, the familiar outline of our hideout comes into view: a decrepit warehouse whose basement has become our sanctuary in recent weeks. Inside, Dame and Jerry are already waiting, their faces etched with anticipation and nerves.

Jerry steps forward, his eyes blazing with fierce determination. "Alright, boys, this is it," he says, his voice ringing like a clarion call. "Tomorrow, we take our shot at a better life. We've been through hell together and come out stronger for it. Whatever happens, I want you to know I'm proud to call all of you my brothers."

The words hit me like a physical blow, forming a lump in my throat as I felt the full weight of our bond. In this moment, I realized that no matter what the future holds, these men will always be a part of me, a testament to the unbreakable ties that bind us.

As we huddle together, our hands clasped in a final show of solidarity, I feel a surge of emotion coursing through me—fear, hope, and overwhelming love for these men who have become my family. And as we step out into the night, ready to face whatever challenges lie ahead, I know that I will always carry this moment with me, a beacon of light in the darkness surrounding us.

I am still stuck in this seemingly long Groundhog Night that I can't escape as I still see Dame hunches over the blueprints. His brow furrowed in concentration as he traced the escape route with his finger. "I've gone over this a hundred times," he mutters, more to himself than to us. "But I keep coming back to this stretch of road. It's too exposed, too risky."

I watch him silently, marveling at his meticulous care in every detail. It's a side of Dame I've always admired, the way he can lose himself in the intricacies of a plan, his mind working overtime to ensure no stone is left unturned.

"And then there's the matter of the split," he continues, his voice tinged with frustration. "Fifty percent to Slick and his crew? It doesn't sit right with me, but I guess that's the price we pay for their help."

Russell claps him on the shoulder, a gesture of solidarity. "We knew what we were getting into, Dame. It's a small price to pay for a chance at something better."

Dame nods, but I can see the conflict in his eyes, the unease that comes with compromising one's principles. I know this feeling too well: the constant push and pull between what we want and must do to survive in this unforgiving world.

As the meeting winds down, I find myself lost in thought, my mind jumbling with conflicting emotions. The weight of our decision presses down on me; the enormity of what we are about to do is suddenly all too real.

I think of the lives we will impact, the people who suffer because of our actions. And yet, I cannot shake the sense that this is our only way out, our one chance to break free from the cycle of poverty and despair that has defined our lives for so long.

Ultimately, it all comes back to the harsh realities of life on the West Side—the crumbling buildings, the shattered dreams, the constant struggle to keep our heads above water. This world has shaped and molded us into the men we are today, for better or worse.

And as I sit there, surrounded by the friends who have become my family, I realize that perhaps there is no easy answer, no clear path forward. We are all fumbling in the dark, trying to find our way in a world that seems determined to break us.

But in that moment, I also feel a flicker of hope, a tiny spark that refuses to be extinguished. Because despite all the darkness that surrounds us, we still have each other. And maybe, just maybe, that will be enough to see us through, to guide us towards a future that we can finally call our own.

The soft glow of the streetlights filters through the cracks in my blinds, casting eerie shadows across my bedroom walls. I lie there, eyes fixed on the ceiling, my mind a whirlwind of thoughts and emotions that refuse to be silenced. The result was the same each time my mind went through the groundhog loop.

Tomorrow. The word echoes through my head like a drumbeat, pulsing with anticipation and dread. Tomorrow, we'll put our plan into action, taking a leap of faith that could either set us free or destroy us completely.

I close my eyes, trying to picture a different life, a future beyond the confines of the West Side. In my mind's eye, I see myself walking down a bustling city street, briefcase in hand, a man with a purpose and a destination. It's a fantasy, I know, but it has kept me going through the darkest times.

And yet, even as I cling to that imagined future, the doubts creep in, insidious whispers that I cannot ignore. What if something goes wrong? What if one of us gets caught or worse? The thought of my friends and brothers paying for my dreams is almost too much to bear.

I roll onto my side, my gaze falling on the faded photograph on my nightstand. It's a picture of us, the four amigos, taken on a rare day of laughter and lightness. Looking at their faces, frozen in time, I feel a surge of love and loyalty that threatens to overwhelm me.

"I won't let you down," I whisper to the empty room, my voice barely audible over the distant wail of a siren. "No matter what happens, we're in this together."

But even as the words leave my lips, I feel the weight of uncertainty pressing down on me, a suffocating force that seems to grow stronger with each passing moment. I think of the families we'll be impacting and the lives we'll be disrupting, and I wonder if I have the strength to carry that burden.

Sleep feels like a distant memory, an elusive reprieve from my turmoil. I know I should rest and conserve my energy for the challenges ahead, but my mind refuses to quiet, spinning endlessly like a top that has lost its balance.

And so I lie there, caught between the promise of tomorrow and the fears that threaten to consume me. The night stretches on, each minute an eternity, until the first tentative rays of dawn begin to paint the sky in hues of orange and gold.

It's a new day, a new beginning. As I finally drift off into a fitful slumber, I can only pray that our choices will lead us to a break of light, not darkness.

Chapter 4: The Heist

The crisp morning air nipped at my skin as I huddled in the alleyway with Jerry, Dame, and Russell. Our breaths mingled in anxious clouds, crystallizing the heavy tension between us. Jerry's eyes darted back and forth, his fists clenching and unclenching at his sides. Dame chewed on his bottom lip, lost in thought. Russell shifted his weight from foot to foot, his gaze fixed on the grimy pavement.

"It's time," I said, my voice barely above a whisper.

We exchanged glances, a silent understanding passing between us. The weight of what we were about to do pressed down on our shoulders. With leaden steps, we climbed into the car, the doors slamming shut like a gavel, sealing our fate.

As the engine roared, I gripped the steering wheel, my knuckles turning red. The city streets blurred past, a kaleidoscope of rundown buildings and flickering traffic lights. Each mile brought us closer to the bank and the uncertain future ahead.

My mind raced, and memories of our hardscrabble upbringing flashed before my eyes. The laughter echoing through crumbling basketball courts, the late-night heart-to-hearts on stoops, and the dreams we whispered under starlit skies led to this crossroads.

"You sure about this, Turland?" Dame asked, his voice cutting through the tense silence.

I met his gaze in the rearview mirror, seeing the same determination and apprehension in his expression. "No turning back now," I replied, my words heavy with resignation.

As we approached the bank, the weight of our decision settled in the pit of my stomach. The adrenaline coursed through my veins, a dizzying cocktail of fear and exhilaration. We exited the car, footsteps echoing against the pavement like a foreboding drumbeat.

I paused, taking in the imposing facade of the bank - a symbol of the world that had always seemed just out of reach. The gravity of our choices bore down on me, threatening to crush my resolve. But beneath the fear, a flicker of hope still burned, a desperate yearning for something more than the hand we'd been dealt.

With a deep breath, I squared my shoulders and strode forward, my friends stepping beside me. Each step carried the weight of our shared history, the bonds that had held us together through thick and thin. As we neared the entrance, I couldn't help but wonder if those bonds would be strong enough to weather the storm that lay ahead.

The bank loomed before us, a monolith of glass and steel. My heart hammered against my ribcage, a frantic reminder of the magnitude of this moment. There was no turning back now—we had crossed the threshold and committed ourselves to this path. Whatever lay beyond those doors, we would have to face it together, for better or worse.

As we entered the bank, the bustling atmosphere enveloped us, a jarring contrast to the tension that thrummed through our veins. Customers and tellers went about their routines, blissfully unaware of the chaos that was about to unfold. The normalcy felt surreal, like a dream that could shatter any moment.

I scanned the room, taking in the details I had spent weeks committing to memory - the layout, the exits, the security cameras. My gaze lingered on the faces of the people around me, ordinary folks going about their lives, oblivious to the desperation that had driven us to this point.

We fanned out, each moving to our designated positions with a practiced synchronicity that belied the nerves that threatened to overwhelm us. I caught Jerry's eye from across the room and saw the fierce determination that blazed there, a silent promise to see this through no matter the cost.

Time seemed to stand still momentarily, the air heavy with anticipation. And then, with a sudden, violent motion, Jerry drew his weapon, his voice ringing out across the room like a thunderclap.

"Everybody on the ground, now!"

The words hit me like a punch to the gut, even though I had known they were coming. Panic and fear rippled through the crowd like a shockwave, and the atmosphere shifted instantly. Screams pierced the air, and customers and staff dropped to the floor, their faces etched with terror.

I forced myself to move, to play my part in this twisted drama. But even as I went through the motions, a part of me remained detached, watching it all unfold as if from a distance. The weight of what we were doing crashed over me in waves, a sickening mix of guilt and adrenaline.

As the chaos erupted around us, I caught a glimpse of my reflection on the polished marble floor - a distorted image of the man I had become. At that moment, I saw the culmination of every choice and every mistake that had led me to this point. And beneath the bravado and desperation, I saw a flicker of doubt, a silent question that echoed in the depths of my soul:

Was this the only way out, or had we just sealed our fates forever?

My feet swiftly carried me to the teller's counter, a mask of calm determination hiding the turmoil. I could feel my heart pounding against my ribs, a relentless drumbeat that threatened to drown out everything else. The teller before me trembled, her eyes wide with fear, as I leaned in close, my voice low and steady.

"The money. Now." The words tasted bitter on my tongue, a stark contrast to the dreams I had once whispered in the safety of my mind—dreams of a better life, of a future beyond the confines of the West Side. But those dreams seemed like distant memories now, lost in the harsh reality of our choices.

As the teller fumbled with the cash, her hands shaking, I glanced over my shoulder. Dame and Russell had taken up positions near the exits, their postures tense and alert. I could see the same conflicting emotions on their faces, the weight of our actions bearing down on them like a physical force.

Dame's eyes met mine for a fleeting moment, and we conversed silently. In that brief exchange, I saw the depths of our friendship, the bond forged through years of shared struggles and fleeting joys. But beneath that connection, I also saw the cracks forming, the unspoken doubts and fears that threatened to tear us apart.

Russell, ever the watchful guardian, scanned the room with determination and apprehension. His gaze darted from one face to another, searching for any sign of resistance or recognition. I could see the tension in his shoulders and how his fingers twitched near the weapon concealed beneath his jacket.

As the teller pushed the stacks of cash across the counter, I felt a sudden wave of nausea wash over me. The money felt heavy in my hands, a tangible reminder of our crossed line. At that moment, I couldn't help but wonder if this was the price of our freedom or if we had just signed away our souls for a fleeting taste of power.

The seconds stretched like an eternity as I shoved the money into a bag, my movements mechanical and precise. Around me, the sounds of fear and chaos blended into a discordant symphony, a haunting backdrop to the unfolding scene.

As I turned to signal to Dame and Russell, I saw something in their eyes—a flicker of uncertainty, a silent plea for reassurance. At that moment, I realized that we were all grappling with the same internal struggle, each desperately trying to reconcile the people we had once been with and our roles.

But there was no turning back now. We had set this course in motion and would have to see it through to the bitter end. As we began to move towards the exit, the weight of our choices hung heavy in the air, a suffocating presence that threatened to engulf us all.

The security guard's eyes narrowed as he approached Russell, his hand hovering near his holster. My heart raced, pounding against my ribcage like a caged bird desperate for freedom. Russell stood his ground, his gaze unwavering, his posture relaxed yet alert.

"Everything alright here, sir?" the guard asked, his voice laced with suspicion.

Russell's lips curved into an easy smile, a mask of nonchalance that belied the tension thrumming beneath the surface. "All good, officer. Just waiting for my friend to finish up his business."

The guard's eyes flicked towards me, then back to Russell. At that moment, I saw the gears turning in his mind, the puzzle pieces slowly clicking into place. But before he could voice his doubts, Russell spoke again, his words smooth and confident.

"We appreciate you monitoring everyone's safety. It's good to know that people like you are still looking out for the community. However, we need you to understand that this isn't the time to be a hero."

The guard hesitated, caught off guard by the unexpected compliment. His stance softened slightly, his hand drifting away from his holster. "I am just doing my job," he muttered, but I could see the flicker of pride in his eyes.

Russell nodded, his smile widening. "And we're grateful for it. We want you to continue to have a good day, officer."

With that, the guard moved to the ground. I released a breath I hadn't realized I'd been holding, my lungs burning with the effort. Russell caught my eye, silently acknowledging the bullet we had just dodged.

As I turned back to the task at hand, the weight of the money in my hands seemed to double, pulling me down like an anchor. The thrill of the heist was fading, replaced by a creeping sense of unease, a sinking realization of the consequences that awaited us.

My fingers curled around the cash, its crisp edges biting my skin. At that moment, I was torn between the exhilaration of our success and the crushing guilt of our actions. We had done it and accomplished the impossible, but at what cost?

The voices in my head warred, one reveling in the adrenaline rush and the other whispering of the lives we had just shattered. I tried to push them aside to focus on the task, but they clung to me like a second skin, a constant reminder of my choice.

As I stuffed the last of the money into the bag, I couldn't help but wonder if this was indeed the beginning of a new life or just another chapter in a never-ending cycle of desperation and regret. The weight of the cash in my hands felt like a promise and a curse, a symbol of our success and our damnation.

The piercing wail of alarms filled the air as we regrouped near the exit, a cacophony of chaos and fear. The once mundane bank interior had transformed into a scene of pandemonium, with customers cowering behind overturned chairs and tellers frantically reaching for emergency buttons. The urgency of our escape thrummed through my veins, a pulsing reminder that every second counted.

"Go, go, go!" Jerry shouted, his voice barely audible above the din. We moved as one, a well-rehearsed unit propelled by adrenaline and desperation. Dame led the charge, his eyes darting from side to side, searching for any signs of resistance. Russell brought up the rear, his imposing figure a silent warning to anyone who dared to stand in our way.

I clutched the bag of money tightly to my chest, the weight of our actions bearing down on me with each step. The sounds of screams and sobs faded into the background as we burst through the doors, the cool city air hitting my face like a sobering slap. My heart raced, a drumbeat of exhilaration and fear, as we sprinted towards our getaway vehicle.

The streets blurred past us, a kaleidoscope of color and motion. Pedestrians jumped out of our way, their expressions a mix of confusion and alarm. We moved with a single-minded focus, our feet pounding against the pavement in a frantic rhythm. The car was waiting for us, its engine humming with anticipation, a promise of escape and freedom.

As we piled into the vehicle, a moment of stillness descended. We looked at each other, our chests heaving and eyes wide with disbelief. The reality of what we had just done slowly sank in, settling into the crevices of our minds like a heavy fog.

"We did it," Dame whispered, his voice trembling with relief and uncertainty. "We did it."

I nodded, unable to find the words to express my turmoil. The money sat between us, a tangible reminder of our success and the price we had paid for it. As the car sped away from the scene, the city streets becoming a distant memory, I couldn't shake the feeling that this was just the beginning of a long and treacherous journey.

The weight of our choices hung in the air, a palpable presence that threatened to suffocate us. We had crossed a line and stepped into a world from which there was no turning back.

The future stretched out before us, a blank canvas stained with the colors of our actions.

I leaned back against the seat, my eyes drifting towards the horizon. The adrenaline was fading, replaced by a creeping sense of unease. We had gotten what we wanted, but at what cost? The road ahead was uncertain, a winding path filled with obstacles and dangers we could scarcely imagine.

As the car sped onwards, the city fading into the distance, I wondered if we had escaped or were running towards a fate we could no longer control. The money in my hands felt like a blessing and a curse, a reminder of our choices and the consequences we would have to face.

At that moment, as the world rushed by in a blur of uncertainty, I realized that our lives had been forever changed. We had taken a leap of faith, a desperate gamble for a better future, but the price of that gamble was yet to be determined. All we could do now was hold on tight and pray that our choices would lead us to a brighter tomorrow, even as the shadows of our past threatened to swallow us whole.

The car slowed to a stop, gravel crunching beneath the tires as we pulled into a secluded lot. As we stepped out, the air was thick with tension, our breaths still ragged from the escape. Slick emerged from the shadows, flanked by a dozen unfamiliar faces, their eyes glinting with anticipation and menace.

"Well, well, well," Slick drawled, his voice dripping with satisfaction. "Looks like you boys did good."

I glanced at Jerry, Dame, and Russell, their faces etched with the same apprehension I felt. We had no idea there would be so many others here, a sea of strangers who seemed to care little for our alliance with Slick.

The silence stretched on, broken only by the rustle of fabric as Slick reached into the bag, his fingers curling around the stacks of cash. He tossed a bundle to each of us, the weight of the money a tangible reminder of our choices.

A wave of conflicting emotions crashed over me as I caught my share. The thrill of the heist, the rush of adrenaline that had carried us this far, was quickly overshadowed by the looming consequences of our actions. My mind reeled with the implications, the lives we had forever altered, and the path we had set ourselves upon.

I watched as the others took their cuts, their faces mirroring my inner turmoil. We had done this for a reason: to break free from the chains of poverty and desperation that had bound us for so long. But standing there, surrounded by the cold eyes of Slick's gang, I couldn't help but wonder if we had traded one set of shackles for another.

My gaze drifted to the horizon, the city skyline a distant memory. The world we knew, the life we had left behind, seemed like a fading dream. We had crossed a line, and there was no going back. Our choices hung heavy in the air, a suffocating reminder of the uncertain future ahead.

As the last of the money was divided, Slick's predatory smile grew wider, sending shivers down my spine. "Congratulations, boys," he said, his voice a low purr. You're part of the big leagues now."

I swallowed hard, the taste of bile rising in my throat. We had wanted this, dreamed of this moment for so long, but now that it was here, I couldn't shake the feeling that we had made a terrible mistake. The price of our ambition, the cost of our desires, loomed large before us, a debt that we would spend the rest of our lives trying to repay.

As we climbed back into the car, our silence was deafening. Each lost in our thoughts, fears, and doubts, we drove on into the gathering darkness, the weight of our choices bearing down upon us like a physical force. The road ahead was uncertain, a twisting path filled with dangers and temptations we could scarcely imagine.

But there was no turning back now. We had made our bed and had to lie in it. As the city lights faded in the rearview mirror, I closed my eyes and prayed for the strength to face whatever lay ahead. I knew that our choices today would echo through the rest of our lives, a haunting reminder of the price we had paid for our dreams.

The cracked concrete steps of my stoop felt cold beneath me, a stark contrast to the feverish heat coursing through my veins. I sat there, elbows resting on my knees, my gaze drifting to the horizon where the sun was setting, painting the sky in hues of orange and red. The colors bled together, a fitting metaphor for the blurred lines of my life, the choices I had made, and the consequences that now loomed over me like a gathering storm.

In the distance, the church bells rang out, a familiar sound that once brought comfort but now only reminded me how far I had strayed from the path of righteousness. The money weighed heavy in my pocket, a tangible reminder of the gravity of my actions and the price I had paid for a chance at a better life.

"What have we done?" I whispered to myself, my voice barely audible above the gentle rustling of the wind through the trees. The question hung in the air, unanswered, as I grappled with the reality of our choices, the realization that there was no going back, no reset button to undo the damage we had wrought.

I thought of Jerry, Dame, and Russell, my brothers in arms, who had stood by me through thick and thin. We had always dreamed of a better life, of escaping the suffocating confines of our neighborhood, but now that we had taken that first step, I couldn't shake the feeling that we had crossed a line from which there was no return.

I closed my eyes, trying to picture a future where we had made different choices and found another way out, but the images wouldn't come. Instead, all I could see was the inevitable consequences of our actions, the price we would pay for our transgressions.

I felt a profound sadness wash over me, realizing that this was the path I had chosen, the life I had embraced with eyes wide open. There was no Groundhog Day, no chance to relive this moment and make a different choice. This was my reality, the bed I had made, and now I had to lie in it, come what may.

With a heavy sigh, I pushed myself to my feet, the world's weight pressing down my shoulders. I turned my back on the horizon, on the fleeting hope of a better tomorrow, and made my way inside, ready to face the consequences of my choices to navigate the treacherous waters of the life I had chosen. The future was uncertain, but one thing was clear: there was no turning back now.

Chapter 5: A Taste of Freedom

The rush still echoes in my ears, our laughter reverberating off the pristine walls of the bank lobby as we bolted, cash clutched tight. It's been days, but that high lingers like a sweet song I can't shake.

I stroll down the bustling Chicago street, past glittering storefronts, and the weight of the bills in my pocket is a tangible reminder. Untouchable. That's how I feel; nothing can bring me down from this perch.

A glint catches my eye—a jewelry store's window, a kaleidoscope of gold and diamonds. I step inside, the door chiming my arrival—the chains beckon, each link a promise of something more. I let a thick gold rope glide through my fingers, imagining how it would feel against my skin. A symbol of making it, of rising above the hand I'd been dealt.

"I'll take this one," I tell the clerk, slapping a wad of cash on the counter.

The weight of the chain around my neck feels right as I exit the store, a king adorned in his riches. But the weight of this amazing girl's gaze stops me in my tracks.

Across the street, amidst a trio of beautiful women, she stands out like a rose in a field of daisies. Her mahogany skin glows in the sunlight, her smile radiant and knowing as our eyes meet. A spark ignites within me, a pull I can't resist.

I approach, confidence in my stride, the gold chain a gleaming beacon. She watches me, her eyes dancing with curiosity and something more—perhaps a recognition of kindred spirits.

For the first time in a long time, I feel alive, the thrill of possibility thrumming through my veins. My past sins fade away, eclipsed by the promise of this moment, of her.

I know I should walk away, leave this angel untainted by the choices that led me here. But I'm drawn to her light, a moth to a flame, ready to risk everything for a taste of redemption in her embrace.

"Madamn," I greet her, the word rolling off my tongue like honey, the emphasis on the "damn" a testament to her breathtaking beauty. "I couldn't help but notice you from across the street. Your radiance outshines the sun itself."

She laughs a melodic sound that sends shivers down my spine. "Is that so?" Her voice is smooth, with a hint of playfulness. "And what brings you here on this fine day, sir?"

"Fate, perhaps," I reply, my smile easy, masking the turmoil within. The weight of the cash in my pocket, the spoils of our heist, feels suddenly heavy, a reminder of my chosen path. "Or maybe it's just my lucky day, running into a goddess like yourself."

Her friends giggle, but she holds my gaze, her eyes searching mine as if trying to unravel the secrets hidden beneath my charm. "Fate works in mysterious ways," she says, her words laced with a wisdom beyond her years.

As we talk, the world around us fades away, the bustling streets of Chicago reduced to a distant hum. Her presence is intoxicating, a balm to the wounds I've carried for so long. The laughter we share and the stories we share feel like a glimpse into a life I never dared to dream of.

But even as I lose myself in the magic of this moment, the guilt simmers beneath the surface, a constant reminder of the choices that led me here. The money, the heist, the rush of adrenaline—they all pale in comparison to the connection I feel with this stranger, this beautiful soul who sees beyond the mask I wear.

Impulsively, I take her hand in mine, the warmth of her skin sending electricity through my veins. "Come with me," I whisper, my voice urgent and pleading. There's something I want to show you."

She hesitates momentarily, her eyes searching mine again, before nodding, a smile playing at the corners of her lips.

I lead her back to the jewelry store, my heart pounding in my chest, my mind racing with the weight of what I'm about to do. The clerk looks up, recognition flickering in his eyes as I enter, my goddess by my side.

"Back so soon?" he asks, his gaze darting between us.

"I found something else that caught my eye," I reply, my voice steady, betraying none of the nervousness within me.

I guide her to the display case, my fingers trailing over the glass until they land on the most exquisite piece—a delicate and intricate gold chain with a pendant that sparkles like the stars.

"This one," I breathe, my eyes locked on hers, watching surprise and delight dance across her features. "For you."

The clerk carefully removes the chain from the display, the gold glinting under the lights as he places it in my hands. I step behind her, my fingers brushing against the soft skin of her neck as I fasten the clasp, the pendant resting just above her heart.

She turns to face me, her eyes shining with emotion, the chain a perfect complement to her beauty. Right then, I realized I would give her the world and lay everything I had at her feet to see that look in her eyes forever.

But even as I revel in the joy of this moment, the guilt gnaws at my insides, a constant reminder of the sins that shadow my steps. Can I ever truly escape the choices of my past and my life? Or will they forever haunt me, tainting even the purest of connections?

As we step out of the store, her hand in mine, I push those thoughts aside, determined to lose myself in the magic of her presence, even if only for a little while. The future is uncertain, but anything feels possible right now with her by my side.

The gold chain sparkles against her skin, a tangible symbol of our new connection, even if only for this fleeting moment.

"Madamn," I say, the words flowing from my lips like honey, "would you do me the honor of spending the day with me?"

Her friends exchange knowing glances, their smiles broad and encouraging. "Go on, girl," one of them urges, nudging her gently. "Live a little."

She looks up at me, her eyes filled with excitement and curiosity. "I'd love to," she replies, her voice soft and inviting.

A rush of satisfaction courses through my veins, temporarily overpowering the nagging guilt that lurks beneath the surface. In her presence, the weight of my past seems to fade, replaced by a newfound sense of possibility.

Hand in hand, we make our way through the bustling streets, our laughter intertwining with the city's pulse. I find myself drawn to her like a moth to a flame.

Our steps lead us to Navy Pier, the iconic Chicago landmark that beckons with its promise of adventure and wonder. The Ferris wheel looms above us, its colorful lights twinkling against the azure sky while the scent of buttery popcorn and sweet cotton candy fills the air.

Children's laughter echoes through the pier, mingling with the distant crash of waves against the shore. The energy is palpable, and I feel it coursing through my veins, igniting a spark of hope that I thought had long been extinguished.

As we stroll along the pier, our fingers intertwined, I allow myself to be lost in the moment, to forget the choices that led me here, and to bask in the warmth of her presence.

We go to the Ferris wheel, its towering presence a beacon of joy and excitement. As we enter the gondola, the girl's eyes sparkle with anticipation, mirroring the glistening lights that adorn the pier. The gentle rocking motion of the wheel carries us higher and higher, offering a breathtaking view of the city skyline and the vast expanse of Lake Michigan.

"It's beautiful, isn't it?" she whispers, her voice barely audible above the hum of the wheel.

I nod, my gaze fixated on how the setting sun casts a rosy hue across her features. "Not as beautiful as you," I reply, the words tumbling from my lips before I can stop them.

A shy smile graces her face, and she leans into me, her head resting on my shoulder. At that moment, the world seems to stand still, and I feel a sense of peace wash over me, a respite from the turmoil that has long plagued my mind.

As the wheel descends, we disembark, our hands still clasped together. We weave through the crowds, stopping to play games and share cotton candy, its sugary sweetness melting on our tongues. Laughter spills from our lips as we challenge each other to carnival games, the thrill of victory and the joy of shared experiences binding us together in ways I never thought possible.

The evening unfolds, and we find ourselves at the McVicker's Theater, drawn in by the promise of a karate movie marathon. As we settle into our seats, the flickering images on the screen casting shadows across our faces, I feel a sense of contentment wash over me. In the darkened theater, the outside world fades away, and all that matters is the connection we share, the unspoken understanding that seems to flow between us.

As the movies play out before us, we lean into each other, our shoulders touching, our breath mingling in the space between us. It's a simple gesture, yet it holds a profound intimacy, a silent acknowledgment of the bond that has formed between us in such a short time.

The marathon draws to a close, and we emerge from the theater, the cool night air a welcome respite from the intensity of the day. Our steps are leisurely as we go down the street, the city's vibrant energy thrumming around us.

"I know a place," I say, my voice barely above a whisper. "A restaurant where we can enjoy a nice dinner if you're up for it."

She nods, her eyes shining with a mixture of excitement and curiosity. "Lead the way," she replies, her hand tightening around mine.

We arrive at the high-end restaurant, its elegant facade contrasting with the gritty streets we've left behind. The maître d' greets us with a polite smile, guiding us to a table bathed in the soft glow of candlelight. The clinking of glasses and the gentle murmur of conversation fill the air, creating an intimate atmosphere that seems to surround us from the outside world.

As we perused the menu, our eyes meeting over the top of the leather-bound folders, I felt a sense of gratitude wash over me. At this moment, the weight of my past seems to lift, replaced by a feeling of hope, a glimmer of possibility that I never dared to entertain.

We order our meals, and the waiter's attentive service is a testament to the restaurant's refined ambiance. As we wait for our food to arrive, we fall into easy conversation, our words flowing like a gentle stream, carrying us deeper into each other's worlds.

The girl's laughter is a melody that fills the space between us, her eyes sparkling with genuine joy. In her presence, I find myself opening up and sharing stories and dreams I've long kept hidden beneath the weight of my past mistakes.

As our dinner arrives, the aroma of perfectly prepared dishes wafting through the air, we raise our glasses in a toast. The soft clink of crystal against crystal seems to seal the moment, a promise of something more, a future that may be uncertain but is filled with possibility.

We savor each bite, the flavors dancing on our tongues, a symphony of culinary delights. But the company, the connection we share, truly nourishes our souls. In this intimate setting, the world falls away, and all that remains is the two of us, lost in the moment's magic.

As the evening draws close, we linger over dessert, reluctant to let go of the spell woven around us. The restaurant's soft lighting casts a warm glow across our faces, and I find myself studying the contours of her features, committing every detail to memory.

Ultimately, we enter the night, the city's energy enveloping us again. But something has changed, a shift that is both subtle and profound. The connection we've forged and shared moments have left an indelible mark on my soul, a reminder that hope can be found in the most unexpected places, even in the darkest times.

As we walk hand in hand, the city's lights twinkling above us, I feel a sense of possibility, a glimmer of a future I never imagined.

A gentle breeze caresses our skin as we leave the restaurant, promising a new beginning. Our steps fall into sync, a natural rhythm that speaks to our shared connection. The city's vibrant energy pulses around us, but it fades into the background as we make our way to the shores of Lake Michigan.

We find a quiet spot along the shore, the sand beneath our feet a soft cushion as we sit side by side.

For a moment, we exist in the beauty of the moment, the gentle lapping of the waves against the shore a soothing melody. But as I gaze out at the horizon, the weight of my actions, the choices that led me to this point, begins to settle heavily on my shoulders.

"I never thought I'd find myself here," I confess, my voice barely above a whisper. "With someone like you in a moment like this."

She turns to me, her eyes searching mine, a flicker of understanding in their depths. "Sometimes, the most beautiful moments come when we least expect them."

Her words strike a chord within me, a resonance that echoes through my very being. The guilt that has been my constant companion, the shadow that has clung to my every step, begins to recede in the face of her gentle wisdom.

"I've made mistakes," I admit, the words catching in my throat. "Choices that I can never take back."

She reaches for my hand, her fingers intertwining with mine, a silent gesture of support. "We all have our pasts, our regrets. But they don't have to define us."

In that moment, I feel a shift within myself, a glimmer of hope that pierces through the darkness. The path ahead may be uncertain, the road to redemption a long and winding one, but with her by my side, I feel a strength I never knew I possessed.

The city lights flicker to life, casting a soft glow across the water's surface.

"Thank you," I whisper, my voice thick with emotion. "For seeing beyond my mistakes, for giving me a chance."

She smiles, her radiant expression seeming to light up the night. "Everyone deserves a chance to start anew, to find their way back to the light."

As we sit there, the world around us fading into the background, I know that this moment, this connection, will stay with me forever. It reminds us that even in the darkest times, hope can be found in the most unexpected places and that the power to change and become something more lies within us all.

As the night deepens and the city's hustle and bustle fades into a distant hum, the realization that our time together is ending settles heavily upon me. The weight of the day's experiences, the joy, the laughter, and the bittersweet ache of knowing that this connection may be fleeting all converge in a single moment.

I turn to face her, my heart pounding in my chest, and I find myself at a loss for words. How do I quickly convey my gratitude and her profound impact on me? I take a deep breath, my voice wavering slightly as I speak.

"I don't even know your name," I confess, a rueful smile tugging at the corners of my lips. "But I feel like I've known you forever."

She laughs softly, her eyes sparkling in the moonlight. "Sometimes, names are just labels. The connection matters how two souls can understand each other without needing words."

I nod, understanding the truth in her statement. We have shared so much and revealed parts of ourselves that we keep hidden from the world, and yet, the simple act of exchanging names seems almost trivial in comparison.

"I don't want this night to end," I admit, my voice barely above a whisper. "I'm afraid that once we part ways, I'll wake up and realize it was all just a dream."

She reaches out, her hand finding mine, and the warmth of her touch sends a shiver down my spine. "It's not a dream. This moment, this connection, it's real. And even if we never see each other again, it will always be a part of us, a reminder that we are capable of so much more than we ever believed possible."

I close my eyes, savoring the feeling of her hand in mine, the gentle breeze caressing my face, and the sound of the waves lapping against the shore. At this moment, every-thing else fades away, and I am left with a sense of peace, a glimmer of hope that I thought I had lost forever.

"Thank you," I whisper, my voice thick with emotion. "For everything."

She smiles, and in that smile, I see a reflection of my soul, a kindred spirit who understands the struggles and the triumphs that have shaped me.

As the night deepens, the city's lights twinkling like distant stars, Turland and the girl find themselves standing outside her hotel, their hearts heavy with the impending goodbye. The girl's gaze meets Turland's, and in that moment, he sees a reflection of his longing, a desperate desire to hold onto this fleeting connection for just a bit longer.

"I'm supposed to spend the night with my friends," the girl says softly, her voice barely above a whisper. "But I don't want this to end. Not yet."

Turland's heart races, his mind torn between the euphoria of the day and the weight of his past choices. He knows that he should let her go, that their paths were never meant to cross for more than a brief moment. But the thought of watching her walk away, her silhouette fading into the night, is more than he can bear.

"I don't want it to end either," he admits, his voice raw with emotion. "Today, with you, it's been like a dream. A glimpse of a life I never thought I could have."

The girl reaches out, her fingertips grazing Turland's cheek. He leans into her touch, savoring the warmth of her skin against his. "Then let's make it last a little longer," she whispers, her eyes shining with hope and uncertainty.

Turland nods, his heart pounding as they enter the hotel lobby, their hands intertwined. As they make their way to her room, he can't help but wonder if this is a mistake, if he's setting himself up for even greater heartbreak. But the feeling of her hand in his, the way her presence fills the emptiness inside him, is too powerful to resist.

They stand facing each other inside the room, the silence heavy with unspoken emotions. Turland's gaze traces the contours of her face, committing every detail to memory, knowing that this moment may be all they ever have.

"I don't even know your name," he whispers, his voice tinged with a bittersweet realization.

The girl smiles a soft, tender expression that makes Turland's heartache. "Does it matter?" she asks, her fingers tracing the chain around his neck. "Sometimes, the most precious moments are the ones we can't put a name to."

Turland nods, understanding the truth in her words. They move closer, their lips meeting in a gentle, tentative kiss that slowly deepens, a physical manifestation of their forged connection. As they lose themselves in each other's embrace, Turland's mind races with a torrent of emotions – the exhilaration of the day, the guilt of his past, and the bittersweet knowledge that this moment is as fragile as it is beautiful.

As they lay entwined, their bodies and souls bare, Turland knows the challenges ahead will be greater than ever. But for now, in the sanctuary of this room, with the girl who has awakened a part of him he thought long dead, he allows himself to believe in the possibility of redemption, in the power of human connection to heal even the deepest wounds.

Chapter 6: Whispers on the Street

The flickering streetlights cast a dim glow over the neighborhood, shadows dancing across cracked sidewalks and crumbling brick facades. I shoved my hands deep into the pockets of my worn jacket, the autumn chill seeping into my bones as I made my way to our usual spot. Each step carried the weight of our shared history, the ghosts of laughter and tears that echoed through these streets.

As I approached the corner, my heart pounded with excitement and dread. The anticipation of seeing my boys again battled with the unease that had settled in my gut since our last meetup. I scanned the familiar surroundings - the abandoned lot where we used to play ball, the boarded-up storefront that once housed old man Jenkins' corner store. Memories swirled like leaves caught in an updraft, bittersweet reminders of simpler times.

I took a deep breath, steadying myself against the rush of emotions. I leaned against the graffiti-covered wall and watched three figures emerge from the shadows. Jerry, Dame, and Russell - my brothers in everything but blood. As they drew closer, the tension in the air thickened, their faces etched with the same weariness I felt in my bones.

"Turland," Dame greeted me, his voice low and strained. He clasped my hand briefly, the warmth of his grip a fleeting comfort.

Jerry nodded, his jaw clenched tight. "Been a minute, huh?" The words hung between us, heavy with unspoken truths.

Russell remained silent, his eyes darting nervously around the empty street. The carefree grin that once lit up his face was nowhere to be seen.

I swallowed hard, searching for the right words. "How y'all been holding up?" The question felt inadequate, a hollow echo of the bond we once shared.

Jerry scoffed, kicking at a loose pebble. "Same old, same old. Just trying to stay afloat in this messed-up world."

Dame sighed, running a hand over his face. "It ain't been easy, T. The weight of it all... sometimes it feels like it's going to crush me."

I nodded, understanding all too well the burden they carried. The choices we'd made, the paths we'd taken - they haunted us like restless spirits. But even amid our struggles, I couldn't help but cling to the hope that we could find a way out and that redemption was still within reach.

"We gotta stick together, y'all," I said softly, my voice barely above a whisper. "Ain't nothing gonna change if we don't have each other's backs."

Russell's gaze met mine, a flicker of the old camaraderie sparking in his eyes. "You right, T. We have been through too much to let it all fall apart now."

Those words hung heavy in the air, a palpable tension settling over us like a thick fog. The reality of our situation was sinking in, and I could feel the weight of it pressing down on my chest, making it hard to breathe.

Jerry's eyes flashed with a familiar heat, his hotheaded nature flaring up like a spark igniting dry kindling. "Nah, man, we ain't running," he insisted, his voice firm. "We lay low, keep our heads down, and wait for this shit to blow over. Ain't no way they got enough on us to make anything stick."

But beneath the bravado, I could hear the undercurrent of fear in his tone, the slight tremor that betrayed his doubts. We were all grappling with the consequences of our choices, the specter of our past actions looming over us like a gathering storm.

Russell shifted uneasily, his gaze darting between us as he searched for the right words. "Maybe we should think about getting out of town for a while," he suggested, a hint of desperation creeping into his voice. "Just until things cool off, you know? We could start fresh somewhere else, leave all this behind."

I listened to my friends, their words washing over me like a tide of conflicting emotions. Part of me wanted to run, to escape the suffocating grip of our mistakes and the looming threat of the law. But another part of me still clung to the tattered remnants of my ideals and whispered that there had to be another way.

"We can't keep running forever," I said softly, my voice barely audible above the pounding of my own heart. "Sooner or later, we gotta face up to what we've done. Maybe it's time we thought about turning ourselves in, making things right."

The words felt foreign on my tongue, a concept so alien to the world we'd built for ourselves. But even as I spoke them, I could feel a flicker of hope stirring in my chest, a fragile ember that refused to be extinguished.

Jerry scoffed, shaking his head in disbelief. "You've lost your damn mind, T. Ain't no way we're turning ourselves in. We'd be signing our death warrants."

Dame's expression was pensive, his brow furrowed as he grappled with the weight of our choices. "I don't know, man. Maybe Turland's right. We can't keep living like this, always looking over our shoulders, waiting for the hammer to drop."

The air between us crackled with tension, our differing opinions threatening to tear apart the fragile bonds that held us together. But even as we argued, our voices rising and falling like the tide, I couldn't shake the feeling that we were standing on the precipice of something meaningful, a turning point that would define the rest of our lives.

The wail of police sirens pierced the night, an ominous chorus cutting through our heated words like a knife. In that instant, the world around us seemed to be still, our breaths catching in our throats as realization dawned. The flashing red and blue lights reflected in my friends' wide, panicked eyes, a kaleidoscope of fear and urgency.

"Shit, shit, shit," Jerry muttered under his breath, his voice tight with barely controlled panic. His gaze darted around the alleyway, searching for an escape route that wasn't there.

Russell's movements were frantic, his hands trembling as he tugged at his hair. "We gotta get out of here, man. We gotta move now!"

Dame stood frozen, his eyes locked on the approaching lights. I could see the terror etched into every line of his face, a mirror of the dread that gripped my own heart.

My mind raced, thoughts tumbling over each other in a dizzying spiral. How had it come to this? The choices we'd made and the paths we'd taken led to this moment, this suffocating fear that threatened to consume us whole.

The sirens grew louder, the sound reverberating through my bones. Time seemed to slow, each heartbeat an eternity as I stood there, paralyzed by the weight of our actions.

In the moment's chaos, I saw something in my friends' eyes - a flicker of regret, a silent plea for redemption. But the night offered no mercy or reprieve from the consequences upon us.

We had to move, run, and cling to the fading hope that, somehow, we could outpace the shadows of our past. The future we'd dreamed of, the lives we'd imagined—they hung in the balance, teetering on the edge of this single, terrifying moment.

As the sirens reached a deafening crescendo, I knew that our fates were intertwined, our destinies forever altered by our choices. The bonds of our friendship, forged in the crucible of hardship and shared dreams, would be tested like never before.

In that fleeting instant, suspended between the life we knew and the uncertain path ahead, I saw a glimmer of the strength that had carried us this far—a strength born of resilience, of hope in the face of overwhelming odds.

"Split up!" Jerry hissed, his voice barely audible above the wail of the sirens. "Meet at the old factory in an hour!"

The words hung in the air for a heartbeat, a fragile lifeline amid the chaos. I locked eyes with each of my friends, our gazes conveying a thousand unspoken emotions. Fear, determination, loyalty – all etched into the lines of our faces, a testament to the unbreakable bonds that had carried us through the trials of our lives.

Dame's hand clasped mine, his grip fierce and urgent. "Stay safe, Turland," he whispered, his voice rough with emotion. "Don't let them catch you."

I nodded, my throat too tight to speak. Russell clapped me on the shoulder, his eyes glinting with a fierce resolve. "We'll see you on the other side, brother."

And then, as if on some unspoken signal, we scattered. Our footsteps echoed through the night, a staccato rhythm against the relentless pulse of the sirens. I ran, my heart hammering in my chest, the world narrowing to the pounding of my feet against the pavement and the ragged rush of my breath.

The city blurred around me, a kaleidoscope of shadows and flickering streetlights. I ducked into alleys and vaulted over fences, my mind a whirlwind of fear and desperation. The weight of our choices bore down on me, a suffocating burden that threatened to crush the air from my lungs.

"Keep moving," I muttered, a mantra against the rising tide of panic. "Don't stop, don't look back."

But even as I ran, memories came flooding back—the laughter and the tears, the dreams we'd shared, and the battles we'd fought. The bonds of our friendship, forged in the crucible of hardship and hope, had brought us to this moment, this desperate bid for freedom.

I thought of Jerry, whose quick wit and fierce loyalty were a constant light in our world's darkness. I thought of Dame, whose quiet strength and unwavering compassion are a balm to our battered souls. And Russell, with his unyielding determination and fierce protectiveness, is a shield against the cruelties of fate.

As I raced through the night, the city's familiar landmarks passing in a blur, I clung to the hope that somewhere, somehow, we would find our way back to each other.

The sirens faded into the distance, their echoes lingering like the ghost of a fading nightmare. But even as the immediate danger passed, I knew our journey was far from over. The road ahead was uncertain, a winding path through a world that had never been kind to dreamers like us.

But at that moment, as I ran beneath the starless sky, I felt a flicker of something profound within – a spark of resilience, of hope that refused to be extinguished. It was the same fire that had sustained us through the darkest times, the unquenchable spirit that had carried us from the depths of despair to the brink of freedom.

But most of all, I ran towards the hope that somewhere, in the vast and unforgiving expanse of the world, there was still a place for us – a place where the bonds of friendship and the power of our dreams could transcend the cruel machinations of fate and carry us towards a brighter tomorrow.

Jerry's lungs burned as he sprinted through the labyrinth of alleyways, his feet pounding against the cracked pavement. The distant wail of sirens spurred him onward, a relentless reminder of the fate that awaited if he faltered. He could feel the weight of his past bearing upon him, the choices that led them to this desperate flight.

Beside him, Dame's breath came in ragged gasps, her eyes wide with fear that mirrored his own. They exchanged a fleeting glance, a silent acknowledgment of the chasm that had opened between them—the unspoken truths and unresolved wounds that hung heavy in the air.

"We can't keep running forever," Dame panted, her words punctuated by the staccato rhythm of their footfalls.

"We don't have a choice," Jerry shot back, his voice raw with emotion. "It's either this or..."

He trailed off, unable to give voice to the alternative that loomed like a specter on the horizon.

As they rounded a corner, Jerry caught a glimpse of Russell's retreating form, his silhouette swallowed by the shadows. A pang of regret pierced his heart, a longing for the days when their bond had been unshakable – a fortress against the world's cruelties.

But those days were lost to the relentless march of time and the weight of their mistakes.

Turland's mind raced as he sought refuge in the city's depths, his thoughts a whirlwind of fear and regret. The choices that had seemed so evident in the moment now took on a different hue, the consequences of their actions painting a grim portrait of the future that awaited them.

He paused for a moment, his back pressed against the cool brick of a derelict building, his chest heaving as he struggled to catch his breath. The night air was thick with the scent of desperation, the echoes of their fractured lives reverberating through the empty streets.

He closed his eyes, drawing in a deep breath, and felt the familiar warmth of hope blossoming in his chest – a promise whispered on the wind, a secret language known only to those who dared to dream.

And so, with a final glance over his shoulder at the city that had shaped him, Turland pushed himself away from the wall and stepped forward into the unknown – ready to face whatever fate had in store, armed only with the strength of his convictions and the unshakable bonds of friendship that had sustained him through it all.

The night swallowed Turland as he ventured deeper into the labyrinth of city streets, his footsteps echoing against the cracked pavement like a lonely heartbeat. The distant wail of sirens faded into the background, replaced by the mournful whisper of the wind and the hollow rustling of discarded newspapers dancing across the asphalt.

He moved purposefully, his lean frame cutting through the shadows like a blade, his eyes scanning the darkened alleys and boarded-up storefronts for any sign of trouble. The weight of their fractured bond pressed against his chest, a constant reminder of the choices that had led them to this moment –

a tapestry of mistakes and misunderstandings woven together by the threads of their shared history.

Turland's mind wandered to his friends, scattered to the winds like leaves in a storm. He could almost see them in his mind's eye – Jerry, with his quick wit and fierce loyalty; Dame, with his quiet strength and unwavering determination; and Russell, with his infectious laughter and boundless optimism. They were a part of him, as much as the blood in his veins and the air in his lungs, and the thought of losing them was almost too much to bear.

Chapter 7: The Walls Close In

Turland is perched on the edge of his grandmother's faded floral couch, his legs bouncing restlessly as the flickering light from the television dances across his face. The news report droned on, each word about the bank robbery sending a fresh jolt of panic through his veins.

"Authorities are still searching for the four suspects..." the anchor announced, her voice cold and clinical.

Turland's heart pounded against his ribs, a sickening rhythm that echoed the fear consuming his thoughts. He clenched his fists, nails digging into his palms, as the reality of what they had done crashed over him in relentless waves.

"What were we thinking?" he muttered under his breath, the words catching in his throat. "This ain't no game. This is real-life consequences."

Unable to sit still longer, Turland pushed himself up from the couch, the worn springs creaking beneath him. He paced the small living room, his footsteps heavy on the scuffed hard-wood floors. The dim light filtering through the tattered curtains cast long shadows across his face, mirroring the darkness that clouded his mind.

He thought of Jerry, Dame, and Russell - his brothers in this mess. Were they safe? Had the police already caught up to them? The questions raced through his mind, each more urgent than the last.

Turland ran a hand over his close-cropped hair, his fingers trembling slightly. The weight of their shared decision pressed down on his shoulders, a suffocating burden he couldn't shake. They always had each other's backs, but the stakes were higher this time.

As he turned to pace back across the room, the floorboards groaned beneath his feet, a mournful sound that seemed to echo the turmoil in his heart. Turland paused by the window, peering through a gap in the curtains at the empty street outside. The neighborhood was eerily quiet as if holding its breath in anticipation of the storm.

The phone's shrill ring shattered the silence, jolting Turland from his thoughts. He lunged for the receiver, his heart pounding against his ribs as he pressed it to his ear.

"Yo, T," Jerry's voice crackled through the line, barely above a whisper. "You see the news?"

"Yeah, man," Turland replied, his voice tense. "Cops everywhere. They are on the hunt."

"No doubt. Dame and Russ, they lay low?"

"Far as I know. Ain't heard nothing else."

Jerry let out a shaky breath, static hissing through the connection. "We gotta stay ghost, T. Can't let them catch us slippin'."

"I hear you." Turland glanced over his shoulder, half-expecting to see the flashing lights of a police car outside the window. "We ride this out. Stay outta sight. They'll move on soon enough."

"Let's hope so, man. Let's hope so."

The line went dead, leaving Turland alone with the weight of their choices. He set the phone back in its cradle, his hand lingering on the cool plastic as he fought to steady his breathing.

In the silence that followed, memories flooded his mind - the four of them, laughing and dreaming on street corners, their bond forged in the fires of struggle and survival.

But now, as the consequences of their actions closed around them, Turland couldn't help but question their chosen path. The money, the rush, and the promise of something better seemed worth the risk. Yet, standing in his grandmother's living room, the flickering light of the television casting shadows on the walls, he felt the weight of responsibility pressing down on him like a physical force.

The creak of the floorboards shattered the heavy silence, and I turned to see Grandma standing in the doorway, her weathered face etched with lines of worry and suspicion. Her eyes, once bright with laughter, now were melancholy as they darted between my face and the television screen, where images of the robbery continued to flash.

"Turland, baby," she began, her voice soft but laced with an undercurrent of steel, "what's going on? You've been pacing around like a caged animal all day."

I swallowed hard, and my mouth suddenly dried as the Sahara. How could I tell her? How could I admit to the woman who had raised me and poured her love and wisdom into my soul that I had betrayed everything she stood for?

"Grandma, I..." My voice faltered, the words sticking in my throat like shards of glass.

She took a step closer, her gaze never leaving mine. "I know that look, child. I've seen it before, on the faces of too many young men in this neighborhood. That haunted, hunted look."

I wanted to look away and hide from the truth in her eyes, but I couldn't. She had always seen through me, straight to the heart of who I was.

"You're in trouble, aren't you?" It wasn't a question but a statement of fact, speaking with a quiet resignation that shattered my composure.

Tears burned behind my eyes, and I blinked them back furiously. I couldn't break, not now. But as Grandma reached out and laid a gentle hand on my shoulder, the dam inside me burst, and the words came pouring out in a torrent of anguish and regret.

"I messed up, Grandma. We all did. The robbery... it was us. Jerry, Dame, Russell, and I thought we could make a quick score and change our lives. But it all went wrong, and now..." A sob tore from my throat, raw and jagged. "Now, I don't know what to do. The cops, they're closing in, and I'm so scared. I'm so sorry..."

Her grip on my shoulder tightened, and her voice was fierce with love and sorrow when she spoke. "Oh, my sweet boy. I knew this day would come. I've watched you and your friends see the hunger and desperation in your eyes. This world is not kind to boys like you, with dreams too big for these narrow streets."

She drew me into her arms, and I clung to her like a drowning man to a life raft, my tears soaking into the soft fabric of her blouse. At that moment, I was a child again, seeking comfort in the only safe harbor I had ever known.

"Listen to me, Turland," Grandma whispered, her breath warm against my ear. "You've made a mistake, a terrible one. But it's not too late. You have a choice, even now. You can let this define you. Let it drag you down into the abyss. Or you can face it head-on, take responsibility, and start the long, hard road to making things right."

I pulled back, searching her face for the condemnation I deserved, but found only love and a fierce, unwavering belief. Something shifted inside me, a flicker of hope amid the darkness.

"I don't know if I'm strong enough, Grandma. I don't know if I can do this alone."

She smiled then, a sad, knowing smile. "You're never alone, child. You have me, and you have your friends. Together, we'll weather this storm. It won't be easy, but nothing worthwhile ever is."

As I let her words wash over me, I felt a glimmer of something I hadn't dared to think about in a long time: the possibility of redemption, of a future beyond the choices that had brought me to this moment. And as the television continued to flicker in the background, casting shadows on the walls, I knew the road ahead would be long and arduous. But with Grandma by my side and the bonds of friendship to guide me, I would find a way to make things right, no matter the cost.

The phone's shrill ring shattered the moment, jolting me back to the harsh reality of our situation. I reached for the receiver with a heavy heart, already knowing who would be on the other end.

"Turland, it's Dame." His voice was strained, the usual bravado replaced by a palpable fear. "The cops, man. They're everywhere. Asking questions, knocking on doors. We gotta do something, and fast."

I closed my eyes, the weight of our choices bearing down on me like a physical force. "I know, Dame. I know. But what can we do? We're in too deep."

"We gotta run, Turland. Get out of the city and lay low until this all blows over. It's the only way."

His desperation was a mirror of my own, the realization that our actions had finally caught up with us. But even as the words left his mouth, I knew that running wasn't the answer—not this time.

"We can't run forever, Dame. Sooner or later, we'll have to face what we've done. And I don't know about you, but I'm tired of running."

There was a long pause on the other end, the sound of Dame's heavy and difficult breath. "So what do we do, then? Turn ourselves in? Let them lock us up and throw away the key?"

I glanced at Grandma, her eyes still fixed on me with unwavering love and support. And in that moment, I knew what I had to do.

"We do the right thing, Dame. We take responsibility for our actions and face the consequences, whatever they may be. It's the only way to make things right."

The words tasted bitter on my tongue, the reality of what I was proposing sinking in like a lead weight. But even as the fear threatened to consume me, I knew it was the only path forward.

"I don't know if I can do that, Turland. I don't know if I'm strong enough."

"You are, Dame. We all are. And we'll do it together, just like we always have because that's what friends do. They stand by each other, no matter what."

As the words left my mouth, I felt a calm wash over me, a clarity that had eluded me for far too long. As I hung up the phone, I knew the road ahead would be long and complicated, but with Grandma's love and the bonds of friendship to guide me, I would find a way to make things right, no matter the cost.

The decision had been made, and the path set.

Grandma sat quietly across from me, her weathered hands folded in her lap as she listened to my side of the conversation with Dame. The weight of her gaze pressed upon me, a silent reminder of the unwavering support she had always provided, even in the darkest of times.

I began to pace, my footsteps heavy against the worn floorboards. The walls seemed to close around me, the air thick with the weight of my thoughts. I could feel the panic rising in my chest, the fear that had been my constant companion since we had made that fateful decision.

"What have we done, Grandma?" I whispered, my voice barely audible over the pounding of my heart. "We've ruined everything. There's no way out of this."

Grandma rose slowly from her chair, her movements deliberate as she crossed the room to stand before me. Her eyes, so full of wisdom and understanding, locked with mine, and for a moment, I felt as though she could see straight into my soul.

"There's always a way, Turland," she said softly, her hand resting on my shoulder. "It may not be easy, and it may not be what you had planned, but there's always a way forward."

I shook my head, the tears I had held back finally spilling over. "Not this time, Grandma. We've gone too far. The police... they'll be here any minute. And then what? Prison? For how long? Our lives... they're over."

Grandma's grip on my shoulder tightened, her voice firm as she spoke. "Your life is not over, Turland. It's just beginning. And I will always be here for you no matter what happens, where you go, or what you face. Always."

I clung to her then, my face buried in her shoulder as the sobs wracked my body. And at that moment, with her lavender perfume filling my nostrils and the warmth of her embrace surrounding me, I felt a glimmer of hope, a sense that maybe, just maybe, there was still a chance for redemption.

But even as Grandma comforted me, I couldn't shake the growing sense of dread that had taken root in the pit of my stomach.

I pulled away from Grandma's embrace, my eyes red and swollen as I met her gaze once more. "I'm scared, Grandma," I admitted, my voice barely above a whisper. "I'm so scared of what's going to happen to us."

Grandma's expression softened, her hand coming up to cup my cheek. "I know, Turland. I know. But fear is a part of life. It's what we do with that fear that matters. And I know you have the strength to face whatever comes next, no matter how difficult."

I nodded, drawing in a shaky breath as I tried to steady myself.

As I leaned into my grandmother's touch, a sudden memory flooded my mind, transporting me back to a simpler time. The laughter of my friends echoed in my ears, and I could almost feel the sun's warmth on my skin as we sat together on the stoop, trading jokes and dreams for the future.

Jerry's smile was wide and carefree then, his eyes sparkling with mischief as he told us tales of his latest exploits. Dame's laughter was infectious, his joy a balm to the harsh realities of our lives. And Russell, ever the quiet observer, watched us with a contented smile, his presence a steady anchor in the chaos of our world.

The memory was bittersweet, a reminder of our lost innocence and the bonds forged in the crucible of our shared struggles.

But as quickly as the memory had come, it faded, replaced by the cold, hard truth of our present reality. The sound of a car engine, growing louder with each passing second, jolted me back to the present, and I felt a renewed surge of fear course through my veins.

I moved to the window, my heart pounding as I peered through the curtains. The sight of the police vehicle, its lights flashing in the gathering darkness, was like a punch to the gut, a confirmation of my worst fears.

"They're here," I whispered, my voice trembling as I turned back to face my grandmother. "The police. They've found us."

Grandma's expression was solemn, her eyes filled with sadness and resignation. She stood up slowly, her movements heavy with the moment's weight. "Then we face them together," she said, her voice steady and sure. "As a family."

I nodded, drawing strength from her words even as fear threatened to overwhelm me. The future was uncertain, and the consequences of our actions were still unknown. But in that moment, as I stood beside my grandmother and prepared to face the reckoning that awaited us, I knew I was not alone.

The bonds of love and friendship that had sustained me through the darkest times would be my anchor in the storm. And though the road ahead was fraught with danger and uncertainty, I knew I would face it with the courage and resilience forged in the fires of my past.

A knock echoed through the house, each rap against the weathered wood reverberating in my bones. My heart raced, pounding against my ribs as if it sought to escape the confines of my chest. I felt my grandmother's hand on my shoulder, a reassuring touch that steadied my fraying nerves.

"Remember, Turland," she whispered, her voice a soothing balm amidst the chaos, "you are more than your mistakes. You are a good man, and I will stand by you no matter what comes next."

I placed my hand over hers, feeling the warmth of her skin, the love that radiated from her very being. In that moment, I drew strength from her presence, from the unwavering support that had been my constant throughout the years.

With a deep breath, I steeled myself for what lay ahead. The weight of my choices and the consequences of our actions seemed to converge upon this singular point in time. As I stepped forward, my hand reaching for the doorknob, I felt a kaleidoscope of emotions swirling within me—fear, regret, determination, and a flicker of hope that refused to be extinguished.

The door creaked open, revealing the stern faces of the officers on the porch. Their badges gleamed in the fading light, a reminder of the authority they represented. I met their gazes, my eyes filled with trepidation and acceptance.

"Turland Deville?" the lead officer asked, his voice gruff and uncompromising.

I nodded, my throat tight with emotion. "Yes, that's me."

As the officers stepped forward, their intentions clear, I felt my grandmother's presence beside me, a silent pillar of strength. Together, we faced the unknown, ready to confront the consequences of our past and the challenges ahead.

And though the future was shrouded in uncertainty, I knew I would face it with the love and support of those who believed in me, those who saw beyond my mistakes and recognized the potential for redemption that flickered within my soul.

Chapter 8: Tears and Handcuffs

The moonlit street fractured into chaos. Sirens wailed, red and blue lights flashed, and suddenly, I was drowning in a sea of cops. My heart hammered against my ribs as they swarmed around me, their faces complicated and unreadable.

"Turn around! Hands behind your back!" A gruff voice barked.

I froze, mind reeling. This can't be happening. Not now. Not like this.

Rough hands grabbed me, shoving me against the wall. The patterns of the wall bit into my cheek as they wrenched my arms behind my back, cold metal handcuffs biting into my wrists.

"You're under arrest." The words hung in the air, heavy and final.

They hauled me out of the door. I caught a last glimpse of the neighborhood - the crumbling bricks, the vibrant murals, the faces of my people - before they shoved me into the squad car. The door slammed with a bang of finality.

At the station, they paraded me down sterile corridors that reeked of despair. The cuffs chafed as I shuffled past holding cells, the faces of the detained haunting me with their hollow eyes. Thieves, junkies, gangbangers - all caged like animals, a menagerie of misery.

The oppressive weight settled on my chest as I realized this was my fate. I was one of them. Just another statistic, another life the system had chewed up and spat out.

They left me in a cell, the metal bars slamming shut with a resounding clang. I slumped against the cold concrete, my head in my hands.

Echoes of laughter and jeers from the surrounding cells washed over me, a cruel soundtrack of hopelessness. The dreams I clung to, the future I dared to imagine, crumbled to ash in my mouth.

In this bleak labyrinth of broken souls, only one certainty remained - my life would never be the same. As my situation's gravity crashed, dread coiled around my heart.

Yet, buried deep beneath the fear, a stubborn ember of hope remained. In the darkness, I closed my eyes and whispered a prayer.

Shouts from the corridor jolted me out of my thoughts. A familiar voice, laced with defiance, cut through the din. Jerry.

I scrambled to my feet, pressing against the bars. Two officers wrestled him down the hall, his feet lashing out at every step. They slammed him against the wall, pinning his arms behind his back.

"Get off me, man!" Jerry snarled, his face contorted with rage. "I ain't done nothin'!"

The officers grappled with him, their frustration evident. Jerry's fiery spirit burned bright, even in the face of overwhelming odds. He locked eyes with me as they dragged him past, a silent exchange of fear and solidarity.

In that fleeting moment, I saw the same desperation that clawed at my own heart. We were brothers in this struggle, bound by the chains of circumstance.

As they hauled Jerry away, his shouts fading into the station's depths, a heavy silence descended. I slid down the wall, my head thumping against the concrete.

Across town, Dame ducked into a quiet alley, his breath coming in ragged gasps. The distant sirens' wail spurred him, and his feet pounded against the pavement.

He darted around a corner, only to skid to a halt. Two officers blocked his path, their hands on their holsters.

"Don't move!" one barked, his voice sharp with authority.

Dame's eyes widened, panic rising in his throat. He spun on his heel, desperate to escape, but it was too late.

They were on him in an instant, tackling him to the ground. The air whooshed from his lungs as they pressed him into the asphalt, the rough surface scraping his cheek.

Dame struggled against their grip, his bravado crumbling. A wave of resignation washed over him as the cuffs clicked around his wrists.

"I'm sorry, Mama," he whispered, his voice cracking. "I'm so sorry."

The officers hauled him to his feet, their faces impassive. Dame's head hung low, his spirit broken.

The city's indifferent bustle mocked his plight as they led him to the waiting car. The world moved on, uncaring, while his life unraveled.

In the holding cell, I closed my eyes, my mind drifting to happier times—laughter in the park, the warmth of friendship, the promise of a brighter future.

But those memories felt like fragile mirages, shimmering just out of reach. The cold reality of our situation pressed down on me, suffocating in its intensity.

I thought of the girl I had just met and didn't even know her name. I left her behind, her smile a fleeting light in the darkness. Would she wait for me? Could love survive the ravages of time and distance? Or was it even love?

Questions swirled in my mind, unanswerable and tormenting. The uncertainty of our fate gnawed at my soul, a relentless hunger that could not be satisfied.

Yet even in the depths of despair, a flicker of hope persisted. It whispered of redemption, second chances, and a future beyond these walls.

I clung to that hope, a fragile lifeline in the storm of my emotions. It was all I had left in this bleak landscape of shattered dreams.

Russell's eyes darted frantically as the officers closed in, his trademark grin faltering. "Come on, fellas," he pleaded, his voice strained with desperation. "Can't we talk about this?"

The officers exchanged glances, their expressions unyielding. "You're under arrest," one of them stated flatly, reaching for Russell's wrists.

Russell's charm, his constant companion, deserted him in that moment. The handcuffs clicked into place, cold metal against his skin, and his smile crumbled like a house of cards. The mask of bravado slipped, revealing the raw fear beneath.

Russell's shoulders slumped as they led him away, his predicament bearing down on him. The streets he once roamed with carefree abandon now felt like a prison, the city's pulse a mocking reminder of his lost freedom.

The holding cell was a cacophony of despair, the air thick with the stench of sweat and hopelessness. As the door closed behind Russell, he found himself face to face with his friends; their eyes mirror his anguish.

"Russ..." Dame whispered, his voice hoarse with emotion.

Russell stumbled forward, falling into their embrace. They clung to each other like drowning men, their tears mingling in a silent chorus of shared pain.

"How did it come to this?" Jerry murmured, his usual fiery spirit dimmed by the weight of their circumstances.

I shook my head, words failing me. The disbelief, the sheer incredulity of our situation, hung heavy in the air.

"We're in this together," I managed, my voice barely above a whisper. "No matter what happens, we've got each other."

The others nodded, their faces etched with a grim determination. In that moment, our bond was a lifeline, a fragile thread of hope in the darkness.

As we huddled together, the cold walls of the cell seemed to close in around us. The future stretched out before us, bleak and uncertain, a twisted path paved with the consequences of our actions.

Yet a flicker of defiance persisted even in the depths of our despair. It whispered of resilience, of the strength that had carried us through the trials of our past.

We would face this challenge as we had faced all others - together, united by the unbreakable ties of our friendship. In this crucible of adversity, our loyalty to each other was the only thing that mattered.

The road ahead was shrouded in shadows, but we would walk it side by side, our steps in unison, our hearts beating. And perhaps, in the end, we would find the redemption we desperately sought.

The door to the interrogation room swung open with a metallic clang, jolting me from my thoughts. A stern-faced detective, his features chiseled from years of witnessing the darker side of humanity, stepped inside. The fluorescent lights cast harsh shadows across his weathered skin as he sat across from me, a thick file in his hands.

"Turland Deville," he began, his voice a low rumble. "You've got quite a rap sheet here. Burglary, assault, and now this." He tapped the file, his eyes boring into mine. "It's time to come clean, son. Tell me what happened."

I swallowed hard, my mouth suddenly dry. The weight of my choices and our situation's gravity pressed upon me like a physical force. I could feel the detective's gaze, searching for cracks in my composure for any sign of weakness.

"I... I don't know what you want me to say," I managed, my voice barely above a whisper. "We didn't do anything wrong."

The detective leaned forward, his elbows resting on the table. "Listen, kid. Your friends are in the other rooms, spilling their guts. You don't want to be the odd man out."

A wave of anger surged through me, hot and fierce. The thought of my brothers, my ride-or-die crew, turning on each other was almost too much to bear. We had sworn an oath, a sacred vow of loyalty that transcended the laws of men.

"You're lying," I said, my jaw clenched tight. "They would never do that. We stick together, no matter what."

The detective's eyes narrowed, a flicker of something unreadable crossing his face. "You think this is some game? You're looking at serious time here, Turland. Don't throw your life away for a misplaced sense of loyalty."

I closed my eyes, reverting to a different time and place. The sun-dappled grass of the park and my friends' laughter echoed through the air. We were young then, untouched by the harsh realities of the world.

"Yo, T!" Jerry called out, his grin wide and infectious. "Catch!"

He tossed a football in a perfect spiral, the ball arcing through the clear blue sky. I leaped up, my fingers grazing the worn leather as I snatched it from the air.

"Nice catch, man!" Dame shouted, his voice filled with admiration.

Russell clapped me on the back, his smile brighter than the sun. "That's our boy, always coming through in the clutch."

We collapsed onto the grass, our chests heaving with exertion and joy. Our bonds were unbreakable, forged in the fires of shared struggles and triumphs.

"We're gonna make it out of here someday," I said, my eyes fixed on the endless sky above us. "All of us, together."

The others nodded, their faces alight with the same fierce determination that burned within me.

"Ain't nothing gonna stop us," Jerry declared, his voice ringing with conviction. "We're brothers, now and forever."

The memory faded, the colors bleeding back into the stark reality of the interrogation room. The detective was still watching me, his expression a mix of frustration and something almost resembling pity.

"Those were just kids' dreams," he said, his voice softer now. "The world doesn't work that way, Turland. Sooner or later, you've got to face the consequences of your actions."

I shook my head, a bitter smile tugging at the corners of my mouth. "You don't understand. Those dreams, that loyalty... it's all we've got. It's what keeps us going when everything else is falling apart."

The detective sighed, leaning back in his chair. "And look where it's gotten you. Is it worth throwing your life away for?"

I met his gaze, my eyes burning with a fierce intensity. "They're my brothers. I'd do anything for them, no matter the cost."

The detective's eyes narrowed, his frustration palpable in our tense silence. He leaned forward, his elbows resting on the cold metal table as he fixed me with an unwavering stare.

"Listen, Turland," he began, his voice low and insistent. "I get it. You're loyal to your friends. But you've got to think about your future, too. You're young. You've got your whole life ahead of you. Don't throw it all away for some misguided sense of brotherhood."

I felt my resolve wavering, his words settling heavily on my shoulders.

"I'm not telling you anything," I said, my voice barely above a whisper. "I can't... I won't turn my back on them."

The detective's jaw clenched, his frustration boiling over into barely contained anger. He slammed his hand down on the table, the sudden noise making me cringe.

"Damn it, Turland! Don't you see what you're doing? You're throwing your life away for nothing!"

I met his gaze, my anger rising to match his. "It's not nothing. It's everything."

The scene shifts to another interrogation room, where Jerry sits across from a different detective. His eyes blaze with defiance, his posture rigid and unyielding as he stares down the man before him.

"I ain't saying a word," he spits, his voice dripping with contempt. "You can't make me turn on my brothers."

The detective leans back in his chair, a smirk playing at the corners of his mouth. "You think you're tough, don't you? Think you can handle whatever comes your way?"

Jerry's jaw tightens, his hands clenching into fists beneath the table. "I can handle anything you throw at me. I'm not afraid of you."

But beneath the bravado, there's a flicker of fear in his eyes, a glimpse of the uncertainty that gnaws at his gut. He knows the stakes, knows the price of loyalty in a world that's determined to tear them apart.

The detective sees it, too, his smirk widening into a predatory grin. "You say that now, but we'll see how long that tough-guy act lasts when you're facing a lifetime behind bars. Your friends aren't going to be there to save you then."

Jerry's resolve wavers, the weight of the detective's words settling heavily on his shoulders. He thinks of the years stretching out before him, the endless days and nights locked away from the world he knows.

But even as the fear takes hold, he clings to the memories of their friendship, the unbreakable bonds that have carried them through the darkest times. He knows he can't betray them, not now, not ever.

"Do your worst," he says, his voice thick with emotion. "I'm not turning my back on them. Not now, not ever."

The detective shakes his head, a mixture of frustration and something almost resembling admiration in his eyes. "You're a fool, Jerry. But I guess that's the price of loyalty in your world."

Jerry meets his gaze, his own eyes burning with a fierce intensity. "It's the only world I know. And I'll be damned if I let you take that away from me."

The metal chair scrapes against the concrete floor as Dame settles into it, his expression carefully blank. The interrogation room starkly contrasts the vibrant streets of the West Side, all cold fluorescent lights and oppressive silence.

"Damien Johnson," the detective says, flipping open a file. "Quite the rap sheet you've got here. Petty theft, assault, drug possession. Seems like you've been busy."

Dame shrugs, his eyes fixed on a point just beyond the detective's shoulder. "A man's gotta do what he's gotta do to survive out there."

"And that includes robbing banks with your buddies?" The detective leans forward, his elbows resting on the table. "You're looking at some serious time here, Damien. Unless you start talking."

Dame's jaw clenches, a muscle twitching in his cheek. He thinks of Turland, Jerry, and Russell, the years of friendship that have seen them through countless scrapes and close calls. The memories flicker through his mind like a grainy film reel - late nights on the basketball court, shared laughter over a game of dice, the unspoken understanding that they would always have each other's backs.

"I ain't got nothing to say," Dame says, his voice low and steady. "We did what we had to do. That's all there is to it."

The detective sighs, leaning back in his chair. "Loyalty is a noble thing, Damien. But it won't keep you warm at night when doing a 30-year bid. Think about that."

In another room, Russell sits across from a female detective, his trademark charm already wearing thin. She regards him with a cool, appraising gaze, her pen tapping against the table in a rhythmic cadence.

"Russell Dixon," she says, her voice crisp and businesslike. "I've heard a lot about you. The ladies' man, the smooth talker. But your silver tongue won't do you much good here."

Russell flashes her a smile, but it doesn't reach his eyes. "I'm sure we can come to some understanding, Detective. There's no need for things to get unpleasant."

She laughs a short, humorless sound. "You think this is a game, Russell? You and your friends are in serious trouble. And no amount of charm is going to change that."

Russell's smile falters, the reality of the situation sinking in like a lead weight. He thinks of the girl he left behind and his promises to her under the glow of the streetlights—promises of a better life, a future far away from the grim realities of the West Side.

But those dreams seem impossibly distant now, lost in the harsh glare of the interrogation room. Russell feels a rising panic, a desperate need to escape, to flee back to the familiar streets and the comforting embrace of his friends.

"Look, I didn't... we weren't trying to hurt anyone," he says, his voice trembling slightly. "It was just supposed to be a quick score, you know? Something to keep us afloat."

The detective shakes her head, a flicker of something almost resembling pity in her eyes. "There are no quick scores in this life, Russell. Only hard choices and even harder consequences."

As the interrogations continue, the four friends cling to the memories of their shared past, the unbreakable bonds that have sustained them through the darkest times. But as the walls close in and the future grows ever more uncertain, they must confront the bitter truth - that the world they once knew is gone, and the price of survival may be higher than they ever could have imagined.

The courtroom is a sea of somber faces, the air heavy with shattered dreams and broken promises. I stand alongside my brothers, our hearts pounding in unison as we await our fate. The judge's gavel falls like a thunderclap, each striking a death knell for the lives we once knew.

"Turland Deville, Jerry McMillan, Dame Johnson, and Russell Dixon," the judge chants, his voice a cold, impassive murmur. "You have been found guilty of armed robbery and assault. This court judges that you be sentenced to thirty years in the state penitentiary without the possibility of parole."

The words crash over me like a tidal wave, dragging me under, stealing the breath from my lungs. Thirty years. Three decades of my life were gone in an instant, sacrificed on the altar of youthful folly and desperate choices.

I feel the hot sting of tears in my eyes, the ache of a future ripped away, the weight of my grandmother's gaze boring into my back. I force myself to turn, meet her eyes one last time, and see the pain, love, and fierce, unyielding pride that has always been my anchor.

Her face is a map of sorrow, the lines etched deep by a lifetime of struggle and sacrifice. But even now, in this moment of ultimate despair, I see the flicker of hope in her eyes, the unspoken promise that she will never stop fighting for me, for us.

"I'm sorry," I whisper, my voice cracking under the strain of emotions too vast to contain. "I'm so sorry, Grandma."

She nods, a single tear tracing a path down her weathered cheek. "I know, baby. I know. But you're strong, Turland. Stronger than you know. You'll make it through this, and we'll be waiting for you on the other side."

As the bailiffs lead us away, the clang of the handcuffs a harsh reminder of our new reality, I cling to my grandmother's words like a lifeline. The road ahead is long and dark, the challenges immense, but I know I am not alone. I have my brothers beside me and the love of my family to guide me through the storms to come.

And somewhere, deep in my heart, a tiny flame of hope still flickers, a stubborn reminder that even in the darkest of nights, the promise of a new dawn endures.

The cold metal of the handcuffs bites into my wrists, a stark contrast to the warmth of Jerry's shoulder brushing against mine as we're led out of the courtroom. The weight of our shared fate hangs heavy in the air, a palpable presence threatening to crush us beneath its unyielding grip.

I dare to glance at my friends, their faces mirroring my anguish. Dame's jaw is set, his eyes fixed straight ahead, but I can see the tremor in his hands, the silent scream of a spirit in torment. Russell's head is bowed, his once-bright smile now a distant memory, replaced by a mask of despair that tears at my heart.

As we pass through the doors, the sounds of our families' muffled sobs echo in my ears, a haunting chorus of grief and loss. I want to turn back the clock, run to them, and promise that everything will be okay, but the cold reality of our situation holds me in its merciless grip.

"Keep your head up, Turland," Jerry whispers, his voice rough with emotion. "We'll get through this together. We must stay strong for each other and our families."

I nod, swallowing back the lump in my throat. "I know, man. It's just... it's hard, you know? Thinking about all the time we'll lose, the life we could have had."

"That life is not gone," Dame says, his voice low but fierce. "It's just on hold. We'll do our time and come out stronger on the other side. This isn't the end of our story, brothers. It's just the beginning of a new chapter."

As we step out into the harsh light of day, the sun a mocking presence in the clear blue sky, I cling to Dame's words, to the fragile thread of hope that binds us together. The road ahead is long and uncertain, the challenges immense, but I know I am not alone.

We are brothers forged in the fires of adversity.

As the prison van looms before us, a hulking beast ready to swallow us whole, I take one last deep breath of free air, letting it fill my lungs with the promise of redemption. For in this moment, even as the shadows of our fate close in, I know that the light of hope still burns within us, a stubborn flame that will never be extinguished.

Chapter 9: Welcome to Hell

The shackles rattle against my ankles as I shuffle off the bus. The weight of the chains is nothing compared to the dread settling in my chest. Jerry, Dame, and Russell are close behind, our wrists bound, our futures uncertain. We exchange glances, a silent conversation of shared fear and forced bravery. The reality of our situation sinks in like a stone, cold and unyielding.

The intake area is a sterile expanse of concrete and metal, the air heavy with the stench of sweat and despair. We're herded into a line, cattle to the slaughter, as the guards bark orders with practiced indifference.

"Strip," a guard commands, his voice echoing off the walls. "Everything off. Now."

My fingers tremble as I shed my clothes, layer by layer, until I stand exposed and vulnerable. The others do the same, our nakedness a stark reminder of how far we've fallen. The humiliation burns hot on my cheeks as the guards' eyes roam over our bodies, searching for contraband, for secrets, for anything to assert their power.

I fight back the tears that threaten to spill, blinking hard against the sting. *Can't let them see me break,* I tell myself, even as my mind races with thoughts of shame and helplessness. *get through this moment. Just breathe.*

"Open your mouth. Lift your tongue," the guard demands, his latex-gloved fingers invading the last shreds of my dignity.

I comply, my jaw clenched so tight it aches. The strip search is methodical and clinical; each prodding touches a violation of the self. They examine every crevice, every hidden space, leaving no part of us untouched by their degradation.

Is this what I've become? The thought whispers through my mind as I stand there, naked and shivering. *A body to be searched, a number to be filed away?*

I catch Jerry's eye, a flicker of understanding passing between us. We are now stripped bare in more ways than one, and the crucible of confinement tests our brotherhood. Dame and

Russell stand resolute, their jaws set, their eyes fixed straight ahead. We cling to our dignity by a threadbare string, knowing it's all we have left.

As the guards finish their inspection, I feel a part of myself slip away, left behind on the cold concrete floor. They toss our prison uniforms, the rough fabric a harsh embrace against my skin. We dress silently, our movements stiff and mechanical, as if our bodies are no longer ours.

This is just the beginning, I realize, the weight of the years ahead pressing down on my shoulders. *But I won't let this place break me. I won't let it define who I am.*

I straighten my spine, squaring my shoulders as best I can in the ill-fitting uniform. The chains may bind my limbs but cannot shackle my spirit. I will endure this, day by day, holding onto the hope that flickers like a distant star. Even the faintest light can guide us home on the darkest nights.

The guard's gruff voice shatters the silence, barking out our cell block assignments like a judge delivering a verdict. "Deville, block A. Johnson, block C. Dixon and McMillan, block B."

My heart clenches, and a wave of panic rises in my throat. Separated. The word echoes in my mind, a haunting refrain. I catch Jerry's gaze, his eyes mirroring the same fear and desperation that threaten to consume me. Our bond is our lifeline in this place, and now it's being severed.

"Keep your head up, Turland," Dame whispers, his voice steady despite the tremor in his hands. "We'll find a way."

Russell nods. His silence speaks volumes. A promise, unspoken but no less powerful, passes between us. We will survive this. We will find each other again.

As the guards lead us away, I feel a part of my heart tear, left behind with my brothers. The corridors stretch before me, a labyrinth of concrete and steel, each step taking me further from the world I once knew. The weight of the shackles, the stale air, the echoing footsteps—all reminders of the reality I now inhabit.

One foot in front of the other, I tell myself, a mantra to keep the despair at bay. *Breathe in, breathe out. Survive.*

We reach the junction where our paths diverge, and I cast one last glance over my shoulder. Jerry, Dame, and Russell—their faces etched with grim determination, their eyes holding a fierce love that transcends these walls. At this moment, I make a silent vow. I will carry their strength with me, a beacon in the darkness.

As I turn to face the unknown, a small voice whispers within me, a flicker of hope amidst the shadows. *This is not the end. It's just the beginning of a new chapter, a story yet to be written.*

With a deep breath, I step forward, ready to meet whatever lies ahead. For in the depths of my soul, I know that even in the darkest places, the human spirit can find a way to shine.

The guard's grip on my arm tightens as he leads me down the narrow corridor, the fluorescent lights casting an eerie glow on the concrete walls. The sound of metal doors slamming shut reverberates through the air, each one a jarring reminder of the finality of my situation. I feel the weight of a thousand unseen eyes upon me, judging, assessing, waiting for a moment of weakness.

keep walking, I urge myself, trying to ignore the growing sense of isolation that threatens to consume me. *Don't let them see you break.*

We stop abruptly before a cell; the rusted bars starkly contrast the sterile surroundings. The guard unlocks the door with a clang that sends a shiver down my spine. "Your new home," he grunts, shoving me inside with a rough push.

As I stumble into the cell, I see a figure lounging on the top bunk. He's a mountain of a man, with biceps the size of my head and a gaze that could cut through steel. The tattoos that adorn his skin tell stories of a life lived on the edge, of battles fought and won.

"Fresh meat," he rumbles, his voice a low growl that fills the small space. "What's your name, kid?"

I swallowed hard, and my throat suddenly dried. "Turland," I croak out, hating how my voice wavers.

The man leans forward, his eyes narrowing as he studies me. "Turland, huh? Well, let me tell you how things work around here. I'm Big Mike, and this is my cell. You follow my rules, and we won't have any problems. Got it?"

I nod, not trusting myself to speak. The tension in the air is palpable, a pulsing energy that sets my nerves on edge. I can feel Big Mike's gaze boring into me, assessing my every move, searching for any sign of weakness.

Stay calm, I remind myself, taking a deep breath. *You've faced worse than this. You can handle whatever comes your way.*

As I settle onto the bottom bunk, the thin mattress offering little comfort, I can't help but wonder what the future holds. Will I find a way to navigate this new world, forge alliances, and survive? Or will the weight of this place crush me, leaving me a shell of the man I once was?

Only time will tell, but one thing is sure: in this moment, in this cell, I am utterly alone. And yet, even in the depths of my isolation, I cling to the hope that somewhere, beyond these walls, there is still a glimmer of light waiting to guide me home.

Big Mike leans against the wall, his gaze never leaving my face. "Listen up, young blood," he says, his voice a low rumble. "In here, it's all about respect. You show respect. You get respect. You disrespect someone, you better be ready for the consequences."

I nod, absorbing his words like a sponge. "I understand," I reply, my voice steady despite the fear coursing through my veins.

"Good." Big Mike nods, a hint of approval in his eyes. "Now, let me give you some advice. First, mind your own business. Don't go stickin' your nose where it doesn't belong. Second, watch your back. Not everyone here is your friend, no matter how nice they seem. And third," he leans forward, his voice dropping to a whisper, "never, ever show weakness. The moment you do, they'll eat you alive."

I swallow hard, the weight of his words settling like a stone in my gut. *This is my reality now,* I think, *a world where every move I make could be my last.*

As the night wears on, I lie awake, my mind racing with thoughts of the past and fears for the future. The sounds of the prison-the clanging of metal doors, the shouts of inmates, the echoing footsteps of guards-assault my ears, a cacophony of despair and hopelessness.

How did I end up here? I wonder, staring at the cracked ceiling above me. *What choices led me to this moment, to this cold, unforgiving place?*

I close my eyes, trying to block out the world around me, but the cell smells, the acrid tang of sweat, the musty odor of old mattresses, and the faint whiff of mildew invade my nostrils, a constant reminder of my new reality.

You can do this, I tell myself, clenching my fists beneath the thin blanket. *You've survived worse than this. You've faced down demons and come out the other side. This is just another challenge, another obstacle to overcome.*

But even as I repeat the words like a mantra, I can feel the weight of the prison bearing down on me, the walls closing in, the darkness threatening to swallow me whole.

Please, I pray to anyone who might be listening. *Give me the strength to endure this. Please give me the courage to face whatever comes my way. Above all, it gives me the hope to keep going, to believe that someday, somehow, I will find my way back to the light.*

A glimmer of light catches my eye as I lay there, lost in my thoughts. I turn my head towards the small, barred window, a mere slit in the concrete wall. I can see a patch of night sky through the narrow opening, a tiny fragment of the world beyond these walls.

The stars twinkle in the darkness, distant and unreachable, yet somehow comforting in their constancy. They whisper to me, reminding me there is still beauty in this world, something to hold onto, even in the depths of my despair.

I fix my gaze on those stars, letting their light wash over me and fill me with a sense of peace and possibility. They become my anchor, my lifeline, a promise that there is more to life than this cramped cell and the monotony of prison routine.

Remember, they seem to say, *you are more than your mistakes and circumstances. You can change, grow, and become the person you were meant to be.*

As I stare at that patch of sky, I feel a flicker of determination ignite within me, a spark of resilience that refuses to be extinguished. I think of Jerry, Dame, and Russell, my brothers, in this struggle, and I know that I cannot let them down or let myself down.

We will get through this, I vow silently, my eyes still locked on the stars. *We will find a way to rise above this place and reclaim our lives and dreams. We will not let this prison define us or let it break us.*

With each passing moment, the stars seem to grow brighter, their light filling the cell, filling my heart with a renewed sense of purpose. They become my silent companions, my guardians, a reminder that even in the darkest times, there is always a reason to keep going, hoping, and fighting for a better tomorrow.

As the night wears on, I find myself drifting into a restless slumber, my mind still clinging to the image of those stars, to the promise they hold. The sounds of the prison—the clanging of metal doors, the distant shouts of inmates, the crackling of the guards' radios—fade into the background, replaced by the steady rhythm of my breathing.

In my dreams, I am back on the streets of the West Side, walking alongside Jerry, Dame, and Russell. The sun is shining down on us, warm and bright, and the air is filled with laughter and music. We are young again, unburdened by the weight of our choices, free to imagine a future not defined by the confines of a prison cell.

But even as I lose myself in this vision of what could have been, a part of me knows that it is just a dream, a fleeting escape from the reality that awaits me when I wake. And yet, I cling to it, cling to the feeling of hope that it brings, the reminder that there is still a world beyond these walls, a world that I have not yet lost.

As the first rays of sunlight begin to filter through the small window, I stir from my slumber, my eyes blinking open to the sight of the gray concrete walls surrounding me. For a moment, I am disoriented, the images from my dream still lingering in my mind, but then the weight of my surroundings comes crashing down on me again.

This is my reality now, I remind myself, sitting on the thin mattress and stretching my stiff limbs. *This is the hand I have been dealt, the path I must walk.*

But even as I acknowledge the challenges ahead, I feel a new sense of resolve settling over me, a determination to face whatever comes my way with the same strength and resilience I saw in those stars.

I will survive this, I tell myself, my voice a whisper in the stillness of the cell. *I will find a way to make it through and become stronger on the other side.*

With that thought, I rise to my feet, ready to face another day in this place and begin the long journey toward redemption and hope.

Chapter 10: Adapting to Prison Life

The book's weathered spine cracks as I open it, my fingers delicately tracing the yellowed pages. I find solace in this prison library, surrounded by towering metal shelves and the musty scent of old paper—a brief escape from the cold concrete walls that have confined me for the past year.

I lose myself in the words, each a window to a world beyond these bars. Images of rolling hills and open skies flood my mind, starkly contrasting the gray monotony that envelops me. For a fleeting moment, I am free.

A distant shout shatters my reverie. I glance up, the book still cradled in my hands like a fragile lifeline. Through the small, rectangular window, I heard from the yard beyond.

Jerry's voice carries across the yard, his words sharp as shattered glass. "Back off, man! Leave the kid alone."

I rise, placing the book gently on the scarred wooden table. As I approach the window, my breath fogs the glass. Jerry stands tall, his shoulders squared, facing off against another inmate. The more petite prisoner cowers behind him, fear etched into his youthful features.

The aggressor sneers, his face a twisted mask of bravado. "This ain't your business, Jerry. Walk away."

Jerry steps forward, undeterred. "I'm making it my business. The kid's off-limits, you hear?"

I watch, my heart pounding against my ribcage. Jerry's always been the protector and stands up for the weak. Even here, where strength is currency and compassion a liability, he refuses to let injustice prevail.

The other inmate hesitates, weighing his options. Jerry's reputation precedes him—a hothead fiercely loyal to those he deems worthy of his protection. After a tense moment, the aggressor backs down, cursing as he slinks away.

Jerry turns to the young prisoner, his voice softening. "You alright, kid?"

The boy nods, gratitude shining in his eyes. "Thanks, Jerry. I... I didn't know what to do."

Jerry clasps his shoulder, a gesture of camaraderie in this unforgiving place. "Stick with me, kid. I got your back."

A flicker of warmth ignites in my chest as I watch their exchange. Amid this cold, harsh world, Jerry's unwavering spirit reminds me that humanity persists and that a spark of hope can endure even in the darkest places.

I turn from the window, my gaze falling upon the abandoned book. Its pages whisper untold stories of lives lived beyond these walls. At that moment, I understood that our story was still being written. Even here, in our confinement, we can shape our destiny.

With renewed resolve, I return to the table and gently close the book. Its weathered cover holds the promise of tomorrow, a testament to the resilience of the human spirit. As I sit in the library's quiet, the distant echoes of Jerry's laughter filtering through the air, I believe redemption is possible. Like the pages before me, that hope is worth holding onto.

Silence hangs heavy in the cell, the air thick with unspoken thoughts. Dame sits on his bunk, his gaze fixed upon the ceiling as if searching for answers in the cracks and stains. His once vibrant eyes now hold a distant, haunted look, reflecting the inner turmoil that consumes him.

I watch as I walk up to the cell, my heart aching for the friend I once knew. The distance between us grows with each passing day, a chasm carved by the relentless tide of prison life. Where once we shared laughter and dreams, now only stillness remains.

Dame's voice, when he finally speaks, is barely a whisper. "I can't do this anymore, Turland. I can't keep pretending everything's okay."

His words pierce the silence, a painful admission of our struggle. I long to reach out, to offer comfort and reassurance, but the words catch in my throat. How can I promise a better tomorrow when each day feels like an eternity?

Instead, I nod, silently acknowledging the burden we bear. At this moment, there are no easy answers, no quick fixes for the wounds that run deep.

The sound of a bell echoes through the prison, signaling the start of another mundane routine. Inmates rise from their bunks, the weight of our thoughts still clinging to our shoulders as we make our way to the mess hall.

Amidst the clatter of trays and the murmur of voices, I spot Russell in the line ahead. His once confident demeanor has vanished, replaced by a hunched posture and darting eyes. The change in his appearance is startling—his hair now braided tightly against his scalp, his lips glistening with a sheen that resembles lip gloss.

As he navigates the crowded hall, I sense the tension radiating from his every move. The predatory gazes of other inmates follow him, their intentions clear in their leering and whispering. Russell's charm, once his most significant asset, now seems like a distant memory, overshadowed by the vulnerability that clings to him like a second skin.

I watch as he sits at a table in the corner, his hands trembling slightly as he picks at his food. The sight of my friend reduced to a shell of his former self sends a surge of anger through my veins. I am angry at the injustice of it all, the way this place strips away our humanity piece by piece, leaving us raw and exposed.

But even during this darkness, I cling to the hope that flickers within—the hope that somewhere deep inside, the Russell I once knew still exists, that beneath the layers of fear and trauma, his spirit endures.

As I sit beside Dame, the silence between us feels heavier than ever. The weight of our shared history, of the bonds that once held us together, threatens to crumble under the strain of this place.

Yet at that moment, as our eyes meet at the table, I see a flicker of understanding between us. A recognition that we are not alone in this struggle, that our friendship, however strained, still holds the power to sustain us.

And so, with a deep breath, I reach out and rest my hand on Dame's arm. It is a simple gesture but one filled with meaning. It reminds me that even in the darkest of times, we have each other. Hope, however fragile, still lives within these walls.

As the din of the mess hall swirls around us, I believe redemption is possible.

The weight of Russell's situation hangs heavy in the air as Turland, Jerry, and Dame gather in a cell. The space feels even more cramped than usual, the walls pressing in on them as they confront the harsh reality of their friend's vulnerability.

Turland breaks the silence, his voice low but urgent. "We can't let them hurt him. Russell's not cut out for this place, and those guys... they'll tear him apart."

Jerry paces the small cell, his anger simmering just beneath the surface. "I heard them talking in the yard. They're planning to jump him during rec time tomorrow. We gotta do something, man."

Dame remains seated on the bunk, his eyes fixed on the floor. The distance between them seems to stretch even further at this moment, but Turland refuses to let it consume them.

"Dame, I know you've been dealing with your shit, but we need you. Russell needs you. We're all he's got in here."

Dame looks up, his gaze meeting Turland's. At that moment, a flicker of the old connection sparks between them, a reminder of the bond they once shared.

"I'm here," Dame says, his voice quiet but persistent. "Whatever it takes, I'm with you."

Turland nods, a sense of relief washing over him. "Okay, so here's the plan. Jerry, you and I will stick close to Russell during rec time. We'll make sure he's never alone. I need you to check to see if you can learn more about their plans."

As they discuss the details, the situation's urgency settles over them like a suffocating blanket. The thought of their friend, the boy they once knew, facing such a brutal fate tears at their hearts.

"We're not gonna let them win," Jerry says, his voice a low growl. "We've been through too much together to let them break us now."

But now, those memories feel like they were from a lifetime ago. The reality of their present crashes down upon them, and the prison walls are a stark reminder of how far they've fallen.

As they finalize their plan, Turland reaches out, clasping Jerry and Dame's hands in his own. "We're gonna get through this," he says, his voice filled with a quiet determination.

At that moment, the distance between them seems to shrink, the prison walls fading away as they cling to the strength of their connection.

The prison yard stretches before us, a sea of concrete and chain-link fences. The air is heavy with tension, thick with the anticipation of what's to come. I feel it in the pit of my stomach, a gnawing sense of dread threatening to consume me.

But I push it down, focusing instead on the task at hand. Beside me, Jerry stands tall, his muscles coiled and ready for action. We move through the crowd, our eyes scanning the faces of the other inmates, searching for any sign of Russell.

And then we see him, huddled in a corner of the yard, his braids hanging limp around his face. He looks small and fragile, like a bird with a broken wing. My heart aches at the sight of him, at the knowledge of what he's been through.

We approach slowly, careful not to draw too much attention. The other inmates watch us, their eyes hard and calculating. I can feel their gazes boring into my back, wondering what we're up to.

As we draw closer, I see the fear in Russell's eyes, the way his body tenses at our approach. "It's okay," I say softly, holding my hands in peace. We're here to help you, Russell. We're not going to let anything happen to you."

He looks up at me, his eyes brimming with tears. "I'm scared, Turland," he whispers, his voice barely audible over the yard's din. I don't know what to do."

I crouch down beside him, placing a hand on his shoulder. "I know you're scared," I murmur, my voice gentle but firm. "But you're not alone, Russell. You've got us, and we'll ensure you're safe."

Jerry takes up a position on Russell's other side, eyes scanning the yard for any signs of trouble. I can see the tension in his jaw, the way his fingers twitch at his sides, ready to strike at a moment's notice.

And then we hear it, the sound of footsteps approaching. I look up to see a group of inmates heading our way, their faces twisted with anger and hatred. I recognize them as targeting Russell and seeing him as an easy mark.

I rise to my feet, squaring my shoulders as they draw closer. "That's far enough," I say, calm but commanding. "We don't want any trouble here."

The leader of the group sneers at me, his eyes glinting with malice. "This ain't none of your business, Deville," he spits, his voice dripping with venom. "That little bitch owes us, and we're gonna collect."

I feel angry at his words but force myself to remain calm. "Russell doesn't owe you anything," I say evenly, my gaze locked on the leader. "And if you try to lay a hand on him, you'll have to go through us first."

Beside me, Jerry cracks his knuckles, his stance shifting subtly as he prepares for a fight. I can see the calculations running through his mind, how he's sizing up our opponents, looking for weaknesses to exploit.

But I focus on the leader, my eyes never leaving his. "Listen," I say, my voice low and intense. "I know you think you're tough and can take what you want. But this ain't the streets, and we ain't just going to roll over and let you hurt our brother."

I take a step forward, closing the distance between us. "So here's what's going to happen. You're gonna turn around, walk away, and leave Russell alone from now on. Because if you don't, if you even think about coming near him again, you're gonna have to deal with all of us."

For a moment, the leader hesitates, his eyes flickering between me and Jerry. I can see the calculations running through his mind, the way he's weighing his options. And then, slowly, he takes a step back.

"This ain't over, Deville," he growls, his voice low and menacing. "You and your little crew better watch your backs."

But I smile a cold, humorless thing. "We'll be waiting," I say softly, my voice like steel. "And we'll be ready."

As the group slinks away, I feel relief wash over me. I turn to Russell, helping him to his feet. "You okay?" I ask, my voice gentle once more.

He nods, his eyes still wide with fear. "I don't know what I would've done without you guys," he whispers, his voice trembling.

I pull him into a quick hug, feeling the way his body shakes against mine. "We've got you, Russell," I murmur. "Always have, always will."

And as we make our way back across the yard, I feel a sense of purpose settle over me. This is what we do, what we've always done. We look out for each other, no matter the cost. Because in this harsh and unforgiving world, our bond is all we have left in this place.

The cell door clangs shut behind us, echoing through the cramped space. I sink onto my bunk, feeling the day's weight settle heavily on my shoulders. Across from me, Jerry paces back and forth. His muscles coiled tight with restless energy.

"That was too close," he mutters, running a hand over his close-cropped hair. "We can't keep doing this, Turland. Sooner or later, our luck's gonna run out."

I lean back against the cold concrete wall, momentarily closing my eyes. "What choice do we have?" I ask softly. "We can't just let them tear Russell apart."

Dame sits silently on a bunk, his gaze distant and haunted. "But how long can we keep this up?" he whispers, his voice barely audible over the constant hum of the prison. "How long before we end up in the infirmary ourselves, or worse?"

The question hangs heavy between us, the unspoken fear we've grappled with for months. Here, there are no guarantees, no promises of safety or survival. Every day is a gamble, a desperate fight to make it through to the next.

"We just gotta stay smart," I say finally, my voice low and determined. "Watch each other's backs, like we always have. It's the only way we're gonna make it through this."

Jerry nods slowly, some of the tension easing from his broad shoulders. "You're right," he sighs, sinking onto the bunk. "We've been through worse than this before. We'll find a way."

But even as he speaks the words, I can see the flicker of doubt in his eyes, the unspoken fear that maybe this time, things are different. Perhaps this place will break us in ways we never thought possible.

I reach out, clasping his shoulder firmly. "We will," I promise, my voice fierce with conviction. "No matter what it takes, we're gonna make it out of here together."

A swell of emotion rises in my chest as I look around at these men who have become my brothers.

We may be scared, battered, and bruised, but we have each other. And that's enough to keep us fighting and holding on to the hope of a better tomorrow.

The cell door clangs open, and a guard's gruff voice shatters the moment. "Deville, you've got a visitor."

Surprise flickers across my face as I stand, my mind racing with possibilities. Who could be coming to see me in this godforsaken place?

As I follow the guard down the echoing corridor, my heart pounds with anticipation and dread. The visiting room is a stark, colorless space divided by a thick pane of glass. And there, on the other side, sits his grandmother.

She looks sad and fragile in the harsh fluorescent light, her eyes wide and haunted. As I sink into the chair opposite her, I smile reassuringly. "Hey. How are you holding up?"

"That's what I need to ask you because I'm scared for you, Turland," she whispers, her voice trembling. I don't know what to do with all this and you being in here."

My heart clenches at the desperation in her tone, and I lean forward, pressing my hand against the cool glass. "Listen to me. You've taught me more than you know. My friends are all in this together, and we're not gonna let anything happen to each other."

She meets my gaze, a flicker of hope igniting in her eyes. "You believe that?"

"I do," I say firmly. "I know it's hard to see it now, but there's a future beyond these walls. You taught me that, so we hold on."

His grandmother nods slowly, a shaky breath escaping her lips. "I'll keep praying," she murmurs. "It's just... it's so hard to see you in here, and I don't know if I'll even be around when you get out."

"Please, Let's not talk about stuff like that," I acknowledge, my voice softening. We have to continue to lean on God and each other. We're family. Only God knows what's gonna happen to any of us, and this place isn't going to change his plans for us."

A glimmer of a smile touches her face, then a fleeting moment of warmth in the bleak surroundings. "God bless you, Turland," she says quietly. "Keep praying."

As the guard signals the end of our time, I hold Grandma's gaze, trying to convey everything I can't say—the love and the support.

And then she's gone, and I'm being led back to my cell, my mind whirling with the weight of our conversation.

Later that night, as I lay in my bunk, staring at the shadowed ceiling, I couldn't shake the feeling of unease in my chest—the knowledge that in this place, our lives hang by a thread, our futures balanced on a razor's edge.

And so I close my eyes, my resolve hardening like steel in my veins. No matter what tomorrow brings or how long we're trapped in this concrete hell, I will fight for them. I will hold on to the hope of a better future, even when it seems impossibly out of reach.

With that thought, I let myself drift into a restless sleep, my dreams haunted by the faces of the men I would die for—the men who are my family, my reason for surviving in this place where hope goes to die.

As the first rays of morning light filter through the narrow window, I blink awake, my mind still hazy with the remnants of my dreams. The weight of yesterday's events settles upon me like a heavy shroud, and I feel the familiar ache of uncertainty in my chest.

Swinging my legs over the edge of the bunk, I let my bare feet touch the cold concrete floor, the sensation grounding me in the present. Around me, the soft snores of my cellmates fill the air, a reminder that for now, at least, we are all still here. Still breathing.

I rise quietly, careful not to disturb the others, and go to the small sink in the corner of the cell. The water is frigid as I splash it over my face, but it helps to clear the cobwebs from my mind, bringing the world into sharper focus.

And as I stare at my reflection in the small, scratched mirror above the sink, I am struck by a sudden realization. The man looking back at me is not the same one who entered this place a year ago. There is a hardness in his eyes, a set to his jaw that speaks of battles fought and scars earned.

But something else glimmers beneath the surface like a hidden gem—a strength born of adversity, a resilience forged in the crucible of this unforgiving place.

"Never thought I'd see the day when Turland Deville was up before the rest of us," Jerry's voice cuts through my thoughts, a note of amusement in his tone.

I see him propped in his cell across the hall on one elbow, his hair tousled from sleep. "Guess there's a first time for everything," I reply, a faint smile tugging at the corners of my mouth.

"Seems like it," he agrees, swinging his legs over the side of his bunk. "But seriously, man. You okay? Yesterday was...intense."

I nod slowly, considering his words. "I'm alright," I say at last, my voice quiet but steady. "Just thinking about how much has changed. How much we've changed."

Jerry is silent for a moment, his gaze distant. "Yeah," he murmurs finally. "This place...it does something to you. Makes you realize what matters."

At that moment, I understood the truth of his words with a clarity that took my breath away. Ultimately, not the trials we face but how we choose to face them define us. The bonds we forge in the darkness light our way home.

I glance over at Russell's sleeping form in the cell with Jerry and how his face looks so much younger in repose. And I know that no matter what the future holds, I will never stop fighting for him. For all of them.

Because that is what family does; that is what love means.

As the prison begins to stir to life around us, as footsteps and slamming doors echo through the halls, I feel a renewed sense of purpose settling over me like a mantle.

We will survive this place. We will find our way back to the light. And we will do it together, bound by the unbreakable ties of brotherhood and hope.

It is a promise to myself and the men who have become my world. A vow that I will carry with me, no matter where the road ahead may lead.

For now, I am not just Turland Deville, the dreamer from the west side of Chicago. I am a survivor, a protector, a beacon of hope in a world that so often seems devoid of it.

And that is a truth that no prison can ever take away.

Chapter 11: The Riot

The sun was beating down on the concrete yard, glinting off the razor wire that lines the chain-link fences. I had to squint against the glare, taking a drag from my cigarette as I leaned against the bleachers. Jerry, Dame, and Russell sat in our usual spots beside me.

"Another day in paradise," Jerry says amusingly, scratching his stubbled cheek. His bruised knuckles still show the marks from his last scuffle.

"Could be worse," I shrug, exhaling a plume of smoke. "At least the weather's decent." I'm always trying to find that silver lining, however thin.

Dame chuckles, low and rough. "Listen to you, Turland. Regular ray of sunshine, ain't you?" He reaches over and snatches the cigarette from my fingers to take his pull.

"Someone's gotta keep the hope alive in here." I quirk a half-smile. "So what's on the agenda today, gentlemen?"

Russell opens his mouth to reply when a sudden roar erupts from the other end of the yard. Shouts and curses ricochet off the concrete walls. We all snap our heads toward the commotion, instantly alert.

Across the way, near the weight benches, a group of inmates clash violently. Fists fly, connecting with flesh in sickening thuds. Crimson splatters on the ground. Makeshift blades flash under the unrelenting sun.

"Shit..." Dame breathes out, flicking the cigarette to the ground. We rise as one, muscles coiled, ready to move.

The guards rush in, batons raised, and whistles shrieking. But their presence only seems to fuel the frenzy. More bodies surge into the fray, unleashing an avalanche of pent-up rage.

I catch Jerry's eye and see my trepidation mirrored there. Dame and Russell flank us. Their stances are defensive. None of us are strangers to violence here, but this feels different—bigger. Uglier.

The riot spirals outward, tendrils of chaos snaking through the yard. Cons shove and swing everywhere, old grudges and new slights erupting in a cacophony of brutality. The anger is a living, seething thing.

My heart pounds against my ribs as the tide of violence inches closer. I swallow hard, mouth gone bone-dry. Is this it? The day our luck finally runs out?

"We need to move," I hiss to the others, urgency sharpening my words. "Find some cover, ride it out." Easier said than done in this powder keg.

We start pushing through the edges of the brawl, trying to skirt the worst of it. Elbows and shoulders slam into us from all sides. Angry faces contort in wordless snarls, caught up in the fever pitch.

The stink of sweat and blood clogs my nostrils. Screams mingle with the meaty thump of fists on flesh, a hellish symphony. Panic claws at my guts, my mind racing to find an escape from this nightmare.

But there's nowhere to run, nowhere to hide. We're trapped in this seething mass of rage and desperation, just more fodder for the relentless machine of the system that ground us down to this.

I think wildly we must stay together, frantically scanning for the others in the crush of bodies. We have to watch each other's backs, like always. It's the only way we'll survive this, the only way we've ever survived anything in this godforsaken place.

As the riot rages on, I pray to a god I'm not sure listens to the prayers of condemned men. I pray for a miracle, salvation, and a glimmer of that hope I've tried so hard to keep kindled in my chest.

But in the churning sea of violence and fury, hope feels like a distant dream, fading fast under the cold, cruel light of day in the prison yard turned battleground.

My heart hammers against my ribs as I lunge forward, grabbing Jerry's arm in a vice-like grip. "Stay close!" I yell over the din, my voice raw and desperate. "We gotta stick together!"

Jerry nods, his eyes wide with fear, but his jaw is set determinedly. We forge ahead, pushing through the crowd, our bodies battered by the tide of humanity. It's like swimming against a rip current, every step a battle.

Dame and Russell are somewhere in this chaos. I know it. We can't leave them behind. Panic rises in my throat at the thought of losing sight of them, of being separated in this madness.

"There!" Jerry shouts, pointing towards the far side of the yard. I glimpse Dame's tall frame, his arms raised to fend off an attacker. Russell's beside him, ducking a wild swing.

We fight our way towards them, desperate to close the gap. But the crowd surges again, a wave of bodies crashing against us. I'm ripped away from Jerry, my fingers slipping from his arm. "No!" I scream, but my voice is lost in the roar.

I'm spinning, disoriented, buffeted on all sides. I catch sight of the kitchen door, a tiny island of hope in the sea of violence. If I can get there, maybe I can find the others and regroup.

I sprint for it, dodging blows, my lungs burning. I'm almost there when I collide with someone, hard. We tumble to the ground in a tangle of limbs. I scramble to my feet, ready to fight, but it's Dame, his face contorted in pain and relief.

"Turland," he gasps, "thank God. Where's Russell? Jerry?"

"I don't know," I pant, hauling him up. "Lost them in the crowd. We gotta get inside, find them..."

We battle our way to the kitchen together, shouldering through the door and slamming it shut behind us. Dame grabs a heavy table, upending it to barricade the entrance. We collapse against it, chests heaving, the wood shuddering under the impact of bodies on the other side.

In the sudden, eerie quiet, the aftermath of the adrenaline rush hits me like a truck. My hands shake uncontrollably. Tears sting my eyes. Jerry, Russell... they're still out there. Guilt twists in my guts like a knife.

Dame meets my gaze, his expression haunted. "We'll find them," he says as if reading my thoughts. "We'll figure this out. We always do."

I nod, trying to believe him and cling to that fragile thread of hope. But as the riot rages on beyond the barricaded door, doubt coils in my chest like a cold and heavy snake.

At this moment, surrounded by chaos and fear, with my brothers lost in the madness, I've never felt so helpless, so utterly alone. All I can do is pray that somehow, against all odds, we'll find a way through this nightmare... together.

In the laundry room, Russell crouches behind a row of industrial washers, his heart hammering against his ribs. The cold metal presses into his back, a stark contrast to the heat of his fear. He strains his ears, listening for any sign of his friends amidst the muffled shouts and thuds from beyond the door.

"Come on, Turland," he mutters under his breath, his voice barely audible over the hum of the machines. "Where are you, man?"

His mind races, imagining the worst: Jerry and Dame, lost in the chaos, and Turland, alone and outnumbered. The thought of his brothers facing this madness without him is a lead weight in his gut, a suffocating pressure that threatens to crush him.

Russell clenches his fists, his nails biting into his palms. He's always been the protector, watching out for the others. But now, trapped in this room, he's never felt so powerless.

A sudden crash from outside jolts him back to the present. He tenses, his muscles coiled like springs, ready to fight or run immediately. The seconds tick by like hours, each heartbeat an eternity.

And then, through the chaos, he hears it—a voice, faint but unmistakable.

"Russell! Russ, where you at?"

It's Turland calling for him. Relief floods through Russell's veins, so intense it's almost painful. He leaps to his feet, rushing to the door.

"Turland!" he shouts, pounding on the metal. "I'm here, man! In the laundry!"

For a moment, there's no response. Russell's heart sinks, fear clawing at his throat. But then, the door swings open, and there's Turland, his face bruised and bloody but alive.

"Thank God," Russell breathes, pulling his friend into a fierce hug. "Where's Jerry? Dame?"

Turland's expression darkens, his eyes haunted. "I don't know. We got separated. Dame's in the kitchen, but Jerry..."

He trails off, unable to finish the thought. Russell nods, understanding all too well the fear that grips them both.

"We'll find him," he says, his voice steady despite the tremor in his hands. "We'll find a way out of this together. No matter what it takes."

Turland meets his gaze, and in that moment, a flicker of hope sparks between them. They were silent promises, vows to never give up on each other.

And as they step out into the chaos again, shoulder to shoulder, Russell knows that whatever happens, they'll face it as brothers. Always.

Turland peers through the small, grimy window of the kitchen door, his heart pounding against his ribs like a caged bird desperate for freedom. The riot rages on in the prison yard, a sea of bodies crashing against each other in a brutal, primal dance. Screams and shouts mingle with the sickening thud of fists against the flesh, a cacophony of chaos that threatens to shatter the very foundations of this concrete hell.

"Do you see them?" Dame asks, his voice tight with worry as he crouches beside me.

I shake my head, my eyes straining to make sense of the madness. "Not yet. There's too many—wait!" My breath catches in my throat as a familiar figure emerges from the fray. "It's Jerry!"

But the relief is short-lived. Jerry is caught in the open, surrounded by a group of inmates with murder in their eyes. They circle him like vultures, their faces twisted with a hatred born of years of suffering and despair.

"We have to do something!" I shout, my hands slamming against the window in helpless frustration.

Dame grabs my arm, his grip fierce. "Turland, no! We can't go out there. It's suicide!"

I whirl to face him, my eyes wild with desperation. "That's our brother out there, Dame! We can't just leave him!"

But even as the words leave my lips, I know he's right. The riot was a maelstrom of violence, a force of nature that would swallow us whole the moment we stepped outside—my mind races, searching for a way to save Jerry without losing ourselves in the process.

And then, the unthinkable happens. The inmates descend upon Jerry like a pack of wolves, their fists and feet raining down on his defenseless body. His screams pierce the air, a sound that will haunt me until my dying day.

"Jerry!" I scream, my voice raw with anguish. "No!"

Dame holds me back, his own eyes glistening with unshed tears. "We can't help him, Turland. Not like this."

I sink to my knees, my forehead pressed against the cold metal of the door. Sobs wrack my body, the weight of my helplessness crushing me like a stone. At this moment, I am not a dreamer or a survivor. I am a broken man, watching his world crumble to dust.

I take a shuddering breath, my tears mingling with the sweat and grime on my face. As I rise to my feet, a new resolve takes hold in my heart—to honor Jerry's memory and fight for a better life, not just for myself but all the lost souls trapped in this endless cycle of pain and suffering.

"We'll make them pay," I whisper, trembling with grief and determination. "For Jerry, for every brother we've lost. We'll find a way to make this right."

Dame nods, his jaw set with the same fierce resolve. And together, we turn our backs on the window, ready to face whatever challenges lie ahead.

For in this moment, we are more than prisoners. We are survivors, bound by a love that transcends these walls of stone and steel. And no matter what the future holds, we will never stop fighting for each other, for the dream of a better tomorrow.

The heavy clang of the cell door slamming shut behind us resonates through the cramped space, a stark reminder of our confinement. The air hangs thick with the weight of our shared grief, the silence broken only by the distant echoes of the prison's never-ending rhythm.

I sink onto the thin mattress, my body heavy with exhaustion and sorrow. The image of Jerry's lifeless form, sprawled across the blood-stained concrete, is seared into my mind, an indelible scar that I know will haunt me for the rest of my days.

Dame leans against the wall, his gaze fixed on the tiny window that offers a glimpse of the world beyond these walls. "We can't let this break us, Turland," he says, his voice low and fierce. "Jerry wouldn't want that. He'd want us to keep fighting, to find a way out of this hellhole."

I nod, my throat tight with emotion. "You're right. But how? The odds are stacked against us, and now we've lost one of our own."

Dame turns to me, his eyes glinting with a fiery determination. "We start by remembering who we are and where we come from. The West Side taught us to be survivors and never to give up, no matter how hard life hits us. And that's exactly what we're going to do."

His words ignite a spark of hope in my chest, a flicker of light amidst the darkness.

"The guards, the warden, they think they've won," I say, my voice growing stronger with each word. "But they don't know the strength within us, the power of our brotherhood. We'll find a way to make them pay for what they've done, to honor Jerry's memory and fight for the justice he deserves."

Dame clasps my shoulder, his grip firm and reassuring. "Together, brother. We'll do this together. For Jerry, for the West Side, for every soul trapped in this godforsaken place."

As we sit in the stillness of the cell, the weight of our resolve settles over us like a mantle. The road ahead is long and treacherous, but we know we are not alone. The spirits of our fallen brothers, the love of our community, and the indomitable will that has carried us through countless trials flow through our veins, a source of strength that cannot be extinguished.

So, we begin to plan, dream, and hold fast to the hope that even in the darkest of nights, dawn will eventually break.

Remembering the weight of Jerry's lifeless body in my arms is a burden I never thought I'd have to bear. The guards let us see him one last time, and his blood seeps into my prison uniform, staining the fabric with a cruel reminder of the life that's been stolen from him and all of us. I cradle his head, my fingers trembling as they brush against his face, hoping for a flicker of life, a sign that this is all just a terrible nightmare.

But there's nothing. Only the stillness of death and the echoes of the chaos brought us to this moment.

Dame stands beside me, his presence a silent anchor in the storm of my grief. I can feel his gaze upon me, his pain etched into the lines of his face. We've seen our share of loss, Dame and I, but nothing could have prepared us for this.

"He didn't deserve this," I whisper, my voice cracking under the strain of my emotions. "Jerry was good, Dame. He had dreams. He had hope. And now..."

I trail off, unable to express the finality of it all. Dame kneels beside me, his hand resting on my shoulder, a gesture of solidarity amidst the sorrow.

"I know, Turland. I know." His words are heavy with understanding, with the shared weight of our grief. "This place, it takes, and it takes until there's nothing left but the bones of our hopes and dreams."

We sit silently for a moment, the only sound being the distant echoes of the prison returning to its uneasy rhythm. The guards will momentarily take Jerry away and reduce him to a statistic in their reports.

But for now, he's still ours, a fallen brother cradled in the arms of those who loved him.

As we stand amidst the wreckage of the riot, the weight of our loss is heavy upon us. I know that the road ahead will be long and hard.

And so, we begin to walk, to take the first steps on a journey that will test us in ways we cannot yet imagine.

The guards bark orders as they herd us back to our cells, their voices sharp and unforgiving. But their words barely register, drowned out by the tumult of emotions within me. Each step feels leaden, as if the weight of Jerry's loss has settled into my very bones.

We pass through the corridors, a sea of faces etched with grief and anger. The air is thick with the stench of sweat and desperation, a palpable reminder of the suffocating reality that engulfs us. Yet even amidst this darkness, I catch fleeting glimpses of solidarity - a nod of recognition, a brief clasp of hands, a shared moment of silent mourning.

As the cell door clangs shut behind me, I find myself alone with my thoughts. The day's memories replay a relentless loop of chaos and heartbreak in my mind. I see Jerry's lifeless body, the anguish in Dame's eyes, the sheer helplessness that consumed us in those fateful moments.

But even as the pain threatens to overwhelm me, I feel a flicker of something else - a spark of determination that refuses to be extinguished.

I close my eyes, and in the stillness of my cell, I make a silent promise to Jerry, Dame, Russell, and every soul trapped within these unforgiving walls. We need a commitment to keep fighting, to keep dreaming, and to keep holding onto the hope that someday, somehow, we will find a way to rise above the chaos that seeks to consume us.

In this place of shadows and sorrow, hope sustains us—hope that whispers of a world beyond these walls.

The tears that once flowed freely now give way to a quiet resolve. I know that the scars of this day will linger for years to come.

And so, as the chapter of this day draws to a close, I find myself ready to face whatever tomorrow may bring. I am Turland Deville, a son of the West Side, and no matter how dark the night may seem, I will never stop believing in the dawn that awaits us on the other side.

Chapter 12: Grief Behind Bars

The worn spines of discarded books felt like old friends beneath my fingertips as I traced their faded titles, searching for solace within the prison library's musty stacks. A heavy sigh escaped my lips, the weight of Jerry's absence pressing against my chest like a vice. The books whispered promises of escape, of worlds beyond these confining walls, but the void left by my fallen friend tethered me to the inescapable reality of our loss.

I pulled a tattered volume from the shelf, its pages soft and yielding like the embrace of a trusted confidant. The words blurred before my eyes, and my mind drifted to memories of Jerry—his infectious laughter, the mischievous glint in his eye, the way he could find light in even the darkest corners of this godforsaken place. Now, that light had been extinguished, leaving us to fumble through the shadows of grief.

With the book clutched to my chest, I returned to the cell, each step feeling heavier than the last. The familiar sight of Dame and Russell greeted me, their faces etched with the same sorrow that carved into my bones. We sat in silence, the air thick with unspoken anguish.

"I found this in the library," I said, my voice barely above a whisper as I held out the book. "Thought it might help, you know, to read something... to escape for a bit."

Dame nodded, his eyes fixed on a distant point as if he could see beyond the concrete walls that trapped us. Russell reached for the book, his fingers trembling slightly as they brushed against mine.

"Thanks, Turland," he said, his voice hoarse and strained. "Jerry, he... he would've liked this one."

The mention of Jerry's name hung in the air, a tangible presence that filled the tiny cell. We clung to it, each of us grappling with the realization that he was gone and that the bond we'd forged through countless trials and tribulations had been irrevocably altered.

"Remember when he snuck those extra rolls from the mess hall?" Dame said, a ghost of a smile playing at the corners of his mouth. "Thought the guards were gonna catch him for sure, but he just waltzed right past 'em like he owned the place."

A flicker of laughter danced in Russell's eyes, a fleeting spark amidst the gloom. "That was Jerry, alright. Always had a way of making the impossible seem easy."

As we traded stories and memories, the weight in the room seemed to shift, the oppressive grief giving way to bittersweet nostalgia. The book lay open on my lap, its pages a testament to the power of words to unite, heal, and offer solace when the world outside threatened to break us.

In that moment, huddled in our shared sorrow, I understood that Jerry's legacy lived on through us—through the unbreakable bonds of friendship that even death could not sever. The books on the library shelves whispered of hope and redemption, of stories waiting to be written, and I knew ours was far from over.

Dame sits silently on the lower bunk, his eyes fixed on the gray cinderblock wall before him. The cell feels claustrophobic, and the air is heavy with unspoken grief. I watch him from the corner of my eye, my heart aching at his hunched shoulders and vacant stare.

He's been like this since Jerry's death —withdrawn, selectively mute, a shell of the vibrant friend I once knew. It's as if a part of him died along with Jerry, leaving behind a hollow space that no words can fill.

I glance at Russell, who meets my gaze with a helpless shrug. We've tried to coax Dame out of his silence to offer comfort and support, but our efforts have been met with little more than a nod or a distant, half-hearted smile.

The piercing sound of a whistle shatters the heavy stillness, signaling the start of yard time. Dame rises mechanically from the bunk, his movements stiff and robotic as he falls into line behind Russell and me.

As we step out into the harsh sunlight of the prison yard, the cacophony of voices and the clanging of weights assaults our senses. I watch Dame, hoping the change of scenery might spark some flicker of life in his deadened eyes.

On the other hand, Russell is a coiled spring of tension, his jaw clenched and his fists balled at his sides. I can see the anger simmering beneath the surface, a volatile cocktail of grief and rage threatening to boil over at any moment.

It happens in the blink of an eye—a careless bump from another inmate, a muttered insult, and Russell explodes. His voice rises above the din of the yard, raw and ragged with emotion as he squares off against the other man.

"Watch where you're going, man!" Russell shouts, shoving the inmate hard in the chest. "You think you can just walk all over people? Huh?"

The other inmate, a wiry man with gang tattoos snaking up his neck, sneers at Russell. "You best back off, boy. You don't know who you're messing with."

I move to intervene, but Dame's hand on my arm stops me. For the first time in days, I see a flicker of awareness in his eyes, a silent plea to let Russell have this moment.

The argument escalates, drawing the attention of the guards. They descend upon the scene, batons at the ready, their voices sharp with authority as they order Russell and the other inmate to stand down.

Russell, chest heaving and eyes wild, reluctantly steps back, his hands raised in surrender. The guards escort the other inmate away, shooting warning glances at Russell.

In the aftermath, I approach Russell, my hand resting on his shoulder. "You alright, man?"

He nods, his breath coming in ragged gasps. "Yeah, I just... I couldn't take it anymore. Everything's building up inside me, and I don't know how to let it out."

Dame steps forward, his voice hoarse from disuse. "We're here for you, Russ. We'll get through this together. For Jerry."

A flicker of understanding passes between us, recognizing the shared pain that binds us.

As yard time draws close and we return to our cells, I glimpse something in Dame's eyes—a spark of resilience, a hint of the friend I once knew. A small victory fills me with a renewed sense of purpose.

We may be broken, battered, and scarred, but together, we'll find a way to honor Jerry's memory and forge a path forward, one step at a time.

The worn spines of the library books beckon to me, their faded titles promising escape from the suffocating grief that haunts these prison walls. My fingers trace the cracked leather, seeking solace in the familiar texture as my mind wanders to memories of a life that seems so distant now.

It's here, nestled between the musty pages, that I find it—a tattered copy of "The Adventures of Huckleberry Finn." Seeing it sends a jolt through my heart, transporting me back to a summer long ago when Jerry and I first discovered the power of a shared story.

*****

The sun-drenched streets of our neighborhood shimmer in the heat, the asphalt radiating waves of distortion as Jerry and I make our way to the old oak tree that stands as our sanctuary. Jerry clutches a book, its cover worn and its pages dog-eared.

"What've you got there?" I ask, my curiosity piqued.

Jerry grins, his eyes sparkling with mischief. "It's called 'The Adventures of Huckleberry Finn.' Mrs. Thompson gave it to me and said it's a classic."

We settle beneath the oak's sprawling branches, the leaves casting dappled shadows across the pages as Jerry begins to read aloud. His voice, usually so brash and bold, takes on a new quality—a softness, a reverence for the words that spill from his lips.

As he reads, the world around us fades away, replaced by the winding Mississippi River and the escapades of a boy and his friend, Jim. We laugh at Huck's antics, our troubles forgotten for a few hours.

***

The memory fades, and I'm back in the prison library, the book clutched to my chest like a lifeline. I check it out, a plan forming in my mind as I make my way to the mess hall.

The cacophony of the dining area assaults my senses, but my focus is solely on Russell and Dame, huddled at a corner table.

Russell's eyes are ringed with dark circles, his jaw clenched tight. Dame picks at his food, his gaze distant and haunted.

I slide into the seat beside them, the book hidden beneath the table. "Hey, guys. I found something I think you'll want to see."

Russell barely glances up, his voice flat. "Not now, Turland. I'm not in the mood."

"Just hear me out," I press, revealing the book. "Remember when Jerry first introduced us to Huck Finn? How did we spend that summer reading it, dreaming of adventures beyond the neighborhood?"

A flicker of recognition crosses Dame's face, a ghost of a smile tugging at his lips. "Yeah, I remember. Jerry couldn't stop talking about it for weeks."

I nod, my fingers tracing the book's spine. "I thought maybe we could reread it together. For Jerry."

Russell's eyes meet mine, a glimmer of understanding breaking through the fog of his anger. "You think it'll help?"

"I don't know," I admit, my voice raw with honesty. "But I do know that Jerry would want us to stick together, to find a way to keep going. This book is a part of our history."

Dame reaches out, his hand resting on the worn cover. "I'm in. For Jerry."

Russell takes a deep breath, his shoulders sagging as he nods. "Alright, let's do it. For Jerry."

As we sit there, the book between us, I feel a spark of hope ignite in my chest. It's a small thing, this shared memory, but it's a start—a way to keep Jerry's spirit alive, to find our way back to each other amidst the darkness.

And so, with the din of the mess hall fading into the background, I open the book and begin to read, my voice carrying the words that once brought us together, a reminder that even in the depths of despair, there is still light to be found.

The cell door slams shut, the echo reverberating through the empty corridor. I sit on the edge of my bunk, the book clutched tightly in my hands. The silence is heavy, broken only by the distant sounds of the prison settling into the night.

I glance at Dame, his eyes fixed on the ceiling, lost in thought. Russell paces the small space, his anger simmering just beneath the surface. The weight of Jerry's absence hangs in the air, a tangible presence threatening to suffocate us all.

"You want to read it now?" Dame asks, his voice barely above a whisper.

I nod, my fingers trembling slightly as I open the book. The familiar words stare back at me, a flood of memories rushing through my mind. I clear my throat, my voice cracking as I begin to read.

"'It was the best of times, it was the worst of times...'" The words flow from my lips, each a tribute to the moments that defined us.

As I read, I can feel the tension in the room slowly dissipate, replaced by a gentle warmth that spreads through my chest. Dame sits up, his eyes closed as he listens, a faint smile on his lips. Even Russell stops pacing, his shoulders relaxing as he leans against the wall.

We lose ourselves in the story, the outside world fading away until there's nothing left but the four of us, united by the power of words and the strength of our friendship. At this moment, I can almost feel Jerry's presence, his laughter echoing in the spaces between the lines.

When I finish the chapter, a comfortable silence settles over the cell. Russell sighs, his voice rough with emotion. "He always loved that part, didn't he?"

"Yeah," Dame agrees, his eyes glistening in the dim light. "He'd get this look on his face like he was seeing the world for the first time."

I smile, the memory of Jerry's infectious enthusiasm warming my heart. "He taught us to find beauty in the darkest places, to hold onto hope even when it seemed impossible."

Russell nods, his gaze distant. "I just... I can't believe he's gone. It doesn't feel real."

"I know," I whisper, my grief threatening to overwhelm me. "But we have to keep going for him. We must find a way to make this count, to make our lives mean something."

Dame reaches out, his hand resting on my shoulder. "We will. Together."

As the night wears on, we take turns reading, our voices blending in a symphony of grief and resilience. And somewhere in my heart, I know that Jerry is with us, his spirit guiding us through the storm, a reminder that love endures even in the face of unimaginable loss.

The yard stretches out before us, a vast expanse of cracked concrete and barbed wire. The sun beats down mercilessly, casting harsh shadows across the faces of the inmates milling about. I squint against the glare, my eyes drawn to the far corner where a group of men huddle together, their voices low and urgent.

"What's going on over there?" Russell mutters, his brow furrowed.

I shake my head, a sense of unease settling in my stomach. "I don't know, but it doesn't look good."

We watch as the group disperses, their expressions grim. One of the men catches my eye, his gaze haunted and empty. I recognize him as one of Jerry's friends, who had shared countless hours with him in the prison workshop.

"We should do something," I say, my voice barely above a whisper. "For Jerry."

Dame nods, his eyes fixed on the ground. "But what? It's not like we can bring him back."

I take a deep breath, the weight of Jerry's absence pressing down on my chest. "We can honor him in our way. Show that he mattered, that his life had meaning."

Russell looks at me, his eyes searching. "What did you have in mind?"

I glance around the yard, my gaze settling on a small patch of earth near the wall. "There," I say, pointing. "We can make a memorial, a place to remember him."

We make our way to the spot, our steps heavy with purpose. I kneel, my fingers sinking into the dry, cracked soil. "Jerry always talked about wanting to plant a garden," I murmur, a wistful smile tugging at my lips. "Said it would give him something to nurture, to watch grow."

Dame crouches beside me, his hand resting on my shoulder. "He had a way of finding beauty in the smallest things," he says, his voice thick with emotion.

We work in silence, our hands moving with reverence as we clear away the debris and smooth the earth. Russell finds a small rock and places it at the center of the patch, a makeshift headstone for our fallen friend.

"Remember when Jerry snuck a packet of sunflower seeds from the kitchen?" Russell says, a hint of a smile playing at the corners of his mouth. "He was so excited, said he was going to grow the tallest sunflower in the whole damn prison."

I chuckle, the memory bittersweet. "He never did get to plant them," I say, my voice catching in my throat. "But he never stopped dreaming, never stopped hoping."

We stand together, our heads bowed in silence, as we pay our respects to the man who had brought light into our lives. The sun beats down on our backs, and the heat is oppressive and unrelenting, but at that moment, I feel a sense of peace wash over me.

"He's still with us," I whisper, my eyes stinging with unshed tears. "In every memory, every laugh, every dream we shared."

Dame nods, his hand finding mine. "And we'll carry him with us, always."

As we make our way back across the yard, the weight of our loss still heavy on our shoulders, I feel a flicker of determination spark to life in my chest. Jerry may be gone, but his spirit is a reminder that hope can still bloom even in the darkest places.

The metal doors clang shut behind us as we step back into the dimly lit corridors, the echo reverberating through the empty halls. I feel the weight of our shared grief pressing down on my chest, but there's a newfound strength in our bond, a resilience forged in the fires of loss.

As we return to our cells, Dame's voice breaks the silence. "He wouldn't want us to give up," he says, his words measured and heavy with emotion. "Jerry always believed in second chances, in the power of redemption."

Russell nods, his jaw clenched tight. "We owe it to him to keep going, to make something of ourselves."

I let their words wash over me, a balm to the raw ache in my heart. They're right. Jerry's memory deserves more than our despair; it deserves our hope and determination to be better than our circumstances.

We pause outside our cells, the weight of the future stretching out before us. I look at my friends, at the resolve etched into their faces, and I know that together, we can weather any storm.

"For Jerry," I say, my voice steady and clear.

"For Jerry," they echo, their voices blending with mine in a solemn vow.

As I step into my cell, the door closing behind me with a definitive click, I feel a sense of purpose settle over me.

I sit down on my bunk, my fingers tracing the worn edges of another book I'd found in the library. It's a reminder of the power of words, of the stories that can lift us out of our darkest moments and guide us toward the light.

I open the book, the pages whispering their secrets, and I begin to read, Jerry's memory a constant companion in the stillness of my cell. The future may be uncertain, but at this moment, I am exactly where I need to be, and the promise of a new chapter is waiting to be written.

As the night deepens, I find myself lost in the book's pages, the words weaving a tapestry of comfort and solace. Each sentence, each paragraph, feels like a lifeline, a connection to a world beyond these walls.

I pause, my fingers resting on a passage about the resilience of the human spirit. Its message resonates deep within me, a reminder of the strength that lies dormant, waiting to be awakened.

My thoughts drift to Dame and Russell, to the pain lingering in their eyes. I know that healing will take time and that the scars left by Jerry's absence will never indeed fade. But I also know we can begin to mend, piece the shattered fragments of our lives, and create something new together.

I close my eyes, picturing the three of us standing together in the yard, our faces turned towards the sun. It's a vision of hope, of a future where we are more than the sum of our mistakes and can find redemption in the bonds that unite us.

A soft knock on the cell door pulls me from my reverie. I look up to see Dame standing in the doorway, his expression a mix of sorrow and determination.

"Mind if I join you?" he asks, his voice low and steady.

I nod, making space for him on the bunk. He sits beside me, his gaze fixed on the book in my hands.

"What are you reading?" he asks, genuine curiosity in his tone.

I show him the cover, a small smile tugging at the corners of my mouth. "It's a story about second chances," I say, "about finding hope in the darkest places."

Dame nods, understanding dawning in his eyes. "Sounds like something we could all use right about now."

We sit in silence for a moment, the weight of our shared grief hanging between us. But beneath the sorrow, there's a flicker of something else, a glimmer of resilience that refuses to be extinguished.

"We'll get through this," I say, my voice barely above a whisper. "For Jerry and each other."

Dame reaches out, his hand resting on my shoulder. It's a simple gesture but speaks volumes, a testament to the unbreakable bond that ties us together.

As we sit there, the quiet of the night enveloping us, I feel a sense of peace wash over me.

I open the book once more, the words a beacon in the darkness, and I begin to read aloud, my voice a gentle murmur in the stillness of the cell. And as the story unfolds, I can almost feel Jerry's presence, a whisper of hope in the shadows, guiding us toward the light.

Chapter 13: Paths Diverge

The days, at times, seem to blend. It's just another day with the sun beating down on the cracked concrete of the prison yard, casting those familiar shadows across the faces of my two closest friends. Dame leans back against the wall, his dark eyes glinting with mischief as he recounts a tale from our youth. "Remember when we snuck into that abandoned warehouse on the low end? Thought we'd find some hidden treasure, but all we got was a face full of cobwebs and a near heart attack from that mangy old dog!"

Russell chuckles, his laughter rumbling deep in his chest. "Man, we were some stupid back then. Chasing dreams in all the wrong places."

I can't help but smile, the memories flooding back like a bittersweet tide. Those were simpler times before our choices landed us in this concrete cage. "We had some good times, though," I muse, my voice tinged with nostalgia. We could take on the world, just the four of us against everything."

Dame nods, his gaze distant as if looking back through the years. "Ain't that the truth? Thick as thieves, we were. Thought nothing could break us apart."

A comfortable silence settles over us, each lost in our thoughts of the past. The distant clang of metal doors and the shouts of inmates fade into the background as we sit together, bound by a history that runs deeper than these prison walls.

But the approach of a guard shatters our reverie, his boots crunching on the gravel. A sense of unease prickles along my spine as he stops before us, his face an impassive mask. "Deville, Johnson, Dixon - got news for you. Orders came down from on high. You're being transferred to different facilities. Bus leaves tomorrow morning."

The words hit like a physical blow, stealing the air from my lungs. I glance at Dame and Russell, seeing my shock mirrored in their faces. We've been here ten years, clinging to each other like lifelines in this sea of despair. And now, just like that, they're tearing us apart.

Dame is the first to find his voice, a hint of desperation seeping into his words. "Transferred? But why? We ain't caused no trouble, been model inmates and everything."

The guard shrugs, unmoved by our distress. "It's not my call—just following orders. Better get your goodbyes in now, boys. Come morning, you're going your separate ways." He turns on his heel and strides away, leaving us grappling with his words' weight.

I feel like I'm drowning, the future I'd clung to slipping through my fingers like sand. How will we survive this place or a new one without each other? The thought of facing these bleak days alone, without the comfort of our shared past, is almost too much to bear.

Russell reaches out, gripping my shoulder with a force that speaks of his turmoil. "We'll get through this, Turland. We always do. Ain't nothing going to break us, not even this."

I want to believe him, to cling to that shred of hope like a lifeline. But as I look around at the towering fences and barbed wire, at the despair etched into the faces of the men around us, I can't help but wonder if this is the blow that will finally shatter us beyond repair.

And as we sit in silence, each grappling with the uncertain future that looms, I can't shake the feeling that nothing will ever be the same again.

The heavy cell door clangs shut behind us, the echo re-verberating through the cramped space. We settle onto the thin mattresses, forming a small circle on the cold concrete floor. The silence hangs heavy, weighted with the reality of our impending separation.

Dame clears his throat, his voice rough with emotion. "So, this is it, huh? After all these years, they'll rip us apart like it's nothing."

Russell shakes his head, his eyes glinting with defiance. "Nah, man. They can't break us that easy. We've been through too much together."

I nod, trying to muster the same conviction, but the words feel hollow. "We'll find a way to stay connected. Write letters, maybe even get visits if we're lucky."

My fingers drift to the pocket of my prison uniform, feeling the photograph's worn edges hidden there. I pull it out, and the faded image is a stark reminder of our bond.

"Remember this?" I ask, passing the photo to Dame. "Feels like a lifetime ago."

He takes it, a wistful smile tugging at his lips. "Look at us, all young and stupid. Thought we had the world figured out."

Russell leans in, his gaze softening as he studies the picture. "We were going to be kings, remember? Conquer the streets, make something of ourselves."

I chuckle, the sound tinged with bitterness. "Yeah, look how that turned out."

The photo makes its way back to me, and I trace the lines of our teenage faces, the carefree grins that seem so foreign now. A lump forms in my throat as I think of Jerry, the fourth musketeer, lost to the same violence that once consumed our youth.

"We gotta hold onto this," I say, tapping the photo. "No matter where they send us, we can't let them take away what we have. What we've always had."

Dame nods, his jaw clenched tight. "Damn right. We're brothers, no matter what. Ain't no prison walls going to change that."

We sit silently for a moment, each lost in our memories, in the bittersweet nostalgia of a simpler time. The photo rests in my hands.

Russell breaks the quiet, his voice low and earnest. "We're gonna make it through this, y'all."

I want to believe him, to cling to that glimmer of hope in the darkness. But as I sit in this cramped cell, the weight of uncertainty presses down on me.

As the night wears on, we talk in hushed tones, reminiscing and making promises for a future we can't quite picture. As I clutch the photo close to my heart, I silently vow to keep our connection alive, to hold onto the love and loyalty that have carried us this far.

For in this unforgiving place, where hope is a rare and precious commodity, the strength of our brotherhood may be the only thing that keeps us from losing ourselves entirely.

The morning comes too soon, the harsh fluorescent lights flickering to life and casting an eerie glow across the cell. I blink away the remnants of a restless sleep, my heart already heavy with the knowledge of what's to come.

The prison is a hive of activity, a stark contrast to the usual monotony of our days. Guards bark orders, their voices echoing off the concrete walls as they herd inmates from their cells. The air is tense, a palpable sense of unease that settles over the cellblock like a suffocating blanket.

I move to the small shelf beside my bed, my fingers trembling slightly as I gather my belongings. The photo of us, worn and faded but still cherished, is atop the meager pile. Each item holds a memory, a piece of my life before these walls became my world.

As I pack, my mind wanders to Dame and Russell, wondering if they're going through the same motions in their cells. The thought of facing this day without them by my side is almost too much to bear, and I feel a lump forming in my throat.

The sound of chains rattling fills the air, a harsh reminder of our trapped reality. I take a deep breath, trying to steady myself and find the strength to face what's coming.

"Deville! Let's go!" A guard appears at my cell door, his face an impassive mask.

I nod, not trusting my voice to remain steady as I step out into the chaos of the cellblock; my heart races, and my hands are clammy with sweat. The weight of my belongings feels like an anchor, pulling me into the depths of fear and uncertainty.

Around me, inmates shuffle past, their faces etched with the same expression of resignation and apprehension that I feel in my soul. The guards herd us forward, constantly reminding us of their power over our lives.

I glimpse Dame in the crowd, his usually stoic features tinged with a hint of sadness. Our eyes meet for a fleeting moment, a silent acknowledgment.

As we're led through the winding corridors of the prison, the reality of our impending separation hits me like a physical blow. Each step feels like a lifetime, carrying me further from the only constants in my life, the brothers who have been by my side through every trial and tribulation.

For in a world where hope is a precious commodity, the strength of our brotherhood may be the only thing that can carry us through the darkness and into the light on the other side.

The heavy metal doors of the transport vehicles loom before us, a stark reminder of this moment's finality. I try to catch one last glimpse of Dame and Russell, desperate to etch their faces into my memory, but the sea of orange jumpsuits and the chaos of the transfer process make it nearly impossible.

As I step forward, the weight of my shackles feels heavier than ever, a physical manifestation of the emotional chains that bind us together. The guards roughly push me into the vehicle, their hands cold and impersonal against my skin.

I stumble into the cramped space, my heart pounding as I sit on the hard metal bench. The air is thick with the stench of sweat and fear, the palpable anxiety of the other inmates pressing in on me from all sides.

As the doors slam shut with a resounding clang, I feel a sudden rush of panic, the realization that this is it, the moment I've been dreading. The sound of the locks clicking into place is like a death knell, sealing us off from the world we've known, from the bonds that have sustained us.

I close my eyes, trying to steady my breathing as the vehicle lurches forward, carrying us toward an uncertain future. In the darkness behind my eyelids, I see the faces of my friends, the memories of our time together playing out like a bitter-sweet film.

"Stay strong, Turland," I whisper to myself, my voice barely audible over the engine's rumble. "You've got to hold on, for them, for yourself."

As the prison disappears from view, I feel a tear slip down my cheek, a silent tribute to the brotherhood I'm leaving behind. But even in this pain, I cling to the hope that some-day, somehow, we'll find our way back to each other and that the bonds forged in adversity will prove unbreakable.

For now, I have no choice but to face the road ahead.

The journey stretches on, each mile taking me further from the familiar, from the known. I watch the landscape change, the urban sprawl giving way to open fields and distant horizons, a world so different from the one I've known. As the prison transport rumbles along the highway, my thoughts drift to the past, the moments that shaped us, and the choices that led us here.

I remember the laughter, shared dreams, and the mis-chief we got into. I remember the way we looked out for each other and the way we faced every challenge together. But most of all, I remember the love and the unshakable loyalty that bound us, four brothers in all but blood.

The weight of the years settles on my shoulders, a reminder of all we've lost and endured. Yet, even in the depths of this uncertainty, I find a flicker of hope, a quiet resilience that refuses to be extinguished.

As the transport slows, my heart quickens, a mix of apprehension and determination flooding me. The gates of the new prison loom before us, a stark reminder of our reality. I take a deep breath, steeling myself for what lies ahead.

The processing is a blur of faces and forms, a monotonous routine that strips away the last vestiges of our individuality. I'm led through corridors of cold concrete and harsh fluorescent lights, the echoes of my footsteps mingling with the distant clamor of unfamiliar voices.

And then, I'm there, standing in the doorway of my new cell, a small, barren space that will be my home for the foreseeable future. The emptiness of it hits me like a physical blow, a stark contrast to the warmth and camaraderie I've known.

But as I step inside, as the door closes behind me with a definitive click, I feel a flicker of determination, a quiet resolve that grows with each passing moment.

I sit on the edge of the narrow bed, my gaze drawn to the small window that offers a glimpse of the world beyond these walls. At that moment, I made a silent promise, a vow to myself and the brothers I held dear.

I will endure this, find a way to keep our connection alive and nurture the hope that we'll be together again someday. In the end, it's that hope, that love, that will see us through, that will give us the strength to rise above the darkness and find our way back to the light.

With a sigh, I unpack my meager belongings, each item a tangible reminder of the life I've left behind. As I reach into my pocket, my fingers brush against the worn edges of a photograph, and I carefully pull it out, a bittersweet smile tugging at my lips.

There they are, my friends, my brothers—Jerry, Dame, and Russell—captured in a moment of youthful exuberance, their faces alight with laughter and dreams not yet shattered. I trace their features with my fingertip, remembering the countless adventures we shared and the bonds we forged in the face of adversity.

Gently, reverently, I place the photograph on the small shelf beside my bed, a tiny altar to the relationships that have sustained me and given me a reason to keep fighting, even in the darkest times. It's a simple, meaningful gesture, symbolizing my unwavering commitment to keeping our connection alive.

"I won't let this break me," I whisper to the silent room, the photograph that serves as my anchor. "I won't let it break us."

Chapter 14: Turland's Solitude

The ceiling stares back at me, cold and unforgiving. I've counted the cracks a thousand times, tracing their jagged lines like scars etched into my soul. Time stretches endlessly in this concrete box, each moment a reminder of the emptiness that consumes me.

Jerry's gone. The thought hits me like a punch to the gut, stealing my breath. I close my eyes, trying to picture his face, but the memory is fading, slipping through my fingers like sand. Dame and Russell, my brothers in this unforgiving world, feel like distant stars, their light dimmed by the vastness of our separation.

I sit up, the thin mattress creaking beneath me. The cell is suffocating, the walls closing in with each passing second. I need to move, to escape the ghosts that haunt me.

My feet hit the floor, the cold seeping through my thread-bare socks. I stand, my muscles protesting the sudden movement. The cell door looms before me, a barrier between the man I am and the man I want to become.

I step out into the corridor, the echo of my footsteps bouncing off the walls. The air is stale, thick with the weight of a thousand shattered dreams. I walk with purpose, my stride determined, my destination clear.

The library is my sanctuary, where I can lose myself in the pages of a book and forget the chains that bind me. I walk faster, my heart racing with anticipation. The corridors stretch endlessly, a labyrinth of despair and lost hope.

But I press on, driven by a hunger that gnaws at my soul. Knowledge is power and my only weapon in this place of powerlessness. I round the corner, the library doors coming into view.

My hand reaches for the handle, and the metal cools against my skin. I pause, taking a deep breath. At this moment, I am not just a prisoner, a number in a system designed to break me. I am a seeker, a dreamer, a man determined to rise above the circumstances that define me.

I push open the door and step inside, the musty scent of old books enveloping me like a warm embrace. A smile tugs at my lips as I walk towards the shelves, the weight on my shoulders lifting with each step.

Here, among the wisdom of the ages, I will find my solace. I will forge my path to redemption, one page at a time. The void within me may never be filled, but I will find the strength to carry on in the pages of these books. I will honor Jerry's memory and fight to reconnect with Dame and Russell.

The journey ahead is long and treacherous, but at this moment, surrounded by the written word, I am alive, whole, and ready to face whatever comes next.

I trace my fingers along the spines of the books, their titles whispering promises of knowledge and escape. Philosophy, history, self-improvement—each volume holds the potential to transform, enlighten, and inspire. I select a few, cradling them in my arms like precious treasures.

The librarian, a gentle soul with kind eyes, nods in recognition as I approach the desk. "Found something interesting, Turland?" she asks, her voice soft and warm.

"Always," I reply, a genuine smile spreading. "These books, they're my lifeline. My connection to a world beyond these walls."

She stamps the due date on each book, and her movements are practiced and precise. "Well, I hope they take you on an incredible journey."

"They always do," I murmur, hugging the books close to my chest as I make my way to a quiet corner of the library.

Settling into a worn but comfortable chair, I open the first book, the pages crisp beneath my fingertips. The words leap out at me, each one a tiny spark igniting my imagination. I lose myself in the pages, my surroundings fading away as I delve deeper into the text.

Time becomes irrelevant as I read, my mind expanding with each new concept and profound insight. The authors become my mentors, their wisdom guiding me through the labyrinth of my thoughts. In these moments, I am not just a prisoner but a student of life, eagerly absorbing the lessons laid out before me.

As I turn the pages, I feel a sense of empowerment growing within me. The knowledge I gain reminds me that even in the darkest circumstances, there is still room for growth, change, and hope. Each word is a tiny light, illuminating the path forward.

The outside world may have taken my freedom, but I find liberation in the pages of these books. I see the strength to confront my past, make peace with my mistakes, and envision a future beyond the confines of this place.

As I read, I make notes in the margins, my thoughts mingling with those of the authors. I am a passive recipient of their wisdom and active in my transformation. These books are an escape and lifeline, tethering me to the person I know I can become.

The library becomes my sanctuary, a place where I can shed the weight of my past and embrace the possibilities of my future. In these quiet moments, surrounded by the written word, I find a sense of purpose, a reason to keep pushing forward.

As I close each book, the spark within me grows brighter, and the path ahead becomes more apparent. Armed with the knowledge and strength I have gained within these walls, I am ready to face whatever challenges lie ahead.

In the pages of these books, I have found an escape, a way to reclaim my story, and a way to write a new chapter for myself. And that, I realize, is the greatest gift of all.

A soft, hesitant voice interrupts my reverie. "Excuse me, Turland?" I glance up from my book to see a young inmate standing before me, his hands fidgeting at his sides. "I was wondering if I could talk to you briefly?"

I set the book aside, a gentle smile tugging at my lips. "Of course, have a seat." I gesture to the empty chair across from me. The young man, barely out of his teens, settles into the chair, his eyes flickering between me and the table.

"I've heard about you," he begins, his voice low and uncertain. "The other guys say you're the one to talk to when you need advice, someone to listen."

I nod, my expression open and inviting. "I'm here to help in any way I can. What's on your mind?"

The young inmate takes a deep breath, his words tumbling out in a rush. "I'm struggling, man. Being in here, it's eating away at me. I keep thinking about my choices and the people I've hurt. I don't know how to move forward or make things right."

I lean forward, my elbows resting on the table, my gaze locked with his. "I understand what you're going through. I've been there myself, trapped in the cycle of guilt and regret. But I've learned that dwelling on the past won't change it. The only thing we can do is focus on the present, on making better choices from here on out."

The young man nods, his eyes glistening with unshed tears. "But how do you do that? How do you let go of the weight of your mistakes?"

I pause, considering my words carefully. "It's not easy, and it doesn't happen overnight. It's a process, a journey of self-discovery and growth. It started with taking responsibility for my actions and owning up to the harm I've caused. And then, it was about seeking knowledge, learning from the wisdom of others, and applying those lessons to my own life."

The young inmate listens intently, his brow furrowed in concentration. "And that's what the books are for?" He gestures to the stack of volumes beside me.

I nod, a smile playing at the corners of my mouth. "The books, they're like a lifeline. They've shown me that there's a world beyond these walls, a world of ideas and possibilities. They've taught me that no matter how far we've strayed, there's always a path back to the light."

The young man leans back in his chair, a glimmer of hope in his eyes. "I want that, Turland. I want to find that path, to make something of myself."

I reach across the table, my hand resting on his shoulder. "You can, and you will. It won't be easy, but you have the power within you to change your story. Embrace the lessons of the past, but don't let them define you. Focus on the man you want to become, and take one step at a time towards that goal."

The young inmate nods, a tentative smile spreading across his face. "Thank you, Turland. I needed to hear that."

I squeeze his shoulder, a gesture of understanding and support. "Anytime, brother. My door is always open, and my ear is always ready to listen. We're in this together and find our way together."

As the young man rises from his chair, his stance determined, I feel a sense of purpose settles over me. I find my path to redemption by helping others and sharing my lessons.

And as I watch him walk away, I know that this is just the beginning, that countless others like him are yearning for guidance and hope. And I vow to be there for them, the light in the darkness, the voice of wisdom amidst the chaos.

For in the act of mentoring, in sharing knowledge and experience, I find my salvation, my way to make amends for past mistakes. And that, I realize, is the true power of redemption, the true meaning of second chances.

Turland sits at the small table in his cell, the cold metal surface contrasting the warmth of the letter he holds in his hands. The paper is worn, the edges softened by the countless times he's unfolded and refolded it, a physical manifestation of the connection he shares with Dame.

He picks up a pen, the weight familiar in his fingers, and begins to write, his words flowing from a place of introspection and hope.

"Dear Dame,

I hope this letter finds you both in body and spirit. I've been thinking a lot about your chosen path and the newfound faith that has brought light into your life. It's a beautiful thing to find something that gives you purpose and peace.

I, too, have been on a journey of sorts, a quest for redemption and understanding. In the quiet moments between the chaos of prison life, I've reflected on the choices that led me here, my mistakes, and the man I want to become.

It's not an easy road, this path of self-discovery and growth. There are days when the weight of my past feels like an anchor, dragging me down into the depths of despair. But then I remember the strength and resilience that has carried me through the darkest times.

I think of you, Dame, and your courage in embracing a new way of life. Your faith has become a beacon of hope, a reminder that change is possible and that redemption is within reach.

I want you to know I'm proud of you and the man you're becoming. I hope that, in some small way, my words can offer you the same comfort and encouragement that your example has given me.

Keep walking in the light, my friend. Keep holding onto that faith that sustains you. And know that you are never alone, no matter the distance between us.

With hope and affection,

Turland"

As he sets the pen down, a sense of catharsis washes over him, the act of writing a balm for his weary soul. He folds the letter carefully, a silent prayer in each crease, and sets it aside, ready to be sent on its journey.

But as he reaches for an envelope, his eyes fall upon another letter, the handwriting on the front achingly familiar. Russell's name stares back at him, reminding him of the friend he left behind and their shared struggles.

With trembling fingers, he opens the envelope, his heart heavy with anticipation. As he reads, his brow furrows, the words on the page painting a picture of frustration and despair.

"Turland,

I don't know how much longer I can do this, man. Every day is a battle to keep my head above water. The guards here are on a power trip, always looking for an excuse to bring the hammer down.

The other inmates are like vultures, circling, waiting for a moment of weakness. I've had to watch my back every second, never letting my guard down, never showing a hint of vulnerability.

It's exhausting, this constant state of alertness, this never-ending survival dance. And for what? What's the point of all this suffering, all this pain?

I thought I was strong and could handle anything this place threw at me. But now, I'm not so sure. I feel like I'm losing myself, losing sight of the man I once was.

I need your help, Turland. I need your guidance, your wisdom. You've always had a level head, able to see the bigger picture.

Tell me how to overcome this and find the strength to keep going. Because right now, I'm hanging on by a thread, and I don't know how much longer I can hold on.

Your friend,

Russell"

Turland feels a wave of concern wash over him as he finishes reading, his heart aching for his friend's struggles. He knows the darkness Russell describes all too well, the hopelessness that can consume even the most potent spirits.

But he also knows the power of connection, the strength that comes from knowing you're not alone. With a renewed sense of purpose, he picks up his pen again, ready to offer the words of comfort and encouragement Russell desperately needs.

For in the act of writing, in sharing his journey, Turland finds a way to bridge the distance between them, offering a lifeline to his struggling friend. And in that moment, he knows that this is his calling, his way of making a difference in a world that often feels cold and unforgiving.

As I sit in the quiet of my cell, the weight of our choices hangs heavy in the air. The paths we've taken and the decisions we've made have led us to this moment, each of us grappling with the consequences in our way. Dame, with his newfound faith, seeks solace in a higher power. Russell, consumed by frustration and despair, his letters are a testament to the battles he fights each day.

And me? I find myself caught between the past and the future, the man I was and the man I long to become. The memories of our youth and shared dreams feel distant now, like echoes of a life that no longer belongs to me. But even in the depths of this place, I refuse to let go of the hope that burns within me.

I close my eyes, picturing the person I want to be—a man of wisdom, compassion, and strength. A man who can look beyond the bars that confine him and see the potential. It won't be easy, I know that.

But I am determined to walk it, to emerge from this prison not just as a free man but as a better one. I will learn from my mistakes and the choices that brought me here and use that knowledge to forge a new path. One step at a time, one day at a time, I will rebuild myself from the inside out.

The sound of footsteps echoing down the hallway pulls me from my thoughts, and I rise to my feet, ready to face whatever challenges the day may bring.

As I enter the prison yard, the sun warms on my face, and I take in the scene before me.

The yard is a microcosm of the world beyond these walls, a tapestry of stories and struggles woven together in a complex dance. I watch the other inmates navigate the space, some with confidence, others with trepidation. The air hums with an undercurrent of tension, the potential for conflict simmering beneath the surface.

But I see something else, too—opportunities for connection, growth, and change. In the faces of these men, I recognize the same longing that resides within me, the desire for something more than this existence. And I know that if I can reach out, offer a word of encouragement or a listening ear, perhaps I can make a difference, however small.

My eyes scan the yard, taking in the dynamics at play, the alliances and rivalries that shape this world within a world. And as I do, I feel a sense of purpose taking root within me, a calling to be a light source in this place of darkness.

I have seen the power of redemption and hope's transformative nature. And I know that if I can hold onto that and nurture it in myself and others, then perhaps we can find a way to break free from the chains that bind us—not just the physical ones, but the mental and emotional ones as well.

And so, I move through the yard, a silent observer and a quiet force for good, ready to lend a helping hand or a word of wisdom wherever needed. In this place of confinement, I have found a new sense of purpose, a reason to keep fighting and believing in the power of the human spirit to overcome even the darkest circumstances.

As I continued my quiet observations, a new figure entered the yard, immediately drawing my attention. The young man moves cautiously, his eyes darting around the space as if assessing potential threats or allies. A familiarity in his demeanor tugs at my memories, pulling me back to my early days within these walls.

I watch as he navigates the yard, his movements measured and deliberate. He keeps his distance from the established groups, the cliques that have claimed their territories with invisible but well-understood boundaries. It's a delicate dance that I remember all too well—the need to find your place without stepping on the wrong toes, the constant balancing act between self-preservation and the longing for connection.

I soon learned the young man's name was Coolidge Patterson. As I study him from afar, I can't help but feel a kinship, a recognition of a kindred spirit. There's a vulnerability beneath his guarded exterior, a flicker of hope that the harsh realities of this place haven't yet extinguished.

My heart aches for him and the journey ahead of him. I know all too well the challenges he will face and the temptations and pitfalls that await him. But I also see the potential for growth, transformation, and finding a new path amidst the darkness.

As Coolidge settles into a quiet corner of the yard, I find myself drawn to him, a magnetic pull I can't quite explain. Perhaps it's the recognition of my younger self in his eyes or the whisper of a higher purpose urging me forward. Whatever the reason, I know I can't stand idly by, not when I can make a difference.

With a deep breath, I approach him, my steps steady and purposeful. The words I will say are not yet clear in my mind, but I trust that they will come when the moment is right. For now, all I know is that I must reach out and offer the guidance and support that I once so desperately needed.

As I draw closer, Coolidge looks up, his gaze meeting mine with wariness and curiosity.

"Hey there," I say softly, offering a small smile. "I'm Turland. Mind if I join you for a bit?"

Coolidge hesitates momentarily, his eyes searching mine for any sign of ulterior motives. But whatever he sees must reassure him, for he nods slowly, gesturing to the space beside him.

As I settle down next to him, I feel the weight of responsibility settling on my shoulders. But it's a weight I am ready to bear, a burden I am willing to carry if it means making a difference in even one person's life.

For in this moment, as I sit beside Coolidge Patterson, I am reminded of the power of human connection and the potential for growth and change that lies within each of us. And I know this is just the beginning, the first step on a journey of redemption and hope that will transform us in ways we cannot yet imagine.

As we sit in silence, the hum of the prison yard fading into the background, I take a moment to gather my thoughts. I know that the words I choose now could make all the difference and could be the spark that ignites a fire of change within Coolidge's heart.

"You know," I begin, my voice low and earnest, "when I first got here, I felt like I was drowning. I'd never see the light of day again like the walls were closing on me."

Coolidge nods, his eyes fixed on the ground before him. "Yeah," he murmurs, "I know that feeling."

"But you know what I've learned?" I continue, leaning forward slightly. "We've got a choice, even in here. We can let this place define us and break us down until there's nothing left. Or we can grow and become better than we were when we walked through those gates."

Coolidge looks up at me, then a flicker of surprise in his eyes. "You believe that?" he asks, his voice tinged with a hint of skepticism.

I nod, holding his gaze. "I do. Because I've seen it happen, not just for myself, but for others too. It's not easy, and it sure as hell isn't quick. But it's possible if you're willing to work."

We fall silent again, each of us lost in our thoughts. I can almost see the gears turning in Coolidge's mind, the seeds of possibility taking root.

Finally, he speaks, his voice barely above a whisper. "I want that," he says, with a quiet determination. "I want to be better than this."

I smile, reaching out to rest a hand on his shoulder. "Then let's make it happen together. One day at a time, one choice at a time."

I realize this is why I'm here—not just to serve my time but to make a difference, to be a light in the darkness for those who have lost their way.

And as I look at Coolidge, seeing the glimmer of hope in his eyes, I know this is just the beginning. Together, we will walk this path of redemption, learning, and growing with each step.

In this place of shadows and sorrow, we have found a reason to keep pushing forward and believing in the power of change. And that, I know, is a gift beyond measure.

Chapter 15: Coolidge Patterson

The prison yard hummed with the restless energy of caged men with the stench of sweat and desperation. I leaned against the wall, my eyes fixed on the rusted metal door that led back into the bowels of the prison. That's when I saw him again - Coolidge Patterson, striding into the yard like a young man on a mission.

His head was held high, shoulders squared, and there was a defiant glint in his eye that I hadn't seen before. It was as if our conversation yesterday had lit a fire inside him, burning away the uncertainty and fear that had once weighed him down. The other inmates took notice, too, their gazes following Coolidge as he crossed the yard with purposeful steps.

Even the guards seemed to straighten up, hands resting on their batons, sensing the shift in the atmosphere.

I figured I would watch Coolidge from a distance, my brow furrowed with concern. That newfound confidence, while admirable, was dangerous in a place like this. It could easily be mistaken for a challenge, an invitation for trouble.

My mind drifted to memories of Jerry. He had that same swagger, that reckless bravado that made him feel invincible. But in here, that attitude could get you killed. I still remember the day they carried Jerry's body out of the prison, his once vibrant eyes staring blankly at the unforgiving sky.

I pushed off the wall and approached Coolidge, weaving through the sea of orange jumpsuits. The closer I got, the more I could see the cracks in his facade - the slight tremble in his hands, the way his eyes darted nervously around the yard. He was putting on a show, but beneath it all, he was still just a scared kid in over his head.

"Coolidge," I called out as I approached, my voice low and steady. "Walk with me."

He turned to face me, his expression a mix of surprise and relief. "Turland, I..."

I placed a hand on his shoulder, steering him away from the prying eyes of the other inmates. "I know, I know. But we need to talk."

As we walked, I could feel the weight of my past bearing down on me—the choices I had made and the people I had lost. I couldn't let Coolidge make the same mistakes. I wouldn't.

We found a quiet spot near the fence, the distant sounds of the prison fading into the background. I turned to face Coolidge, my eyes searching his. "Listen to me carefully, young blood. That fire you're feeling, that hunger to prove yourself? It's going to get you hurt. Or worse."

Coolidge's jaw clenched as he met my gaze. "I can't just be another scared little fish here, Turland. I have to show them I'm not weak."

I shook my head, a sad smile playing on my lips. "Strength isn't about puffing out your chest and acting tough. It's about surviving, being smart, and keeping your head down until you can leave here alive. You trying to fight against the current, young blood?"

Coolidge held my gaze for a long moment before dropping his eyes to the ground, his shoulders sagging under the weight of his newfound understanding. "I just don't want to lose myself here, you know? I don't want this place to change me."

My hand again found its way to his shoulder, a gesture of solidarity and understanding. "It's going to change you, Coolidge. That's inevitable. But you get to decide how it changes you. You can let it break you down, or you can let it build you up. It's your choice, young blood. But I'll guide you through it if you'll let me."

A glint of hope flickered in Coolidge's eyes, a small but significant shift in his demeanor. Maybe, just maybe, he would make it out of here with his soul intact. And maybe, in helping him, I could find a measure of redemption for myself.

The sound of heavy footsteps approaching snapped me out of my thoughts. I turned to see a group of hardened inmates, their expressions a mix of amusement and predatory interest, closing in on Coolidge and me. The atmosphere in the yard shifted, tension crackling like electricity in the air.

"Well, well, well," the group leader, a burly man with a scar running down his cheek, drawled. "What do we have here? The old-timer and the new kid, having a heart-to-heart?"

Coolidge stiffened beside me, his bravado resurfacing as he stepped forward. "Who are you calling a kid?"

I placed a hand on his chest, holding him back. "Easy, young blood," I murmured, my eyes never leaving the group of men. "This isn't a fight you want to pick."

The leader's grin widened, revealing a row of gold-capped teeth. "You should listen to your friend, boy. He knows what's good for you."

Coolidge's jaw clenched, his hands balling into fists at his sides. I could feel the anger radiating off him, the desire to prove himself, to show that he wasn't afraid. But I knew all too well where that path led.

"Coolidge," I said, my voice low and urgent. "Remember what we talked about. Don't let them get under your skin."

I thought he would ignore me momentarily, that he would charge forward and unleash all his pent-up frustration and anger on these men. But then, slowly, he stepped back, his fists unclenching.

The leader of the group let out a bark of laughter. "Looks like the old-timer has you on a leash, boy. Maybe you're not as tough as you think you are."

I could see the humiliation burning in Coolidge's eyes, the desire to lash out warring with the knowledge that doing so would only make things worse. It was a battle I knew all too well, one I had fought countless times.

As the group of men sauntered away, their laughter echoing across the yard, I turned to Coolidge. "You did the right thing," I said softly. "I know it doesn't feel like it now, but engaging with them would have only brought you more trouble."

Coolidge let out a shaky breath, his shoulders slumping. "I just feel so powerless," he admitted, his voice barely above a whisper. "Like I'm just a pawn in their game?"

I nodded, memories of my early days in prison flashing through my mind. The constant tests, the challenges to my manhood, the need to prove myself. It had taken me years to learn that true strength came from within, not from the approval of others.

"You're not powerless, Coolidge," I said, my voice firm but gentle. "You have the power to choose how you respond to their taunts and attempts to dominate you. It's not easy, but it's the only way to survive here with your soul intact."

Coolidge looked at me then, his eyes searching mine for the truth behind my words. I saw a flicker of understanding, a glimmer of hope that maybe, just maybe, he could make it through this ordeal and come out the other side as a better man.

As we stood there in the silence of the prison yard, the weight of our shared experience hung heavy in the air. The sounds of the other inmates faded into the background, and for a moment, it felt as if Coolidge and I were the only two people in the world.

"I want to believe you," Coolidge said, his voice trembling slightly. "But I'm scared, Turland. I'm scared of losing myself here, of becoming someone I don't recognize."

I touched his shoulder, feeling the tension beneath my fingers. "That fear is what will keep you human, Coolidge. Embrace it. Use it as a reminder of who you truly are and who you want to be."

Coolidge nodded slowly, a single tear escaping from the corner of his eye and rolling down his cheek. "I don't know if I'm strong enough," he whispered, his gaze dropping to the ground.

"You are," I said, my voice filled with conviction. "You're stronger than you know, Coolidge. And you don't have to face this alone. I'm here for you, and together, we'll find a way through this darkness."

Coolidge looked up at me then, a flicker of hope sparking in his eyes. "Thank you, Turland," he said, his voice barely audible over the distant sounds of the prison. "For everything."

I smiled, a sense of warmth spreading through my chest. "That's what friends are for, Coolidge. That's what friends are for."

The metal door creaked open, and Coolidge stepped into the small, dimly lit room, his shoulders hunched and his eyes darting nervously. I followed close behind, the weight of the recent confrontation still heavy on my mind.

Coolidge spun around as the door closed behind us, his face still mixed with anger and fear from the confrontation. "I just want you to know, Turland?" he snapped, his voice echoing off the bare walls. "If you weren't around, I would have had it under control."

I leaned against the wall, my gaze steady as I studied the young man before me. "Did you, Coolidge?" I asked softly. "Because from where I was standing, it looked like you were about to get into a whole world of trouble."

Coolidge's jaw clenched, and he looked away, his hands balling into fists at his sides. "I don't need your help, I don't need anyone's help," he muttered, his voice raw with emotion. "I can take care of myself."

I sighed, pushing myself off the wall and stepping toward him. "I know you can, Coolidge. But sometimes, even the strongest among us need a little support, and that's all I did, which was support you."

He shook his head, his eyes glistening with unshed tears. "You don't understand," he whispered, his voice cracking. "You don't know what it's like to be me, to have done the things I've done."

I touched his shoulder, feeling the tension beneath my fingertips. "Then help me understand, Coolidge. Talk to me."

For a long moment, he was silent, his gaze fixed on the floor. Then, slowly, he lifted his head, his eyes meeting mine. "I never meant for any of this to happen," he said, his words tumbling out in a rush. "I just wanted to make something of myself, to prove that I was more than just another kid from the streets."

I nodded, my heart aching for the pain I saw etched on his face. "We all make mistakes, Coolidge. It's what we do after that defines us."

He laughed then, a bitter, hollow sound. "And what if there is no after? What if this is all there is for me?"

I shook my head, my grip on his shoulder tightening. "It's not, Coolidge. You have a choice, a chance to be something more. But you have to be willing to fight for it."

Coolidge's eyes searched mine, a flicker of hope sparking in their depths. "How?" he asked, his voice barely a whisper.

I smiled, a sense of purpose filling my chest. "Take it one day at a time, learn from your past, and use it to shape your future. By believing in yourself, even when the world tells you not to."

He nodded slowly, a tear slipping down his cheek. "I'm scared, Turland," he admitted, his voice raw and honest. "Scared of failing, of letting everyone down."

I hugged him, feeling the shudder of his breath against my chest. "I know, Coolidge. But you're not alone. I'm here, and we'll find a way through this together. I promise."

As we pulled apart, Coolidge wiped his eyes with the back of his hand, a flicker of determination replacing the fear that had clouded his features moments before. "I want to change,

Turland," he said, his voice steadier now. "I don't want this place to define me."

I nodded, understanding the weight of his words. "It won't, Coolidge. Not if you don't let it." I paused, memories of my struggles resurfacing. "When I first got here, I was lost. I thought I had no future, no hope. But then I realized that I had a choice. I could let this place break me or use it to make me stronger."

Coolidge listened intently, his brows furrowed in concentration. "How did you do it?" he asked, genuine curiosity lacing his tone.

I leaned back against the wall, my gaze distant as I recalled those early days. "I started small. I focused on the things I could control, like my thoughts and actions. I read books. I learned new skills. I surrounded myself with people who wanted to be better, who believed in something more than just surviving."

Coolidge's eyes widened, a glimmer of recognition in their depths. "Like you," he said softly, a hint of a smile tugging at the corners of his mouth.

I chuckled, the sound echoing in the quiet of the room. "Yeah, like me. And like you, too." I met his gaze, my expression serious. "You have that same spark, Coolidge. That same desire to be more than what this place tries to make you."

He looked away, his shoulders tensing. "But what if I can't do it? What if I'm not strong enough?"

I reached out, my hand finding his. "You are, Coolidge. You're stronger than you know. And you don't have to do it alone. I'll be here every step of the way."

Coolidge's fingers tightened around mine, silently acknowledging our forged bond. "Thank you, Turland," he whispered, his voice thick with emotion. "For believing in me, for giving me a chance."

I smiled, a warmth spreading through my chest. "That's what friends are for, Coolidge. That's what hope is for."

Turland's words settled into the space between us, their weight comforting and empowering. Turland and I both could feel the shift in our relationship, a newfound depth of understanding and trust that seemed to anchor me amidst the chaos of prison life.

I looked at Turland, my eyes tracing the lines of his face, the wisdom etched into his features. "How do you do it?" I asked, my voice barely above a whisper. "How do you keep hope alive in a place like this?"

Turland leaned back, his gaze drifting to the small window that allowed a sliver of sunlight to penetrate the gloom. "It's not easy," he admitted, his voice low and contemplative. "Some days, it feels like hope is a distant memory, a dream that fades with each passing year."

He turned back to me, his eyes intense. "But then I remember the power of choice, Coolidge. The power to decide who I want to be, no matter my circumstances. And I choose to believe in something better, to hold onto the hope that there's more to life than these walls."

His words struck a chord deep within me, resonating with a part of myself I had long forgotten. "I want that, too," I confessed, my voice trembling. "I want to believe that I can be more than my mistakes and find a purpose beyond survival."

Turland smiled, a gentle, understanding smile that lit up the room. "You can, Coolidge. And you will. It won't be easy, and there will be days when you want to give up. But remember this moment. Remember the choice you made to believe in yourself."

He reached out, his hand resting on my shoulder, a gesture of support and camaraderie. "And remember that you're not alone. I'll believe in you, even when you doubt yourself."

I nodded, a lump forming in my throat as I struggled to find the words to express my gratitude. "I won't let you down, Turland," I promised, my voice filled with determination. "I'll make you proud."

Turland chuckled, a warm, affectionate sound that chased away the shadows. "You already have, Coolidge. You already have."

As we sat there, the weight of our shared journey settling upon us, I felt a flicker of hope ignite within my heart, a small but fierce flame that promised to guide me through the darkest times. With Turland by my side, I knew I could face whatever challenges lay ahead and become the man I had always dreamed of being.

Turland and Coolidge's bond had grown stronger, forged in the fires of shared experience and mutual understanding. And as they looked to the future, they knew that hope would be their constant companion, a beacon guiding them toward a brighter tomorrow.

As Coolidge departed, his footsteps echoing through the hollow corridors, I was consumed by a profound sense of reflection. The weight of our conversation hung heavy in the air, a testament to the transformative power of human connection. I leaned against the cold, unyielding wall, my gaze distant as I pondered the implications of this newfound bond.

In Coolidge, I saw a glimmer of my younger self—a lost soul searching for purpose in a world that seemed intent on breaking him. The parallels between his struggles and mine were striking, a poignant reminder of the universal human desire for redemption. As I closed my eyes, memories of my journey flooded my mind, a kaleidoscope of pain, regret, and hope.

The path to self-discovery had been treacherous, fraught with obstacles and setbacks that threatened to shatter my resolve. Yet, through the darkest times, I had clung to the belief that change was possible, that even the most shattered of souls could be mended with patience, compassion, and unwavering determination.

As I stood in the aftermath of my conversation with Coolidge, I felt a renewed sense of purpose coursing through my veins. The impact of my words, my guidance, and my support could alter the trajectory of his life to steer him away from the pitfalls that had once ensnared me. It was a responsibility I did not take lightly, a sacred trust that I vowed to uphold with every fiber of my being.

My heart swelled with anticipation and trepidation as I pushed myself away from the wall.

Ultimately, not just Coolidge's journey but my own hung in the balance. Together, we would embark on a quest for self-discovery, a pilgrimage of the soul that would lead us to the very essence of our humanity. With each passing day, each shared moment of vulnerability and triumph, we would inch ever closer to the light, to the promise of a future unburdened by the shackles of our past.

Chapter 16: Lessons and Farewells

The library's scent of aged paper and worn bindings engulfed us as I watched Turland lean back in his chair, its creak echoing softly. His eyes met mine, a faint smile on his lips. "You know, Coolidge, this place right here," he gestured to the rows of books, "this is your ticket out."

I furrowed my brow. "What do you mean?"

"Education, man. It opens doors, even for us." Turland's voice held a steadfast conviction. "You'll need more than good intentions when you walk out those gates. You'll need skills, knowledge."

His words settled into the spaces between my thoughts, taking root. I nodded slowly, my gaze drifting to the inmates hunched over their books, pencils scratching against paper. A flicker of something ignited within me—a curiosity, a hunger.

Turland must have seen it in my eyes. He clapped a hand on my shoulder. "Come on, let's put it into practice."

We rose, the chair legs scraping against the worn linoleum. Turland led me through the stacks, purpose in his stride. We emerged into a small room, a handful of inmates gathered around a table. Tools lay scattered across its surface—pliers, wire cutters, screwdrivers.

"Welcome to the workshop," Turland grinned. "Today, we're learning basic electrical work."

I hesitated, doubt creeping in. My hands, accustomed to clenched fists and hasty grabs, seemed ill-suited for such delicate tasks. But Turland's encouragement propelled me forward.

"Here, start with this." He handed me a spool of wire, its copper gleaming. "Strip the ends, then connect it to the circuit board."

My fingers fumbled at first, the wire slipping from my grasp. Turland's patient guidance steadied me. "Take your time. Focus on the task at hand."

As I worked, a sense of calm descended. The world narrowed to the wire between my fingertips and the satisfying click of the pliers. Turland's presence was reassuring, and his instructions were clear and concise.

Time seemed to stretch and contract, marked only by the progress of the wires and the hum of concentration. When I finally looked up, a small circuit board lay complete before me. It wasn't pretty, but it was functional. Pride swelled in my chest.

Turland's smile mirrored my own. "See? You've got this, Coolidge. Just imagine what else you can learn, what you can build."

His words ignited a spark within me, a glimmer of hope that had long lain dormant. For the first time in years, I envisioned a future beyond these walls—a future where my hands were created instead of destroyed, where my mind was my most valuable asset.

As we packed the tools, a newfound determination settled into my bones. The path ahead was uncertain, and the challenges were numerous. But with Turland's guidance and the promise of education, I could feel the first tentative stirrings of a different life—a life I was determined to build, one wire at a time.

The din of the prison cafeteria enveloped us as Turland and I settled onto the hard metal bench, trays on the tables. The scent of overcooked vegetables and mystery meat mingled with the sweat and desperation that clung to every surface. I pushed the limp greens around my plate, my appetite waning under the weight of my thoughts.

Turland's voice cut through the noise, a lifeline in the sea of hopelessness. "You know, Coolidge, this place has a way of making you forget who you are. It's easy to get lost in the monotony, the isolation."

I nodded, eyes fixed on the congealed gravy. "How do you do it? How do you stay sane in here?"

A wistful smile played on Turland's lips. "My friends. Dame, Russell, Jerry. Even when we're apart, the memories keep me going. The laughter, the dreams we shared. They remind me that there's a world beyond these walls, a part of me that prison can't touch."

His words stirred something in me, a longing for connection, a bond that could withstand the test of time and circumstance. "Tell me about them. Your friends."

Turland's eyes took on a faraway look as if he were peering into the past. "Dame, Russell, and Jerry are like brothers to me. We grew up together and got into our fair share of trouble. But we always had each other's backs. No matter what."

I leaned in, hanging onto every word. "What were they like?"

"Dame, he's the serious one. Always thinking and planning. He's got this quiet strength about him. And Russell, he's the heart of the group. The one who could make you laugh even on the darkest days. Jerry was the energy that gave us that go-for-it power."

The affection in Turland's voice was palpable, and their bond was tangible. I marveled at the depth of their friendship, how it seemed to transcend the physical boundaries that separated them.

"I can't imagine what it's like being away from them for so long," I murmured, pushing my tray aside.

Turland's hand found my shoulder, a comforting weight. "It's hard, I won't lie. But in a way, they're always with me. In the memories, in the lessons they taught me. And that keeps me going, the hope that we'll all be together again, on the outside."

I let his words wash over me, a balm to the ache in my chest. The thought of having a friendship like that, a connection that could weather any storm, filled me with a yearning I hadn't known I possessed.

As we rose to return our trays, I felt a new sense of purpose taking root. I wanted what Turland had—not just the promise of freedom but the unbreakable bonds of friendship. With Turland's guidance, I was determined to build those bonds, one conversation, one shared experience at a time.

A guard's gruff voice cut through the cafeteria's quiet hum. "Deville, you got mail."

Turland's face lit up, a rare sight in this place where joy was fleeting. He accepted the envelope with reverence, his fingers tracing the familiar handwriting.

As he unfolded the letter, I saw the words penned in neat, flowing script. The warmth in Turland's eyes told me everything I needed to know—this was a lifeline, a connection to a world beyond these walls.

He read in silence, his lips moving softly as if in prayer. A smile tugged at the corners of his mouth, and for a moment, the weight of the years seemed to lift from his shoulders.

"Good news?" I asked, my curiosity getting the better of me.

Turland nodded, folding the letter carefully. "It's from Russell. He's doing well and got a new job at the prison. He says he's helping kids stay out of trouble, giving them the guidance we never had."

I nodded, understanding the unspoken sentiment. Hope was a rare commodity in prison.

We fell into a comfortable silence, each lost in our thoughts as the minutes ticked by; I thought about my future and the choices ahead.

"Turland," I began, hesitance creeping into my voice. "What do you think I should do when I get out? I know I want to avoid trouble, but where do I start?"

Turland leaned forward, his eyes intense with purpose. "Start with the basics. Find a job, something steady. It doesn't have to be your dream career, but it'll give you structure, a reason to stay on the straight and narrow."

I nodded, mentally cataloging his advice. "What about my old neighborhood? The temptations, the old crowd?"

"You have to be willing to let go," Turland said, his voice firm but not unkind. "It's not easy, but sometimes you must leave the past behind to build a better future. Surround yourself with people who want to see you succeed, who'll hold you accountable."

The words settled over me like a mantle, heavy with responsibility but also a possibility. I knew it wouldn't be easy, and the road ahead would be filled with challenges.

As we left the cafeteria, I felt a sense of purpose.

Turland and I walked the perimeter of the prison yard, our shadows stretching long across the cracked asphalt. The air was heavy with the weight of our conversation, the reality of my impending release settling over us like a shroud.

"You know, it's funny," I said, kicking a pebble with the toe of my worn sneaker. "I've been dreaming of this day for so long, but now that it's almost here, I'm scared."

Turland nodded, his gaze distant as if lost in his memories. "It's normal to be afraid, Coolidge. The world is not the same as when we got locked up. Everything moves so fast, and it's easy to get lost in the shuffle."

I swallowed hard, and my throat suddenly dried. "What if I can't make it? What if I end up back here, or worse?"

Turland stopped, placing a hand on my shoulder. His eyes, usually so guarded, held a softness I rarely saw. "You're stronger than you give yourself credit for, Coolidge. You've grown so much here, learned to face your demons and come out the other side. That takes courage."

I looked away, blinking back the sudden sting of tears. "But what if it's not enough? What if I'm not enough?"

Turland's grip tightened, his voice fierce with conviction. "Listen to me, Coolidge. You are enough. You always have been. The choices you made in the past don't define you. What matters is what you do from here on out."

I met his gaze, seeing the unwavering belief in his eyes. At that moment, I desperately wanted to believe him, to trust in the strength he saw in me.

"I'm scared of failing," I admitted, my voice barely above a whisper. "Of letting everyone down, of letting myself down."

Turland's expression softened, understanding etched in the lines of his face. "We all fail sometimes, Coolidge. It's part of being human. What matters is that we keep trying, keep pushing forward even when it feels impossible."

I nodded, drawing in a shaky breath. "I want to make something of myself, Turland. I want to be someone my mama can be proud of."

Turland smiled, a rare sight that lit up his usually stoic features. "You will be, Coolidge. I've seen the potential in you since the day you arrived. You've got a good heart and a sharp mind. Don't let anyone tell you different."

We resumed our walk, the silence between us now more comfortable, less weighted with the fears that had haunted me.

"You know," Turland said, his gaze fixed on the horizon, "when I first got here, I thought my life was over. I couldn't see a future beyond these walls or imagine a world where I mattered."

I listened intently, knowing how rare it was for Turland to speak of his struggles.

"But then I realized that even here, I had a purpose. I could still make a difference, even if it were just in the lives of the guys around me. That's when things started to change."

I nodded, understanding dawning. "Like with me."

Turland smiled, a touch of pride in his eyes. "Yeah, like with you. Seeing you grow and watching you start to believe in yourself has given me hope. Hope that maybe, just maybe, I've done something worthwhile with my time here."

I felt a lump form in my throat, the weight of Turland's words settling over me. I realized how much his friendship and guidance meant to me at that moment.

"You have," I managed, my voice thick with emotion. "You've done more for me than you'll ever know."

Turland's hand found my shoulder again, a gesture of comfort and camaraderie. "We've got to have each other's backs in here, Coolidge. And when you walk out those gates, I want you to remember that you're not alone. You've got people who believe in you, who want to see you succeed."

I nodded, a newfound determination taking root in my chest. "I won't let you down, Turland. I promise."

The harsh clang of metal against metal jolted me from my thoughts as the cell door swung open, revealing Turland standing in the doorway, a small cardboard box in his hands. The day had finally arrived—my last day in this concrete cage.

"Time to pack up, Coolidge," Turland said, his voice a mix of excitement and something else I couldn't quite place. He entered the cell, setting the box on my neatly made bed.

I nodded, a lump forming in my throat as I glanced around the space that had been my home for the past few years. Once bare and lifeless, the walls now held traces of my journey—a calendar marked with the days until my release, a few worn books stacked on the shelf, and a picture of my family, creased and faded from countless hours of being held in my hands.

With a deep breath, I gathered my belongings, each a tangible reminder of the moments that had shaped me. Turland worked alongside me, his movements steady and purposeful. We moved silently, the weight of the impending farewell hanging heavy in the air.

As I placed the last possessions into the box, Turland cleared his throat, drawing my attention. "You've come a long way, Coolidge," he said, his eyes meeting mine with a fierce intensity. "I remember when you first got here, all that anger and fear bubbling beneath the surface. But look at you now—you've grown, you've learned. You're ready for this."

I swallowed hard, the sincerity in Turland's words hitting me like a physical force. "I couldn't have done it without you," I admitted, my voice barely above a whisper. "You believed in me, even when I didn't believe in myself."

Turland's face softened, a smile tugging at the corners of his mouth. "That's what friends do, Coolidge. They see the best in each other, even in the darkest times."

We settled onto the edge of the bed, the box between us, and let the silence envelop us once more. My mind drifted to our countless conversations in this spot—the laughter, tears, and shared dreams of a better future.

"I'm scared, Turland," I confessed, fingers picking at a loose thread on my jumpsuit. "Out there, it's... it's a whole different world. What if I can't make it? What if I fall back into old habits?"

Turland's hand found my shoulder, his grip firm and reassuring. "You're stronger than you give yourself credit for, Coolidge. You have a good heart and the tools to make something of yourself. It won't be easy, but I know you can do it."

I leaned into his touch, drawing strength from the unwavering faith in his words. "I'll make you proud, Turland. I promise."

"You already have, Coolidge. You already have."

We sat shoulder to shoulder as the minutes ticked, each lost in our thoughts. Once a symbol of confinement and despair, the cell felt like a cocoon—where I had shed the remnants of my past and emerged, ready to spread my wings.

As the distant sound of footsteps echoed down the corridor, signaling the approach of the guards who would escort me to the outside world, I knew that no matter what challenges lay ahead, I would always carry the lessons and love of this place and the man beside me.

The heavy clang of the cell door jolted me from my reverie, and I stood, my heart pounding in my chest as the guards entered. Turland rose beside me, his presence a steadying force as we stepped out into the corridor.

We walked silently, our footsteps echoing the distant sounds of the waking prison. The closer we got to the gates, the more accurate it became—the knowledge that I was leaving behind this place, this life.

As we approached the final checkpoint, Turland turned to me, his eyes glistening with emotion. "This is it, Coolidge. The start of your new journey."

I swallowed hard, my throat tight with gratitude and trepidation. "I wouldn't be here without you, Turland. You... you saved me."

He shook his head, a small smile playing on his lips. "No, Coolidge. You saved yourself. I just helped you see the path."

We embraced, clinging to each other as if trying to imprint this moment and connection onto our souls. When we pulled apart, a final benediction, Turland's hand lingered on my shoulder.

"Remember, Coolidge. You're not alone out there. You've got people who care about you, who believe in you. Lean on them when needed, and never forget your strength."

I nodded, my vision blurring with tears. "I'll make you proud, Turland. I'll make something of this second chance."

"I know you will, Coolidge. I know you will."

With a final squeeze of my shoulder, Turland stepped back, and I turned to face the gates. The guard beside me nodded, a flicker of understanding in his eyes as he unlocked the final barrier between me and the world beyond.

The early morning sunlight spilled across the threshold as the gates creaked open, bathing me in its warmth. I took a deep breath, the sweet scent of freedom filling my lungs, and with one last glance back at Turland, I stepped forward, ready to embrace the challenges and triumphs that awaited me on the other side.

As Coolidge's figure receded into the distance, I stood at the gates, a silent sentinel witnessing the dawn of a new chapter. Pride swelled within me, intermingling with the bittersweet ache of farewell. In the time we had shared within these walls, I had watched Coolidge transform from a frightened, lost soul into a man of purpose and resilience. The knowledge that I had played a part in his journey, that I had helped guide him towards a brighter path, filled me with a sense of accomplishment that transcended the confines of my circumstances.

Yet, as the echoes of Coolidge's footsteps faded, a pang of loneliness settled into the space he had once occupied. The realization that our daily conversations, shared laughter, and tears would now be memories tugged at my heart. But even as I grappled with this newfound solitude, I found solace in the hope that had taken root within me.

Turning my gaze inward, I reflected on the decades I had spent within these walls, the lessons I had learned, and the bonds I had forged. Though uncertain, the path that stretched before me was no longer shrouded in darkness. Coolidge's transformation had rekindled the embers of my dreams, reminding me that redemption was not a destination but a daily choice to embrace the light within.

As I stood there, the morning breeze caressing my face, I allowed myself to imagine the possibilities that awaited me: the chance to rebuild broken relationships, contribute to a world I had once felt estranged from, and create a legacy that extended beyond the confines of my past mistakes. The road ahead would be fraught with challenges, but I felt equipped to face them head-on for the first time in years.

With a deep breath, I turned away from the gates, my heart lighter than it had been in years. As I walked back towards the prison, I whispered a silent prayer for Coolidge, for the strength to persevere in the face of adversity, and for the courage to embrace the unknown. And though the future remained unwritten, I clung to the hope that had blossomed within me, a testament to the transformative power of connection and the indomitable spirit of the human soul.

Chapter 17: The Final Countdown

The crinkle of paper echoes in the quiet of my cell as I unfold Dame's letter, the words already etched into my mind from countless readings. My fingers trace the familiar curves of his handwriting, each letter a lifeline stretching across the miles and years between us.

"Keep your head up, Turland," I read aloud, my voice whispering in the stillness. "Freedom is just around the corner for all of us."

The warmth of those words seeps into my bones, chasing away the chill of the concrete walls.

I fold the letter carefully, smoothing the creases with reverent fingers before placing it beside another worn envelope.

Russell's bold scrawl greets me, a testament to our enduring bond. My mind drifts to memories of laughter shared under the flickering streetlights tears shed over shattered dreams.

A smile tugs at my lips as I recall the mischief we got up to as kids, the grand plans we spun with stars in our eyes.

"You remember when we snuck into old man Johnson's yard?" I murmur to the empty cell, my voice tinged with nostalgia. "Russell nearly got caught in the fence, and you had to sweet-talk our way out of trouble."

Laughter bubbles up from deep within, a sound that has grown rare within these walls.

I lean against the cold wall. The letters clutch my chest like talismans against the loneliness that threatened to creep in. At this moment, I feel them with me—Dame's gentle strength, Russell's unwavering loyalty—their love a lifeline tethering me to the world beyond these bars.

"Just a little longer," I whisper, a promise to them and myself. "We'll be together again, laughing under the open sky."

The letters rustle softly as I tuck them beneath my pillow, cherished reminders of the unbreakable ties that have sustained me through the long years. As I close my eyes, their faces dance behind my lids, and for a moment, the confines of my cell melt away.

The harsh clang of metal on metal jolts me from my reverie, and I find myself standing by the small window of my cell, gazing out at the prison yard. The sight of the concrete and barbed wire stirs a mix of emotions within me, a bitter reminder of the world I've been isolated from for so long.

Beyond these walls, life has marched on, seasons blending into years, while I remain frozen in time, a relic of my mistakes. The realization settles heavily in my chest, a weight I've grown accustomed to bearing.

My fingers absently trace the cool, rusty bars, and I'm transported back to my early days in prison, a young man still grappling with the consequences of his choices.

"Fresh meat!" The jeers of the other inmates ring in my ears as I'm led to my cell, my bravado a flimsy shield against the fear churning in my gut.

I remember the first time I caught my reflection in the stainless steel mirror, barely recognizing the gaunt face staring back at me. The once vibrant eyes were hollow, the cocky grin replaced by a wary grimace.

"You'll learn quick, kid," my cellmate had rasped, his voice weathered by years of smoking and shouting. "Ain't no room for weakness in here."

I learned I did the hard way—through brawls in the yard, sleepless nights listening for the whisper of a shank being drawn, and the constant gnawing hunger that no bland, taste-less food could satisfy.

Yet even in those darkest moments, when despair threatened to swallow me whole, I clung to the memories of my friends, their laughter a distant echo tethering me to the person I once was, the person I hoped to be again.

I blink away the ghosts of the past, my gaze refocusing on the present. The yard bustles with activity—inmates playing basketball, huddled in groups, or pacing the perimeter like caged animals. I watch them, marveling at how far I've come from that reckless youth who first stepped into this unforgiving world.

The lessons I've learned are etched into my very bones, each scar a testament to the resilience that has carried me through the long years. I've learned to listen more than I speak, observe the delicate balance of power, and navigate the treacherous currents of prison politics with a cool head and a steady hand.

But more than that, I've learned the value of compassion, of helping lost people, just as I once was. In the quiet moments, the whispered conversations, and shared secrets, I've found a sense of purpose, a way to make amends for the wrongs of my past.

As I turn away from the window, my gaze falls upon the stack of books on my shelf. The dog-eared pages and creased spines testify to my countless hours lost in their worlds. In the pages of those books, I've found solace, wisdom, and the strength to keep dreaming, even when the walls of my cell felt like they were closing in around me.

"One day at a time," I whisper to myself, a mantra that has seen me through the darkest nights and the loneliest days.

With a deep breath, I square my shoulders, feeling the weight of my past and the promise of my future balanced upon them.

I carry with me the strength of my convictions, the love of my friends, and the unshakable belief that even in the depths of darkness, there is always a glimmer of hope waiting to be found.

I smooth the front of my shirt, the faded blue fabric soft beneath my fingertips, and take a deep breath. The metal door of my cell swings open with a familiar creak, and I step out into the hallway, my footsteps echoing against the concrete floor.

As I make my way toward the counselor's office, prison sounds surround me—the distant clamor of voices, the clanging of metal doors, and the ever-present hum of fluorescent lights. These noises have been the backdrop of my life for so long that they've almost become a strange comfort, a reminder of the world I've known for the past three decades.

I pass by a group of inmates, some of whom I've mentored over the years. They nod in acknowledgment, their eyes conveying respect and understanding. In their faces, I see a reflection of my journey—the struggles, the mistakes, and the hard-fought battles to become something more than our worst choices.

"Keep your head up, Turland," one of them says, his voice rough but sincere. "You've taught us that there's always hope, no matter how dark things seem."

I nod back, a lump forming in my throat. "Thank you," I manage to say, my voice thick with emotion. "Remember, you've got the power to change your story, too."

As I continue down the hallway, my mind wanders to the countless conversations I've had with these men, the shared experiences, and the lessons learned. In mentoring others, I've found a sense of purpose, a way to channel the pain of my past into something positive.

The weight of my impending release sits heavy on my shoulders, a mix of excitement and trepidation coursing through my veins. The world beyond these walls has moved on without me, and the thought of navigating it alone is thrilling and terrifying.

But as I approach the counselor's office, I remind myself I'm not alone. The love and support of my friends, the strength

I've found within myself, and the hope that has sustained me through the darkest of times will guide me forward.

I pause outside the office door, my hand resting on the cool metal handle. This meeting marks the beginning of a new chapter, a chance to rewrite the ending of my story. And though the path ahead is uncertain, I know I am ready to face it, one step at a time.

With a final deep breath, I turn the handle and step inside, ready to embrace the future on the other side of these prison walls.

The counselor's office, with its soft lighting and comfortable chairs, starkly contrasts the rest of the prison. After years of concrete and metal, the space feels almost alien, a reminder of the world I've been separated from for so long.

"Turland, please come in." The counselor's voice is warm and inviting, and I feel a sense of ease wash over me as I sit across from her. "I've been looking forward to this meeting. You've made incredible progress during your time here."

Her words fill me with pride, validation of the hard work and self-reflection I've poured into my journey. "Thank you, ma'am. It hasn't been easy, but I've learned much about myself and what I want for my future."

"That's wonderful to hear," she replies, her eyes crinkling with genuine happiness. "I have some information here that

I think will be helpful as you transition back into society. There are resources for housing, employment, and continued education. I want you to know that you have support beyond these walls."

She hands me a stack of pamphlets and brochures, each a lifeline to a world I've been disconnected from for so long. I flip through them, eyes scanning the pages filled with opportunities and hope.

"I... I don't know what to say," I manage, my voice thick with emotion. "This means more to me than you can imagine."

"You've earned this, Turland. Your dedication and growth have been remarkable. I do not doubt that you will make the most of these resources and build a life you can be proud of."

Her words strike a chord deep within me, and I feel a lump in my throat. The validation of my efforts and the acknowledgment of my progress are almost overwhelming.

"I won't let you down," I promise, my voice steady despite the emotions swirling inside me. "I won't let myself down. This is a new beginning, a chance to make things right."

The counselor smiles, her eyes filled with warmth and understanding. "I have every faith in you, Turland. Remember, your past does not define you, but your future choices do. That's what you tell everyone around here, and it's very much appreciated. Embrace this opportunity, and know that you have people who believe in you, too."

I nod, clutching the pamphlets and contact information like a lifeline. This meeting has solidified my determination to create a life of purpose and meaning.

As I leave, I extend my hand to the counselor, gratitude flowing through every fiber. "Thank you for everything. Your guidance and support have meant the world to me."

She takes my hand, her grip firm and reassuring. "It has been an honor to witness your journey, Turland. I look forward to hearing about all the great things you will accomplish. Remember, my door is always open if you ever need anything."

With a final nod, I turn and exit the office. My heart filled with a renewed sense of hope and determination. The pamphlets in my hand are a tangible reminder of the opportunities that await me, the chance to build a life beyond these prison walls.

As I return to my cell, I feel light in my step, a sense of purpose that has been absent for far too long. The future is uncertain, but I am ready to face it head-on for the first time in years, knowing I can change and grow.

The metal door clangs shut behind me, a familiar sound that once filled me with dread but now carries a hint of finality. I survey the small space that has been my home for the past three decades, the walls bearing silent witness to my struggles and triumphs.

With a deep breath, I begin to gather my belongings, each item a piece of the puzzle that is my life. The worn pages of my journal are filled with thoughts and dreams, hopes and fears. A faded photograph of my grandmother, her loving smile a constant reminder of the strength that runs through my veins. The small wooden cross, carved by a fellow inmate, symbolizes the faith that has sustained me through the darkest times.

As I carefully place each item into my bag, memories flood my mind, a kaleidoscope of images and emotions. The day I first stepped into this cell, I was a frightened young man consumed by anger and regret and the countless hours spent in the prison library, losing myself in the pages of books that offered a glimpse of a world beyond these walls. The moments of laughter and camaraderie shared with other inmates are a reminder that even in the bleakest of circumstances, the human spirit can find connection and joy.

Night falls, and I lie awake on my bunk, the darkness a familiar companion. The weight of the past presses down upon me, a tapestry woven from the threads of my choices and experiences. I think back to those early days, the thrill of running wild through the West Side streets, the adrenaline rush that came with each reckless decision. The faces of my friends, Jerry,

Dame, and Russell, float through my mind, their presence a bittersweet reminder of the bonds that have endured despite our trials.

As the hours tick by, I find myself between the past's pull and the future's promise. The sobering reality of prison life, the endless days marked by the echoes of metal doors and the weight of confinement, juxtaposed against the dreams that have taken root in my heart, the whispered hopes of a life rebuilt, a purpose reclaimed.

In the stillness of the night, I close my eyes, allowing myself to imagine the possibilities that lie ahead. I have the chance to make amends, to create something beautiful from the ashes of my past, to honor the memory of those I've lost, and to carry their legacy forward into a brighter tomorrow.

As I drift off to sleep, the uncertainty of the future mingles with the quiet strength that has grown within me, a testament to the resilience of the human spirit.

The weight of thirty years presses upon my chest as I lie in the darkness, the chill of the concrete seeping through the thin mattress. The anticipation of freedom, so long yearned for, now mingles with a profound sense of trepidation. What will the world beyond these walls hold for a man like me, shaped by the unforgiving hand of time and the consequences of my choices?

I draw a deep breath, the stale air of the cell filling my lungs, and allow my thoughts to drift to the faces that have sustained me through the years. Dame is a beacon of light in the darkest times. Russell, with his strength and resilience, is a constant reminder of the power of the human spirit. And Jerry... the memory of his laughter, his boundless optimism, is forever etched in my heart.

In the calm stillness of daybreak, I make a silent vow, a promise whispered to Jerry's memory and the man I aspire to be. I will honor his legacy by living purposefully and seeking the good in others and myself. I will walk the path of redemption, not as a burden but as a sacred duty, a tribute to the love and faith that have carried me through the darkest nights.

As the prison begins to stir with the familiar sounds of another day, I feel a renewed sense of determination coursing through my veins with each passing moment. The fear of the unknown slowly gives way to a quiet strength, a resilience forged in the crucible of this place.

For in this moment, as I stand on the precipice of a new beginning, I am reminded that even the most shattered of souls can be mended, that the light of redemption can pierce through the deepest darkness. And with each step forward, I will carry the memories of those who have believed in me, the lessons learned within these walls, and the unshakable conviction that a life of purpose and meaning awaits beyond the shadow of my past.

The weight of thirty years seems to lift from my shoulders as I take in the familiar surroundings one last time. The scratches on the walls, the worn fabric of the mattress, the small window that has been my portal to the outside world—each detail etched into my memory, a testament to the life I've lived within these confines.

I stand at the threshold of my cell, my hand resting on the cool metal of the door frame. The corridor stretches before me, a path I've walked countless times, yet today, it feels different. The echoes of my footsteps mingle with the distant chatter of inmates and guards, a symphony of hope and uncertainty. As I step forward, I feel the eyes of those who have shared this journey with me—the men I've laughed with, cried with, and grown alongside. Their silent nods and knowing smiles are a language all their own, a recognition of the transformation we've undergone together.

With each step, memories flood my mind—the late-night conversations, the shared dreams, the moments of despair and triumph. I recall the words of encouragement from Dame and Russell, their unwavering support a beacon in the darkest times. And I remember Jerry, his presence forever etched in my heart, a reminder of the lives we touch and the legacies we leave behind.

As I approach the end of the corridor, the prison gates loom before me, a threshold between two worlds. The moment's weight settles upon me, and I pause, my breath caught in my throat. Thirty years of confinement, growth, and self-discovery led to this singular point. I close my eyes, inhaling deeply, the scent of freedom mingling with the lingering traces of the life I've known.

And then, with a final glance over my shoulder, I take the last step, crossing the boundary between past and present. The gates creak open, and the world beyond stretches before me, a canvas of possibilities waiting to be painted. The sun's warmth embraces me, a gentle reminder of the life that awaits, the second chance I've been given.

I stand tall, my shoulders squared, ready to face the challenges and triumphs ahead. For in this moment, I am not just a man leaving prison behind; I am a testament to the resilience of the human spirit, a living embodiment of the power of redemption. As I take my first steps into the world anew, I carry the love, wisdom, and hope that have been my constant companions on this extraordinary journey.

The prison gates close behind me with a resounding clang, a final punctuation mark on the chapter of my life that has come to a close. As I walk forward, the faces of Dame, Russell, and Jerry are etched in my mind, and I know I am not alone. Their love, faith, and unwavering support will guide me as I navigate the uncharted waters of my newfound freedom.

With each step, I feel the weight of my past growing lighter, replaced by a sense of purpose and determination. The world may have changed in my absence, but I, too, have been transformed. The lessons learned within the walls of the prison, the bonds forged through shared adversity, and the wisdom gained through introspection—these are the tools I will carry with me as I build a new life, one rooted in hope, compassion, and the unwavering belief in the power of second chances.

And so, I embrace the unknown, my heart open to the possibilities that await. I am not just a man leaving prison behind; I am a living testament to the resilience of the human spirit, a beacon of hope for all who have ever dared to dream of a second chance.

Chapter 18: Freedom at Last

I glance back at the prison, which has been my home for three decades. The stark walls and barred windows now seem like a distant memory, a chapter in my life that I'm finally ready to close.

With a deep breath, I turn my face towards the sun, letting its warmth wash over me. The world awaits, and I'm ready to embrace it for the first time in an eternity.

As I walk away from the prison, the echoes of my footsteps fade into the distance. The weight of my past may still linger, but it no longer defines me. I am free, and with that freedom comes the promise of a future filled with hope and possibility.

The journey has just begun, and I am ready to face it, one day at a time.

The world engulfs me in a kaleidoscope of sensations. The vastness of the sky stretches endlessly above, an azure expanse that seems to dwarf the confines of the prison walls. The sun's rays caress my skin, and their warmth reminds me of the life I've been missing. I inhale deeply, the fresh air filling my lungs like a long-lost friend, carrying with it the scents of freedom—the earthy aroma of grass, the faint whiff of exhaust from passing cars, and the sweet fragrance of blooming flowers.

The cacophony of sounds assaults my ears. There's a symphony of life waiting for me that I've nearly forgotten. The distant honking of horns, the chatter of pedestrians, and the rustling of leaves in the breeze will soon create a tapestry of overwhelming and exhilarating noise. It contrasts the prison's oppressive silence, where every sound is muted and controlled.

I stand there, momentarily frozen, my senses overloaded with the sheer intensity of the world around me. It's a world I've been separated from for so long that has continued to evolve while I remained trapped in a static existence.

"Turland Deville?" a calm voice breaks through my reverie.

I see a woman standing a few feet away, her kind eyes meeting mine with a gentle understanding. She's dressed professionally, a stark contrast to the drab uniforms of the prison guards.

"I'm your social worker, Amanda," she introduces herself, extending a hand in greeting. "It's good to meet you."

I take her hand, the physical contact almost foreign after years of limited human interaction. "Nice to meet you too," I manage to say, my voice sounding distant to my ears.

Amanda's reassuring words wash over me, her voice a soothing balm amidst the chaos of my emotions. She speaks of the support of resources available to help me navigate this new chapter in my life. But her words barely register as my attention is drawn back to the world around me, the colors, sounds, and sensations threatening to overwhelm me.

I nod along, trying to focus on her voice, but my mind is already wandering in anticipation, consumed by the details of the streets, the people, and the life that pulses through the city. It's a world I've dreamed of for so long, a world that is now within my grasp.

As Amanda guides me towards her car, I can't help but feel a sense of trepidation mingling with the excitement. I allow myself to bask in the freedom, to let the world wash over me, and to embrace the possibilities that await.

As Amanda and I walk towards her car, a familiar figure in the distance catches my eye. At first, I think it's just a trick of the light, a mirage conjured by my overwhelmed senses. But as we draw closer, the silhouette sharpens, and my heart skips a beat as recognition dawns on me.

It can't be... but it is.

Coolidge Patterson stands near the parking lot, his hands tucked into the pockets of his well-worn jeans. He looks like his prison years haven't dimmed the resilient spark in his eyes. Our gazes lock, and a flood of emotions surges through me—joy, disbelief, and a profound sense of connection that time and distance never erase.

"Coolidge?" His name escapes my lips, barely more than a whisper.

A smile breaks across his face, warm and genuine. "Turland. It's you."

I'm moving before I realize it, my feet carrying me towards him as if pulled by an invisible force. The world around us fades away, and for a moment, it's just the two of us, two old friends reunited against all odds.

As I draw near, Coolidge opens his arms, and I find myself embraced in a hug that feels like coming home. His laughter rings in my ears, a sound I never thought I'd hear again. Tears prick at the corners of my eyes, but for once, they're tears of happiness.

"I can't believe you're here," I mumble into his shoulder, my voice thick with emotion.

Coolidge pulls back, his hands resting on my shoulders as he looks me up and down. "Sorry I'm a little late, but I couldn't miss this day, man. I had to be here for you."

His words strike a chord deep within me, a reminder of the bond we forged during those long years behind bars. In Coolidge, I found not just a friend but a little brother—someone who understood the struggles, the fears, and the dreams that kept us going when hope seemed lost.

Amanda approaches us with a knowing smile. "I take it you two know each other?"

Coolidge nods, his arm still slung around my shoulders. "Turland and I go way back. Back to the days on the inside together. We've been through a lot together."

I glance between them, realization dawning. "Did you.. .?"

"I might have made a few calls," Coolidge admits with a grin. "I wanted to surprise you."

I am surprised, but it's the best kind of surprise. Standing there, with Coolidge by my side and Amanda's support, I feel a glimmer of hope that I haven't experienced in years.

Amanda nods, understanding. "Well, it looks like you're in good hands, Turland. I'll let you two catch up."

She hands me a card with her contact information. "If you need anything, don't hesitate to reach out."

I take the card, grateful for her kindness. "Thank you, Amanda. For everything."

Coolidge turns to me as she walks away, his eyes sparkling with mischief. "So, you ready to get out of here?"

I take a deep breath, the reality of my freedom still sinking in. "More than ready."

We start walking towards the parking lot, our steps falling into a familiar rhythm. Being out in the world again with Coolidge is almost surreal. The years have changed us both, but our shared connection remains unbreakable.

"I can't believe you're here," I say, shaking my head in wonder.

Coolidge shrugs, a hint of pride in his voice. "I've been working hard to get my life back on track."

I nod, understanding the challenges he must have faced. "And your mom? How's she doing?"

A soft smile plays on Coolidge's lips. "She's good, man. Better than good. She's been my rock through all of this."

We reach his car, a modest sedan that speaks of hard work and determination. As I slide into the passenger seat, Coolidge turns to me, his expression serious.

"Listen, Turland, I know it's not much, but my mom and I want you to stay with us for a while. Just until you get back on your feet."

I'm stunned by the offer, a lump forming in my throat. "I... I don't know what to say."

Coolidge grins, patting my shoulder. "You don't have to say anything. We're family, remember?"

And at that moment, I realized that he was right. Through the trials and tribulations, the laughter and the tears, Coolidge has become more than just a friend. He's the little brother I never had, who's been there through thick and thin.

Coolidge navigates the bustling streets easily, the city's energy pulsing through the car like a heartbeat. I lean back in my seat, breathing and taking in my newfound freedom's reality. The weight of the years spent behind bars slowly begins to lift, replaced by a cautious optimism for what lies ahead.

As we drive, Coolidge fills me in on the changes that have taken place since I've been gone. New buildings have sprung up, old ones torn down, and faces have come and gone. But beneath the surface, I can sense that the city's heart remains the same—a place where dreams are born and tested, where hope can flourish even in the darkest times.

"You know," Coolidge says, his voice reflecting, "I never stopped thinking of some of the things you taught me on the inside, Turland. Even when things got tough, you made me see the bigger picture to make it through."

His words strike a chord deep within me, and I am grateful for his unwavering support. "I just found a way to see a world of possibilities through your young eyes, Coolidge. You also never gave up on me, even when quietly I gave up on myself."

Coolidge smiles, a knowing look in his eyes. "That's what friends are for, man. We lift each other, no matter what."

Chapter 19: Homecoming

As Coolidge steers the car through the once-familiar streets of Chicago's West Side, I find myself transfixed by the passing scenery. The buildings, the storefronts, and the very rhythm of the neighborhood seem to have shifted in the decades I've been away. My eyes trace the outlines of streets I once knew like the back of my hand, searching for remnants of the past amidst the unfamiliar present.

"They've put up a new community center over there," Coolidge remarks, pointing to a freshly painted building on the corner. "It's got a library, a gym, even a recording studio for the kids to explore their talents."

I nod, taking in the vibrant murals adorning the center's walls—images of hope, unity, and a brighter future. "That's good," I murmur, my voice rough with emotion. The young ones need a place to dream, create, and be more than what the streets would make of them."

Coolidge glances at me, a flicker of understanding in his eyes. "I hear you, Turland. It's not easy growing up around here. Fighting and surviving is just how it is."

We lapse into silence, the weight of our shared experiences hanging between us. As the car winds through the neighborhood, I can't help but notice the signs of change, both hopeful and heartbreaking. Freshly planted trees line the sidewalks, their leaves a vibrant green against the worn brick of the buildings. Yet, for every new business or renovated home, there are vacant lots and boarded-up windows, stark reminders of the challenges plaguing these streets.

"They tore down the old factory on Lake Street," Coolidge mentions as we pass a sprawling, empty lot. "Used to be the heart of the neighborhood, providing jobs for generations. Now, it's just a reminder of what we've lost."

I feel a pang in my chest, remembering the bustle of the factory in its heyday. The pride in the eyes of the men and women who worked there, the sense of purpose that came with an honest day's labor. "Progress ain't always pretty," I muse, my fingers tracing the weathered fabric of my seat. "But we can't let the ghosts of the past keep us from moving forward, from building something new."

Coolidge nods, his grip tightening on the steering wheel. "That's the dream. To take what we've learned, the good and the bad, and use it to make a difference. To be the change we want to see in the world."

As we continue to drive, I realize that the neighborhood, like myself, is a work in progress. We've both seen our share of darkness, pain, and loss. But in the people's resilience, in the small acts of kindness and community, there is a flicker of hope that refuses to be extinguished.

And maybe, just maybe, that hope is enough to light the way forward, one street at a time.

As Coolidge turns the corner, the familiar silhouette of Mr. Washington's house comes into view. The once-pristine property, with its neatly trimmed hedges and freshly painted facade, now bears the marks of time's relentless march. The paint has faded, chipped away by the elements, and the yard is overgrown, a tangle of weeds and untamed grass.

I feel a tightness in my chest as Coolidge pulls up to the curb, the car coming to a gentle stop. My hand hesitates on the door handle, a sudden wave of emotions crashing over me. Anticipation mingles with dread, a longing for the past warring with the uncertainty of the present.

"You okay, Turland?" Coolidge asks, his voice is soft and concerned.

I take a deep breath, trying to steady myself. "Yeah, I just... I didn't think it would be this hard coming back here. Seeing how much has changed."

Coolidge places a hand on my shoulder, a gesture of silent support. "Change is never easy, but it's a part of life. We can't hold onto the past forever, no matter how much we might want to."

I nod, knowing he's right. But as I step out of the car, the weight of my memories threatens to pull me under. I remember the countless afternoons on this porch, listening to Mr. Washington's stories and soaking up his wisdom. I remember the laughter and the tears, the moments of triumph and the depths of despair.

Each step towards the house feels like a journey through time, the ghosts of my past whispering in my ears. The creak of the weathered wood beneath my feet, the scent of honeysuckle drifting on the breeze—it's all so familiar, yet so distant, like a dream I can't quite hold onto.

As I reach the front door, my hand trembles as I raise it to knock. A part of me wants to turn back, to run from the flood of emotions that threaten to overwhelm me. But I know I can't. I owe it to Mr. Washington, who believed in me when no one else did, to face whatever lies ahead.

With a deep breath, I let my knuckles fall against the door, the sound echoing through the stillness of the afternoon. As I wait, my heart racing in my chest, I can't help but wonder if the past can ever indeed be reclaimed or if we're all grasping at shadows, trying to hold onto something that's already gone.

The door opens slowly, revealing a face I've held in my memory for three decades. Mr. Washington stands before me, his once-robust frame slightly stooped with age. His silver beard, neatly trimmed, frames a face marked by wrinkles that tell stories of their own. His eyes, those gentle eyes that always seemed to see right through me, now squint in confusion as he takes in my presence.

"Can I help you, young man?" His rich, slightly raspy voice washes over me, and for a moment, I'm speechless.

I swallow hard, my throat tight with emotion. "Mr. Washington, it's me. Turland. Turland Deville."

He leans forward, his brow furrowed as he studies my face. I watch recognition slowly dawn like the sun breaking through the clouds. "Turland? Is that you?"

I nod, a smile tugging at the corners of my mouth. "Yes, sir. It's been a long time."

He steps back, opening the door wider. "Come in, come in. Let me get a good look at you."

I follow him inside, the familiar scent of his home enveloping me like a warm embrace. The living room is just as I remember it: the worn leather couch, the bookshelves lined with well-thumbed volumes, the photographs on the walls telling the story of a life well-lived.

Mr. Washington turns to face me, his eyes shining with joy and disbelief. "Look at you, all grown up. I always knew you had it in you, Turland. Always knew you were destined for more than what life handed you."

I feel a lump rising in my throat, the weight of his words settling on my shoulders. "I couldn't have done it without you, Mr. Washington. You were the one who believed in me, who pushed me to be better."

He waves a hand dismissively, a smile playing on his lips. "I just saw what was already there, son. The strength, the resilience, the heart. That was all you."

We stood silently for a moment, the years stretching out between us. I thought of all the times I wanted to give up, to let the darkness consume me in my youth. But Mr. Washington's voice was always in my head, urging me to keep going, to hold onto hope even when it seemed lost. Then, when the time came, and I didn't hear the whispers anymore, I ended up in prison.

"I'm sorry I didn't come back sooner," I say softly, my voice barely above a whisper. "I wanted to, but..."

He places a hand on my shoulder, his touch firm and reassuring. "You're here now, Turland. That's what matters. The past is the past, and the future is what we make of it."

I nod, feeling the weight of the past slowly lifting from my shoulders. As we settle into the familiar rhythm of conversation, the years melting away like snow in the spring, I can't help but feel a sense of hope rising within me—hope for a new beginning, for a chance to make things right.

In the end, that's what Mr. Washington taught me all those years ago. No matter how far we fall or how lost we become, there's always a way back. There is always a chance for redemption if we're willing to fight for it.

As Mr. Washington and I continue our conversation, I can feel Coolidge's presence in the background, a silent observer taking in the moment. I glimpse him from the corner of my eye, standing a respectful distance away, his hands clasped before me. There's an attentiveness in his posture, a sense of understanding that goes beyond mere curiosity.

I realize that Coolidge comprehends the significance of this reunion, the weight of the memories that hang between Mr.

Washington and me. He knows this is more than just a simple visit, more than a casual conversation between two old acquaintances. It's a bridge between the past and the present, a chance for healing and reconnection.

As I listen to Mr. Washington's words, I can't help but reflect on the community that surrounds us, the neighborhood that once thrived with life and purpose. The streets that were once filled with laughter and dreams now bear the scars of neglect and decay. The pride that once defined this place has been slowly eroded by time and circumstance, leaving a sense of dislocation and longing.

I feel a tug at my heart, a yearning for the sense of belonging I once knew. Memories of my childhood and the bonds I shared with my friends and neighbors come flooding back to me. I remember the warmth of Mrs. Johnson's smile as she handed out fresh-baked cookies, the excitement in Jerry's voice as we raced down the street on our bicycles, and the sense of unity that held us all together, even in the face of adversity.

But as I look around me now, I see only the ghosts of those memories, fading like old photographs in the sun. The community that raised me, that shaped me into the man I am today, has become a shadow of its former self. And I can't help but feel a sense of responsibility, a need to do something, anything, to bring back the light that once shone so brightly.

"It's not the same anymore, is it?" I ask softly, my gaze drifting to the window, to the streets beyond. "The neighborhood, the people. Everything's changed."

Mr. Washington nods, a wistful smile playing at the corners of his mouth. "Change is the only constant, Turland. But it's up to us to decide what kind of change we want to see. We can either let the world shape us or shape the world."

His words struck a chord within me, resonating with the thoughts swirling in my mind.

I glance at Coolidge, seeing the determination in his eyes and our shared understanding.

"You're right," I say, my voice filled with a newfound resolve. It's time for us to take back what's ours, to rebuild what's been lost. And I'm not going to rest until I see this community thriving once more and the pride and joy I remember from my childhood."

Mr. Washington reaches out, clasping my hand in his grip firm and unwavering. "Then let's get to work, my boy. Let's show the world what the West Side is truly made of."

As we sit there, our hands joined in a silent promise, I feel a sense of purpose rising and a determination to make things right. This is more than just a neighborhood; it is a collection of streets and buildings. It's a part of me, a part of my very soul.

And I'll be damned if I let it slip away without a fight.

As we bid farewell to Mr. Washington, his weathered hand clasps mine, a fleeting connection bridging the decades between us. His eyes, clouded by age and memories, hold a flicker of the wisdom I once sought so eagerly. "Remember, Turland," he says, his voice a whisper against the weight of time, "the roots run deep here. Tend to them, nurture them, and watch the community bloom again."

I nod, my throat tight with emotion, the words I long to say tangled on my tongue. How can I express my gratitude and reverence for this man who guided me through the turbulent waters of my youth? Ultimately, I settle for a simple "Thank you," hoping he can feel the depth of my appreciation in those two words.

We return to the car. The silence between us is heavy with the echoes of the past, the unspoken understanding of the journey ahead. As we settle into our seats, the engine humming to life, I let my gaze drift over the neighborhood again.

The streets may be cracked, the buildings worn and weary, but I can see the potential, the promise hidden beneath the surface. It's in the eyes of the children playing on the sidewalks, the determined steps of the men and women making their way to work, and the whispered prayers of the elders sitting on their stoops.

Coolidge clears his throat, his voice soft yet filled with conviction. "You know, Turland, it's about rebuilding lives, restoring hope where it's been lost."

I turn to him, my eyes searching his face, seeing the sincerity in every line. "You're right," I murmur, my voice rough with emotion.

He nods, a smile tugging at the corners of his mouth. "And we'll do it together, one brick at a time, one soul at a time."

As we pull away from the curb, the streets of the West Side unfolding before us, I feel a sense of purpose settling over me like a mantle. This is my calling, my chance to make amends for the years lost, to create something lasting and meaningful.

Because this is my home, my heart, and I won't rest until I see it rise from the ashes, a phoenix reborn in the flames of hope and determination.

The car ride back to Coolidge's building is a blur, my mind lost in a whirlwind of thoughts and emotions. As we navigate the bustling streets, I find myself drawn to the faces of the people we pass—the young mother pushing a stroller, the elderly man perched on a stoop, the group of teenagers laughing on a corner. Each one is a story, a life interwoven with the fabric of this community.

I hesitate, trying to put into words the feelings swirling within me. "I'm just... overwhelmed," I admit, my fingers tracing the weathered leather of my seat. "Seeing Mr. Washington, being back here after so long—it's like stepping into a dream, one I never thought I'd have the chance to make real."

As we pull up to the curb outside his building, I take a deep breath, squaring my shoulders.

Coolidge claps me on the shoulder as we climb out of the car, his touch grounding me in the present. "Ready to get started?" he asks, his eyes sparkling excitedly.

I nod, my heart swelling with a newfound sense of purpose. "Ready as I'll ever be."

Together, we ascend the steps to his building, the promise of a brighter future stretching like an open road.

Because in the end, that's what it's all about—not just rebuilding buildings, but rebuilding lives, one soul at a time.

Chapter 20: A New Beginning

As we ascend the steps of the building, each footfall an echoing heartbeat—the worn wood creaks beneath our weight, like a symphony of my past and now present. I inhale deeply. The air is tinged with the faint scent of blooming flowers and freshly cut grass—a new beginning, a chance to grow.

At the threshold, we pause, Coolidge's hand hovering over the doorknob. Coolidge's eyes meet mine, a silent understanding passing between us. "You got this, Turland. One step at a time." His words are a gentle push, propelling me forward.

The door swings open, and a wave of warmth rushes over me, wrapping me in its tender embrace. Golden light spills from the entryway, chasing away the shadows of doubt that cling to my soul. And there, standing in the midst of it all, is Mary Jane Patterson.

Her smile is a beacon, guiding me home. Soft lines frame her eyes, speaking of a life of grace and resilience. She steps forward, her arms outstretched, and I am drawn into her embrace. The scent of lavender and freshly baked bread envelops me, a balm to my weary spirit.

"Welcome, Turland," she says, her voice a soothing melody. "We've been waiting for you." The sincerity in her words settles deep within me, a seed of belonging taking root.

As my eyes drink in the cozy interior, soft, well-worn furniture beckons, promising comfort and rest. Family photographs adorn the walls, capturing moments of laughter and love. Each image whispers a story, inviting me to join their tapestry.

God, is this what home feels like? The thought flickers through my mind, a tentative hope. Thirty years within cold, unforgiving walls have left me praying for a place to call my own. You must be prepared for what you pray for because now, in the warmth of Mary Jane's smile and the gentle touch of Coolidge's hand, It's only with grace that I may have found it.

Mary Jane's hand finds mine, her touch gentle and reassuring. "Turland, I want to thank you," she says, her eyes glistening with emotion. "For being there for Coolidge in that place, for looking out for him when I couldn't."

I shake my head, humbled by her gratitude. "It was a pleasure, ma'am. The truth is, we looked out for each other in there. It was a blessing to have met your son in many ways."

Coolidge steps forward, a grin spreading across his face. "You're family now, Turland. And in this house, family means everything."

The words wash over me, a balm to the scars that prison has left on my soul. Family. It's a concept I had nearly forgotten, lost in the depths of time and the echoes of my past mistakes. But here, in the warmth of this moment, I feel it is blossoming within me once more.

As I look around, my senses come alive. The aroma of home-cooked food drifts from the kitchen, enticing and inviting. It stirs memories long-dormant, of childhood dinners and laughter shared around a table. The ghosts of my past seem to fade, replaced by the promise of new beginnings.

Is this what redemption tastes like? I wonder, savoring the scent of Mary Jane's cooking. It's a flavor I had never dared to imagine, a dream that had seemed too distant to grasp. But now, standing here in the heart of this family, I can almost taste it on my tongue.

"Come on in, Turland," Mary Jane says, gesturing towards the living room. "Make yourself at home. You're part of this family now."

Mary Jane guides me through the living room, her movements graceful and unhurried. As we walk, I can't help but notice the way her casual attire drapes over her elegant frame, accentuating her natural beauty. The soft fabric of her blouse catches the light, and I find myself drawn to the warmth emanating from her presence.

"I hope you don't mind staying in the basement apartment," she says, her voice gentle and reassuring. "It's not much, but a space to start fresh."

I shake my head, overwhelmed by her generosity. "It's more than I could have ever hoped for, Mary Jane. Thank you."

She smiles, and its genuineness reaches her eyes. "You deserve a second chance, Turland. Everyone does."

As we approach the basement door later that evening, Mary Jane pauses, her hand resting on the knob. She turns to face me, her expression serious yet filled with compassion.

"I want you to know that you're safe here," she says, her words weighted with sincerity. "This apartment is yours for as long as you need it. It's where you can heal and regain your footing."

I nod, my throat tight with emotion. "I don't know how to thank you, Mary Jane. For everything."

She reaches out, her hand gently squeezing my shoulder. "You don't need to thank me, Turland. Just promise me that you'll never give up on yourself and keep fighting for the life you deserve."

I promise, I whisper, the words a solemn vow. *I'll make you proud, Mary Jane. I'll make myself proud.*

I feel a sense of peace as she opens the door, revealing the stairs leading down to my new home. It's a feeling I haven't experienced in years, a lightness that comes with knowing I am exactly where I'm meant to be.

This is my chance, I think, descending the steps with a newfound sense of purpose. *My chance to rewrite my story, to become the man I've always known I could be.*

And with each step, I feel the weight of my past growing lighter, replaced by the promise of a future filled with hope and possibility.

The wooden stairs creak beneath my feet as I descend into the basement apartment, each step a gentle reminder of the solidity and permanence of this moment. The air grows more remarkable, a welcome reprieve from the warmth of the house above, and I find myself enveloped in a sense of calm that I haven't known in years.

I pause, my eyes adjusting to the soft light that filters through the small windows lining the top of the wall. The space is modest yet inviting, a far cry from my prison cell's cold, unforgiving confines. The walls are painted a soothing shade of pale blue, the color of a clear sky on a spring day, and I feel a smile tug at the corners of my mouth.

Freedom, I think, is a whisper in my mind. *This is what freedom feels like.*

I take a tentative step forward, my gaze sweeping across the room, taking in every detail. A small kitchenette occupies one corner, its countertops clean and uncluttered. A table and two chairs sit nearby, and a vase of fresh flowers adds color to the simple wooden surface.

In the opposite corner, a bed beckons, its soft, white comforter starkly contrasting with the thin, scratchy blankets I've grown accustomed to. Beside it, a small nightstand holds a lamp and a few books, their spines worn and well-loved.

Books, I muse, my fingers itching to reach and touch them. *It's been years since I held a book outside of prison, felt the weight of its freedom pages, and felt the texture of its freedom cover.*

I cross the room, my footsteps muffled by the plush carpet beneath my feet. As I sink onto the edge of the bed, a wave of emotion crashes over me: a mixture of gratitude and disbelief.

This is real, I tell myself, my hands gripping the comforter, anchoring me to this moment. *This is my life now, my second chance.*

I close my eyes, inhaling the scent of fresh linen and lavender filling my lungs. It's a scent I never thought I'd experience again, a reminder of the simple pleasures I'd taken for granted for so long.

No more cold metal bars, I think, my mind drifting back to the countless nights I spent staring at the ceiling of my cell, dreaming of a different life. *No more concrete walls, no more echoing footsteps in the hallway.*

Here, in this space, I am surrounded by warmth and comfort, by the promise of an entirely my own future. As I lay back on the bed, my head sinking into the soft pillow, I feel a sense of peace wash over me, a peace that comes from knowing that I am exactly where I'm meant to be.

Thank you, I whisper, my words a prayer of gratitude. *Thank you for this chance, moment, and life.*

As I drift off to sleep, the weight of my past growing lighter with each passing second, I know that tomorrow will bring new challenges and obstacles to overcome. But for now, at this moment, I am content, I am safe, and I am free.

Later, as I stood in the center of the room, the reality of my new beginning washed over me like a gentle wave. The walls expand, offering a sense of boundless possibility I had long forgotten.

I walk to the window, my fingers brushing against the cool glass. The world outside is bathed in the warm glow of the setting sun, casting long shadows across the street. It's a world I've been apart from for so long, a world that now beckons me to explore its hidden corners and untold stories.

"A new chapter," I murmur, my voice barely above a whisper. *"A chance to rewrite my story."*

My mind drifts to the choices that led me to this moment—the missteps, the regrets, the moments of weakness. I think of the lives I've impacted, the pain I've caused, and the bridges I've burned. The weight of these memories settles heavily on my shoulders, a reminder of the long road ahead.

But even as I acknowledge my past mistakes, hope ignites within me. It's a hope born from the kindness in Mary Jane's eyes, the warmth of Coolidge's embrace, and the promise of a future that is mine to shape.

With a deep breath, I turn away from the window and move towards the center of the room again. Each step feels lighter, as if the burdens of my past are slowly falling away. As I stand there, surrounded by tangible reminders of my newfound freedom, a sense of purpose settles over me like a warm blanket.

This is my moment, my opportunity to prove to myself and the world that redemption is possible. As I close my eyes, I silently pledge to embrace this journey with an open heart and a steadfast determination to become the man I've always known I could be.

Again, I sink onto the mattress, feeling it yield beneath my weight. The sensation is still almost foreign, starkly contrasting to the thin, unyielding prison cots. I stretch out slowly, savoring how my body settles into the gentle embrace of the bed.

A profound sense of peace washes over me as I lie there.

It's as if the bed is a sanctuary, a place where I can shed the burdens of my former life and emerge renewed.

I close my eyes, letting the tranquility of the moment envelop me. The sounds of the house above fade away, and I find myself drifting into a state of calm anticipation.

As sleep begins to claim me again, I feel profound gratitude. With that gratitude comes a quiet determination to make the most of this opportunity, to rise each morning to become a better man than I was the day before.

The last thought that flickers through my mind before I surrender to the embrace of sleep is a simple one, but it holds the power of a thousand prayers:

"Thank you for everything."

Chapter 21: First Steps

It's my first morning of freedom in three decades, and it's peaceful until the door creaks open. Coolidge steps in and a breakfast tray is carefully balanced in his hands. His eyes meet mine, and he smiles tentatively. Surprise flutters through me at the unexpected kindness, and gratitude wells up and softens my features.

"Morning," Coolidge says, his voice gentle as he sets the tray on the small table by the window. Sunlight streams in, casting a warm glow over the simple spread - toast, eggs, and a few fruit slices. "I wasn't sure what to get at the store. The food in prison was... well, you know. Didn't want to bring back bad memories."

I shake my head, a lump forming in my throat. "No, this is... this is great. Thank you, Coolidge. Really." The sincerity in my words hangs in the air between us.

His smile widens a fraction, shoulders relaxing. "After thirty years of that slop, I bet anything tastes like a gourmet meal, huh?"

A chuckle escapes me, and I nod. "You got that right. This here's a feast fit for kings compared to what we had." I gesture to the tray, marveling at the colors and the freshness of it all.

Coolidge pulls out a chair and sits, his elbows resting on his knees as he leans forward. "Figured it was the least I could do. Wanted to help somehow, you know? Make things a little easier."

The earnestness in his voice and the way his eyes hold mine stir something in my chest. A warmth I haven't felt in ages. "I appreciate it, Coolidge. More than you know."

We sit in comfortable silence for a moment, the sounds of the waking neighborhood filtering through the thin walls. Car engines rumbling to life, distant chatter, a dog barking—the world moving on, as always. But in this small pocket of time, there's a sense of stillness in this basement apartment, of possibility.

I reach for a piece of toast, the bread crisp against my fingertips. Taking a bite, I savor the simple taste and texture—flavors

I'd nearly forgotten. Coolidge watches me, a flicker of understanding in his gaze. He knows. He's been where I've been, feeling the weight of those years pressing down on his soul.

But here, now, there's a lightness—a glimmer of hope, fragile as a butterfly's wing. It's in the way Coolidge's mouth curves into a smile, in the sunlight dancing across the table, in the small acts of kindness, and in the shared moments of silence.

And as I sit across from Coolidge, breaking bread and trading gentle words, I feel a flicker of something long-forgotten stirring in my heart.

Something like hope.

As the last bite of toast disappears, I lean back in my chair, my stomach full and my heart even more so. Coolidge sips his coffee, the steam curling around his face, and I'm struck by the domesticity of it all: two men sharing a meal, a moment of peace amidst the chaos of our pasts.

"I want to find a job," I say suddenly, the words tumbling out before I can stop them. "Contribute to the household, you know? Pull my weight."

Coolidge sets his mug down, his eyes meeting mine. There's no judgment there, no pity—just understanding. "I get that, Turland. Wanting to feel useful, like you're making a difference."

I nod, my fingers tapping against the tabletop. A nervous habit, one I thought I'd left behind in prison. "I don't want to be a burden. You've already done so much for me."

"You're not a burden," Coolidge says firmly, his voice brooking no argument. "You're family now. And family looks out for each other."

Family. The word settles in my chest, warm and heavy. It's been so long since I've had anyone to call my own, anyone who cared whether I lived or died. But here, at this moment, with Coolidge's steady gaze on mine, I feel a sense of belonging. Of home.

I swallow past the lump in my throat, my voice rough with emotion. "Thank you, Coolidge. For everything."

This time, he smiles a genuine smile that crinkles the corners of his eyes. "You don't have to thank me, Turland."

I gather the empty plates and mugs. I wash the dishes, suds clinging to my skin.

I finish the dishes in comfortable silence, and the last plate is set to dry on the rack. Coolidge turns to me, his expression thoughtful. "Turland, there's no rush to find a job. Take some time to adjust, to find your footing."

I nod, my heart full to bursting. "I will. But I want to contribute, Coolidge. I need to."

He claps a hand on my shoulder, his touch warm and solid. "I know you do. And we'll find something, I promise. But for now, let's take it one day at a time."

One day at a time is a philosophy I can support, a mantra to cling to in the face of uncertainty. As Coolidge and I move about the tiny basement apartment, tidying up and making plans for the day ahead, I feel a sense of purpose, of direction.

I have a reason to wake up in the morning for the first time longer than I can remember—to keep going and fighting. I feel a flicker of something like joy. Like hope.

Coolidge's face as he turns to me, his eyes alight with enthusiasm. "You know what we should do today, Turland? Let's ride bikes like you said you wanted to do while we were in prison, see the neighborhood, and see how things have changed."

I hesitated, a flicker of uncertainty in my chest. Even though he was right, I talked about it on the inside because that's what I did as a teenager. It's been so long since I've ridden a bike, let alone explored the streets of my youth. The thought of facing the ghosts of my past, of seeing how the world has moved on without me, fills me with trepidation.

But as I meet Coolidge's gaze, I see the excitement there, the eagerness to share this experience with me. Slowly, I felt my excitement build, pushing past the fear and doubt.

"I'd like that," I say, my voice soft but steady. "It's been too long since I've felt the wind on my face, the freedom of the open road."

Coolidge grins, his smile as bright as the morning sun. "That's the spirit! We'll take it slow, just a leisurely ride to get you back in the saddle."

As we go outside, the fresh air fills my lungs, and the scent of spring blossoms and car exhaust mingles in a heady perfume. The neighborhood is already alive with activity, and the sound of children's laughter and the distant rumble of traffic is a symphony to my ears.

Coolidge leads me to a pair of old bikes leaning against the side of the building, their paint chipped and faded but still sturdy. He hands me one, and as I swing my leg over the seat, I feel a rush of memories of childhood adventures and carefree days.

We set off down the street, the wind whipping my face as we pedaled. The familiar sights and sounds of the West Side surround us, and the dilapidated buildings and vacant lots starkly remind us of our community's challenges.

But there is beauty here, too, in the colorful murals adorning the walls and the laughter and chatter of the people we pass. As we ride, I feel a sense of connection and belonging that I haven't felt in years.

Coolidge points out changes as we go, new businesses that have sprung up in the place of old ones, community gardens where once there was only concrete. And with each discovery, I feel a sense of hope, of possibility.

Maybe, just maybe, there is still a place for me in this world—a chance to build something new, something better. And as Coolidge and I ride on, the sun on our faces and the wind at our backs, I know I am exactly where I am meant to be.

The bikes creak and groan beneath us as we navigate the pothole-ridden streets, but they hold steady, just like Turland and me. We've both seen our share of rough roads and weathered our storms, but we keep pushing forward, one pedal at a time.

As we ride, I find myself stealing glances at Turland, marveling at the change in his demeanor. Gone is the heaviness that seemed to weigh him down, replaced by a lightness, a sense of freedom that radiates from his very core.

He catches me looking and flashes a grin, his eyes crinkling at the corners. "I never thought I'd feel this way again," he confesses, his voice barely audible above the wind. "Like I've got a second chance, a fresh start."

I nod, understanding all too well the power of redemption and forgiveness. "We all deserve that," I reply, my voice thick with emotion. A chance to make things right, to be better than we were before."

We fall into a comfortable silence, each lost in our thoughts as we continue our journey through the neighborhood. I realize that hours have passed since we first set out.

As we turn the corner onto our street, I feel a sudden pang of sadness, knowing our ride is ending. But then I catch sight of Turland's face, his expression one of pure contentment, and I realize that this is just the beginning.

We pull up to the house, dismounting our bikes and leaning them against the porch railing. Turland reaches out and clasps my shoulder in a gesture of gratitude and camaraderie.

"Thank you," he says, his eyes glistening with unshed tears. "For everything."

I nod, my own emotions threatening to overwhelm me. "Anytime," I manage, my voice cracking slightly. "That's what friends are for."

As we head inside, the warmth of the house enveloping us like a comforting embrace, I know that we have forged a bond that will last a lifetime.

Later that evening, as Turland decides to work on the bikes, his hands moving with practiced ease, he shares more stories of his youth, his voice taking on a dreamy, almost poetic cadence.

"You know, Coolidge, this neighborhood used to be different. It was alive, vibrant, full of hope and possibility."

I lean forward, my elbows resting on my knees, my eyes fixed on Turland's face as he speaks. There's a faraway look in his eyes as if he sees not the dusty backyard but the streets of his childhood, teeming with life and energy.

"We had block parties every summer," he continues, a smile tugging at the corners of his mouth. "The whole community would come together, everyone bringing something to share. The air would be filled with the smell of barbecue and the sound of laughter and music."

I nod, trying to picture the scene he describes. Given the state of the neighborhood now, it's hard to imagine, but I can see it in my mind's eye—the colorful streamers, the children playing in the streets, the adults chatting and dancing, their faces aglow with joy.

"What happened?" I ask softly, almost afraid to break the spell of Turland's memories.

He sighs, his hands stilling on the bike frame. "Life happened," he says, his voice tinged with sorrow. "Drugs, violence, poverty. It crept in slowly at first, like a disease, eating away at the fabric of our community. And before we knew it, everything had changed."

I feel a lump forming in my throat, a sense of loss that I can't quite put into words. It's as if Turland's memories have become my own, the weight of his nostalgia settling heavily on my chest.

"But it wasn't all bad," he adds, his eyes meeting mine. "We still had each other, that sense of belonging, of family. Even when things got tough, we knew we could count on our neighbors to have our backs."

I nod, understanding the sentiment all too well. It's the same feeling I had in prison, that sense of camaraderie born of shared hardship and struggle.

"Tell me more," I urge, my curiosity piqued. "What were your friends like? What did you do for fun?"

Turland chuckles, the sound warm and rich. "Oh, we got into all sorts of trouble," he admits, his eyes twinkling with mischief. "But it was innocent trouble, the kind that comes from being young, carefree, and full of life."

As he talks, I find myself lost in his stories, transported to a time and place I've never known but somehow feel a deep connection to. We laugh together at his tales of youthful hijinks and fall silent in shared reverence for the moments of beauty and grace he describes.

And through it all, I feel a bond forming between us, a sense of kinship that goes beyond our shared prison experience. It's as if, in sharing his memories, Turland has opened a door to his soul, inviting me to step inside and see the world through his eyes.

I sat down beside him, our shoulders almost touching. "Nothing stays the same forever," I offered gently. But that doesn't mean it's all lost. There's still hope, still a chance for redemption."

Turland turns to me, his eyes searching mine. "You believe that?"

I nod, my conviction unwavering. "I have to. It's what keeps me going, the thought that maybe, just maybe, we can make things right again. That we can build something new from the ashes of the past."

For a long moment, Turland is silent, his gaze turned inward. Then, slowly, a smile spreads across his face—a smile tinged with sadness but also with fierce, unrelenting hope.

"You're right," he says, his voice growing stronger. "We can't change what's happened but can shape what's to come. And that starts with small things, like getting these old bikes in better shape and taking them out for more rides."

Together, we return to work, our hands moving with renewed purpose. As the bikes begin to take shape under our supervision, I feel a sense of accomplishment swelling in my chest. This restoration act is small but feels significant some-how, like a promise of better things.

Turland and I exchange glances, our smiles mirroring each other. In that moment, I feel a surge of anticipation for more rides ahead—not just the physical journey through the streets of Chicago but the more profound, symbolic journey we've embarked upon together.

As we plan our following rides through the memorable streets of Turland's youth, I want to see the neighborhood through his eyes.

He wants to show me the corner store where he used to buy candy with his friends and the park where they'd play pickup basketball games until the streetlights came on. Some things have changed—buildings have been torn down, new ones erected in their place—but the essence of the community remains vibrant and alive.

Chapter 22: Echoes of the Past

The screen door squeaked as Turland and Coolidge stepped onto the weathered porch, their shoes crunching on gritty floorboards. Turland gripped the handlebars of the rusty bicycle, his palms slick with anticipation. The once vibrant red paint had faded to a dull ember, flecks of chrome peeking through like embers in ash.

"Man, I haven't felt like this in forever," Turland said, his voice a mix of excitement and apprehension. "Not since I was a kid, racing Jerry and them down to the corner store."

Coolidge nodded, a wistful smile playing at the corners of his mouth. "Simpler times, huh?"

"Simpler times."

With a deep breath, Turland swung his leg over the seat, the worn leather creaking under his weight. His feet again found the pedals and muscle memory took over again as he pushed off. He still wobbled for a moment before finding his balance; after all, it was his second ride in thirty years.

The tires hummed against the pavement as they pedaled down the street, past row houses with peeling paint and sagging porches. The wind whipped against Turland's face, a cool caress that sent a shiver down his spine, and he loved every moment of it. His legs pumped, the steady rhythm of the pedals a metronome for his pounding heart.

Freedom. That's what this feeling was, he realized. He'd felt the same rush of independence as a boy, flying down these same streets without care before the choices that led them astray, before the cold metal of handcuffs and the clang of prison bars.

Turland glanced over at Coolidge, who rode beside him with an effortless grace, his eyes closed as if savoring the breeze. In that instant, the years melted away, and they were just two friends, two dreamers, chasing the promise of something better.

But even as the thought formed, reality crept in at the edges. The houses they passed bore scars of neglect, windows boarded up, and grass overgrown—a reminder that time hadn't stood still, that the world he left behind had changed, just as he had.

Turland pushed the thought aside, focusing instead on the burn in his legs, the sweat beading on his brow. For now, he'd let himself have this moment, this fleeting taste of a past untarnished by regret. He'd let himself believe redemption was as simple as the wind in his face and the open road ahead, if only for a heartbeat.

As they turned onto a familiar street, Turland felt his stomach clench. The old school loomed ahead, a once-proud building now worn and faded, like a forgotten memory. He slowed to a stop, his feet planting on the cracked pavement as he stared up at the place that had once held so much promise.

"You okay, man?" Coolidge asked, pulling up beside him.

Turland nodded, his throat tight. "Just... it's different than I remember."

"Yeah, I feel you. It's like looking at a ghost."

They stood silently for a moment, the only sound the distant echo of children's laughter from the playground. Turland closed his eyes, letting the memories wash over him.

"I had this teacher, Mr. Hendry," he said softly. "He used to tell me I could be anything I wanted, that I had a bright future ahead of me."

Coolidge crossed his arms. "He wasn't wrong, you know. You still got that future."

Turland shook his head. "I don't know. Sometimes, it feels like that future died the day my friends and I got arrested. This is just living on borrowed time now."

"Nah, don't think like that. We paid our debt. We got a second chance. That's more than most people get."

Turland looked again at the school, the peeling paint, and the rusted chain-link fence. "I just wish I could go back, you know? Tell that kid to make different choices. To not let this place become just another broken dream."

"You can't change the past, Turland. But you can change what comes next. This is what you kept telling me on the inside, and now I have to remind you of the same stuff. That's what we're doing out here, right? Building something new, something better."

Turland met Coolidge's gaze and saw the determination and unwavering belief in second chances. And for a moment, he let himself believe it, too.

"Yeah, you're right. We have to keep moving forward. For Mr. Hendry, for all the kids who never got the chance."

He swung his leg back over the bike, gripping the handlebars with renewed purpose. The past might be set in stone, but the future was theirs to write.

"Let's ride," he said, pushing off into the wind again. And as they left the old school behind, Turland felt a flicker of something long buried stirring in his chest.

Hope.

As we pedaled away from the school, the sun-faded storefronts and cracked sidewalks blurred past, a testament to the relentless march of time.

The rhythmic creak of bicycle chains filled the air as Turland and Coolidge pedaled down the familiar streets. Turland's heart quickened with anticipation as they rounded the corner towards Mister Johnson's Candy Shop. His mind raced with memories of colorful jars filled with sweets, the tinkling bell above the door, and the warm smile of old Mr. Johnson himself.

"Man, you wouldn't believe the candy they used to have," Turland said, a grin spreading across his face. "Bigger than your fist, I swear."

But as they approached, Turland's smile faded. Where once stood a cheerful storefront with hand-painted signs now loomed a neon-lit liquor store, its windows barred and plastered with advertisements for cheap booze.

Turland's grip tightened on his handlebars. "No... it can't be."

He skidded to a stop, his eyes fixed on the transformed building. The flashy lights seemed to mock him, each flicker erasing another cherished memory.

"This ain't right," he muttered, his voice thick with emotion. "This place... it was more than just candy, you know? It was..." He trailed off, struggling to find the words.

Coolidge dismounted, standing beside his friend. "It was hope," he said softly. "A little piece of sweetness in a bitter world."

Turland nodded, swallowing hard. "We'd save up our pennies for weeks just to get a taste of something good. Something pure." His eyes burned with unshed tears. "Now look at it. Just another poison factory."

The wind whispered through the empty street, carrying with it the faint echoes of children's laughter, now silenced. Turland closed his eyes, overwhelmed by the loss – not just of a building, but of innocence, of possibility.

Coolidge looked over at Turland. "I know it hurts. But m aybe... maybe this is why we're here. To remember what was, and imagine what could be again."

The neon sign flickered, casting an eerie glow across the sidewalk. I was about to suggest we head back when the liquor store's door swung open, and a familiar figure stepped out.

My heart lurched. "Dame?"

He turned, eyes widening in disbelief. "Turland? Man, is that you?"

We collided in a bone-crushing embrace, years of shared history and unspoken pain compressed into that moment. The scent of cheap whiskey clung to his clothes, but underneath was the unmistakable musk of Dame – a smell that transported me back to cramped cells and endless yard time.

"I can't believe it," I choked out, pulling back to study his face. The years had etched new lines around his eyes, but that sharp, calculating gaze hadn't changed. "How long have you been out?"

Dame's lips quirked in a half-smile. "Six months, give or take. You?"

"Just a couple of weeks," I replied, my mind reeling. "I had no idea... I mean, I tried to get word—"

"Yeah, well, the system ain't exactly set up for happy re-unions, is it?" Dame's tone was matter-of-fact, tinged with bitterness.

I nodded, feeling the weight of lost time. "You look good, man. You working?"

"Hustling," Dame shrugged. "Doing what I gotta do. You still chasing dreams, T?"

I felt a flicker of defensiveness. "I'm trying to make something of myself. Got plans."

Dame's eyes softened. "Always did. That's what I loved about you, man. Never let the world beat you down."

A shadow passed over his face. "Unlike..." He trailed off, glancing at the liquor store.

My stomach clenched. "What is it, Dame?"

He took a deep breath. "It's Russell, T. He didn't make it."

The world tilted on its axis. "What do you mean, didn't make it?"

Dame's voice was low, urgent. "Got out at the same time as me. Was doing good, you know? Working, staying clean. But some punks started giving him shit about how prison changed him. Called him soft."

I could see it unfolding, a nightmare in slow motion. "No..."

"Russell knocked one of 'em out cold right here," Dame continued, gesturing to the cracked pavement. "But the other one... he had a gun. Didn't even hesitate."

The words hit me like physical blows. Russell – wild, laughing Russell – gone. Just like that.

"I should've been here," I whispered, my throat raw. "I could've..."

Dame gripped my shoulder. "Nah, T. Don't do that to yourself. We all made our choices."

I looked at him, seeing the hard-won wisdom in his eyes. "How do you do it, Dame? How do you keep going when everything's falling apart?"

He glanced at the liquor store, then back at me. "One day at a time, brother. That's all any of us got."

I felt the weight of Russell's absence pressing down on my chest like a physical ache. My eyes burned, and I blinked rapidly, trying to hold back the tears that threatened to spill over. Coolidge stood nearby, his face a mask of empathy and concern.

"I... I need to see him," I choked out, my voice barely above a whisper.

Dame nodded, his typically sharp gaze softened with understanding. "I got my truck. We can head to the cemetery now if you want."

As Dame went to retrieve his pickup, I turned to Coolidge, my emotions raw and exposed. "I'm sorry, man. I didn't mean for this to..."

Coolidge cut me off with a gentle shake of his head. "Don't apologize, Turland. This is part of your journey. I'm here."

The ride to the cemetery was a blur of gray concrete and faded billboards, the once-vibrant neighborhood now seeming dull and lifeless. I stared out the window, lost in memories of

Russell's infectious laugh, wild dreams, the way he'd always had my back.

"You know," Dame's voice broke through my reverie. Russell talked about you all the time after he got out. He wondered how you were doing if you were staying strong."

I swallowed hard, my throat tight. "I wish I could've told him I was trying."

As we pulled into the cemetery, the weight of our shared history settled over us like a heavy blanket. The rows of weathered headstones were silent witnesses to too many lives cut short.

Dame led the way, his steps sure and purposeful. I followed, each step feeling like I was wading through molasses, Coolidge a steady presence at my side.

When we reached Russell's grave, simple and unadorned, the finality of it all hit me like a sucker punch. I sank to my knees, tracing the letters of his name with trembling fingers.

"I'm sorry, Russ," I whispered, my voice cracking. "I'm so damn sorry."

Dame pulled a bottle of whiskey from his jacket. He unscrewed the cap and poured a generous splash over the grave.

"For you, brother," he murmured, then passed the bottle to me.

I took it, and the glass stayed cool against my palm. As I tilted the bottle, letting the liquor splash onto the earth, memories flooded back – late nights dreaming of freedom, shared laughter echoing off cell walls, Russell's unwavering belief that we could be more than our mistakes.

"I made it out, Russ," I said softly, my voice thick with unshed tears. "Just wish you were here to see me."

Coolidge placed a hand on my shoulder, a silent anchor in the storm of my emotions. I glanced up at him, seeing understanding in his eyes.

"Russell," I continued, turning back to the grave, "was the one who kept us going inside. He was always talking about second chances, about making things right."

Dame nodded, his usually stoic expression softening. "Man had a way of seeing the good in everything, even in that hellhole."

I took a deep breath, the scent of grass and earth mingling with the sharp tang of whiskey. "Being locked up changes you. It makes you see how precious freedom is. Russell... he never lost sight of that."

Coolidge spoke up, his voice quiet but steady. "Sounds like he left quite a legacy."

"Yeah," I agreed, a sad smile tugging at my lips. "He and Jerry did. And we owe it to them both to live up to it."

Dame crouched down beside me, his eyes meeting mine. "We're going to do right by them both, Turland. All of us. No more wasted chances."

I nodded, feeling a spark of hope kindle in my chest. "Together?"

"Together," Dame and Coolidge echoed in unison.

I felt something shift as we stood there, united in our grief and determination, honoring Jerry and Russell's memory with every step forward.

The pickup truck rumbled down the potholed streets, the familiar landscape of the West Side blurring past the windows. I sat sandwiched between Dame and Coolidge, the warmth of their bodies a quiet comfort as the weight of the day's revelations settled into my bones.

As we turned onto my street, I felt a flutter of anticipation. Dame pulled up to the curb, a knowing smile on his face. "Now I know where to find you."

I chuckled, "Thanks to Coolidge and his mother."

Dame replied, his tone warm. "It's good to have you back. For good this time."

As we climbed out of the truck, I felt a shift. The sorrow that had weighed me down at Russell's grave was still there, but it was tempered now by something else – a glimmer of hope, fragile but growing stronger.

"You know," I said, turning to face Dame and Coolidge, "I never thought I'd need to say this, but I'm truly grateful—for this day, for you both."

Dame clasped my shoulder, his grip firm. "I'm grateful for you too, Turland."

The street was quiet, but I could hear the distant sounds of life – children laughing and music drifting from an open window. It was the soundtrack of possibility, of a future waiting to be written.

As we stood there, the three of us were united by the endless possibilities ahead.

"Yeah," I said softly, more to myself than anyone else. "One day at a time."

Chapter 23: Unspoken Truths

The soft glow of the lamp beside me casts a warm light across the worn pages of my journal. The only sound comes from scratching my pen on the paper as I pour out my thoughts. This basement apartment has become more than a place to lay my head. It's a sanctuary, a quiet corner of the world where I can reflect on the unexpected kindness that has enveloped me since arriving at the Pattersons'.

A muffled sob from above shatters my reverie. It's faint but unmistakable. Mary Jane. The pen stills in my hand as concern washes over me. In the short time I've known her, Mary Jane has been a pillar of strength, her gentle spirit never wavering.

To hear her cry, even softly, feels like a fracture in the very foundation of this place.

I hesitate, the journal forgotten. Do I dare intrude on her private moment of vulnerability? My mind reels with the implications, the boundaries I might cross. But my heart, battered and bruised as it may be, knows only the language of empathy. Before I can second-guess myself, I'm on my feet, the stairs creaking beneath my weight as I ascend.

Mary Jane's room door stands slightly ajar, a sliver of light spilling into the hallway. I pause, my hand hovering inches from the wood, uncertainty coiling in my gut. Another sob, this one clearer, propels me forward. I tap my knuckles against the door, the sound barely audible over the thudding of my own heart.

"Mary Jane?" My voice is a whisper, a tentative lifeline cast into the depths of her sorrow. "It's Turland. I... I heard you crying. I just wanted to make sure you're alright."

The words feel insufficient, a paltry offering in the face of her pain. But they're all I have, these tiny seeds of comfort sown in the hope that they might take root and blossom into something more.

I stand there, waiting, an eternity compressed into a handful of heartbeats, until I hear the soft shuffle of footsteps approaching the door. The door swings open to reveal Mary Jane, her eyes glistening with unshed tears.

Her gaze meets mine, and in that moment, I see a kaleidoscope of emotions swirling within their depths—pain, exhaustion, and a flicker of something that might be gratitude. She steps aside, a silent invitation, and I enter the room with cautious respect.

Mary Jane settles on the edge of her bed. Her shoulders slumped beneath the weight of her burdens. I pull up a chair, close enough to offer comfort but far enough to respect her space. She dabs at her eyes with a tissue, a futile attempt to stem the tide of her tears.

"I'm sorry," she whispers, her voice raw and trembling. "I didn't mean for anyone to hear me."

"You have nothing to apologize for," I assure her, my tone gentle yet firm. "I'm here if you want to talk or listen."

She nods, her gaze fixed on her hands as they twist the tissue into a tight coil. The silence stretches between us, broken only by the occasional sniffle or shuddering breath. I wait, my breath held in anticipation, until she finally speaks.

"It's Coolidge," she begins, the name a prayer and a lament all at once. "I've tried so hard to be there for him, to give him everything he needs. But sometimes... sometimes I feel like I've failed him."

The words pour out of her, a torrent of pain and self-recrimination. She tells me of the struggles of raising her son alone, of the nights spent worrying and the days spent working to keep a roof over their heads. She speaks of the guilt that gnaws at her, the belief that somehow, she is to blame for Coolidge's time in prison.

"I know I've done all I can," she admits, her voice barely above a whisper. "But I'm not a man. I couldn't be the father figure he needed. And I thank you, Turland, for the time you spent with my son inside and outside of prison. It might have made a difference in his life if he'd had a man like you to look up to."

Her words strike a chord within me, resonating with the regrets and hopes that have haunted me for so long. I lean forward, my elbows resting on my knees, and meet her gaze steadily.

"Mary Jane, you are an incredible mother," I tell her, each word weighted with conviction. "You've loved Coolidge with everything you have; that love has sustained him through the darkest times. Don't ever doubt the power of that."

She nods, a tentative smile tugging at the corners of her mouth. "Thank you, Turland. I just... I worry about him so much. I want him to have a better life and find his purpose and happiness."

"He will," I promise, though I know it's a vow I can't guarantee. "And he's lucky to have a mother like you, who believes in and supports him no matter what."

We sit in the quiet room, the air heavy with the weight of shared understanding. Mary Jane reflects my hopes and fears and my desperate desire to make a difference in the life of someone we love.

My gaze wanders around the room, taking in the details of Mary Jane's life. Photographs of Coolidge at various ages adorn the walls, each a snapshot of a moment in time, a precious memory captured and preserved. And there, on the dresser, my eyes fall upon a pendant, its intricate design catching the light and drawing me in.

It's a delicate piece, the gold chain holding a small, circular pendant with a swirling pattern etched into its surface. At the center of the design is a single, small gemstone, its deep blue hue reminding me of the endless possibilities of the night sky. I find myself transfixed by the pendant, a sense of familiarity washing over me as I study its curves and lines.

"That's a beautiful pendant," I remark, my voice soft with wonder. "Where did you get it?"

Mary Jane follows my gaze, her eyes landing on the piece of jewelry. A wistful smile plays across her features as she walks over and reaches to touch the pendant, her fingers grazing the cool metal. Then she folds her arms.

"It was a gift," she says, her voice tinged with nostalgia. "From someone I met long ago, before Coolidge was born. Someone who... who made me believe in the goodness of people, even in the darkest of times."

As she speaks, a flood of memories rushes through me, images and sensations from a distant past that I had thought long forgotten. The pendant, the design, the way it catches the light... it's all so familiar, like a dream half-remembered upon waking. And with each passing second, the realization grows stronger, more insistent, until it's impossible to ignore.

I know this pendant. I know the story behind it, the moment that it represents. As I sit there, staring at the delicate piece of jewelry, I feel the weight of that knowledge settling over me, a truth I had never dared to hope for.

My heart races, my mind reeling with the implications of this discovery. How could it be possible? After all these years, all the twists and turns of fate that had brought me to this moment... could it be her? The girl from my memories, the one who had given me hope in my darkest hour?

I swallow hard, my mouth suddenly dry as I struggle to find the words. I know that I must tread carefully, that the revelation of our shared history could change everything between us.

But I also know I cannot keep this truth to myself, not when it burns brightly.

"Mary Jane," I begin, my voice trembling with emotion. "I... I think I know that pendant. I think... I might have been the one who gave it to you all those years ago."

Mary Jane's eyes widened, her gaze darting from the pendant to my face as she processed my words. There was only silence between us for a long moment, heavy with the weight of revelation and disbelief.

"What do you mean?" she asks, her voice barely above a whisper. "How could you have given me this pendant? I've had it for years since..."

"Since you were a teenager," I finish for her, my heart pounding. "Since that day outside the jewelry store when a young man approached you and told you he wanted to buy you something beautiful."

As I speak, vivid and intense memories flood back. I can see the sunlight glinting off the store windows and feel the nervous energy thrumming through my veins as I approach her. I remember her eyes lit up when I showed her the pendant, the delicate gold chain, and the intricate design that seemed to capture the essence of beauty itself.

"I remember," I continue, my voice growing stronger with each word. "I remember how you smiled at me and told me it was the most beautiful thing anyone had ever given you. And I remember promising that I would come back for you, that we would find a way to be together."

Mary Jane's eyes fill with tears, and her hand trembles as she reaches to touch the pendant. "It was you," she whispers, her voice filled with wonder and disbelief. All this time, I never knew... I never thought I would see you again."

I reach out to take her hand, my fingers lacing with hers as I pull her closer. "I never forgot you," I tell her, my voice raw with emotion. "Through all the years in prison, through all the darkness and despair, your memory was the one thing that kept me going. The thought of finding you again, of being able to tell you how much that moment meant to me..."

She looks up at me, her eyes shining with tears and hope. "And now, here we are," she says softly. "After all this time, fate has brought us back together."

I nod, my heart swelling with a joy I had never thought possible. "It has, I agree," my voice barely above a whisper.

She smiles at me, filled with love, promise, and hope. As I want to pull her into my arms, to hold her close as the tears begin to fall finally, I know that this is maybe not the moment for that, but it's the beginning of our story one way or another.

It is a story of second chances, redemption, and healing. This story began with a chance encounter outside a jewelry store and will continue regardless for the rest of our lives.

A silence falls between us, heavy with the weight of this revelation. The world seems to hold its breath as we both struggle to process the magnitude of what has just been revealed. At this moment, there are no words, only the pounding of our hearts and the swirling emotions that threaten to overwhelm us.

I searched Mary Jane's face to gauge her reaction, but her expression was unreadable. She stares at me, eyes wide and filled with disbelief and wonder. The pendant rests in her hand, a tangible reminder of the connection we share, the bond that has endured through years of separation and hardship.

The silence stretches on, seconds ticking by like hours. I can feel the tension in the room, the air thick with the unspoken questions and emotions between us. My mind races, trying to make sense of it all, to reconcile the girl from my memories with the woman sitting before me.

Finally, Mary Jane breaks the silence, her voice tentative and filled with a raw vulnerability I have never heard before. "It was you," she whispers, her words barely audible over the pounding of my heart. "All this time, it was you."

I nod, unable to speak past the lump in my throat. The enormity of this moment threatens to overwhelm me, and I feel like I am drowning in a sea of emotions. Joy, disbelief, fear, and hope all swirl together in a dizzying mix that leaves me breathless.

"I never thought I'd see you again," Mary Jane continues, her voice growing stronger as she speaks. "I always wondered whatever happened to you, if you were okay. And now, here you are, sitting in my home, telling me that I was the one who kept you going all those years."

She shakes her head, a small smile playing at the corners of her lips. "It's like something out of a dream," she murmurs, almost to herself. "A dream that I never dared to hope could come true."

I reach out tentatively, taking her hand in mine. Her skin is warm and soft, and I can feel the tremors that run through her body. "It's real," I assure her, my voice rough with emotion. "This moment, this connection between us... it's real. And I promise you, Mary Jane, that I will never disappear again."

"What happens now?" she asks softly, her voice filled with a vulnerability that tugs at my heart. "Where do we go from here?"

I squeeze her hand gently, offering her a reassuring smile. "Wherever this journey takes us," I reply, my voice filled with a certainty I have never felt before.

The warmth of Mary Jane's presence envelops me as we sit together, our shared history weaving an invisible bond between us. In the room's stillness, I can almost hear the whispered echoes of our past, the memories that have brought us to this moment of reconnection.

Chapter 24: The Truth Unveiled

Turland sat at the kitchen table, his hands gripping the edges as if to steady himself against the wave of shock that crashed over him. The girl of many years ago was indeed Mary Jane. This caused other thoughts to echo in his mind, pulsing with a possible truth he could hardly fathom. Could Coolidge be his son? His son. The revelation struck him like a physical blow, leaving him breathless and reeling. How could this be? After all these years, is it even possible to discover he had a child he never knew existed...

Across from him, Mary Jane stood with her hands clasped tightly together, her knuckles filled with strain. Her voice trembled as she spoke, each word weighted with the burden of a long-held secret finally set free.

"I see that curious look on your face, and yes, it's true, Turland," she said softly, her eyes glistening with unshed tears. Coolidge is your son—our son."

The vulnerability in her words pierced through his stunned disbelief. He could see the years of silent sacrifice etched into the lines of her face, the strength it must have taken to raise their child alone while keeping this truth locked away in her heart.

Turland's mind raced, fragments of memories and emotions colliding in a dizzying whirlwind. That beautiful day they had shared, the connection that had sparked between them... He had no idea it had resulted in a life, a precious child he had never known.

Mary Jane took a shuddering breath, her voice thick with emotion. "I found out I was pregnant a few months after that day. I tried to reach you, but..." She trailed off, a flicker of pain crossing her features. "I named him Coolidge after the cool kid who swept me off my feet." A wistful smile tugged at her lips, even as a tear escaped her cheek.

Turland felt a surge of gratitude and sorrow intertwined, threatening to overwhelm him. The weight of lost years pressed down on his shoulders, mingling with a bittersweet ache for the life he could have had with Mary Jane and their son.

"I'm so sorry, Mary Jane," he whispered, his voice raw with emotion. "I never meant to leave you alone in this. I had no idea..." The words felt inadequate, unable to encompass the depth of his regret and his newfound longing.

As he sat there, the morning light filtering through the kitchen window, Turland felt a flicker of hope amidst the turmoil. A chance for redemption, to be the father he never had the opportunity to be. It was a daunting prospect but one he knew he had to embrace with every fiber of his being.

In that kitchen, with the weight of the past and the promise of the future hanging between them, Turland and Mary Jane sat in shared silence, their hearts heavy with the knowledge that their lives had been irrevocably intertwined. And yet, in that moment, a glimmer of possibility shone through—the chance to forge a new path, heal old wounds, and find redemption in the love of a son they both cherished.

Turland's mind raced as he paced the small kitchen, his footsteps echoing against the worn linoleum. The revelation of his fatherhood had shaken him to his core, and he struggled to make sense of the overwhelming emotions that threatened to consume him.

How could this be? he thought, his brow furrowed in disbelief. *Coolidge, my son... all these years, and I never knew.*

He ran a trembling hand over his face, feeling the weight of lost time pressing down upon him. The memories of his childhood, marked by the absence of a father, flooded his mind. The pain, the longing, the unanswered questions – all of it came rushing back, mingling with the realization that he had unwittingly inflicted the same fate upon his child.

Turland's gaze drifted to the quiet street outside as he paused by the window. He closed his eyes, allowing himself a moment to imagine the life he could have had—the birthdays, milestones, and simple joys of fatherhood that had been stolen from him or that he surrendered by his decisions in the streets.

"I would have been there," he whispered, his voice barely audible. "I would have held, watched him grow, taught him everything I know."

The words felt like a bitter confession, a lament for the years he had lost. And yet, amidst the regret, a flicker of hope began to take root. The knowledge that he had a son, a piece of himself in this world, ignited a fierce desire to make things right.

Turland turned back to face Mary Jane, his eyes shimmering with unshed tears. "I want to be there for him now," he declared, his voice wavering with emotion. "I know I can't change the past, but I'll do everything I can to be the father he deserves."

Mary Jane nodded, her own eyes glistening with understanding. She stepped forward, placing a gentle hand on Turland's arm. "It won't be easy," she cautioned, her voice soft yet firm. "But I believe in second chances, Turland. And I know Coolidge needs you, even if he doesn't realize it yet."

Turland drew in a shaky breath, feeling the weight of responsibility settle upon his shoulders. He would have to confront his past mistakes and earn Coolidge's trust as a son instead of a former cellmate for how they first met.

"I won't let him down," he vowed, his voice steady with resolve. "I'll be the father I never had, the one I always wished for. And maybe, just maybe, we can find a way to heal together."

Turland felt a sense of purpose wash over him as the words left his lips.

Mary Jane's hand lingered on Turland's shoulder, a gentle reminder of her unwavering support.

Mary Jane spoke softly, her words filled with a quiet strength.

"You have a chance to be the father Coolidge deserves, to show him the love and guidance he's been missing all these years." Her eyes shimmered with unshed tears, a testament to the depth of her emotions. "It won't be easy, but you're the man he needs."

Turland nodded, his gaze fixed on the distant horizon beyond the window. The weight of his past pressed heavily upon his heart. He turned to face Mary Jane, his voice thick with emotion as he spoke.

"I don't know how to be a father, Mary Jane. I never had a good example to follow." His words were raw and honest, a confession of his deepest fears. "But I promise you this – I will learn. I will do whatever it takes to be there for Coolidge, to show him that he is loved and wanted."

Mary Jane's lips curved into a gentle smile, her faith in Turland's potential shining through her every gesture. "You already have what it takes, Turland. God gave you a heart that knows how to love, even if it's been buried beneath the pain of your past. Trust in that, and let it guide you."

Turland felt hope ignite within his chest as the words settled between them.

"Thank you, Mary Jane," he whispered, his voice trembling with gratitude. Thank you for believing in me and giving me this chance to be a part of Coolidge's life."

Mary Jane's hand slipped from his shoulder, resting over his heart. "Turland, I finally get to see the man you truly are, and yeah, after thirty years.

The man you've always been beneath the scars and the pain is someone who didn't show any signs of that on the first day we met outside that jewelry store. And that man is ready to be the father Coolidge needs."

Turland's voice, low and earnest, broke the silence that had settled between them. "I can't begin to imagine your sacrifices, Mary Jane. Raising Coolidge alone, never knowing if I'd come back into your life or if I was dead or alive." He paused, his gaze fixed on the worn linoleum floor. "I'm sorry I wasn't there. I'm sorry I couldn't be the man you deserved."

Mary Jane's eyes softened, a gentle smile playing at the corners of her lips. "You're here now, Turland. That's what matters."

He looked up, meeting her gaze with hope and uncertainty. "If Coolidge will let me, I want to be more than just a former cellmate to him. I want to be a father, the kind of father I never had." His voice dropped to a whisper, raw with emotion. "I'm glad our father, who is in heaven, watched over you and Coolidge and ordered our steps back this way."

A moment of silence stretched between them.

Turland felt a shift within himself. The walls he had built around his heart, the defenses he had erected to survive the harshness of prison life, began to crumble.

Mary Jane's eyes glistened with unshed tears, reflecting the hope and love that had sustained her through the years.

Turland nodded, his heart swelling with a mixture of gratitude and resolve.

Turland and Mary Jane stood together, their hands clasped in a promise of support and understanding.

Mary Jane's eyes shimmered with unshed tears, a testament to the hope and relief that washed over her. She had carried this secret for so long, shouldering the burden of raising Coolidge alone, always wondering what could have been. But now, as she gazed at Turland, she saw a man transformed by the power of love and the promise of redemption.

Chapter 25: Bridging the Gap

The soft click of Mary Jane's coffee mug against the worn kitchen table punctuates the morning stillness. Our eyes meet, and the weight of the truth we carry settles like a heavy mantle upon our shoulders in that wordless exchange.

"How long are we going to wait?" Mary Jane asks, her voice a gentle whisper in the quiet kitchen. "He deserves to know, Turland."

I nod slowly, my fingers tracing the rim of my mug. The steam rising from the dark liquid mirrors the swirling thoughts in my mind. "I know. But the timing's gotta be right. I don't want to overwhelm him when he finds his footing."

Mary Jane reaches across the table, her hand warm and comforting as it rests on mine. "You've both come so far. He's stronger than you think."

I feel the corners of my mouth lift in a slight smile. "He gets that from his mama."

A flicker of pride dances in Mary Jane's eyes, tempered by the gravity of our shared secret. "And his daddy," she adds softly.

The words hang between us, a testament to our unspoken bond and the years of love and sacrifice that have brought us to this moment. I squeeze her hand gently, drawing strength from her unwavering support.

"Soon," I promise, my voice steady despite the tangled emotions in my chest. "When the time is right, I'll tell him. We'll tell him together."

Mary Jane nods, her gaze holding mine with a depth of understanding that needs no words. In the stillness of the kitchen, with the aroma of coffee enveloping us like a comforting embrace, I feel a flicker of hope, cautious optimism that somehow, someway, the truth will set us all free.

The morning air is crisp against my skin as Coolidge and I walk toward the community college, our footsteps echoing on the sidewalk. I glance over at my son, taking in the way his shoulders are hunched, his hands shoved deep into his pockets.

The nervous energy radiates off him in waves, and I feel a pang of empathy in my chest.

"You got this, Cool," I say, my voice low and reassuring. "The first day's always the hardest, but you're gonna do great."

Coolidge nods, his jaw clenched tight. "It's been so long, Turland. What if I don't remember how to do this? What if I'm not smart enough?"

I stop walking, placing a hand on his shoulder and turning him to face me. "Listen to me. You are smart enough. You're more than enough. This is your chance to start fresh, to chase your dreams. Don't let fear hold you back."

Coolidge takes a deep breath, his eyes searching mine for the strength he needs. "You think I can do this?"

"I know you can." My words are firm, laced with a conviction from my soul's depths. "You're a fighter, Cool. You've overcome so much already. This is just the beginning."

As we approach the college campus, the energy shifts, the air buzzing with the excitement of new beginnings. Students mill about, laughter and chatter filling the spaces between the buildings. The scent of freshly cut grass mingles with the aroma of coffee wafting from the nearby café, and for a moment, I'm transported back to my dreams of higher education, the ones I let slip away.

Coolidge's steps slow as he takes it all in, his eyes wide with awe and trepidation. I watch as he observes the other students, their backpacks slung over their shoulders, their futures bright and full of promise. I can see the flicker of longing in his gaze, the realization of the opportunities ahead.

"This is it," I say, my voice barely above a whisper. "This is where your story takes a new turn."

Coolidge nods, his shoulders straightening as he draws in a steadying breath. "I'm ready," he says, and I can hear his determination and unwavering resolve to seize this chance and make it his own.

As we climb the steps to the main entrance, I feel a swell of pride in my chest, a fierce love for the man my son is becoming. The doors swing open, and together, we step into the bustling hallway, the energy of new beginnings enveloping us like a promise of brighter days.

The lecture hall buzzes with eager students' chatter, their voices a symphony of excitement and nerves. Coolidge finds a seat near the front, his notebook open and pen poised, ready to capture every word. As the professor begins to speak, I slip quietly into the back of the room, as I just wanted to be there with him at that moment, my presence unnoticed amidst the sea of faces.

The professor's voice fills the space, her words painting vivid pictures of history and culture, of the power of knowledge to transform lives. I watch as Coolidge leans forward, his eyes alight with a hunger I've never seen before. He scribbles furiously in his notebook, his hand struggling to keep pace with the rapid-fire thoughts racing through his mind.

For a moment, I'm lost in the beauty of it all, the sight of my son embracing his potential, reaching for something more significant than the life we've known. A lump forms in my throat, and I blink back the tears that threaten to spill down my cheeks. I've always wanted this for him: a chance to break free from the chains of our past and write his future.

As the lecture draws close, I slip out of the room, my heart full and my spirit soaring. I wait for Coolidge outside, leaning against the sun-warmed brick of the building, a smile playing at the corners of my lips.

When he emerges, his eyes widen in surprise at seeing me. "Turland? Why are you out here?"

I shrug, trying to play it cool, but the pride in my voice betrays me. "Just wanted to let you have the moment for yourself, that's all."

We step beside each other, and the silence between us is comfortable and familiar. As we walk, I open up, sharing stories of my dreams, the ones I let slip through my fingers like grains of sand.

"I always wanted to go to college," I confess, my gaze fixed on the path ahead. "But I got caught up in the streets, thought I could make a quick buck and be somebody. By the time I realized my mistake, it was too late."

Coolidge listens intently. His brow furrowed in concentration. I can see the wheels turning in his head, the realization that our stories are not so different after all.

"But you're here now," he says, his voice soft and full of understanding. "You're making a difference, Turland. In my life, in the lives of everyone you touch."

I nod, swallowing hard against the lump in my throat. "I just want you to have the chances I never did, Coolidge. I want you to know that you're capable of anything, that your past doesn't define you."

We walk on in silence, the weight of our shared history hanging between us like a bridge spanning the gulf of years and mistakes.

As we return to the apartment, Coolidge and I go to the shed, where our old bicycles await our attention. The rust-speckled frames and tangled chains echo the state of our relationship—neglected but not beyond repair.

I hand Coolidge a wrench and a can of oil, our fingers brushing in the exchange. "Let's start with the chains," I suggest, my voice steady despite my emotions swirling. "They're the heart of the bike, you know. If they're not working right, nothing else will."

Coolidge nods, his eyes bright with understanding. We work in tandem, and our movements are synchronized as if we've been doing this for years. The rhythmic click of the chains and the soft rasp of metal on metal filled the air, a soothing symphony of progress.

As we labor over the bikes, I share stories from my youth – the joy of my first ride and the freedom of the wind on my face. Coolidge listens raptly, his hands never faltering in their task. Now and then, he interjects with a question or a memory of his own, and the depth of his curiosity strikes me, the eagerness of his spirit.

"You know," I say, pausing to wipe the sweat from my brow, "riding a bike is a lot like life. It's all about balance, about learning to trust yourself and keep moving forward, even when the road gets rough."

Coolidge looks up at me, his gaze filled with a newfound respect. "I never thought of it that way," he admits, a smile tugging at the corners of his mouth. "But you're right. It's all about the journey, isn't it?"

I nod, my heart swelling with pride and affection. "And the people you share it with," I add, my voice barely above a whisper.

We return to work, the silence between us now comfortable and familiar. As the sun dips below the horizon and the first stars begin to appear, we step back to admire our handiwork. The bikes gleam in the fading light, their frames straight and true, their chains whispering promises of adventure.

Coolidge turns to me, his face aglow with satisfaction and something else – something tender and unspoken. "Thank you," he says, his hand resting on my shoulder. "For everything."

I wrap my arm around him, pulling him close. With the scent of grease and metal mingling with the sweetness of the evening air, I feel a sense of peace wash over me. We have taken something broken and made it whole again, just as we are slowly mending the fractures in our own lives.

We stand there as silhouettes against the gathering dusk.

The growling of our stomachs finally breaks the spell, reminding us that we've worked straight through the morning. "Come on," I say, giving Coolidge a playful nudge. "Let's grab some lunch. I know a spot not too far from here that makes the best polishes in the city."

Coolidge's eyes light up at the mention of food, and he eagerly follows me as we ride our bikes through the bustling streets. The scent of sizzling onions and polishes wafts through the air, guiding us to a small, unassuming stand on the corner.

"Two polishes with everything," I tell the vendor, who greets us with a smile that crinkles the corners of his eyes. As we wait for our order, Coolidge and I lean against the counter, watching the steady stream of people going about their day.

"You know," I say, turning to him, "I used to come here all the time when I was your age. It was like a ritual – every Saturday night, my boys and I would scrape together whatever change we had and treat ourselves to a polish."

Coolidge grins, his face a mirror of my own at that age. "Sounds like you had some good times," he remarks, gratitude coloring his tone.

Our food arrives, the polishes nestled in soft buns and piled high with grilled onions, mustard, and a sports pepper. We find a nearby bench and sit, savoring each bite like a gourmet meal. We trade stories and jokes between mouthfuls, our laughter ringing across the park.

As we finish our lunch, I can't help but marvel at the ease that has grown between us.

We return to the apartment, our steps lighter than before. As we settle back into work, my mind drifts to the bikes before us—once discarded, now cherished. Then, I see the parallels between these machines and our lives.

Like the bikes, Coolidge and I have experienced our share of hardships. We've been beaten down, left to rust and decay in the unforgiving corners of the world. But just as we've poured our hearts into restoring these bikes, we are slowly piecing ourselves together.

I know it will take time and patience. But with each turn of the wrench, each quiet conversation, I can feel the wounds of the past beginning to heal. And as I watch Coolidge work, his brow furrowed in concentration, I am filled with fierce hope for the future.

Coolidge and I make our way to the community center, a humble brick building nestled between the worn facades of the neighborhood. The air is filled with the chatter of children playing and the distant thrum of music from an open window.

As we approach the entrance, a group of volunteers greets us with warm smiles and open arms. "Turland, Coolidge, so glad you could make it," says Ms. Foster, the center's director. "We could use your help with the mural project."

Coolidge and I exchange glances, a flicker of excitement passing between us. "We're happy to help however we can," I reply, my voice steady despite the nerves fluttering in my chest.

We follow Ms. Foster inside, where young people are already working hard, sketching designs and mixing paints. The walls are a blank canvas, waiting to be filled with color and life.

As we settle in, Coolidge immediately gravitates towards a group of teenagers, his easy smile and gentle demeanor putting them at ease. I watch as he listens intently to their ideas, offering suggestions and encouragement.

"Coolidge has a real gift with people," Ms. Foster remarks, her eyes twinkling with admiration. "He's a natural leader."

Pride swells in my chest as I nod in agreement.

As the hours pass, the mural begins to take shape – a vibrant tapestry of colors and images that tell the story of our community.

But it's Coolidge who truly shines. He moves among the volunteers quickly, offering a kind word or a helping hand here and there. Watching him, I am struck by the realization that he was meant to inspire, guide, and lead.

Coolidge and I step back to admire our handiwork as the day draws closer. The mural is a testament to the resilience and beauty of our community – a reminder that even in the darkest of times, there is always hope.

"You did good today, Coolidge," I say, my voice thick with emotion. "I'm proud of you."

He turns to me, his eyes shining with gratitude. "I couldn't have done it without you, Turland. Thank you for being here – for believing in me."

Coolidge and I find ourselves sitting on the steps of his mother's house, the weight of the day's accomplishments settling upon us like a comforting blanket. The silence stretches between us, but it's not uncomfortable – instead, it's a silence born of understanding, shared experiences, and unspoken bonds.

"You know," I begin, my voice soft and contemplative, "your mother is so proud of you for returning to school. She told me the other day, her eyes shining with tears of joy."

Coolidge looks down at his hands, a small smile playing at the corners of his lips. "I'm doing it for her, you know? For all the sacrifices she made, all the hardships she endured to give me a better life."

I nod, understanding the depth of his words. "And you're doing an amazing job, Coolidge. You're showing her that her faith in you was not misplaced."

He takes a deep breath, his eyes meeting mine with an intensity that catches me off guard. "I couldn't have done it without you, Turland. You've been there for me, guiding me, supporting me. I... I don't know how to thank you because it was truly rough in prison, and it could have gone really bad for me if you didn't step in when you did."

The following words slip from his lips before he can catch them, a whisper carried on the evening breeze. "Thanks, Da-"

He stops himself, his eyes widening in realization of what he almost said, a flicker of uncertainty crossing his features. Was it something he had felt for a while? But at that moment, my heart swells with an emotion I can hardly contain—a mixture of joy and longing, hope and yearning.

I want to tell him that it's okay, that he can call me whatever he wants, and that I'll always be there for him. But the words stuck in my throat, held back by the weight of our truth yet to be revealed and how the secret would feel once it became a reality for him.

Instead, I reach out and place a hand on his shoulder, squeezing gently. "You don't have to thank me, Coolidge. I'm here because I want to be because I believe in you."

We sit there in silence, watching as the stars peek out from the darkening sky, each lost in our thoughts. But a sense of peace settles over us, a feeling of rightness that comes from knowing we're precisely where we're meant to be.

As the night wraps us in its gentle embrace, I allow myself to dream of a future where the truth is spoken, where the walls between us crumble and fall away. a future where Coolidge would understand the depth of my love for him and where we could walk side by side, not as mentor and mentee but now as father and son.

As I step into my basement apartment, the warmth of the day's events still lingers on my skin, a gentle reminder of our progress. The room is small, the walls bare, but tonight it feels different, infused with a sense of hope that I haven't felt in years.

I sink onto the edge of the bed, my mind replaying the moments from earlier, the way Coolidge's eyes shone with pride as he shared his first day of class, and the ease of our conversations as we worked side by side. And then, that moment, the one that caught us both by surprise, when he almost called me "Dad." Not knowing how true that is.

My heart swells with joy and longing, the weight of the unspoken truth pressing against my chest. I want to tell him, to reveal the bond that ties us together, but I know it's not the right time. Not yet.

Instead, I close my eyes and whisper a silent prayer of gratitude. "Thank you, God, for this chance."

The words hang in the air, a sacred vow between myself and the divine. And as I sit there, surrounded by the quiet of the night, I know that everything happens for a reason, that every struggle, every moment of darkness, has led me to this point.

I rise from the bed and move to the window, gazing at the city lights that flicker in the distance. Each one represents a story, a life, a dream.

A smile tugs at my lips, and I whisper into the night, "I'm proud of you, son. And I can't wait to tell you you're my son."

Chapter 26: Community Ties

The kitchen hums with energy as we prepare for the Thanksgiving feast. Mary Jane bustles between the stove and counter, her movements quick and purposeful. Coolidge stands beside me at the table. His eyes fixed on my hands as I shape the dough for my Aunt Ruby's famous rolls.

"Like this?" Coolidge asks, mimicking my motions. His brow furrows in concentration as he kneads the soft, pliable dough.

I nod, a smile tugging at my lips. "That's it. Gentle but firm. Let the dough tell you when it's ready."

My hands move on instinct, the memory of Aunt Ruby's patient guidance echoing through the years. *How often did she stand beside me, her weathered hands guiding mine? Teaching me the secrets of her kitchen, the stories of our family woven into every dish.*

Coolidge's hands are young and strong, untouched by time's cruel march. But there's an eagerness in his touch, a hunger to learn and understand. *To be a part of something bigger than himself.*

"Now we let it rest," I say, covering the dough with a clean damp cloth. "Give it time to rise, to become something new."

Coolidge meets my gaze, a flicker of understanding passing between us. *We both know the weight of waiting.*

Mary Jane's laughter breaks the moment, her smile brighter than the autumn sun streaming through the window. "You boys and your bread," she teases, her voice warm with affection. "Save some magic for the pies, you hear?"

This, I think as we return to our tasks, the kitchen filled with the scent of spices and promise. *This is what I fought for all those years. The chance to stand in this light, to pass on the wisdom in my hands. To build a new legacy, one roll at a time.*

The aroma of roasting turkey mingles with the scent of cinnamon and nutmeg, a symphony of flavors that wraps around me like a warm embrace. *How long has it been since I've felt this sense of belonging? This feeling of home?*

I watch Mary Jane move through the kitchen with the grace of a dancer, her hands blurring motion as she chops carrots and celery. There's a rhythm to her movements, a confidence born of countless meals prepared with love.

She is the heart of this place, I realize, my chest tightening with an emotion I can't quite name. *The steady beat that keeps us all in time.*

"Turland, can you pass me the thyme?" Mary Jane asks, her voice soft yet clear above the sizzle of the stove.

Our fingers brush as I hand her the delicate sprigs, a fleeting touch that sends a jolt of electricity through my veins. *How can such a small gesture hold so much power?*

Mary Jane's eyes meet mine, and the world disappears momentarily. In her gaze, I see a reflection of my longing, a yearning for connection that transcends the wounds of our pasts.

She sees me, I think, my breath catching in my throat. *Not the man I was, but the man I'm trying to become.*

"Thank you," she murmurs, her lips curving into a smile that could light up the darkest nights.

I nod, unable to find the words to express the gratitude that swells within me. *For this moment, this chance, for the hope that blooms in the space between us.*

As we return to our tasks, the kitchen hums with a newfound energy, a sense of purpose beyond the meal we're preparing. *This is more than just a dinner,* I realize, observing Coolidge arrange the rolls on a baking sheet.

The oven door closes with a soft thud, sealing in the heat and the promise of the feast. *And maybe,* I dare to hope, *sealing in the beginnings of a new family, one forged in the fires of adversity and tempered by the strength of our shared humanity.*

A knock at the door pulls me from my reverie, and I wipe my hands on a dish towel, exchanging a glance with Mary Jane as I answer it.

I open the door to find Mr. Washington standing on the threshold, his weathered face creased with a gentle smile. He leans heavily on his cane, but his eyes sparkle with the wisdom of a life well-lived. "Turland," he greets me, his voice rich and warm. "It's good to see you, son."

"Mr. Washington," I reply, stepping aside to usher him. "Please, come in. Let me help you get a seat."

He nods, allowing me to guide him to the living room, where I settle him into the worn but comfortable armchair. "The neighborhood's changing," he remarks, his gaze drifting to the window. "New faces, new stories. But the heart of it remains the same."

I perch on the edge of the couch, leaning forward to listen. "How so?" I ask, genuinely curious.

Mr. Washington chuckles, a deep, rumbling sound that seems to come from the very depths of his soul. "The struggles, the triumphs, the way folks come together when times get tough. That's the essence of this place, the spirit that keeps us going."

I nod, understanding dawning in the silence that stretches between us. *The neighborhood, like the people who call it home, is a survivor,* I muse. *Battered and bruised, but never broken.*

Another knock at the door interrupts our conversation, and I rise to answer it, my heart quickening with anticipation. Dame stands on the other side, his face splitting into a grin as he sees me. "Turland," he says, clasping my hand firmly. "Wow, this is nice."

"Dame," I reply, returning his grin. "You made it."

He steps inside, his presence filling the room with a crackling energy. Our eyes meet, and a lifetime of shared experiences passes between us in that moment. The laughter, tears, moments of despair, and the flickers of hope are all there, unspoken but understood.

We've been through hell together, I think, my throat tightening with emotion. *And somehow, against all odds, we've come out the other side.*

Dame's gaze shifts to Mr. Washington, who inclines his head in a respectful nod. "Mr. Washington," he greets the older man. It's an honor to be here."

Mr. Washington smiles, his eyes crinkling at the corners. "The honor is mine, young man. It warms my heart to see the two of you together, building something good out of the ashes of the past."

I swallow hard, blinking back the sudden sting of tears. *Building something good,* I echo silently. *A future, a family, a life worth living.*

As I stand there, surrounded by the people who have shaped my journey, I feel a flicker of something I haven't allowed myself to think of in a long time: hope, pure and radiant, burning bright in the darkness of my soul.

As we settle around the table, the soft clink of glasses and the gentle murmur of conversation fill the air. I look around at the faces of those gathered here, each one a thread in the tapestry of my life, and I feel a surge of emotion that threatens to overwhelm me.

Dame sits to my right, his presence a solid, reassuring anchor amid the swirling currents of my thoughts. Mary Jane is on my left, her hand resting lightly on my arm, a silent reminder of her unwavering support. Coolidge and Mr. Washington complete the circle, their faces illuminated by the warm glow of the candles flickering at the center of the table.

We sit silently for a moment, each of us lost in our reflections. Then Mr. Washington clears his throat, his deep, rich voice cutting through the stillness like a night beacon.

"I remember," he begins, his eyes distant with memory, "when I first came to this neighborhood. It was a different time then, a different world. But even amid all the change and upheaval, one thing remained constant: the strength of our community."

He pauses, his gaze sweeping around the table, meeting each of our eyes. "We've been through a lot, all of us. We've seen and experienced things that no one should ever face. But through it all, we've had each other. We've had the bonds of friendship, family, and love."

I feel a lump rising in my throat, and I swallow hard, blinking back the sudden sting of tears. *He's right,* I think, my heart aching with the weight of the memories. *We've had each other. And that's what's kept us going even more now than ever.*

Mr. Washington's voice takes on a note of quiet intensity, his words resonating with the wisdom of a lifetime. "But it's not enough just to survive," he says, his eyes burning with a fierce, unwavering conviction. "We have to thrive to stand the test of time."

He leans forward, his hands clasped together on the table before him. "That's what we're doing here tonight. We're planting the seeds of hope, renewal, and redemption."

I feel a shiver run down my spine, and I know, with a sudden, unshakable certainty, that he's right.

Dame's voice cuts through the respectful silence, his words tinged with a bittersweet nostalgia. "Remember that time when Russell, Jerry, you, and I snuck out of the cell block to catch a glimpse of the stars?" he asks, his eyes distant with memory. "We knew we'd get caught, knew we'd pay the price, but for those few precious moments, we were free."

I nod, a lump forming in my throat as I recall Russell's face lit up that night, the way he'd thrown his head back and laughed, his voice echoing off the prison walls. "He always said that the stars were a reminder that there was something bigger out there, something beyond the bars and the concrete and the pain," I murmur, my voice thick with emotion.

Dame smiles a sad, wistful smile that speaks of a lifetime of loss and longing. "And Jerry, he was the dreamer too," he says, his voice soft with remembrance. He was always talking about the life he would live when he got out, the places he was going to go, the things he was going to see."

I feel a pang of grief, sharp and sudden, as I think of Jerry's bright, hopeful eyes, now forever closed. "They deserved better," I whisper, my hands clenching into fists beneath the table. "They deserved a chance, a future, a life too."

Dame reaches out, his hand covering mine, his touch warm and steadying. "We all did," he says, his voice fierce with conviction. "And that's why we're here."

Across the table, Coolidge leans forward, his eyes alight with a fierce, unquenchable curiosity. "Tell me more," he says, his voice eager and earnest. "Tell me about Russell and Jerry, about their dreams and lives they wanted to live."

I feel a surge of pride, hope, and love as I look at Coolidge, at the way he drinks in every word, story, and lesson. *He's the future,* I think, my heart swelling with a fierce, unshakable certainty. *He's the one who will carry on our legacy.*

And so I begin to speak, my voice low and sincere, painting pictures of the past, lost dreams, and shattered hopes.

Hope, I think, my eyes meeting Coolidge's, my heart beating in time with his. *Hope for a better tomorrow.*

As the evening wears on, the warmth of the gathering begins to give way to a subtle undercurrent of tension. It's there in the way Dame's eyes flicker to the side, in the way Mr. Washington's hands tighten around his glass, in the way Mary Jane's smile falters for just a moment before she catches herself.

I also feel a prickling sense of unease, a whisper of something unspoken lurking beneath the surface. It's in the silences that stretch between stories, the half-finished sentences that trail off into nothingness, and the way the laughter sometimes rings too loud or forced. I know it's all in my head because of the secret that still is lingering.

Chapter 27: The Revelation

Across the living room, Turland's eyes locked with Mary Jane's. An unspoken truth passed between them in that glance, a secret yearning to be set free. The air grew thick with anticipation, yet the others remained oblivious, their laughter and chatter filling the space.

Turland's heart quickened. He knew the moment had come. There could be no more hiding, no more pretending. He had to speak the truth. Consequences be damned.

Mary Jane gave him an almost imperceptible nod, her eyes shining with encouragement and something more profound - was it love? Turland drew strength from her gaze.

He cleared his throat, the sound slicing through the revelry like a knife. Slowly, the room fell silent. Curious eyes turned his way - Coolidge, Dame, Mr. Washington, and Mary Jane. The festive atmosphere evaporated, replaced by a taut expectancy.

Coolidge cocked his head, fork still poised over his plate heaped with turkey and stuffing now resting on a TV tray as the football game is in the background. "What's up, Turland? Everything okay?"

Turland's mouth went dry. He licked his lips, pulse hammering in his ears. "I...I have something I need to say. Something important."

Dame leaned forward, elbows on knees, shrewd gaze studying Turland's face. Mr. Washington straightened up, wiping his mouth with a napkin, his wise eyes encouraging Turland to continue.

Mary Jane's hands clasped tightly in her lap, knuckles pale. Her unwavering stare sent a surge of courage through Turland's veins. It was now or never.

He breathed deeply, the words burning in his throat like molten lava. Everyone was watching him, waiting. In the stillness, the announcer's voice crackled from the forgotten TV: "First down!"

But a first down was the last thing on anyone's mind. All eyes were fixed on Turland as he parted his lips to speak, to give voice to the truth that would change everything finally...

"I met Mary Jane once before," Turland began, his voice steady despite the tremor in his hands. "Years ago, outside a jewelry store. We spent the day together, talking and laughing. It was the best day of my life up to that point."

Turland felt a weight lift from his shoulders as the words left his lips. The secret he'd carried for so long, the connection he'd cherished in his heart, was finally out in the open.

Coolidge's brow furrowed, confusion clouding his features. He set his fork down, the clatter of metal against ceramic unnaturally loud in the stillness. "What are you saying, Turland? You knew my mother before?"

Turland nodded, his gaze never leaving Coolidge's face. He watched as myriad emotions flickered across his friend's eyes—disbelief, uncertainty, a glimmer of something unreadable.

"I didn't know God had plans for her to be your mother then," Turland continued, his voice softening. "But that day, that connection, it meant everything to me. It gave me hope during the darkest times."

Coolidge leaned back in his chair, his expression unreadable. The gears turned behind his eyes as he processed Turland's revelation, trying to piece together the implications and hidden truths lurking beneath the surface.

The room held its breath, the tension palpable. Dame's gaze darted between Turland and Coolidge, his streetwise instincts sensing the moment's gravity. Mr. Washington's eyes shone with a knowing light, a flicker of understanding dawning on his wise face.

Turland's heart raced, his palms damp with sweat. He'd taken the leap, bared his soul, and now he could only wait for Coolidge's reaction. Would he be angry or betrayed, or would he see the beauty in the unexpected bond that had brought them together?

The weight of the past hung heavy in the silence, the echoes of laughter and shared memories whispered through the room. As Turland met Coolidge's gaze, he saw a glimmer of something that gave him hope—a flicker of recognition, a spark of the unbreakable connection that had always been there, waiting to be discovered.

Mary Jane's gentle voice breaks the silence, a soothing balm amidst the swirling emotions. "Turland was the coolest guy in the world to me," she says, her eyes glistening with the weight of memories. "I didn't know his name then, but that day, that wonderful day, it stayed with me forever."

My mother's words wrapped around me like a warm embrace, confirmation of a truth. The puzzle pieces of my world are falling or sinking into place, each revelation a brushstroke on the canvas of my life, painting a picture I, Coolidge, never knew existed.

I feel the room's gaze upon me, the weight of their curiosity and anticipation bearing down on my shoulders. But at this moment, there is only the pounding of my heart, the rush of blood in my ears, and the overwhelming surge of emotions that threatens to consume me.

Confusion, disbelief, and anger dance within me, a chaotic whirlwind that leaves me breathless. How could this be? The man I've known as a stranger, a figure from the prison where I once lived, now intertwined with the very fabric of my being.

I search Turland's face, seeking answers in the depths of his eyes. And there, amidst the swirling emotions, I find a glimmer of truth, a reflection of the connection that has always been there, hidden beneath the surface.

The silence stretches on, heavy and thick, as the room holds its breath. I can feel their eyes upon me, waiting for my reaction, for the words that will shatter the stillness. But I am lost in the tumult of my thoughts, in the realization that my world has shifted beneath my feet.

I close my eyes, seeking solace in the darkness, trying to make sense of the revelations that have upended everything I thought I knew. The faces of our guests swim before me—Dame, his loyalty unwavering to Turland and Mr. Washington, his wisdom a guiding light for Turland, their support a steadfast anchor in this newest storm.

As I open my eyes, I meet my mother's gaze. In her eyes, I see the love that has always been there, the unwavering belief in second chances, and the power of redemption. And at that moment, I knew I was not alone no matter what happened.

The silence continues, a pause in the threads of time, as the room awaits my response. But for now, I am lost in the labyrinth of my own emotions, searching for the words that will give voice to the truth that has been revealed.

Dame leans forward, his elbows resting on his knees, his gaze flickering between Turland and me. "You know," he begins, his voice low and steady, "I always thought there was something familiar about you, Coolidge. The way you carry yourself and talk reminded me of someone, but I couldn't quite put my finger on it." He pauses, a slight smile tugging at the corner of his mouth. "But seeing you two together, it's like a puzzle piece falling into place. The resemblance is there."

I feel the weight of Dame's words settling upon me, confirming the truth that has been revealed. His streetwise nature, honed by years of navigating the harsh realities of life, lends a grounding presence to the room, a solid foundation amidst the emotional upheaval.

Mr. Washington, who has been listening intently, clears his throat, drawing all eyes to him. "I remember young Turland," he says, his voice rich with the wisdom of age. "He was a bright boy, full of potential, even in the face of adversity." He turns to me, his gaze warm and knowing. "And now, looking at you, Coolidge, I see that same spark and resilience."

As Mr. Washington speaks, I feel a sense of connection, a bridge spanning the generations. His words, infused with empathy and understanding, wrap around me like a comforting embrace, offering reassurance in the face of uncertainty.

The room seems to breathe a collective sigh, releasing tension as more puzzle pieces fall into place for them. Once a source of confusion and turmoil, the revelation takes on a new meaning, a glimmer of hope in the darkness.

I glance around the room, taking in the faces of those who have gathered here, the people who have become a family. In their eyes, I see a reflection of my emotions—a mixture of surprise, understanding, and acceptance.

The following silence is different now, no longer heavy with anticipation but filled with the quiet hum of contemplation.

Each person is lost in their thoughts, processing the implications of this newfound truth.

As I sit there, surrounded by the warmth of this makeshift family, I feel a new sense of belonging. Perhaps my path and struggles have led me to this moment, to this place of understanding and connection.

As the weight of the revelation settles upon my shoulders, I find myself rising from the sofa, my movements deliberate and measured. The room seems to blur around me, the faces of those I love fading into the background as I focus on the tumultuous emotions swirling within my heart.

I take a step forward, then another, my feet carrying me toward the door, towards the solitude I so desperately crave. I can feel their eyes upon me, the unspoken questions hanging in the air, but I cannot bring myself to meet their gazes, face the concern and compassion I know I will find there.

Instead, I let my steps guide me, each footfall a metronome, steady and purposeful, a rhythm that echoes the beating of my own heart. I reach for the door handle, the cool metal a stark contrast to the heat that seems to radiate from my very core, and with a gentle twist, I step out into the hallway.

The silence that greets me is a welcome reprieve, a moment of stillness amidst the chaos that threatens to consume me. I lean against the wall, my eyes closing as I draw in a deep, shuddering breath, the air filling my lungs and granting me a momentary sense of clarity.

In the solitude of this space, I allow myself to feel, to truly experience the depth of the emotions that have been building within me. Anger, sharp and biting, courses through my veins, a sense of betrayal that stings like a physical wound. How could they have kept this from me, this truth that has the power to reshape the very foundation of my existence?

Yet, even as the anger burns, I can feel something else stirring beneath the surface, a flicker of hope that refuses to be extinguished. Amid this turmoil, I cannot help but wonder what this revelation might mean, what doors it might open, what paths it might illuminate.

I think back to the stories Turland shared, the memories of a young man full of promise and life. In those stories, I see a reflection of myself, a kindred spirit forged in the fires of adversity, shaped by the trials and tribulations of a world that often seems stacked against us.

Perhaps, in the end, this is not a betrayal but a gift, a chance to understand the man who gave me life, to forge a connection that transcends the boundaries of time and circumstance. As I stand there, my hand resting upon the door, I feel a sense of determination rising within me, a resolve to embrace this truth and let it guide me toward a future I have yet to imagine.

With a deep breath, I push myself away from the wall, my steps no longer heavy with uncertainty but imbued with a newfound sense of purpose. I know that the path ahead will not be easy, that obstacles will be overcome, and that wounds will be healed, but I also know that I am not alone and have the love and support of those who matter most.

And so, I turn back towards the living room, ready to face whatever lies ahead, secure in the knowledge that, no matter what the future may bring, I will face it with the strength and resilience that has always been a part of me, a testament to the unbreakable spirit that resides within the very heart of who I am.

As Coolidge's footsteps lead him back inside, the living room falls into a heavy silence. I can feel Mary Jane's gaze upon me, a silent question lingering between us. I turn to meet her eyes, and at that moment, a wordless understanding passes between us, a shared resolve to stand by Coolidge's side no matter what the future may bring.

Mary Jane reaches for my hand, her fingers intertwining with mine, a gesture of unity and support. "We'll get through this together," she whispers, her voice barely audible above the soft hum of the television. "He needs us now more than ever."

I nod, my throat tight with emotion. "I know," I manage to say, my voice rough and unsteady. "I just wish I could take away his pain and make this easier for him somehow."

Mary Jane squeezes my hand, a gentle reminder of her presence. "We can't take away his pain, but we can be there for him, show him that he's not alone."

The other guests stir around us, their hushed conversations gradually filling the room. Dame rises from his seat, his movements deliberate and purposeful. He approaches us, his eyes filled with concern and determination.

"I'm here for you both," he says, low and earnest. "Anything you need, just say the word."

I am grateful for Dame's unwavering loyalty and willingness to stand by us through the storm. "Thank you," I say, my voice thick with emotion. It means more than you know."

Mr. Washington joins us, his weathered face etched with lines of wisdom and compassion. "Coolidge is a strong young man," he says, his voice rich and soothing. "He'll find his way through this with the love and support of those who care for him."

As the guests begin to leave, each offering encouragement and support, I feel a sense of hope rising within me, a glimmer of light amidst the darkness.

As the last guest departs, leaving Mary Jane and me alone in the living room, I feel a renewed sense of purpose, a determination to be the father Coolidge deserves, to help him navigate the challenges ahead, and to build a future filled with hope and possibility.

In the quiet of the living room, the weight of the evening's revelations hangs heavy in the air. I sit beside Mary Jane, our bodies close, seeking comfort in each other's presence. The lamp's soft glow casts shadows across her face, highlighting the worry lines etched into her forehead.

"I never imagined it would be like this," Mary Jane whispers, her voice barely audible above the refrigerator's hum. "Seeing his face, the confusion, the hurt..."

I reach for her hand, intertwining our fingers, feeling the warmth of her skin against mine. "I know," I murmur, my heart aching with the memory of Coolidge's expression, how his eyes widened in disbelief and then narrowed in anger. But we did the right thing, telling him the truth. He deserved to know."

Mary Jane nods, her gaze distant, lost in thought. "I just hope he can find it in his heart to forgive us, to understand why we kept it from him for so long."

I squeeze her hand, trying to convey the depth of my hope and the fierce love that burns within me for her and our son. "He will," I say, my voice steady with conviction. It may take time, but he'll see we only wanted to protect and give him the best life possible."

We sat silently momentarily, the years of separation and longing settling over us like a blanket. I think back to that day outside the jewelry store, the spark of connection that had ignited between us, the promise of a future that had seemed so bright, so full of possibility.

And now, here we are, our lives intertwined once more, facing a new set of challenges, a new journey that will test the strength of our love and the resilience of our spirits. But as I look at Mary Jane, her eyes shining with fierce determination, I know we will weather this storm together and build a life of hope and redemption for ourselves and Coolidge.

"We'll make it through this," I say, my voice barely above a whisper but filled with a quiet strength, a certainty coming from my soul's depths. "Together, we'll find a way to heal, grow, and love."

Mary Jane smiles, a soft, tender curve of her lips that warms my heart. "Together," she echoes, her voice a promise, a vow that will carry us through the darkest of nights into the light of a new dawn.

Chapter 28: Aftermath

Coolidge sat at the kitchen table, his eyes fixed on the cup of steaming coffee before him as if it held some answers to the revelation that shook his world: Turland, his cellmate, his friend—his father. The thought brought conflicting emotions crashing through his mind, fragmenting his concentration.

He leaned back in the chair, the subtle tension in his shoulders betraying the turmoil. Images flashed through his head--shared laughs in their cell, heart-to-heart conversations, a bond forged in the crucible of imprisonment. But now, those memories took on new shades, a deeper meaning that terrified and intrigued him.

Coolidge's hands trembled slightly as he reached for the mug, seeking solace in the familiar warmth. He took a sip, the bitter liquid scalding his tongue, but he barely noticed. His mind raced with unanswered questions and unprocessed emotions. A father—something he'd longed for all his life—was now within reach, yet utterly complicated.

Turland paced the floor in the basement apartment, his footsteps echoing off the bare walls. His heart hammered in his chest as he realized the enormity of the truth he'd recently discovered: a son—a piece of himself in the world, unknowingly connected by blood.

Turland paused before the mirror, his reflection staring back at him with hope and apprehension. He ran a hand over his face, the lines etched by years of hardship and regret. How could he approach Coolidge now? What words could bridge the chasm of time and circumstance that complicated everything for them?

He practiced the words under his breath, rehearsing a conversation he'd never imagined. "Coolidge, I...I never knew. I'm sorry. I want to make things right." The words felt inadequate, mere pebbles tossed into the vast ocean of their shared history.

Yet, beneath the fear and uncertainty, a flicker of hope danced in Turland's eyes—a chance for redemption, for connection, for the family he'd always yearned for. He straightened his shoulders, a newfound determination settling over him. No matter the obstacles, he would find a way to reach out to his now-son to forge a bond that could transcend the mistakes of the past.

Coolidge's grip tightened around the mug in the quiet kitchen, his knuckles turning tense. The weight of the revelation pressed down upon him, a burden he wasn't sure he was ready to bear. Yet, deep within, a small voice whispered—a longing for connection, understanding, and the piece of himself that had always been missing.

He closed his eyes, allowing himself a moment to imagine what could be—a relationship, a family, a chance to rewrite the narrative of his life. The path ahead was uncertain, fraught with emotional landmines and painful truths. But at that moment, Coolidge made a decision. He would confront this new reality head-on with the same resilience that had carried him through his trials.

Two men, father and son, separated by circumstance but bound by blood. Their journeys had taken divergent paths, but now, fate had brought them to a crossroads. In the stillness of their respective spaces, Coolidge and Turland grappled with the weight of their connection, the promise, and the pain it held. The road to reconciliation, very different now, would be long and winding, but a flicker of hope started a slow dance between them at that moment, a fragile bridge spanning the distance of years and secrets.

Mary Jane stepped into the kitchen, her gentle footsteps breaking the heavy silence. She paused, her eyes falling upon Coolidge's hunched form, the tension radiating from his body like heat from a furnace. At that moment, she saw not the grown man before her but the little boy who had once sought comfort in her arms, his tears soaking through her shirt as she whispered soothing words against his hair.

"Coolidge, baby," she murmured, her voice a balm to his frayed nerves. "I know it's a lot to take in. But I'm here for you, no matter what."

Coolidge lifted his gaze, his eyes meeting hers, and in their depths, Mary Jane saw a swirl of emotions—confusion, anger, and beneath it all, a desperate yearning for connection. She moved closer, pulling out a chair and settling beside him, her hand resting on his arm.

"I don't know what to do, Mama," Coolidge confessed, his voice barely above a whisper. "I've spent my whole life wondering about him, and now..."

Mary Jane squeezed his arm, a gentle reminder of her presence. "Take your time, baby. There's no rush. You've got a right to feel however you feel."

Coolidge nodded, his eyes drifting back to the mug cradled in his hands. The steam curled upward, dissipating into the air, and he wished his troubles could vanish just as quickly.

***

Across town, Turland stood before Mr. Washington's gate, his heart pounding against his ribcage. He had come seeking wisdom, guidance, anything to help him navigate the uncharted waters of fatherhood. Yet now, faced with the prospect of baring his soul, he hesitated.

"Turland? Is that you, son?" Mr. Washington's voice carried from the backyard, warm and inviting.

Turland stepped through the gate, his feet carrying him towards the sound. He found the older man kneeling in a bed of vibrant flowers, his hands caked with rich, dark soil. Mr. Washington looked up, a smile crinkling the corners of his eyes.

"Come to help an old man with his gardenin'?" he asked, a knowing twinkle in his eye.

Turland managed a smile, the tension in his shoulders easing slightly. "If you'll have me, sir."

He knelt beside Mr. Washington, his fingers sinking into the damp earth. For a moment, they worked in companionable silence; the only sound was the gentle rustling of leaves and the distant chirping of birds.

"What's on your mind, son?" Mr. Washington asked, his gaze never leaving the delicate seedling he was planting.

Turland swallowed, the words sticking in his throat. "When I found out I... I have a son. Coolidge. And I don't know how to be a father to him now, not after everything."

Mr. Washington hummed a contemplative sound. "Seems to me, the first step is showin' up. Bein' there, even when it's hard. Even when you don't have all the answers. Kind of like you did for him in prison."

Turland nodded, his eyes stinging with unshed tears. "I want to make things right, Mr. Washington. I want to be the father he deserves."

The older man turned, fixing Turland with a steady gaze. "It won't happen overnight. It'll take time and patience. But if you're willin' to put in the work, to be honest, and open... well, there's no tellin' what kind of beauty can grow from that."

Turland looked down at the seedling cradled in his palm, a fragile promise of new beginnings. At that moment, he understood. The road ahead would be difficult, and the soil of their relationship would be rocky and uneven. But with care and nurturing, perhaps something beautiful could bloom between him and Coolidge—a bond that could weather any storm.

As I walk through the neighborhood, the weight of memory settles upon my shoulders like a familiar, well-worn coat. The streets, once vibrant with the laughter of children and the chatter of neighbors, now lie quiet as if holding their breath in anticipation. Boarded-up windows and crumbling facades stand as silent testaments to the passage of time, to the dreams that have faded like the peeling paint on the walls.

I pause before a weathered basketball hoop, its net frayed and swaying in the gentle breeze. Echoes of past games, triumphant shouts, and the pounding of feet against asphalt whisper in my ear. How many hours did we spend here, lost in the thrill of competition, in the camaraderie of shared victories and defeats? Those moments, once so vivid, now feel like the sepia-tinted photographs that line the walls of my memory.

As I continue my journey, the scent of honeysuckle drifts in the air, a sweet reminder of summers past. I close my eyes, allowing myself to be transported back to a time when the future stretched like an endless horizon, full of promise and possibility. But reality, with its sharp edges and unforgiving truths, reshapes even the most idyllic of landscapes.

The sound of a screen door slamming draws my attention, and I catch a glimpse of a young boy racing down the steps, his laughter trailing behind him like a banner. For a moment, I see myself in his carefree stride, in the unbridled joy that radiates from his small frame. The nostalgia is a bittersweet ache in my chest, a reminder of the innocence lost and the hard lessons learned.

I stand before the Patterson home as the sun dips below the rooftops. Once a beacon of warmth and love, the house now seems to hold its breath, waiting for the wounds of the past to heal. I know Mary Jane is preparing dinner within those walls, her heart heavy with unspoken hopes and fears.

Inside, Mary Jane moves through the kitchen with practiced grace, her hands steady as she chops vegetables and stirs pots. But beneath the veneer of domestic tranquility, her mind is a whirlwind of emotions. She thinks of Turland and Coolidge, of the chasm that has grown between them, and the desperate longing for reconciliation that burns in her heart.

As she sets the table, Mary Jane's gaze lingers on the empty chairs, a poignant reminder of the absences that have shaped their lives. She remembers the nights spent in silent prayer, the tears shed in the solitude of her bedroom, and the unwavering belief that love, in all its resilient beauty, could bridge even the widest of divides.

With each place setting, Mary Jane lays down a silent wish, a sincere hope that the meal she prepares will be more than just sustenance for the body. She yearns for it to be a balm for the soul, a catalyst for healing and understanding. In the steam rising from the dishes, she sees the tendrils of a future where forgiveness and acceptance reign, where the past is not forgotten but woven into the tapestry of their shared story.

The wooden stairs creak beneath Coolidge's feet as he descends into the basement, the musty air enveloping him like a familiar embrace. Shadows dance along the walls, cast by the single bare light bulb hanging from the ceiling. Coolidge ran his fingers along the rough shelves, searching for the box of old records he'd promised to dig out for Mary Jane a while ago.

Instead, his hand brushes against a worn, leather-bound journal, its edges frayed and its pages yellowed with age. Coolidge hesitates, his heartbeat quickening as he realizes what he has stumbled upon. Turland's prison journal is a glimpse into the mind of the man he was struggling to understand and forgive.

Part of Coolidge wants to push it back into the shadows, to pretend he never found it. But there's another part, a whisper in the depths of his soul, urging him to open it, to see the world through Turland's eyes.

With trembling hands, I lift the journal from its resting place, its weight heavy in my grasp. I sink to the floor, my back pressed against the cool concrete wall, and I open to the first page.

Turland's raw and honest words wash over me as I read, painting a vivid picture of his life behind bars. The pages are filled with pain and hope, despair and resilience. But one passage catches my eye and makes my breath catch.

"I met a beautiful girl right before coming here with a smile that could light up even the darkest cells. That day, we talked for hours about everything and nothing at all. At that moment, she made me forget what I'd done; even now, the thought of her makes me forget the chains that bound me today. She made me feel alive again and even possible to dream of a future beyond these walls."

Tears blur my vision as I read on, as I witness the depth of Turland's longing, his desperate desire for connection in a world that had cast him aside. With each word, I see him in a new light, not as the distant figure I'd resented for so long when I didn't know he existed, but as a man fighting to hold onto his humanity in the face of unimaginable odds.

"I never got her name, but I'll never forget how she made me feel. In this place where hope is a rare commodity, she was a beacon, a reminder that beauty still exists. And that's what I'll hold onto; that's what will keep me going when the nights grow long and the walls start closing in."

I close the journal, my heart aching with a newfound understanding. All this time, I'd been so focused on my pain and my sense of abandonment that I'd failed to see the scars that Turland carried, the dreams he'd clung to in the darkest of times.

Rising to my feet, I tuck the journal under my arm, a new-found determination coursing through my veins. I know now that the path to healing and forgiveness begins with empathy and a willingness to see the world through another's eyes.

As I go back up the stairs, the aroma of Mary Jane's cooking wafting down to greet me, I feel a sense of purpose and hope. The road ahead may be extended, the wounds deep, but with each step, each shared story, we'll find our way back to each other.

And in the end, that's all that matters.

Turland pushes open the front door, his shoulders slumped with exhaustion, yet his heart lighter than in years. Mr. Washington's words echo in his mind, a soothing balm to the doubts and fears that have plagued him for so long.

As he steps into the dimly lit hallway, a floorboard creaks beneath his feet, announcing his presence. He pauses, listening for any signs of life, unsure of what reception he'll find.

And then, emerging from the shadows, Coolidge clutches a worn journal in his hands, his expression unreadable.

Turland's breath catches in his throat, a flicker of recognition sparking in his eyes as they settle on the familiar cover. It's a relic from another time, a testament to the man he once was, the dreams he once harbored.

"Coolidge," he begins, his voice barely above a whisper, "I..."

But Coolidge holds up a hand, silencing him. There's no anger in his eyes, no resentment, only a quiet understanding, a shared pain that needs no words.

"I read it," Coolidge says softly, his fingers tracing the journal's spine. "I read about my mother, about how she made you feel, about the hope she gave you."

Turland nods, a lump forming in his throat. "She was a lifeline," he murmurs, "a reminder that there was still beauty in the world, even in the darkest places."

Coolidge takes a step closer, his posture softening, the journal held out like an offering. "I'm sorry," he whispers, his voice thick with emotion. "I'm sorry I didn't see it before. I didn't understand..."

Turland reaches out, his fingers closing around the journal, a bridge spanning the gap between them. "I'm sorry too," he says, his eyes glistening with unshed tears. "For not being there, for not finding a way..."

But Coolidge shakes his head, a small smile tugging at the corners of his mouth. "We're here now," he says, his voice growing more confident. "And that's what matters."

With those words, the years of silence hurt, and misunderstanding began to melt away, replaced by tentative hope and a fragile yet unbreakable bond.

In the kitchen's warmth, Mary Jane watches from a distance, her heart swelling with joy as she sees the two men she loves most take their first steps towards healing, towards a future brighter than any of them had dared to dream.

The silence stretches between them, but it's no longer heavy with unspoken words and painful histories. Instead, it's a silence filled with understanding, with the gentle rustling of turning pages as Turland and Coolidge sit beside the journal on the table before them.

Turland's voice is soft, hesitant at first, as he begins to share the stories he'd never thought he'd have the chance to tell. He speaks of the little joys, the moments of laughter and camaraderie that had sustained him during those long years behind bars. He speaks of the dreams he'd held close to his heart, the hopes for a future he'd never dared to voice aloud.

Coolidge listens, really listens, as he speaks, his eyes wide with wonder and empathy. He sees his father in a new light, not just as the man absent from his life but as a person in his own right, with fears, desires, and a capacity for love that had never been fully realized.

Mary Jane continues to watch from her place in the doorway, her hands clasped together as if in prayer. She sees how Turland's shoulders relax and how Coolidge leans closer, hanging on to every word. And she knows, with a certainty that goes beyond mere hope, that this is the beginning of something beautiful, something transformative.

Mary Jane steps forward, her footsteps soft against the worn linoleum. She places a gentle hand on Turland's shoulder and Coolidge's arm, feeling the warmth of their skin beneath her fingers.

"I'm so proud of you," she whispers, her voice trembling. "Both of you."

And in that moment, as the three of them stand for a family hug, united by love and forgiveness, the past falls away, and the future stretches before them, bright with promise and possibility.

There will be obstacles to overcome, wounds to heal, and bridges to build. But as they look into each other's eyes, seeing their hope and determination reflected, they know they will face whatever comes together as a family.

Coolidge sits back down and leans forward, his elbows resting on his knees, his gaze on Turland's face. "Tell me more," he says, his voice soft, almost pleading. "About your life, about... everything."

Turland's breath catches in his throat, a lump of emotion rising to choke him. He swallows hard, blinking back the tears that threaten to spill over. "You want to know?" he asks, his voice rough with disbelief.

Coolidge nods, a small smile playing at the corners of his mouth. "I do," he says. "I want to know everything, to be honest. At times when you told me stuff in prison, it just went in one ear and out of the other because I was dealing with myself at the time."

And so, Turland begins to talk, his words hesitant at first but gathering strength as the memories come flooding back. He tells Coolidge about his childhood, growing up in the neighborhood, the dreams he once had, and his choices that led him down a different path.

He talks about his time in prison, about the loneliness and the fear, about the moments of despair when he thought he would never see the outside world again. But he also talks about the hope that kept him going, the vision of a future that sustained him through the darkest times.

As Turland speaks, Coolidge listens, his eyes never leaving his father's face. He sees the pain etched into the lines around Turland's mouth and the weariness in his eyes, but he also sees the strength, resilience, and unbreakable spirit that has carried him through so much.

As the minutes turn into hours, Coolidge feels a sense of connection and understanding that he has never known. He sees his father not as a stranger or a mystery but as a man, flawed and human but also brave, loving, and authentic.

In the kitchen, Mary Jane busies herself with the dishes, her hands moving automatically as she listens to the murmur of voices from the living room. She feels a warmth spreading through her chest, a sense of rightness and completion that she has been waiting for all her life.

Mary Jane walks softly into the living room with a tray of steaming mugs. She sets them down on the coffee table, the rich scent of hot chocolate filling the air.

"I thought you might like something warm," she says, her voice gentle, almost shy.

Turland looks up at her, his eyes shining with unshed tears. "Thank you," he whispers, reaching out to take her hand.

And as they sit together, sipping their chocolate and whispering, the past and the present intertwining in a tapestry of love and forgiveness, they know they have found something precious, rare, beautiful, and authentic.

The future is uncertain, but at this moment, they are together, and that is enough. More than enough. It is everything.

Chapter 29: Rebuilding

The soft snow starting to tap against the basement window stirs me from my slumber. I blink and sit in bed, the blanket falling away as I rub my eyes. A shiver runs through me, and I reach to pull the covers back up, but then I pause. This chill is different from what I'm used to. It's the cold of winter, but it's muted, gentler somehow. I breathe in and appreciate the warmth surrounding me, the feeling of safety and home.

Swinging my legs over the side of the bed, I stand and stretch, muscles popping. The wooden floorboards are cool under my bare feet as I pad toward the tiny kitchen. Morning light filters in and catches on the swirling dust motes in the air. It's peaceful, serene almost.

I set a pan on the stove and turn the knob, watching the small blue flames leap to life. As I crack eggs into a bowl, my mind drifts to the day ahead. Reality settles on my shoulders like a weight.

"Another day, another job hunt," I mutter, perhaps more vigorously than necessary, whisking the eggs—the yellow liquid sloshes and froths.

As I watch the eggs sizzle and hiss in the pan, the anxiety bubbles up inside me, too, hot and churning. How many rejections will it be today? How many doors will slam in my face once they see my record, branding me as nothing more than an ex-con? I grip the handle tightly. I have to keep trying, though, for Mary Jane and Coolidge. For the future, I desperately hope we can still have.

Sliding the eggs onto a plate, I sit heavily at the small table. I clasp my hands and bow my head. "Please. Please let today be the day," I whisper, a fervent prayer. "I just need one person to give me a chance."

I glance out the small kitchen window as I raise a forkful of eggs to my mouth. The snow drifts down softly, blanketing the world in white—pure, unblemished, and full of promise.

As I watch it fall, a tiny ember of determination sparks to life within me.

My past may be riddled with mistakes and regrets, but it doesn't have to define my future. Each day is a chance to be better than I was yesterday. Each snowflake is a reminder that even the darkest of landscapes can be made new again.

I set my fork down, the clang against the plate unnaturally loud in the stillness. Wiping my mouth, I stand and carry my dishes to the sink. I have a renewed sense of purpose as I start my day.

Whatever happens, I won't give up. I'll weather this storm. Spring always comes eventually, after all. And with it, the promise of new beginnings. I have to keep believing that mine is on its way.

The creak of the basement door snaps me out of my reverie. I glance up to see Coolidge descending the stairs, a grin already spreading across his face. "Morning, Turland," he greets me, his voice warm and rich like honey. "You're up early."

I shrug, returning his smile. "Couldn't sleep. Figured I might as well get a head start on the day."

Coolidge nods, understanding in his eyes. He's been where I am, knowing the restless energy of wanting to prove yourself worthy of a second chance. "I feel you, man. I've got an idea."

He leans against the counter, folding his arms across his chest. "Why don't you swing by the community center today? I heard they've got some job training programs that might be right up your alley."

I raise an eyebrow, surprise and gratitude mingling in my chest. "For real? You think they'd take a chance on a guy like me?"

Coolidge's grin widens. "Absolutely. They're all about giving folks a fresh start. And with your skills? They'd be lucky to have you."

A flicker of hope ignites within me, small but persistent. "Alright, let's do it. I'm in."

We bundle up against the biting cold, tugging on hats and gloves and wrapping scarves around our necks. As we step out into the brisk Chicago morning, our breath curls like smoke, dissipating into the gray sky above.

As we walk, the snow crunches beneath our boots, a satisfying rhythm that echoes through the quiet streets.

A mural stretches across the side of an old brick building, a vibrant splash of color against the muted winter landscape. People hurry past, their faces a blend of determination and resilience, a testament to the unbreakable spirit of this city.

As we round the corner, the community center is seen as a beacon of hope amidst the snow-covered streets. I pause momentarily, taking a deep breath, steadying myself for whatever lies ahead.

Coolidge places a hand on my shoulder, grounding me in the present. "You've got this, Turland. One step at a time, right?"

I nod, squaring my shoulders, ready to face the future head-on. "One step at a time," I echo, my voice filled with determination.

Together, we ascend the steps of the community center, each footfall bringing me closer to the possibility of a brighter tomorrow. And for the first time in a long time, I believe it might just be within reach.

As we step inside the community center, a wave of warmth envelops us, chasing away the chill that had settled deep in my bones. The bustling energy of the place is palpable, a stark contrast to the quiet streets outside. People of all ages move about purposefully, their conversations blending into a symphony of hope and possibility.

Despite the welcoming atmosphere, I can't shake the unease that coils in my gut. The weight of my past presses down on me, threatening to drag me back into the shadows I've fought so hard to escape. I falter, my steps slowing as doubt creeps in, whispering that I don't belong here and'll never be more than the mistakes I've made.

But then Coolidge is there, his presence steady and reassuring. "You've come this far, Turland."

His words cut through the fog of uncertainty, and I draw strength from the unwavering belief in his eyes. With a deep breath, I nod, pushing forward, determined to seize this chance at a new beginning.

We approach the front desk, where a woman with kind eyes and a warm smile greets us. "Welcome to the community center. How can I help you today?"

Coolidge takes the lead, his voice confident and clear. "We're here to learn more about the job training program. My... Turland is looking to get back on his feet, and we heard this was the place to start."

The woman's smile widens, and she nods in understanding. "You've come to the right place. Let me introduce you to our counselor, Ms. Johnson. She'll happily walk you through the program and answer any questions."

As she leads us down a hallway, I feel hope ignite in my chest. The walls are lined with photos and testimonials from people whose lives have been transformed by the center's programs. Their stories echo my tales of struggle, perseverance, second chances, and hard-won victories.

We enter a small office where a woman with silver hair and a no-nonsense demeanor sits behind a desk. She looks up as we enter, her eyes sharp and assessing but not unkind.

"Ms. Johnson, this is Turland and Coolidge. They're interested in learning more about our job training program," the receptionist says before excusing herself and closing the door behind her.

Ms. Johnson gestures for us to take a seat, her gaze lingering on me for a moment. "It's a pleasure to meet you both. I've seen that look before, Turland. The one that says you're not sure if you belong here, if you're worthy of this chance."

I swallowed hard, and my throat suddenly dried. "I've made mistakes in my past, Ms. Johnson. I'm not proud of them, but I'm here because I want to do better, to be better."

She leans forward, her eyes softening. "And that, Turland, is what matters most. The fact that you're here, that you're willing to put in the work to change your life, speaks volumes about your character."

As she begins to outline the job training program, a sense of purpose settles over me. I think I'm exactly where I'm meant to be.

A warm smile spread across my face as I shook Ms. Johnson's hand, her words of encouragement still echoing in my mind.

"Thank you for this opportunity," I say, my voice filled with gratitude. "I won't let you down."

Coolidge claps me on the back, his eyes shining with pride.

The training sessions fly by in a blur of hard work and determination, and before I know it, I'm being offered a maintenance job at the center itself.

"Congratulations, Turland," Ms. Johnson says, handing me my new uniform. "You've earned this. Your work ethic has been truly impressive."

I run my fingers over the fabric, a lump forming in my throat. "I don't know what to say. Thank you for believing in me, for giving me a chance to prove myself."

"You did that all on your own," she replies, her smile warm and genuine.

***

The savory aroma of roasted chicken and herbs fills the air as I enter the house, and the kitchen's warmth is a welcome respite from the brisk Chicago evening. Mary Jane looked up from the stove, smiling as she saw me.

"There's our working man," she says, wiping her hands on her apron before pulling me into a tight hug. "I'm so proud of you, Turland."

Coolidge emerges from the living room, a grin spreading across his face. "Look at you, now. A regular member of the workforce now."

I duck my head, feeling a flush of pride creep up my neck. "It feels good, you know? To contribute, to be a part of something bigger than myself."

We gather around the table, the conversation flowing easily as we pass dishes of steaming vegetables and fluffy mashed potatoes. Mary Jane regales us with stories of her day at the library, her eyes sparkling with passion as she describes the children's enthusiasm for reading. Discovering her love for the library was another surprise to my soul.

"You should see their faces when they find a book they love," she says, her voice filled with warmth. "It's like watching a whole new world open up for them."

Coolidge reaches across the table, squeezing her hand. "You're making a real difference in their lives, just like Turland is at the community center."

A swell of emotion rises in my chest, the sense of belonging almost overwhelming. "I never thought I'd have this," I admit, my voice cracking slightly. "A family, a purpose, a place where I feel like I matter."

Mary Jane reaches over, her hand resting on mine. "You've always mattered, Turland."

As the evening winds down and we clear the dishes, I can't help but reflect on how far I've come. From the hopelessness of prison to the warmth and love of this home, from the weight of my past to the promise of my future.

As I settle into bed that night, the soft glow of the streetlights filtering through the curtains, I feel a sense of peace over me. For the first time, I'm not just surviving now; I'm living.

The following day, I wake to the aroma of freshly brewed coffee and the sizzle of bacon from the kitchen above. Stretching, I take a moment to savor the contentment that has become increasingly familiar in recent weeks.

As I make my way upstairs, I'm greeted by the sight of Mary Jane and Coolidge, who are already busy at the stove. "Morning, sleepyhead," Mary Jane teases, her eyes sparkling joyfully. "We thought you might need some extra rest after getting off from work last night."

Coolidge slides a plate piled high with fluffy scrambled eggs and crispy bacon in front of me as I sit at the table. "You know, I've been thinking," he begins, his tone thoughtful. This is all nice for you with your work and everything, but what if we did something else besides working for others? What if we start a small bakery for Mama? We all know she can bake with the best of them. I'm just thinking of something we could do together."

Mary Jane's face lights up at the suggestion. "That's a great idea! I never thought about it before. Maybe we could find a way to showcase a few of our family's best recipes and see how people respond."

As we dive into the details, my mind buzzes with excitement. The challenges that once seemed impossible now feel like opportunities to prove ourselves and build something meaningful.

"I could talk to some of the folks at the community center," I offer, my voice eager. "See if anyone might be interested in helping or even investing in the business."

Mary Jane reaches over, her hand finding mine. "We're doing this, aren't we? Building something, a future together?"

The weight of her words settles over me, a warm blanket of hope and possibility. "Yeah," I reply, my voice thick with emotion. "We are."

As the morning unfolds, our plans shape, each idea building upon the last. And with every passing moment, I feel the bonds of our little family growing stronger, our shared dreams knitting us together in ways I never thought possible.

Looking around the table, I see not just the faces of my loved ones but the reflection of a man I barely recognize - a man with purpose, hope, and a future worth fighting for. I am no longer alone, adrift.

I am home.

There seems to be a soft halo around Mary Jane as she leans forward, her eyes sparkling excitedly. "I've been thinking," she begins, her voice low and conspiratorial, "about the bakery's name. What do you think of 'Sweet Dreams'? It's a nod to the power of dreaming big, of believing in ourselves and each other."

I let the name roll around in my mind, savoring how it feels on my tongue. "Sweet Dreams," I repeat, a slow smile spreading. It's perfect—just like you."

Mary Jane ducks her head, a bashful grin playing at the corners of her mouth. "You're too kind, Turland. But this new chapter of our lives is about all of us, and it couldn't be possible to do this without Coolidge and your support and belief in me and my baking."

I reach across the table, my fingers brushing against hers. "We're in this together, remember, because that's what I keep being told? Every step of the way."

Coolidge, who's been quietly observing our exchange as he tries to get used to the idea that we only dated for one day, and sometimes we seem to carry on like we never missed a beat, clears his throat. "I might have a few ideas for the logo," he offers a hint of hesitation. I've been sketching some designs in my free time before I brought up the idea to you two."

Mary Jane and I exchanged glances, our eyes wide with surprise and pride. "So, you have?" she asks, her voice warm with encouragement. "And we'd love to see them."

Coolidge retrieves a worn sketchbook from his room, flipping through the pages until he finds what he wants. He slides the book across the table, revealing intricate designs - swirling fonts, delicate flourishes, playful pastries, and coffee cup illustrations.

We pour over the sketches, our fingers tracing the lines and curves, our voices rising excitedly as we point out our favorite elements. And as we do, I feel a swell of pride in my chest, a fierce love for this woman and this boy who have become my family, my reason for being.

"These are incredible, Coolidge," I say, my voice rough with emotion. "You've got a real talent."

He shrugs, a shy smile tugging at his lips. "It's nothing. Just something I enjoy doing."

But I shake my head, my gaze intense. "No, it's not nothing. It's a gift, a way of making the world slightly brighter and sweeter. Just like your mom's baking."

Mary Jane reaches over, pulling Coolidge into a tight hug. "He's right, baby. You've got something special that deserves to be shared with the world."

As we sat there, we huddled around the kitchen table. I felt something different as I watched us all keep discovering something else about each other daily; I never knew how this felt in real life, even though I've seen it on TV screens for thirty years in prison. This is a lot better than what I thought it would feel like.

We can build a future filled with sweet dreams and even sweeter realities.

As the night wears on, our laughter echoing off the walls and our hearts full to bursting, I know this is just the beginning—the start of a journey that will lead us to places we never dared to imagine, to a life beyond our wildest hopes and dreams.

The stairs creak beneath my feet as I descend into the basement, the day's events playing through my mind like a movie reel. I can still feel the warmth of Mary Jane's embrace, the fire in Coolidge's eyes as he spoke of his mother's legacy. Their words echo in my ears, a symphony of hope and possibility that drowns out the doubts that once plagued me.

As I settle onto the worn mattress, the moonlight filtering through the tiny window, I can't help but marvel at the twists and turns that have brought me to this moment. Just a few short months ago, I was a man adrift, haunted by the ghosts of my past and the weight of my failures. But now, as I lie here in the stillness of the night, I understand God has a reason for everything, and I need to remain quiet enough to keep hearing his voice because it gives me a glimmer of something I thought I'd lost forever - hope.

My thoughts drifted to the plans and dreams we dared to voice aloud. A bakery is where Mary Jane's talents can shine, and Coolidge can honor his mother's memory with every pastry and every smile. It's definitely a sweet dream that seemed impossible just yesterday, but now, with each other's love and support, it feels within reach.

I close my eyes, letting the possibilities wash over me. I see myself working alongside Mary Jane and Coolidge, our hands covered in flour and our hearts full of joy. I know the bakery is a warm and welcoming space that draws in the community, where people can unite and find solace in life's simple pleasures.

As sleep begins to claim me, I whisper a silent prayer of gratitude to God and his wisdom for bringing me to this place and these people. I may not have all the answers, and I don't need to because God does. I know that anything is possible.

Tomorrow is a new day, a blank page waiting to be filled with the stories of our lives. And as I drift off to sleep, I can't wait to see what it will bring.

Chapter 30: Confronting the Past

The sound of a ball bounces rhythmically against the polished wooden floor, echoing through the community center gym. I grin, feeling the energy of the kids around me as we move back and forth across the court. "Pass it here, Turland!" shouts Jamal, his eyes excitedly bright. I fake left, then spin right, sending the ball sailing into his waiting hands. The kids laugh and cheer, their joy infectious.

In moments like these, the weight of the past feels lighter. The worries fade away, replaced by the simple pleasure of connecting with these young souls, sharing a love for the game that once brought me solace. As we play, I can't help but marvel at their resilience and their ability to find happiness amid struggle.

The game ends in a flurry of high-fives and fist bumps, the kids' laughter ringing like a melodic anthem of hope. But as I catch my breath, a familiar figure enters the gym, his presence instantly shifting the atmosphere. Marcus, the gang leader I once knew as Slick, stands near the door, his gaze locking with mine.

Time seems to slow as memories flood back, a tidal wave of emotions crashing over me. Surprise, tension, a hint of the old anger – they all swirl inside, threatening to pull me under. Yet I steady myself, drawing in a deep breath. The kids, oblivious to the moment's gravity, continue their playful chatter, their innocence starkly contrasting the history that hangs heavy between us.

Questions race through my mind, unspoken yet potent. Why is he here? What does he want? The years have changed us both, etching lines onto our faces and scars onto our souls. But in that shared gaze, I see a flicker of something—recognition, perhaps even a glimmer of the neighborhood bond he and I and my friends once shared before our choices tore it asunder.

I approach Marcus, my steps measured, my heart pounding a staccato rhythm against my ribcage. The kids' voices fade into the background as I focus on the man before me who once held the power to shape my destiny.

"Slick," I say, the old name slipping out before I can catch it. "It's been a long time."

He nods a flicker of something – regret, perhaps – passing over his features. "It's Marcus now, Turland. I'm not that man anymore."

The words hang between us, a fragile bridge spanning the chasm of our shared history. I want to believe him, to trust that change is possible. But the memories of that fateful day—the bank robbery gone wrong, the betrayal that shattered our lives—cling to me like a second skin.

"Why are you here, Marcus?" I ask, my voice steady despite the turmoil within. "Why now, after all these years?"

He takes a step closer, his eyes searching mine. "To make amends, Turland. I heard you were working here, and I thought... I would try and right the wrongs of the past."

The sincerity in his tone catches me off guard, a crack in the armor I've built around my heart. I think of Jerry, my friend who never made it out of prison, of Russell, whose life was also cut short due to the choices we made. The weight of their absence presses down on me, a constant reminder of the price we paid.

***

I watch the exchange between Turland and the man he slipped and called Slick from across the gym—Coolidge is my name as a tribute to a man my mother thought was the coolest guy ever to her, and now I understand how it represents my family's resilience. As I see the tension in Turland's shoulders, the way his hands clench and unclench at his sides, I decide to remain cool.

A part of me wants to rush over, to stand by his side and face whatever demons have resurfaced. But I hold back, understanding that this is a moment he must face alone. With all its complexities and secrets, the past is a burden he's carried for too long.

As I observe their interaction, a kaleidoscope of emotions swirls within me: curiosity about their history, concern for the weight Turland bears, and a deep yearning to understand the man he was before I knew him. The scars he carries, both visible and invisible, are a testament to the battles he's fought and the sacrifices he's made.

Yet even in this moment of confrontation, I see the strength in Turland's stance, the quiet dignity with which he faces his past.

As I watch, I silently offer a prayer, a plea for healing and understanding. In this gym, where children's laughter still echoes, I sense a shift in the air – a chance for old wounds to mend and forgiveness to take root. And I know, with a certainty that settles deep in my bones, that Turland will emerge from this encounter stronger, his spirit unbroken, his love for us unwavering.

The cool evening air washes over me as I step outside, a temporary respite from the suffocating tension within the community center. The distant hum of traffic and the faint laughter of children playing nearby create a dissonant soundtrack to my troubled thoughts. I lean against the rough brick wall, its solidity starkly contrasting my turmoil.

Seeing Marcus after all these years has unleashed a torrent of memories I thought I had buried deep. The ghosts of our shared past—the heist, the betrayal, the lives lost—clamor for attention, demanding acknowledgment. I close my eyes, take a deep breath, and try to center myself amidst the chaos.

In the stillness of this moment, I find clarity. The path forward is not vengeance or bitterness but reconciliation and growth. My family—Mary Jane, Coolidge, and the new life we've built together—is the beacon guiding me through this storm. They are my anchor, my reason for striving to be a better man.

The sound of footsteps draws me back to the present, and I open my eyes to see Coolidge approaching, his face etched with concern. "Dad, are you okay? I saw what happened with that man, Marcus..."

When I first heard my son call me Dad, I almost wanted to cry, but instead, I offered a weary smile, appreciating his straightforwardness, which made this whole day worth it.

"It's a long story, son. Marcus and I go way back. We were part of something that went wrong, costing us more than we could imagine."

Coolidge nods, his eyes filled with a desire to understand. "What happened? I mean, if you want to talk about it..."

I take a moment to gather my thoughts, the weight of the past pressing against my chest. "Seeing Marcus again, after thirty years... it brought back everything. The friends I lost, the mistakes I made, the toll it took on all of us. It's a pain I thought I'd left behind, but it's still there, raw and real."

My voice wavers, but I push on, determined to share this piece of myself with my son. "At that moment, when I looked into Marcus's eyes, I saw the same regret and guilt I carry daily. And I realized that holding onto this anger, this resentment... it's only hurting me, hurting us."

Coolidge places a hand on my shoulder, a gesture of support and understanding. "I can't imagine what you've been through, Dad. But I'm here for you, no matter what. We all are."

I nod, my heart swelling with gratitude for the love and strength of my family. "I know, son. And that's why I need to find a way to make peace with this, to forgive Marcus and myself. Because you, your mother, our family... you matter most. You're my reason for fighting, for becoming the man I want to be."

As we stand there, the evening breeze carries the distant echoes of the neighborhood.

Coolidge and I stand together, the weight of our shared emotions hanging between us. He takes a deep breath, his eyes flickering with an intensity I've rarely seen before.

"You know, growing up without you... it wasn't easy," he begins, his voice raw with honesty. There were times when I felt lost or abandoned. I was missing a piece I could never quite find. Then I met someone who was a great mentor in prison, and I wished I had known that man sooner."

His words pierce my heart, a reminder of the years I've lost and the moments I can never reclaim: "I'm sorry, son. I'm sorry I wasn't there for you when you needed me most, but I'm glad I met that young man in prison. If I had a son, I wish he would be like that young man."

Coolidge shakes his head, a gentle smile playing on his lips. "But you know what? It made me stronger, so my Father in Heaven ordered all my steps the way he did. To teach me to rely on him and to find my way in this world. And even though it hurt like hell sometimes, I never lost hope that I would one day also meet my earthly father."

I nod, understanding the depth of his resilience, the strength he's had to summon in the face of adversity. "When I met you, I could tell you were always a fighter, Coolidge. I could see that fire in your eyes; now I know where it came from. That determination to rise above your circumstances, to make something of yourself."

He chuckles softly, a hint of pride in his voice. "I guess I get that from you, huh? The never-give-up attitude, the refusal to let the world break you down."

"Maybe so, but God made it shine through you," I admit, a warmth spreading through my chest at the thought of our shared spirit. "Because you've taken it to a whole new level, son. You've become a man I'm proud to call my own, who faces his challenges head-on and never backs down."

Coolidge's eyes shine with emotion, his voice trembling slightly as he speaks. "That means more to me than you know, Dad. All I've ever wanted was to make you proud if I ever got to meet you and show you that despite everything, I turned out alright."

I hug him tightly, pouring all my love and admiration into that single gesture. "You've done more than alright, Coolidge.

You've become a shining example of what it means to overcome, to rise above the hand you've been dealt. And I couldn't be more proud of the man you are today."

As we stand there, holding onto each other like a lifeline, I feel a sense of peace wash over me, and I think of a scripture I used to read all the time in prison.

It came from the Second Thessalonians chapter three and verse sixteen. Now, may the Lord of peace himself give you peace at all times and in every way. The Lord be with all of you.

A gentle hand rests on my shoulder, and I see Mary Jane standing beside us, her eyes glistening with unshed tears. Her presence brings a sense of comfort, a reminder of the unwavering support that has been my anchor through the storms of life.

"Turland, Coolidge," she says softly, her voice a soothing balm to our raw emotions. "Seeing you two together like this, opening your hearts to each other, is beautiful. It's a testament to the power of love and the strength of family."

I reach out and take her hand, interlacing our fingers as I draw her closer. "It's a strength you've been a big part of, Mary Jane. Your love and faith in us—it's what's kept us going all these years. We're two people on two different paths but connected to you. How great is God?"

She smiles a radiant beam of light amidst the shadows of the past. "I've always believed in you both, especially you, Turland, even when I had no clue where you were. But you gave me a gift, my precious son; there's so much goodness within both your hearts. And seeing you both now, embracing each other and hoping for a better future, fills me with a joy I can't describe."

Coolidge looks at Mary Jane, his eyes shining with gratitude. "Thank you, Mom. For being there, for never giving up on us because we both know I put your life on such a bumpy road. Your love has been a constant light, guiding me through all the darkest times."

I am reminded of the beauty that can be found even in the most unlikely places, the hope that springs eternal from the depths of the human spirit.

For in this world of painful smiles and resilient struggles, we have found something precious, something worth holding onto with all our might.

Turland nods, a stubborn glint in his eyes as he speaks, his voice steady and unwavering. "I think it's time I reached out to Marcus to offer forgiveness and try to make things right. We all played a part in that crime, and holding onto this anger and resentment will only eat away at my soul."

Coolidge places a hand on his father's shoulder, a gesture of support and understanding. "That takes a lot of courage, Dad. I'm proud of you for wanting to take that step."

Mary Jane's eyes shimmer with tears, a soft smile gracing her lips as she hears Coolidge for the first time, her son saying, "Dad." Then she hesitates for a moment. "Forgiveness is the path to healing, Turland. It won't be easy, but we'll be right beside you every step of the way."

I feel a surge of determination coursing through my veins. "I need to do this, not just for myself, but for all of us. It's time to break the cycle, to let go of the past and embrace a future filled with hope and possibility."

I reach into my pocket, pulling out the worn slip of paper that bears Marcus's phone number, a tangible reminder of the journey ahead. As I clutch it tightly in my hand, I feel a sense of anticipation, a fluttering in my chest that speaks of new beginnings and second chances.

For in this moment, as the day gives way to night and the stars begin to twinkle overhead, I know that I am taking the first step towards redemption, towards a future unburdened by the mistakes of the past.

Chapter 31: Seeds of Change

"Dreams have power," Turland whispered to himself as he watched children playing a spirited game of tag in the community center, their laughter as vibrant as wildflowers in bloom. Their youth and energy ignited a spark of hope within him--that no matter what, a new dawn could arise.

"Their innocent joy, pure as first raindrops," he mused, "untouched by life's harsh gales." The echoes of the kids' glee rippled against the yellowing walls, breathing life into a place both sanctuary and symbol of their community's faded glory.

Turland's gaze drifted to the window, where the silhouettes of Mr. Washington's garden swayed in a silent, arthritic dance. The old man's gnarly hands had coaxed beauty from barren soil—peppers, tomatoes, and cucumbers bursting with color—a testament that broken things could bear sweetness again if tended with care.

"What are you thinking, Turland?" Coolidge sidled beside him, hands tucked in his pockets, shoulders hunched with a timid and bright hopefulness in his eyes.

Turland turned to him, a smile stretching across his face, slow and golden as a new sunrise. "I have a vision, Coolidge. A garden for our people, right here in the heart of our 'hood. A place to plant not just seeds but dreams. To grow together, to bloom."

Coolidge cocked his head, brow furrowed. "A garden? Here?" He gestured at the cracked sidewalks, the empty bottles glinting in the gutters. "In this concrete desert?"

"Yes. Imagine it." Turland's voice rose with fervor, hands painting pictures in the air. "Tomatoes fat as fists, corn stalks stretching to the sky. Our elders pass on their wisdom as they till the earth. Our youngsters are learning to nurture, not destroy."

Coolidge's eyes widened, catching Turland's fire. "It could change everything. Bring people together, give them purpose." His words tumbled out in a hopeful rush.

"Exactly! We'll call it 'Hope's Harvest.' A symbol of renewal rising from the rubble of broken dreams." Turland gripped

Coolidge's shoulders, eyes blazing. "This is how we start to heal our home."

***

Bent over a small kitchen table, shoulders touching, Turland and Coolidge studied dog-eared maps of the neighborhood, tracing streets they'd wandered as boys, now men on a mission.

"There." Coolidge stabbed a finger at a splotch of green, a rare slash of life amidst the gray. "That vacant lot off Pulaski. It's big enough, gets good light..."

Turland nodded, excitement thrumming in his veins. "It's perfect. And that abandoned building next to it? Imagine fixing it and turning it into the bakery one day, like Mary Jane's always dreamed..."

Coolidge grinned, its brightness a balm. "She'd be over the moon! Serving up her famous sweet potato pie, that peach cobbler..."

They laughed, thinking of Mary Jane's treats and the cinnamon-scented warmth of her hugs.

Turland rifled through a stack of city hall paperwork. His brow furrowed in concentration. "Now, to navigate this bureaucratic maze, dot all our i's and cross our t's..."

Coolidge reached over and squeezed his hand. "We've got this. Together. One step, one seed at a time. We're going to make this happen."

Emotions swelled in Turland's chest: gratitude, love, and an aching, desperate hope. He met Coolidge's eyes and saw his determination reflected. "Brick by brick," he murmured."

As if summoned by their shared vision, Mary Jane swept into the room, a whirlwind of vibrant colors and infectious energy. Her presence filled the space with warmth, chasing away the lingering shadows of doubt and despair, if there were any at all.

"My boys," she exclaimed, her voice a soothing balm to our battered souls. "I heard whispers of your plan, and I couldn't be more proud." She enveloped us both in a fierce hug, the scent of vanilla and cinnamon clinging to her like a promise of better days.

Turland leaned into her embrace, drawing strength from the unwavering love and support that radiated from her very being. "None of this would be happening without you, Mary Jane," he confessed, his voice thick with emotion. Your faith and heart in this project... it's everything."

Mary Jane pulled back, her hands gentle on our shoulders as she fixed us with a determined gaze. "I'm not just here to cheer you on from the sidelines, boys. I'm here to roll up my sleeves and get my hands dirty alongside you." Her eyes sparkled with a mischievous glint. "And you know I've got connections in this neighborhood that run deeper than the roots of an oak tree. I'll rally the troops, get everyone on board with this garden of yours."

Coolidge let out a low whistle, shaking his head in admiration. "Never underestimate the power of Mary Jane Patterson," he chuckled, his smile wide and genuine.

We pored over the maps and paperwork, and Mary Jane's keen eye and practical suggestions guided us through the labyrinth of permits and permissions. Her unwavering belief in our vision of this project's transformative power fueled our determination and our shared excitement crescendo with each hurdle cleared.

***

The sun beat down on the overgrown lot, the air thick with the scent of wild grass and untamed weeds. Turland, Coolidge, and Mary Jane stood at the edge of the space, their eyes filled with a heady mix of trepidation and anticipation.

Turland surveyed the scene before him, his heart racing with the weight of possibility. The lot was a tangle of waist-high grass peppered with the rusted remnants of a forgotten past—a broken-down car, a pile of discarded tires, and a twisted metal fence that had long since surrendered to the ravages of time.

But beyond the decay, Turland saw the promise of new life. He imagined the rich, dark soil teeming with earthworms and nutrients, ready to nurture the seeds they would sow. He envisioned neat rows of vegetables—vibrant green lettuce, plump red tomatoes, and golden squash—a riot of color and abundance where once there had been only neglect.

His gaze drifted to the abandoned building that loomed beside the lot, its boarded-up windows and crumbling bricks a testament to the neighborhood's decline. Yet, in his mind's eye, he saw it transformed—the boards torn away to reveal gleaming glass, the bricks scrubbed clean and painted a welcoming hue. He pictured Mary Jane's bakery, alive with the scent of fresh bread and the laughter of neighbors gathering over steaming cups of coffee.

"Can you see it?" Mary Jane whispered, her voice trembling with barely contained excitement. "The garden, the bakery... a beacon of hope for this community."

Coolidge reached out, his fingers intertwining with Turland's and Mary Jane's. "A place where we can grow more than just plants," he murmured, his eyes glistening with unshed tears. "Where we can cultivate healing, second chances, and a brighter future than we dared to dream. It's crazy how God can use anyone to do his will if they're willing."

Together, they stood on the precipice of change, their shared vision a palpable force that seemed to shimmer in the heat-soaked air.

"Brick by brick," Turland said softly, echoing the words that had become their mantra, their promise to each other and the community they loved. "We'll rebuild our world, one seed, one smile, one story at a time."

As we filed in, the community center buzzed with palpable energy, a sea of familiar faces etched with curiosity and apprehension. I felt the weight of their gazes, the unspoken questions hanging in the air like a thick fog. Beside me, Coolidge and Mary Jane stood tall, their presence a steadying force as we faced the gathered crowd.

I stepped forward, my heart pounding a fierce rhythm against my ribcage. "Thank you all for coming," I began, echoing in the hushed room. "We've asked you here today because we have a vision—a dream for our community that we believe can change lives."

As I spoke, I watched their expressions shift—some skeptical, others intrigued. I told them of our plan for the vacant lot, the garden that would symbolize growth and renewal. I spoke of Mary Jane's bakery, where warmth and nourishment would be served equally.

But even as I poured my heart into the words, I could see the doubt flickering in some of their eyes. "And how do we know this isn't just another scheme?" a voice called out, cutting through the murmurs. "How can we trust that you're not just looking for a new place to grow your drugs?"

The accusation stung, a bitter reminder of the past I had fought so hard to escape. I opened my mouth to respond, but a figure emerged from the back of the room before I could find the words.

Dame strode forward, his presence commanding instant attention. "Listen up," he said, his voice a low, insistent rumble. "I've known Turland for forty years, and I'm telling you right now—he's a changed man."

He turned to face the crowd, his gaze unflinching. "We've all made mistakes. We've all got scars. But Turland and Coolidge have paid their debt to society. They did their time and came out with a purpose."

I felt a surge of gratitude as Dame spoke, his words a balm to the doubts that had begun to fester. He spoke of our shared history, trials, and the unbreakable bonds forged in the depths of our struggles.

"Turland has never dealt drugs," Dame said, his voice ringing with conviction. "He loves this community, just like I do. Like all of you do, this garden, this bakery—it's not about the past. It's about our future."

Out of the blue, Dame bent down and started writing with his finger in the dust and dirt on the floor while occasionally looking up at some of the people. Then Dame whispered, "There was a story when Jesus was writing on the ground similar to what I'm doing now, and we don't know what he wrote, but one thing for sure: people stop complaining, that's for sure."

As he spoke, I saw the tide turning, the skepticism giving way to a tentative hope. Mary Jane reached for my hand, her fingers lacing with mine in a silent solidarity.

"We're asking for your trust," I said, my voice steady despite my emotions swirling. We need your support and your belief in the possibility of change. Together, we can make this dream a reality."

"So what do you say?" I ask, my gaze sweeping the room. "Will you join us in this endeavor? Will you help us build something beautiful that will last long after we're gone?"

For a moment, the room is silent, the weight of the decision hanging heavy in the air. Then, slowly, a hand rises from the crowd, followed by another.

At that moment, as I looked out at the faces of my community, I saw a flicker of the future we had envisioned—a future where hope bloomed in the cracks of our broken sidewalks, where redemption was a seed that could take root and flourish.

And I knew, with a certainty that settled deep in my bones, that we would make it happen. One step at a time, one seed at a time, we would rebuild our world from the ashes of our past.

Slowly, the tension in the room dissipates, replaced by a cautious optimism. I feel gratitude towards Dame; his words are a balm to my battered spirit.

A smile spreads as I watch the community unite in purpose and vision. As the meeting draws close, I feel a renewed sense of hope, determination, and certainty that we can create something extraordinary together.

***

As the sun rises over the horizon, its golden rays illuminate the vacant lot, casting long shadows across the overgrown grass and debris. The air is crisp and cool, filled with the promise of a new day and the potential for change.

I stand at the edge of the lot with a shovel, watching as the community begins gathering. They come from all walks of life—young and old, men and women, each with their own story and reasons for being here. Some carry tools, others carry seeds, but all have a sense of purpose and determination.

"Good morning, everyone," I call out, my voice carrying across the lot. "Thank you for coming out today. I know it's early, and there's a lot of work ahead of us, but together, we can transform this space into something truly special."

As I speak, I feel a hand on my shoulder, and I turn to see Mr. Washington standing beside me, a knowing smile on his weathered face. "You're doing a good thing here, Turland," he says, his voice deep and reassuring. "This community needs more people like you, willing to roll up their sleeves and get their hands dirty."

I nod, grateful for his support and his wisdom. "I couldn't do it without all of you," I reply, gesturing to the crowd. "This is a community effort, and it's going to take all of us working together to make it happen."

With that, we set to work, dividing into teams and tackling the lot from all angles. Some begin clearing the debris, hauling away old tires and broken bottles, while others start tilling the soil, preparing it for planting.

Working alongside my neighbors, I feel a sense of camaraderie and shared purpose that I've never experienced before. We laugh and joke as we work, sharing stories and dreams and learning about each other's lives and struggles.

Mr. Washington moves among us, offering advice and encouragement, his knowledge of gardening and life in equal measure. "Remember," he says, pausing to wipe the sweat from his brow, "a garden is like life. It takes time and patience, but with a little love and care, it will always bear fruit."

I nod, absorbing his words and feeling them take root in my heart. And as I look around at my neighbors' faces, determination and hope in their eyes, I know that we are planting more than just seeds today. We are planting the seeds of change and a better tomorrow.

The hours pass quickly; before we know it, the sun is high in the sky, and the lot has been transformed. Where once there was only chaos and neglect, now there is order and purpose, neat rows of freshly tilled soil waiting to be planted.

As we gather to admire our handiwork, Mr. Washington steps forward, twinkling in his eye. "You know," he says, "I've been saving these seeds for a special occasion, and I can't think of a better time than now."

He reaches into his pocket and pulls out a small packet, holding it up for all to see. "These are heirloom tomato seeds," he explains, "passed down from my grandfather to my father to me. They're a little piece of history, a reminder of where we've been and are going."

With reverence, he begins to pass the seeds around, inviting us to take a few and plant them in the soil. Holding the tiny seeds in my palm, I feel a sense of connection to something larger than myself, a sense of being part of a story that stretches back generations and will continue long after I'm gone.

As we plant the seeds, our hands working together in harmony, I feel that sense of peace again wash over me, knowing it's God.

As the days turn into weeks, the garden begins to take shape before our eyes. Tender green shoots push through the soil, reaching toward the sun with a determination that mirrors our own. The tomato plants are the first to emerge, their leaves unfurling like tiny banners of hope.

Coolidge and I find ourselves drawn to the garden at every opportunity, marveling at our progress. "Can you believe it?" he asks me one day, his voice filled with wonder. "Look at what we've created, Turland. Look at how far we've come."

I nod my throat tight with emotion. "It's like a dream come true," I whisper, touching a delicate flower petal. "Like something out of a storybook."

We are silent, breathing in the sweet scent of blooming life. The garden is a riot of color now, with vibrant reds, deep purples, sunny yellows, and soft pinks. The air hums with the gentle buzz of bees and the chirping of birds, a symphony of renewal.

As I let my gaze wander over the verdant oasis we've brought to life, a sense of pride swells within me. This garden is more than just a collection of plants; it symbolizes our resilience and ability to create beauty and meaning out of the most barren circumstances.

Coolidge's hand finds mine, his grip firm and reassuring. "We did this," he says softly, his eyes shining with unshed tears. "We made something good, something real."

I nod, swallowing past the lump in my throat. "And we'll keep doing it," I vow, my voice fierce with conviction. "No matter what it takes, we'll keep fighting for this community, for each other."

This garden is just the beginning, a tiny seed of hope that we will nurture and grow until it blossoms into something even more extraordinary.

The aroma of freshly baked bread wafts through Mary Jane's cozy living room, mingling with the lively chatter of a few neighbors gathered to celebrate the garden's progress. I take in the scene, marveling at how Mary Jane has brought us together, her warm smile and open heart drawing people in like a beacon of hope.

"I can't believe how far we've come," she says, her eyes sparkling with pride as she looks around the room. "Every one of you has played a part in making this garden a reality, and I couldn't be more grateful."

The room erupts in applause, and I feel a swell of emotion rising in my chest. These people, my neighbors, and my community have rallied around us, lending their time, energy, and unwavering support to a dream that once seemed impossible.

As the evening wears on, I am drawn into conversation after conversation, listening to stories of struggle, triumph, hardship, and resilience. In each face, I see a reflection of my journey, a shared understanding of what it means to fight for something better.

Days later, as the first harvest celebration arrives, the garden is a hive of activity. The air is filled with the rich scent of ripe tomatoes and fragrant herbs, a bounty of nature's blessings. Children dart between the rows of plants, their laughter ringing like a joyful symphony.

I watch neighbors fill baskets with the fruits of our collective labor, their faces alight with wonder and gratitude. The vibrant hues of the produce - deep red tomatoes, glossy purple eggplants, and crisp green lettuce - paint a picture of abundance and vitality.

Mary Jane moves through the crowd, her presence a calming anchor amidst the excitement. She stops to embrace an elderly woman, whispering encouragement and thanks. At that moment, I saw the true power of what we'd created - not just a garden but a tapestry of connection and support.

As the celebration peaks, I stand at the garden's edge, taking in the scene before me. The laughter, the smiles, the sheer joy radiating from every corner - a testament to this community's unbreakable spirit.

Coolidge appears at my side, his eyes misty with emotion. "I would have never thought all of this would have come from a couple of former inmates," he murmurs, his voice thick with pride. This is a good thing."

I nod, my eyes stinging with unshed tears. "This is just the beginning," I whisper, my heart swelling with fierce determination. We had no clue what we were doing, and God used us because he knew we would trust what he told us to do. So, we'll keep building, growing, and fighting for a better future."

As the sun begins to set over the garden, casting a golden glow across the faces of those gathered, I know with unshakable certainty that this is more than just a harvest celebration—it is a celebration of hope, redemption, and the unbreakable bonds that tie us all on the west side of Chicago together.

The celebration winds down, and the last of the neighbors disperse; Coolidge, Mary Jane, Dame, and I find ourselves drawn back to the garden as if pulled by an invisible force. We stand shoulder to shoulder, gazing over the flourishing plants and the now-quiet lot.

The soft evening breeze carries the sweet scent of tomato vines and freshly turned soil, a fragrance that seems to embody the essence of growth and renewal.

"We did this," Mary Jane murmurs, her voice filled with awe. "We took a barren patch of land and turned it into something beautiful, alive."

I nod, my heart swelling with a profound sense of accomplishment. "It's more than just a garden," I say softly, my gaze drifting over the carefully tended rows. "It's a symbol of what we can achieve when we come together and believe in each other."

Dame claps a hand on my shoulder, his grip firm and reassuring. "You've shown them, Turland," he says, his voice gruff with emotion. "You've shown them that change is possible, that hope can take root and flourish, even on the west side."

Coolidge lets out a soft chuckle, shaking his head in wonder. "Who would have thought," he muses, "that a couple of ex-cons and a determined mother could bring a community together like this?"

We share a laugh, the sound mingling with the gentle rustling of leaves and the distant hum of the city and standing here with the people who have become my family.

"This is amazing," I say, my voice ringing with quiet conviction. "We've seen what we can do, the lives we can touch. And we won't stop here."

Mary Jane reaches out, taking my hand in hers. Her touch is warm and comforting. "Together," she says softly, her eyes shining with unshed tears.

I close my eyes, allowing the moment to wash over me, etching it into my memory, a snapshot of triumph against all odds.

"You know," Dame says, his voice low and thoughtful, "when you first told me about this crazy idea of yours, I had my doubts. But seeing all this..." He gestures to the garden, the community center, and the faces of the people who have become more than just neighbors - they've become family. "It makes me believe that maybe, just maybe, we can change things. Not just here, but everywhere."

Coolidge nods, a smile tugging at the corners of his lips. "We've started something special here, something that has the power to ripple out, to inspire others. And who knows where that might lead?"

I think back to those long days in prison, to the moments when hope seemed like a distant memory, a fading dream.

"We've all got our demons," I say, my voice barely above a whisper. "We've all made mistakes and got lost along the way. But if there's one thing this journey has taught me, it's never too late to start over, to find your way back to the light."

As the moon rises above the rooftops, casting its silvery glow over the garden, I feel a sense of peace settle over me, a quiet understanding that God has more for us to do, and this is only the beginning.

"Tomorrow," I say, my gaze drifting over the tranquil scene before us, "we start planning for the bakery. We've got a lot of work ahead of us, but I know we can make it happen."

Mary Jane smiles, her eyes sparkling with anticipation. "I can already smell the cinnamon rolls," she says, her voice warm with affection. "And the look on the kids' faces when they bite their first cookie..."

We linger there a moment longer, savoring the stillness and the sense of accomplishment in the air. As we head inside to begin the next chapter of our story, I feel a renewed sense of determination, a fierce resolve to keep pushing forward and fighting for the future we know is possible.

Because, in the end, that's what this is all about - the belief that change is possible, that hope can triumph over despair, and that even the most broken among us can find a way to heal, grow, and thrive.

And with each step we take, each seed we plant, each life we touch, we move closer to that shining vision, that promised land where every dream is within reach, where every heart can find its way home.

Chapter 32: Family Foundations

The morning air was crisp, and our breath was visible as we approached Patterson's Sweet Dreams Bakery. Coolidge raised his eyebrows at me.

"Are you Ready to put in some work today?" he said with a slight grin. His eyes danced with the early morning light, full of determined anticipation.

I nodded, my excitement building in my chest. "Let's get started. We've got a lot to do."

As Coolidge unlocked the door, my fingers tingled. I was itching to transform this blank canvas of a storefront into something special—a place of warmth and community.

We stepped inside, our shoes echoing on the bare hardwood floors. Dust motes hung suspended in shafts of sunlight that streamed through the smudged front windows. The space seemed to whisper with possibility.

I set my tools down with purposeful movements, envisioning built-in shelves lining the walls, soft seating in cozy nooks, the mingled scents of sweet pastries, and rich coffee filling the air.

Coolidge surveyed the space, hands on his hips. "Alright, we start by patching that hole in the back wall, then sanding and refinishing these floors. Get some primer on the walls, too."

"That sounds good," I replied. I'll take measurements for the shelving units while you work on the drywall. We can brainstorm color schemes as we go."

With each piece of sandpaper and each plank of wood, we were building something meaningful—not just a bakery but a haven, a place for second chances.

The steady rhythm of work was meditative. Scraping old layers of paint, smoothing rough edges, and slowly revealing the potential beneath the surface. It felt symbolic somehow.

As I labored alongside Coolidge, I couldn't help but reflect on my journey. I remembered the mistakes of my past, the years lost to bad choices and unfortunate circumstances, but also the glimmers of hope and unexpected blessings. People like Coolidge, a newfound son who now believed in me, saw something worthy in the unfinished parts of my soul.

Perhaps we were all works in progress, I mused, running a hand along the newly sanded wall. Flawed and unfinished but full of promise. We need care, effort, and vision to become our best selves. To find redemption.

As the morning light shifted and strengthened, the old bakery seemed to come alive under our hands, like a chrysalis on the brink of transformation. I could almost taste the sweetness of what was to come.

The gentle creak of the door drew my attention, and I turned to see Mary Jane entering, a tray of freshly baked muffins she brought in from home balanced on her outstretched hands. The aroma of cinnamon and vanilla wafted through the space, mingling with the scent of sawdust and old memories.

"I thought you boys could use a little sustenance," she said, her warm smile illuminating the room. "Nothing like homemade muffins to fuel a hard day's work."

Coolidge and I set down our tools, drawn by the promise of a well-deserved break. Mary Jane's eyes swept over the space as we gathered around the tray, taking in our progress.

"It's already starting to transform," she mused, her voice soft with wonder. "I can feel it; there is potential here. This place will be a perfect beacon of hope for the neighborhood."

I nodded, understanding the depth of her vision. "It's more than just a bakery," I said, picking up a muffin and inhaling its comforting scent. "It's a chance to create something meaningful, to bring people together."

Mary Jane's gaze met mine, her eyes shining with gratitude and determination. "Exactly. This place, it's not just about the bread and pastries. It's about the connections we'll forge, the lives we'll touch."

As we savored the muffins, the sweetness on our tongues a promise of future delights, I felt renewed. Mary Jane's words had painted a vivid picture, a tapestry of community and hope that we were weaving together, one brushstroke at a time.

We returned to our tasks, the rhythm of our work now infused with a deeper meaning. Coolidge sanded the surfaces with a newfound reverence, his movements smooth and purposeful. I measured and cut the shelving wood, envisioning the rows of fresh-baked goods that would soon line these walls.

And through it all, Mary Jane moved among us, offering guidance and encouragement. Her optimism was infectious, a light that chased away the shadows of doubt and weariness.

"Let's add some color to these walls," she suggested, tracing the newly smoothed surface. "Something warm and inviting, like the glow of a hearth. A shade that says 'welcome home.'"

We nodded in agreement, the idea of color a burst of life amidst the dust and debris. At that moment, I realized that we were not just renovating a space but creating a canvas for the stories yet to be written here—stories of redemption, second chances, and generations to come.

The once-neglected space began to breathe new life, each brush of paint and turn of the screwdriver a testament to the transformation within these walls and ourselves.

As I retreated to admire our progress, I caught Mary Jane's eye. Her smile reflected the satisfaction and gratitude that swelled within my chest.

In that shared moment, I understood the true magic of what we were creating here—a place where broken pieces could be made whole again, where the aroma of fresh beginnings would forever mingle with the sweetness of dreams reborn.

As the day wore on, the once-empty space began to fill with the echoes of our laughter and the steady rhythm of our work. Coolidge, his brow furrowed in concentration, meticulously sanded down an old wooden shelf, his hands coaxing new life from the weathered surface.

"Hey, check this out!" he called, his voice tinged with excitement. A small, worn box was nestled in the corner, hidden beneath a layer of dust and debris. Carefully, he extracted it from its resting place, his fingers leaving trails in the grime.

Mary Jane and I gathered around him, our curiosity piqued. As Coolidge lifted the lid, a cascade of photographs and mementos spilled forth, each a tiny window into the neighborhood's vibrant past.

"Look at this," Mary Jane breathed, her hands gently cradling a faded photograph. "The old barbershop on the corner, before it closed down. And here, the Community Center, back when it was a hub of activity."

We sifted through the treasures, each image and trinket a testament to the rich tapestry of lives that had once thrived here. The smiling faces and captured moments of joy stood in stark contrast to the current state of the neighborhood, a bittersweet reminder of what had been lost.

"We should display these in the bakery," I suggested, my mind already envisioning the way these relics of the past could breathe life into the present. "A wall of memories, to honor those who came before and to inspire those who will come after."

Mary Jane's eyes sparkled with approval, and her hand squeezed mine. "That's a beautiful idea, Turland. It's a way to bridge the gap between then and now, to remind everyone of the community's roots and resilience."

As we continued to explore the box's contents, our conversation turned to the changes that had swept through the neighborhood over the years. The once-thriving streets had fallen into disrepair, the vibrant storefronts shuttered, and the sense of connection frayed.

"But that's why we're here, isn't it?" Coolidge mused, his gaze lingering on a photograph of children playing in the park. "To bring back some of that old spirit, to create a place where people can come together again."

I nodded, the weight of our mission settling onto my shoulders like a mantle of purpose. "We have to honor the past while embracing the future," I said, my voice steady with conviction.

Mary Jane's hand found its way to my shoulder, her touch a gentle affirmation of our chosen path. "And we'll do it together," she said, her words promising and praying. "Brick by brick, memory by memory, until this place is a shining new beacon of hope once more."

As the sun descended towards the horizon, casting a golden glow through the bakery's newly polished windows, we stood together, the box of memories at our feet. In that moment, I felt the stirrings of something powerful, a sense of destiny and purpose that transcended the boundaries of time and circum-stance.

This bakery, this labor of love, was more than a dream. It was a testament to the enduring spirit of a community, a symbol of the unbreakable bonds that tied us together. As we prepared to weave these precious memories into the very fabric of our creation, I knew that we were not just building a business but a legacy—one that would endure long after we were gone, a shining reminder of the power of hope, resilience, and the unending capacity of the human heart to heal, to grow, and to love.

As the hours ticked by, the storefront transformed before our eyes. The once-bare walls now boasted a fresh coat of paint, the soft hues of cream and pale green creating a soothing ambiance. Sturdy and gleaming shelves stood ready to hold the promise of my mother's delectable creations.

I stepped back, wiping the sweat from my forehead with the back of my hand, and surveyed our handiwork. Pride swelled in my chest, mingling with a deep sense of accomplishment. *We did this,* I thought, my gaze drifting to Turland. *Togeth-er.*

Turland caught my eye, a grin spreading across his face. "It's coming together, isn't it?" he said, his voice filled with quiet satisfaction.

I nodded, my smile mirroring his. "It's more than I ever could have imagined," I admitted my voice barely above a whisper.

As the day drew to a close, Turland and I stepped outside, the cool evening air a welcome respite from the heat of our labors. We stood side by side, admiring the transformed storefront, the weight of our shared accomplishment settling over us like a comforting blanket.

Turland reached into his pocket, pulling out a carefully folded fabric. He handed it to me, his eyes shining with anticipation. "I made this design for the bakery," he said, his voice soft and hesitant. "For Mary Jane."

I unfolded the fabric with trembling fingers, revealing a model for a beautifully crafted sign. The words "Patterson's Sweet Dreams" were painted in elegant, flowing script, the letters shimmering with a soft, golden hue. The design was a work of art, a testament to Turland's skill and dedication.

"It's perfect," I breathed, my heart swelling with emotion. "She's going to love it."

I carried the design inside. Our footsteps light with excitement. Mary Jane stood in the center of the room, her eyes wide with wonder as she took in the transformed space. When she saw the design, her hand flew to her mouth, tears welling in her eyes.

"You made this?" she whispered, her voice trembling with emotion. "For me?"

Turland nodded, his own eyes glistening. "For you," he confirmed, his words heavy with meaning. "For all of us."

Mary Jane embraced us both, her tears falling freely as she held us close. In that moment, I understood the true meaning of family, of love that transcended blood and circumstance. With its shimmering letters and heartfelt sentiment, the design represented more than just a name; it symbolized our unbreakable bond, our shared journey of healing and redemption.

As we stood there, wrapped in Mary Jane's warmth, I felt a sense of peace settle over me, a certainty that we would face the future together no matter what. The bakery, with its promise of sweet dreams and new beginnings, was just the start of a story that would unfold in ways we could never have imagined.

At that moment, surrounded by my family's love and support, I knew anything was possible.

The once dilapidated storefront had been transformed, its freshly painted walls and gleaming windows a testament to the power of hard work and unwavering determination. Turland's hand rested on my shoulder, a gentle reminder of the bond we had forged through the trials we had faced together.

"Look at what we've accomplished," he murmured, his voice filled with pride and awe. "Who would have thought two guys like us could make something so beautiful?"

I nodded, my throat tight with emotion. "It's more than just a bakery," I said. Those words were now weighted with a new realization that now hits a little differently because of all this place now represented. "It's a symbol of hope, of second chances."

Mary Jane stood beside us, her eyes shining with unshed tears. "You boys have given me the greatest gift," she said, her voice trembling with gratitude. "You've shown me that love can heal even the deepest wounds, that there's always a reason to keep dreaming."

As we gazed at the transformed storefront, I couldn't help but feel a sense of anticipation, a tingling in my veins that spoke of the endless possibilities ahead. This was the beginning of our journey, a first step toward a brighter future.

Turland's voice broke through my thoughts, a gentle reminder of the work still ahead. "We've got a lot of dreams to make come true," he said, a smile playing at the corners of his mouth. "But with each other and my mother by our side, I know we can do anything."

I nodded, my heart swelling with a newfound sense of purpose. The bakery was more than just a place to make pastries;

it was a haven where we could nurture all the seeds of change and watch them blossom into something beautiful.

Chapter 33: Helping Hand

The phone buzzes, interrupting the quiet Saturday morning with my little television watching me rest my eyes. A glance at the screen - Dame's name flashes. My heart quickens as I answer, a sense of unease rising in my chest.

"Turland, it's Big Mike. He's out, man. Released last week." Dame's voice crackles through the speaker.

I sink into the couch, my mind reeling. Images of Big Mike flood back - the first time we met as cellmates, both wide-eyed and wary. How he took me under his wing taught me to navigate the treacherous waters of prison life.

"Wow, that's... that's big news," I manage, my voice catching. "How's he doing?"

"You know how it is. Adjusting ain't easy. He could use a friend right about now."

I nod, forgetting Dame can't see me. Memories of my release surface - the disorientation, the fear, the desperate longing for something familiar in an alien world. Then, there was Coolidge waiting for me on that harrowing day.

"I hear you. Let me... let me figure something out. I'll reach out to him."

We say our goodbyes, and I sit silently, the weight of responsibility heavy on my shoulders. Big Mike was there for me when I needed him most. Can I do any less?

I went upstairs and found the aroma of coffee mingling with the sizzle of eggs in the pan.

Mary Jane looks at me as I'm lost in thought. Her gentle touch on my arm brings me back.

"Everything okay?" Her eyes search mine, concern etched in the furrow of her brow.

I take her hand, drawing strength from her warmth. "It's Big Mike, my first cellmate. He's out of prison. I just found out."

Coolidge wanders in, catching the tail end of my words. He leans against the door frame, arms crossed, curiosity and caution warring on his face.

"Your old cellmate? The one who had your back inside?"

I nod, meeting his gaze. "Yeah. He's a good man, Coolidge. He taught me a lot about surviving in there. About holding onto hope when everything seems darkest."

Coolidge nodded slowly, processing the information. I could see the wheels turning, the cautious curiosity in his eyes. He knew the world I'd come from, the bonds forged in adversity.

"Oh, how you did for me when you first met me. You gotta do what you gotta do," he said, his voice steady. "We understand."

Mary Jane squeezed my hand, her voice soft and understanding. "He must be going through a lot right now. It's not easy, starting over like that."

"I know. I remember how lost I felt when I first got out. If it wasn't for you two..." I trail off, emotion choking my words.

Coolidge shifts, his expression thoughtful. "So, what are you going to do? How can we help?"

I look between them, my heart full. This is what family means - showing up, even when the path is uncertain.

"I need to be there for him like he was for me. But I don't want to let you down, either. I promised to be here to continue building this new life with you. But I'm trying to establish myself with you and Coolidge, this new life together now. I can't just drop everything."

Mary Jane cups my face, her eyes shining with love and pride. "You've got such a big heart, Turland. Helping Big Mike, that's part of who you are. And we love all of you, you hear me? We're in this together."

Coolidge nods, a small smile tugging at his lips. "Mom's right. If Big Mike's important to you, then he's important to us. We'll figure it out as a family."

I pull them both into a fierce hug, tears pricking at my eyes. At this moment, I feel the full weight of their love, their acceptance. It's a balm to my troubled soul, a reminder that I'm not facing this alone.

As we break apart, I take a deep breath, my mind already spinning with possibilities. Big Mike once took a chance on me and saw past the scared kid to the man I could become. Now, it's my turn to extend that same lifeline to help him find his way in this uncharted territory.

So, while walking away from the table, I gathered my thoughts, preparing for the journey ahead. I kissed Mary Jane softly on her cheek; her love had become a steady anchor in the tempest of my emotions. Coolidge clasped my shoulder in a silent gesture of support, his eyes conveying a depth of understanding that belied his years.

As I exited onto the cracked sidewalk. The air was thick with the tang of exhaust fumes and the distant sizzle of frying oil. I pulled my coat tighter around me, a flimsy shield against the chill that seemed to seep into my bones.

Each step feels heavy, weighted with the memories of a past I can't quite shake. Once familiar and foreign, the streets are a patchwork of boarded-up windows and faded graffiti tags. I search for glimmers of the neighborhood I once knew, the vibrant pulse of life that thrummed beneath the surface, but time has a way of erasing even the most indelible marks.

As I round the corner, the decrepit hulk of the old factory looms into view, its rusted pipes and shattered windows a testament to the relentless march of decay. How many lives were upended when those doors slammed shut for good? How many dreams were left to wither on the vine, starved of sunlight and hope?

I quicken my pace, eager to leave the ghosts of yesteryear behind. The address Dame gave me is seared into my brain. A lifeline is tethering me to the present. With each stride, I feel the weight of responsibility settling on my shoulders, the gravity of the task ahead.

As I navigate the labyrinthine streets, dodging potholes and shattered glass, snippets of conversation drift past me, the cadence of the West Side's unique patois a bittersweet melody. Laughter mingles with shouts, joy intertwined with sorrow -

the eternal dance of a community clinging to life in the face of unrelenting adversity.

Finally, I arrive at the address, a nondescript brick building with peeling paint and a sagging stoop. I pause for a moment, my heart hammering in my chest. Big Mike is waiting somewhere beyond that door, a man adrift in a world that's moved on without him.

I think of the countless hours we spent hunched over dog-eared books, the whispered conversations that sustained us through the long, lonely nights. Big Mike was more than just a cellmate - he was a lifeline, a reminder that even in the darkest places, a flicker of humanity could endure.

With a deep breath, I climb the steps, my hand poised to knock. The future is an unwritten page, a story yet to be told. But at this moment, as the shadows lengthen and the city holds its breath, I know one thing for sure: I won't let Big Mike face this journey alone.

My knuckles rap against the weathered wood, a staccato beat that seems to echo through the stillness. As I wait for the door to open, I feel a flicker of something long dormant stirring in my chest, guiding me forward into the unknown.

The door creaks open, revealing Big Mike's haggard face. Once bright with mischief, his eyes are shadowed by a weariness that seems to seep into his very bones. For a moment, we stand there, two men haunted by the ghosts of our shared past.

"Turland," Big Mike rasps, his voice rough with emotion. "I didn't think you'd come."

I step forward, clasping his shoulder with a firmness that belies the tremor in my fingers. "I made a promise, Big Mike. I don't intend to break it now."

He nods, a flicker of gratitude softening the hard lines of his face. Stepping aside, he ushers me into the cramped apartment, the air heavy with the tang of cigarette smoke and the musty scent of neglect.

We settle onto the threadbare couch, the silence stretching between us like an invisible chasm. I can see the toll that prison has taken on Big Mike, how his shoulders sag beneath the weight of countless disappointments.

"It's not easy out here, Turland," he murmurs, his gaze fixed on the stained carpet. "The world's moved on, but I'm still stuck in the same old cycle."

I lean forward, catching his eye with an intensity that burns through the haze of despair. "You're not alone, Big Mike. We've been through hell together and found our way out, one step at a time."

He looks up, a flicker of hope igniting in the depths of his eyes. "You believe that?"

"I have to," I reply, my voice fierce with conviction. "Because if I don't, what's the point of this? We've been given a second chance, Big Mike. It's up to us to make something of it."

Big Mike nods slowly, a faint smile tugging at the corners of his mouth. "You always were the dreamer, Turland. You never lost sight of the light, even in the darkest places."

I chuckle softly, the sound a balm to my battered soul. "Maybe that's why we survived, Big Mike. Because we had something to hold onto, even when the world tried to tear us apart."

We talk then, the words flowing freely as we navigate the twists and turns of our shared history. The memories are bittersweet, tinged with the ache of lost time and the hope of new beginnings.

With the sun setting, casting the room in a soft, golden glow, I rise to my feet, a renewed sense of purpose thrumming through my veins.

"We've got work to do, Big Mike," I say, my voice steady with resolve. "But we'll face it together, just like we always have."

He stands beside me, his shoulders squared and his eyes bright with determination. "Lead the way, Turland. I'm right behind you."

As we step outside into the gathering dusk, the city stretches before us like a canvas waiting to be painted.

A gentle breeze caresses my skin as I guide Big Mike through the winding streets of our neighborhood, the familiar sights and sounds of the West Side enveloping us in a comforting embrace. The community garden comes into view, a vibrant oasis amidst the concrete and asphalt; its lush greenery and colorful blooms are a testament to the resilience and determination of our people.

"This is it, Big Mike," I say, gesturing to the garden with a sweeping hand motion. "This is where we'll start."

He takes in the scene before him, his eyes widening with awe and apprehension. "It's beautiful, Turland. But I don't know the first thing about gardening."

I placed a reassuring hand on his shoulder. My voice was soft but firm. "That's okay, Big Mike. I didn't either, and we all learned together. This place is not just about growing plants. It's about growing as people, finding a way to put down roots and create something beautiful, even amid the chaos."

He nods slowly, a glimmer of understanding dawning in his eyes. "I think I see what you mean. It's a fresh start, a chance to build something new."

"Exactly," I reply, a smile tugging at the corners of my mouth. "And speaking of fresh starts, there's something else I wanted to talk to you about."

I lead him to the garden's edge, where the bakery stands, its warm, inviting aroma wafting through the air. "The apartment above the bakery is yours if you want it. It's not much, but it's a place to call your own, a chance to start over."

Big Mike's eyes widen, his voice thick with emotion. "Turland, I don't know what to say. I can't believe you'd do this for me after everything."

"We're in this together, Big Mike. Always have been, always will be." I extend my hand, a silent invitation. "What do you say? Ready to take that first step?"

He grasps my hand firmly, his grip firm and steady. "I'm ready, Turland. Let's do this."

As I make my way home, the weight of the day's events settles upon my shoulders, a mix of exhaustion and exhilaration coursing through my veins. I push open the door, the familiar scent of home enveloping me in its warm embrace.

Mary Jane and Coolidge look up from their seats at the kitchen table, their eyes wide with curiosity and concern. "How did it go?" Mary Jane asks, her voice soft and gentle.

I sink into a chair beside her, my hand finding hers beneath the table. "He's in, Mary Jane. He will work in the garden and move into the apartment above the bakery."

Coolidge leans forward, his brow furrowed with a mix of emotions. "Are you sure about this? I know what it's like being in there, but..."

I meet his gaze, my eyes filled with understanding and compassion. "I know it's not easy. But we've all been given a second chance to make things right. Big Mike deserves that chance, just like we did."

Mary Jane nods, her eyes shining with pride and love. "Your father's right, Coolidge. We've all made mistakes, but what we learn from our mistakes defines us."

Coolidge sits back in his chair, his expression contemplative. I can see the wheels turning in his mind, the struggle to reconcile his past with the present. "I get it. I do. It's just... it's a lot to take in."

I reach across the table, my hand resting on his arm. "I know, son. But we'll face it together, as a family. That's what we do."

As the conversation continues, the complex emotions swirling through the room, I feel a sense of hope and determination settle in my chest. I know that anything is possible.

***

The next evening, at sunset, Turland and Big Mike go through the rows of vibrant plants in the community garden. The air is thick with the scent of fresh soil and the hum of bees darting from flower to flower. Turland breathes deeply, feeling a sense of peace over him as he surveys the thriving garden.

"This is it, Big Mike," Turland says, gesturing to the lush greenery surrounding them. "This is where it all happens, where we'll grow something good in the soul."

Big Mike nods, his eyes wide with wonder as he takes in the sight before him. "It's beautiful, Turland. I never knew a place like this could exist in the middle of the city."

Turland smiles, clapping Big Mike on the back. "That's the magic of it, my friend. We've made a little piece of the world our own, where we can cultivate hope and new beginnings."

As they walk deeper into the garden, Turland points out the various plots, each one tended to with love and care. "Over there, we've got the tomatoes, and here, we've got the squash and zucchini. And those sunflowers, they're Mrs. Johnson's pride and joy."

Big Mike listens intently, his fingers brushing against the plants' leaves as they pass. Turland can see the glimmer of excitement in his eyes, the spark of possibility that comes with the promise of a fresh start.

"So, what do you think, Big Mike? You ready to get your hands dirty?" Turland asks, handing him a pair of gloves and a trowel.

Big Mike takes the tools, a grin spreading across his face. "More than ready, Turland. Let's do this."

As they set to work, the sun sinking lower on the horizon, Turland feels a sense of contentment in his bones. Here, among the plants and the soil, he knows he's exactly where he's meant to be, helping a friend find his way back to the light.

As he watches Big Mike dig into the earth, his movements tentative at first but growing more confident with each passing moment, Turland knows that the seeds they're planting today will bear fruit far beyond the boundaries of this little garden. They're planting the seeds of hope, redemption, and a brighter future than any of them could have ever imagined.

Big Mike wiped the sweat from his brow as he knelt in the rich, dark soil of the community garden. The sun-warmed earth felt alive beneath his hands, starkly contrasting with the cold concrete and steel that had been his world for so long. He focused on the delicate seedling before him, his fingers trembling slightly as he eased it into the ground.

"Take your time," Turland said softly, crouching beside him. "There's no rush. Let the plant guide you."

Big Mike nodded, his throat tight. This simple act of nurturing new life felt foreign, almost sacred. As he patted the soil around the seedling, a sense of purpose began to flicker within him like a candle in the darkness.

Days turned into weeks, and Big Mike found himself drawn to the garden, to the rhythm of growth and renewal. He marveled at the tiny green shoots pushing through the earth, reaching for the sun. Each new leaf, each unfurling petal, felt like a small victory, a testament to his resilience.

Turland was a constant presence; his patient guidance and unwavering support were a balm to Big Mike's battered soul. In the quiet moments between planting and pruning, they talked—about their pasts, hopes, and fears. The words flowed easily, bridging the gap between them and forging a bond beyond the prison walls they once shared.

One evening, as the sun dipped below the horizon, Turland invited Big Mike to dinner. "Mary Jane and Coolidge would love to have you," he said, his eyes warm with understanding.

Big Mike hesitated, uncertainty clouding his features. Sitting at a family table and being welcomed into their lives felt like a dream he didn't dare to grasp. But as he looked at Turland, the man who had become his anchor in this new world, he found the courage to nod.

As Big Mike stepped inside, the Patterson home was filled with the aroma of home-cooked food and the soft murmur of conversation. Mary Jane greeted him with a gentle hug and embraced him with a balm of his weary soul. Coolidge, his eyes filled with curiosity and caution, offered a firm handshake.

Big Mike felt a sense of belonging as they gathered around the table. The laughter, the stories, the easy camaraderie—it was a glimpse into a life he had never dared to imagine for himself. Turland, his face alight with joy, looked at ease, a far cry from the haunted man Big Mike had first met in prison.

At that moment, as the candlelight flickered and the conversation flowed, Big Mike felt hope ignited within him. Maybe, just maybe, he could find his place in this world. Maybe, with the support of this unlikely family, he could learn to grow, thrive, and reach for the sun once more.

As the evening progressed, the conversation turned to the past, to the memories that had shaped them all. Turland, thick with emotion, turned to Big Mike and said, "I want to thank you, Big Mike. For looking out for me when I was just an eighteen-year-old kid in prison. For teaching me how to focus and how to be a man. I wouldn't be here today if it weren't for you."

Big Mike felt his throat tighten, his eyes stinging with unshed tears. He looked around the table at the faces of these people who had opened their hearts to him and shook his head. "It wasn't me, Turland. It was God. He had a plan all along. I'm just glad I did the part he entrusted me to do."

Mary Jane reached across the table, her hand resting on Big Mike's. "And we're so grateful that you did, Big Mike. You've touched our lives in ways you can't imagine by doing what God had you to do regarding Turland."

Coolidge's eyes shining with newfound respect, added, "I never really understood what he went through in his early prison days. But seeing you, hearing your story... it's given me a whole new perspective and understanding of why and how he was prepared to help me during my prison time. Thank you for sharing it with us."

Big Mike felt a warmth spread through his chest, a sense of peace he had never known. In this moment, surrounded by the love and acceptance of these incredible people, he knew that he had found his home.

As the night drew close, Turland walked Big Mike to the door, his hand resting on the older man's shoulder. "You're always welcome here, Big Mike. Always. We're your family now."

Big Mike nodded, his voice too choked with emotion to speak. He stepped out into the cool night air, his heart full and his spirit renewed.

Turland watched him go, a sense of fulfillment washing over him. The evening had been a testament to the power of second chances, of the resilience of the human spirit. As he closed the door and turned back to his family, he knew this was just the beginning of a new chapter filled with hope and the promise of a brighter future.

Turland reflected on the journey that had brought him to this moment in the quiet of his room that night. The pain, the struggle, the endless days in prison—they had all led him here, to this place of love and belonging. He thought of Big Mike and the countless others still trapped in the cycle of incarceration and despair, and he knew that his work was far from over.

But for now, he allowed himself to bask in the warmth of this moment, in the knowledge that he was loved, worthy, and finally home. As he drifted off to sleep, he dreamed of a world where every lost soul could find their way back to the light, where the power of compassion and grace could heal every broken heart.

Chapter 34: Rising Challenges

A pale morning light bathed the street with a soft glow as we approached the bakery, our hearts brimming with anticipation. Mary Jane wore her favorite floral dress, which she saved for special occasions. Coolidge walked tall beside me, his face etched with a quiet pride I had never seen before.

"Can you believe it, Mama?" Coolidge said, his voice trembling slightly. "Our very own bakery. I never thought I'd see the day."

Mary Jane reached for his hand, her eyes shining. "The Lord works in mysterious ways, baby. This is a new beginning for all of us."

I nodded, a lump forming in my throat. For so much of his life, Coolidge's future had seemed as bleak as the gray walls of his prison cell. But here we were, on the cusp of something extraordinary. Something none of us had dared to dream of before learning to dream together.

As we rounded the corner, our steps quickened, propelled by an almost childlike eagerness. But the sight that greeted us stopped us dead in our tracks.

The bakery's large front window had been shattered, jagged shards of glass littering the sidewalk like fallen stars. Ugly red graffiti marred the freshly painted walls, the hateful words searing into my eyes.

Mary Jane let out a strangled gasp, her hand flying to her mouth. Coolidge stood rigid, his fists clenched at his sides, a vein pulsing in his temple.

"Who would do this?" Mary Jane whispered, her voice raw with disbelief. "Why?"

I swallowed hard, a bitter taste flooding my mouth. This was supposed to be a day of celebration of new beginnings. But someone had tried to snuff out that hope before it even had a chance to flicker to life.

Coolidge took a deep breath, his jaw set with determination. "We can't let this break us. Not now. Not after all the work we put into this and everything we've been through."

Mary Jane nodded slowly, straightening her shoulders. "You're right, baby. We've come too far to let hate win."

I looked at the two of them, marveling at their strength. They had endured so much—the long years of separation, the stares and whispers of judgment. Yet here they stood, united in the face of adversity.

As the morning sun started to cast gentle rays over the broken glass and hateful words, I felt hope reignite in my chest. This was only a setback, a bump in the road. Together, we would find a way to mend what had been broken and create something beautiful from the ashes of this cruel act.

For that was the true power of redemption—the ability to rise above the darkness and let the light shine through, no matter how many times it tried to be extinguished.

With a heavy heart, I followed Mary Jane and Coolidge into the bakery, the door creaking softly as we stepped inside. The once vibrant space now felt hollow, the weight of the vandalism pressing down on us like a suffocating blanket.

Coolidge slumped into a chair, his head in his hands. "I don't know if we can do this, Mama. Maybe we should postpone the opening and give ourselves time to regroup."

Mary Jane's eyes flashed with a fierce determination. "No, baby. We can't let them win. This bakery is more than just a business—it symbolizes hope for our community."

I leaned against the counter, my mind racing. "But how can we open today with the storefront looking like that? It'll take hours to clean up the mess."

Mary Jane's gaze softened as she looked at me. "Turland, sweetheart, we've got to have faith. The Good Lord didn't bring us this far to abandon us now."

Her words settled into my heart, a gentle reminder of the strength that had carried our family through many trials. I nodded slowly, a small smile tugging at my lips. "You're right, Mary Jane. We'll find a way."

Coolidge lifted his head, his eyes glistening with unshed tears. "I just wanted this day to be perfect, you know? A fresh start for all of us."

Mary Jane wrapped her arm around his shoulders, pulling him close. "And it will be, baby. We'll make it perfect, no matter what it takes."

As I watched them, a flicker of an idea began to take shape in my mind. "What if we ask the community for help? I bet plenty of folks out there'd be willing to lend a hand."

Coolidge's brow furrowed. "You think they'd do that? After they see everything that's happened here today?"

I grinned, feeling a surge of hope rising in my chest. "I know they would. This neighborhood is like a family. When one of us is hurting, we all come together to make things right."

Mary Jane's face lit up with a proud smile. "That's the spirit, Turland. We'll show them that love is stronger than hate every time."

As we sat there, surrounded by the remnants of someone's cruelty, I felt a renewed sense of purpose taking root in my soul. This bakery was more than just a dream—it was a testament to the resilience of the human spirit, a beacon of light in a world that so often seemed shrouded in darkness.

The tinkling of the bell above the bakery door drew our attention, and Dame strode in, his lean, muscular frame radiating a sense of urgency. His sharp, observant eyes swept over the scene, taking in the damage with practiced efficiency.

"I heard what happened," he said, calm and authoritative. "But we're not going to let this stop us. I've already rallied the community to get everyone out here to help clean up and prepare for the opening."

Mary Jane's eyes widened, a glimmer of hope sparking in their depths. "You think they'd come?"

Dame nodded, his jaw set with determination. "They're on the way as I speak. This neighborhood has got a lot of heart. When one of us is in trouble, we all stand together, and that's the way it's always been."

As if on cue, the door swung open again, and Mr. Washington entered, followed by a group of neighbors, their faces etched with a mixture of concern and resolve. The old man's once robust frame might have been stooped with age, but his presence still commanded respect, his silver beard and sharp, gentle eyes a testament to a lifetime of wisdom and hard work.

"We're here to help," Mr. Washington declared, his rich, deep voice filling the space. "This bakery, it's not just yours—it belongs to all of us. It symbolizes hope and the good things that can grow even in the toughest times."

As he spoke, I felt a lump forming in my throat, the day's emotions threatening to overwhelm me. But I swallowed them back, focusing instead on the incredible outpouring of support surrounding us.

Mr. Washington began to organize the cleanup effort, his authoritative presence infusing the scene with a sense of unity and purpose. He assigned tasks with the practiced ease of a man who had spent a lifetime leading and guiding others, his calloused hands gesturing with a gentle strength.

As I watched the community come together, their faces determined and their spirits unbroken, I felt a profound sense of gratitude washing over me. This was the true power of the West Side—not the abandoned buildings or the vacant lots, but the unbreakable bonds of love and solidarity that tied us all together.

And in that moment, I knew that no matter what challenges lay ahead, we would face them as one, our hearts beating in unison to the rhythm of hope and redemption.

As the cleanup effort progressed, snippets of conversation drifted through the air, weaving together a tapestry of resilience and determination.

"We ain't gonna let this break us," declared a woman in a vibrant headwrap, her voice ringing with conviction. "This bakery serves as a shining example of positivity for our community., and we're gonna make sure it shines brighter than ever."

Beside her, a young man nodded in agreement, his hands busy sweeping up shards of glass. "That's right," he affirmed. "We've been through worse than this and always come out stronger on the other side."

Their words echoed the sentiments of countless others, each voice adding to the chorus of hope that swelled around us. In the face of adversity, the West Side had chosen to stand together, to rise above the hatred and the fear, and to prove that our spirit could not be broken.

As the last of the debris was cleared away, Mr. Washington called everyone to gather outside the bakery. The crowd formed a semicircle around him, their faces upturned in anticipation.

"Friends," he began, eyes sweeping over the assembled group. Today, we have witnessed the power of our community. In the wake of this senseless act of vandalism, we have chosen to respond not with anger or despair but with love and unity."

He paused, letting his words sink in before continuing. "You see, life is a lot like a garden. Various vegetables are growing together—cucumbers and tomatoes, carrots and lettuce. Each one is different, with its unique flavor and purpose. But it's those very differences that make the garden thrive."

Mr. Washington's voice took on a poetic cadence as he spoke, his words painting vivid images in our minds. "Just like those vegetables, we all have our roles and gifts to bring to the table. The cucumber can never be the tomato, and that's the beauty of it all. Because together, we can create something far more beautiful and nourishing than any of us could achieve alone."

He fixed us with a piercing gaze, his following words ringing with a quiet intensity. "But understanding, true understanding, it only lasts for a season. What matters is what you do with that season and how you grow and contribute to the garden of life. You don't want to be the spoiled vegetable that rots on the vine and spoils the harvest for everyone else."

As he spoke, I felt a shiver run down my spine, the weight of his wisdom settling deep within my bones. Around me, I could see the faces of my neighbors, their expressions a mix of reflection and resolve.

"So let this day be a reminder," Mr. Washington concluded, his voice rising with the strength of his conviction. "A reminder that no matter what challenges we face or storms may come our way, we have the power to rise above them. We have the strength to cultivate a garden of hope and resilience that will nourish our community for generations to come."

As he finished speaking, a hush fell over the crowd, the silence broken only by the distant hum of traffic and the soft rustling of leaves in the breeze. And then, as if moved by some invisible force, we began to applaud, our hands coming together in a thunderous ovation that echoed through the streets.

At that moment, I felt another swell of pride rising in my chest, a fierce love for this community that had shaped, nurtured, and taught me the true meaning of resilience. And I knew, with a certainty that went beyond words, we would face it together, our roots intertwined, and our hearts forever united regardless of what the future may bring.

As the applause began to fade, I saw Mr. Washington step down from his impromptu podium, his eyes shining with emotion. He made his way through the crowd, shaking hands and exchanging words of encouragement with those he passed.

When he reached me, he placed a hand on my shoulder, his grip firm and reassuring.

"You remember what I said, Turland," he said, his voice low and earnest. "This is your season, your time to grow and flourish. Don't let anyone tell you otherwise."

I nodded, my throat tight with emotion. "I won't, Mr. Washington. I promise."

He smiled, a slow, knowing smile that seemed to hold all the wisdom of the ages. "I know you won't. You've got good roots, boy. Strong roots. And that's what matters most in this life."

With that, he moved on, leaving me to ponder his words as the crowd dispersed. I watched people huddled in small groups, their voices animated with excitement and determination.

This was my community, my people. And even in the face of adversity, we had come together, united by a common goal and a shared sense of purpose. We had taken a stand against hatred and bigotry, and in doing so, we had proven that love and compassion would always triumph in the end.

As the crowd's energy swelled with renewed determination, the sudden arrival of local media added an unexpected layer of intensity to the scene. Reporters and photographers descended upon the bakery, their cameras flashing and voices clamoring for attention. I watched as the young man I recently met named Coolidge and his parents, one of whom was my childhood friend with whom we previously spent time in prison together, navigated this new spotlight, their expressions a mix of vulnerability and strength.

Coolidge stepped forward, his voice steady as he addressed the reporters. "What happened here today was a tragedy, but it's not the end of our story. We're going to rise above this, together, as a community."

His words resonated with the crowd, drawing nods and murmurs of agreement. I could see the pride in his mother, Mary Jane's eyes as she watched her son, her hand resting gently on Turland's arm. Even in the face of such scrutiny, they stood tall, united in their resolve.

As the interviews continued, I was drawn back to the bakery, where the final preparations were underway. The scent of fresh paint mingled with the aroma of baking bread, a tangible reminder of the love and care that had gone into every detail.

Everywhere I looked, I saw the community's support in action. Neighbors worked side by side, hanging decorations and arranging displays. Children carried trays of pastries, their faces lit with excitement. And in the midst of it all, Coolidge and his parents moved with purpose, their hands busy and their hearts full.

I watched as Turland paused to survey the scene, his eyes misty with emotion. "I never thought I'd see the day," he murmured, more to himself than anyone else. "After everything we've been through, to have this... it's a miracle."

Mary Jane wrapped an arm around his waist, her smile gentle. "It's not a miracle, love. It's the result of hard work, faith, and the love of a community that refuses to give up."

This was more than just the opening of a bakery. It was a new beginning, a chance to write a different story.

The doors of the Sweet Dreams Bakery swung open, and the crowd's joyful chatter swelled like a symphony. Neighbors and friends poured in, their faces alight with excitement and pride. The aroma of freshly baked bread and sweet pastries wafted through the air, mingling with hope and triumph.

I watched as Coolidge greeted each person with a warm embrace, his eyes shining with gratitude. Mary Jane moved through the crowd, her laughter ringing out as she thanked everyone for their support. Turland stood by the counter, his hands clasped behind his back, a quiet smile playing on his lips as he entered the scene.

It was a moment of pure, unadulterated joy. The past struggles, pain, and heartache seemed to melt away in the face of this incredible achievement. The vandalism, doubts, and fears were washed away by the love and support of a community that refused to be broken.

As I made my way through the bakery, I caught snippets of conversation, each one a testament to the impact of this moment.

"I never thought I'd see the day," Mrs. Johnson said, her voice thick with emotion. "After everything this family has been through, to see them standing tall like this... it's a miracle."

Mr. Washington nodded, his eyes misty. "It's more than a miracle," he said softly. It's a triumph of the human spirit, a reminder that dawn will always come no matter how dark the night."

I stood beside Coolidge, Mary Jane, and Turland, watching the celebration unfold. For a moment, we stood there, basking in the moment's warmth.

"We did it," Coolidge whispered, his voice choked with emotion. "After everything, we did it."

Mary Jane took his hand, her fingers intertwining with his. "We did it together," she said softly. "All of us. This is what community looks like, Coolidge. This is what love can do."

Turland smiled, his eyes distant as if remembering something from long ago. "When I was in prison," he said quietly, "I used to dream of moments like this—moments of pure, unbridled joy—moments when the world felt right and everything seemed possible."

I looked at him, my heart full. "And now?" I asked softly.

He turned to me, his smile wide and genuine. "Now, I know that those moments aren't just dreams. They're real, and they're worth fighting for. Every single day."

Mr. Washington stepped forward, his presence commanding the attention of the gathered crowd. He held a small, unassuming candle, its wick unlit. The chatter quieted as he asked someone to turn the lights off inside the bakery and raised the candle, his voice ringing with clarity and purpose.

"Today, we stand together as a community, united in the face of adversity," he began, his eyes sweeping over the sea of faces. "This candle represents the light within each of us, the resilience and hope that cannot be extinguished by hatred or fear."

He paused, letting his words sink in. I felt Mary Jane's hand tighten around mine, her eyes glistening with unshed tears.

"Now, let us light this candle together," Mr. Washington continued, "as a symbol of our collective strength and the promise of a brighter future."

He lowered the candle, and Turland stepped forward, a match in his hand. He struck the match swiftly and surely and touched it to the wick, igniting a steady flame.

As the candle flickered to life, a hush fell over the crowd. The world seemed still at that moment as if the universe held its breath.

And then, slowly at first, a ripple of applause began to build. It started as a whisper, a gentle murmur of hands coming together, but soon, it grew into a roar, a thunderous ovation that seemed to shake the very foundations of the earth.

I looked around, my heart swelling with emotion. In the faces of my neighbors, friends, and family, I saw a reflection of my joy and hope. We had suffered and struggled, but in that moment, we were unbreakable.

As the applause reached its crescendo, Mr. Washington raised the candle again, its light casting a warm glow over the crowd.

"Let this light be a reminder," he called out, his voice rising above the din, "that even in the darkest times, hope will always find a way to shine through."

And with those words, he blew out the candle, plunging us into a moment of darkness. But as my eyes adjusted, I realized the darkness was incomplete. All around me, tiny points of light began to appear, as one by one, the members of our community raised their candles, their symbols of resilience and hope.

I had never experienced so much unity and purpose. We were not just individuals struggling to make our way in the world. We were a community bound together by love, hope, and the unshakable belief that we could overcome anything together.

As I looked at Mary Jane and Turland, their faces illuminated by the soft glow of the candles, I knew this was just the beginning of cementing a legacy.

We all stepped forward into the light, ready to embrace the promise of a new day and the endless daily possibilities that lay before all of us.

Chapter 35: Ripple Effects

There was no way I could have known I would be this nervous as I shifted in my seat. My palms are sweaty as I smooth the wrinkled pages of my notes. The modest living room feels spacious and suffocating simultaneously, the weight of this moment pressing against my chest. I glance at the clock—ten minutes until the interview—ten minutes to crystallize my thoughts, to find the words that might spark change.

My fingers trace the bullet points I've scribbled, each a glimmer of hope amidst our challenges. "Community renewal," I murmur, my voice barely a whisper. "Potential for growth, for healing." The words feel small and inadequate against the magnitude of our struggles. But they're a start, a seed that might take root if nurtured with care.

I rise, pacing the worn carpet, my footsteps echoing the rhythm of my heartbeat. The ghosts of my past linger in the corners—the choices that led me here, the regrets that cling like shadows. But there's light in the faces of those who believe in the strength of a community that refuses to surrender.

"You got this, Turland," I tell myself, squaring my shoulders. "Just speak from the heart."

***

The camera lights bathe me in a harsh glow, but I focus on the interviewer's face. Her eyes are kind beneath the veneer of professionalism. She leans forward, her voice gentle.

"Tell us about the West Side, Mr. Deville. What challenges does your community face?"

I take a breath, the words flowing with an ease that surprises me. "Our neighborhood is a place of contrasts. There's beauty here in our people's resilience and how we come together when times are tough. But there's pain too, wounds that run deep."

My mind drifts to the shattered glass and the slurs scrawled across Mary Jane's bakery: "We've faced vandalism, crime, and a sense of hopelessness that can seep into the cracks if we let it. But that's not the whole story."

I lean forward, my voice growing stronger. "When I was a teenager, I felt lost, like there was nowhere to turn. But this community has the power to change that narrative. We have the potential to create opportunities, to show our young people that their dreams matter."

The interviewer nods, her pen poised above her notepad. "And how do you propose we do that?"

I think of the garden, the way the earth yielded beneath our hands as we planted seeds of hope. "It starts small," I say, a smile tugging at my lips. It started with our community garden, a gathering place to grow food and relationships. Then, our Sweet Dreams bakery also serves as a beacon of warmth and a welcoming place for everyone. Mentorship programs that connect our youth with leaders who believe in them."

The words pour out, painting a picture of the future we dare to imagine. "Change happens when we invest in our people and recognize the strength within each of us. It happens when we choose compassion over condemnation and offer second chances and a path forward."

My voice softens, heavy with the weight of memory. "I've seen the inside of a prison cell and felt the despair of feeling forgotten. But I've also seen the power of redemption, how a single act of kindness can alter the course of a life. That's the potential that lives here, on the West Side. And it's up to us to nurture and watch it bloom."

As the interview concludes, I step outside, my heart racing with exhilaration and disbelief. Now, the sun warms my face more than the lights from the cameras, and I squint against its brightness, marveling at how the world seems to shimmer with possibility.

My phone vibrates in my pocket, and I pull it out to find a flood of messages. Local politicians, community organizations, and even a few old friends from the neighborhood are all reaching out to express their support and admiration for the words I spoke.

As I scroll through the messages, a lump forms in my throat. I never imagined that my story, my vision, could resonate with so many that the seeds we planted in that small garden could spread beyond the confines of our block.

With each message, I feel gratitude and the realization that our efforts are not in vain. Others believe in this community's potential and will stand beside us in the fight for change.

I go to Mary Jane's bakery. My steps light with a once again newfound sense of purpose. As I push open the door, the sweet aroma of freshly baked bread envelops me, and I'm greeted by the sight of Coolidge and Mary Jane, their faces etched with anticipation.

"Turland!" Mary Jane exclaims, rushing from behind the counter to embrace me. "We saw the interview. You were incredible."

Coolidge grins, his eyes shining with pride. "Man, you had them hanging on every word. I couldn't have said it better myself."

I sink into a chair. My cheeks flushed with a mixture of embarrassment and joy. "I just spoke from the heart," I say, shaking my head in wonder. But the response—it's been overwhelming."

Mary Jane settles into the seat beside me, her hand resting gently on my arm. "People are hungry for hope," she says softly. "You gave them a glimpse of what's possible when we come together and believe in each other."

I nod, the weight of responsibility settling on my shoulders. "We have to keep pushing forward," I say, my voice filled with determination. "This is just the beginning."

Coolidge leans forward, his elbows resting on the table. "The garden, the mentorship program, the community events—we'll make them happen. We'll show the world what the West Side is made of."

There's a fire in his eyes, a fierce determination that mirrors mine. I feel a swell of pride, knowing that I'm not alone in this fight. Together, we can break the cycle of despair and build something lasting.

Mary Jane smiles, her gaze drifting to the window, where the sun dances on the sidewalk. "Change is coming," she murmurs, her words like a prayer. "I can feel it in my bones."

As we sit in the warmth of the bakery, our hearts full of hope and purpose, I know that she's right. The seeds we plant today will bear fruit tomorrow. The West Side will rise, stronger and more vibrant than ever.

The council chamber buzzes with anticipation as I step up to the podium, my heart pounding. I take a deep breath, scanning the faces of the council members, some curious, others skeptical. The weight of my past, of the choices that led me here, presses down on me, but I refuse to let it define me.

"Esteemed council members," I begin, my voice steady and clear. "I stand before you today not as a former prisoner but as a member of the West Side community. A community that has been overlooked and underserved for far too long."

I pause, letting my words sink in. The room is silent, all eyes fixed on me.

"When I was a teenager, I made mistakes. I won't make excuses for them. But I also didn't have many options. The

West Side was where dreams went to die, where hope was a luxury we couldn't afford."

I see a flicker of recognition in some of their eyes, a glimmer of understanding.

"But it doesn't have to be that way," I continue, my voice growing stronger. "We have the power to change the narrative, to give our young people a chance at a better future."

I talk about the community garden, the mentorship program, and vibrant murals that could adorn many more walls of abandoned buildings. I speak of the potential that lies dormant in our streets, waiting to be awakened.

"Investing in the West Side isn't just about resources," I say, gaze locking with each council member. "It's about believing in our people, our resilience, and our ability to rise above our circumstances."

The room is electric now, and the air is crackling with possibility. I see some council members leaning forward, their expressions thoughtful, while others remain guarded.

"I know firsthand the cost of neglect, of indifference," I say, my voice raw with emotion. "But I also know the power of second chances, of redemption. The West Side is ready for change, ready to write a new chapter in our story."

As I finish speaking, the room erupts into a cacophony of voices, some raised in support, others in opposition. But I stand tall, unshakable, my resolve unwavering.

I remember when we started the garden, planted seeds, and the shoots that broke through the soil. I realize change is like that—fragile at first but unstoppable once it takes root.

As I step down from the podium, surrounded by the din of debate, I feel a flicker of hope ignite in my chest. The road ahead won't be easy, but every journey begins with a single step. And today, we've taken that step towards a brighter, more just future for the West Side.

The sun's warmth caressed my skin as I returned to the community garden. The vibrant colors of blooming flowers and lush vegetables greeted me like an old friend. Coolidge walked beside me, his eyes widening as he took in the transformation before us.

"Can you believe this?" he exclaims, gesturing towards the bustling garden. "Look at all these people, working together, making something beautiful."

I nod, a smile tugging at my lips. "It's amazing what a little hope and hard work can do."

We go through the garden, chatting with volunteers as they tend to the plants. There's a palpable sense of camaraderie in the air, a shared sense of purpose transcending age, race, and background.

An elderly woman, her hands caked with soil, looks up at me with a twinkle in her eye. "You know, young man, I've lived in this neighborhood for over fifty years and never seen anything like this. You've started something special here."

Her words fill me with pride and responsibility. I think back to my struggles, to the choices that led me down a path of darkness. But here, in this garden, I recognize the strength in second chances and the possibilities for growth and redemption.

As Coolidge and I continue our walk, I find myself lost in thought, marveling at the resilience of the human spirit. Against all odds, in the face of adversity and neglect, the people of the West Side have come together to create something beautiful, something hopeful.

The sound of laughter jolts me from my reverie, and I look up to see a group of children, their faces smudged with dirt, giggling as they chase each other through the rows of plants. In their eyes, I can see the future of our community and the promise of a brighter tomorrow.

We leave the garden, our hearts full and our spirits lifted, and walk towards Mary Jane's bakery. As we approach, the aroma of freshly baked bread and the chatter of customers spill out onto the street, a testament to the bakery's success.

Inside, Mary Jane greets us with a warm smile, her apron dusted with flour. "Well, if it isn't my two favorite men," she teases, pulling us both into a hug.

I look around the bakery, taking in the lively atmosphere. People from all walks of life sit at the tables, enjoying pastries and coffee, their conversations mingling in a symphony of community.

"Business is booming, huh?" Coolidge remarks, his eyes widening at the sight of the packed bakery.

Mary Jane nods, pride evident in her voice. "It's been incredible. People come from all over the city now, not just for baked goods, but for the sense of community and belonging."

As I listen to her words, I'm struck by the realization that the bakery, like the garden, has become a symbol of the West Side's resilience, a symbol of optimism in a neighborhood that had been written off by so many.

I think back to the city council meeting and the skepticism and doubt I faced from some members. But here, in the heart of the West Side, I see the proof of our potential, the evidence of what can happen when we believe in ourselves and each other.

"You know," I say, thick with emotion, "this is what it's all about. Building something together fosters a feeling of belonging and purpose. This is how we change the narrative and write a new chapter for the West Side."

Mary Jane and Coolidge nod, their eyes shining with the same hope and determination I feel in my heart. As we stand there, surrounded by the warmth and vitality of the bakery, I know that we are on the cusp of something extraordinary that will transform not just our lives but the lives of generations to come.

Inspired by the positive changes in the community, I find myself compelled to take action and contribute in my own way. The idea of a youth mentorship program takes root in my mind, growing each day until it becomes an undeniable force, a calling I can no longer ignore.

I reach out to local business owners, my voice trembling with nervousness and excitement as I share my vision. To my surprise, they embrace the idea wholeheartedly, their enthusiasm matching mine. Together, we recruit mentors who have walked the path of redemption and emerged stronger, wiser, and more compassionate.

As the program takes shape, I find myself standing before a group of teenagers, their eyes filled with curiosity and apprehension. I take a deep breath, my heart pounding as I share my story, the journey that led me to this moment.

"I know what it's like," I say, my voice barely above a whisper, "to feel lost, like the world has given up on you. But I'm here to tell you there's hope and a chance for a new beginning."

The teens lean in, their attention rapt as I recount the struggles and triumphs of my past, my mistakes, and the lessons I learned. I speak of the power of forgiveness, of the strength that comes from facing one's demons head-on and emerging victorious.

As I look around the room, I see a glimmer of recognition in their eyes, a flicker of possibility that wasn't there before. The atmosphere shifts, the air crackling with newfound energy as the teens open up, sharing their stories, dreams, and fears.

At that moment, I realized that redemption truly means transforming one's life and its ripple effect on those around us. By sharing our experiences and offering guidance and support, we have the power to ignite change, to spark a chain reaction of hope and healing that extends far beyond ourselves.

As the meeting draws close, I experience a profound sense of purpose engulfing me, a clarity of vision I've never experienced before. I know this is just the beginning, and there will be challenges and setbacks. But I also know we have the strength to overcome them and build a brighter future for ourselves and future generations.

With renewed determination, I step forward, ready to embrace the journey ahead and be the change I wish to see in the world. As I do, I feel the weight of my past lifting, filled with hope and possibility that is limitless bounds.

***

As I stand in my modest living room, the weight of the invitation in my hand sends a shiver down my spine. This is a conference on urban renewal, a chance to share our story and inspire others with the transformative power of community. It's a testament to the progress we've made, the lives we've touched, and the hearts we've changed.

But even as pride swells within me, I can't help but feel a twinge of apprehension, a fluttering in my stomach that threatens to overtake me. Who am I to stand before an audience, to speak of hope and redemption when the scars of my past still linger? Can I do justice to our journey and the countless lives our efforts have impacted?

I take a deep breath, closing my eyes as I envision the faces of those who have walked this path with me—Coolidge, with his unwavering determination; Mary Jane, her gentle strength, a beacon in the darkness of my heart for years; and the countless others who have joined us along the way. Their stories, triumphs, and struggles are woven into the fabric of my own, a tapestry of resilience and hope that cannot be denied.

With trembling hands, I reach for a pen, my mind racing as I sketch out the words that will give voice to our collective experience. I know I must speak from the heart, be raw and honest, and be unafraid to bear my soul's depths. Only through vulnerability can we truly connect and inspire others to embark on their transformation journeys.

As the hours pass, the words flow from me like a river, a torrent of emotion and truth that threatens to overwhelm me. I write of the darkness that once consumed me, of the despair that nearly drove me to the brink. But I also write of the light that emerged from within, the spark of hope that refused to be extinguished, no matter how fierce the storm.

While writing, a wave of clarity envelops me, igniting a fresh determination that drives me forward. This is my calling and the path I was meant to walk. While the journey ahead might be filled with challenges, I am ready to face them head-on, armed with the strength of my convictions and the support of those who stand beside me.

With a final flourish, I set down my pen, my heart racing as I survey the words before me. They are a testament to the power of the human spirit and the resilience and courage that lies within us. As I prepare to step onto that stage and share our story with the world, I know that I am not alone and carry the hopes and dreams of an entire community.

This is not just my journey but the journey of us all—a reminder that even in the darkest times, there is always the promise of a brighter tomorrow. And it is up to us to seize that promise, to be the change we wish to see in the world, one heart, one soul, one story at a time.

***

The soft glow of the streetlights filters through the bakery window, casting a warm hue across Mary Jane's face as we sit, our hands wrapped around steaming mugs of tea. The silence between us is comfortable, a testament to the bond we've forged through shared struggles and triumphs.

"You know," Mary Jane says, her voice barely above a whisper, "I never thought I'd see the day when our little corner of the world would be filled with so much hope."

I nod, a smile tugging at the corners of my lips. "It's been a long road. But look at how far we've come, Mary Jane. Look at the lives we've touched, the change we've inspired."

She reaches across the table, her hand finding mine, and I feel the warmth of her touch, the strength of her spirit. "And it's all because of you, Turland. Your courage, your resilience, your unwavering belief in the goodness of people."

I shake my head, humbled by her words. "No, Mary Jane. It's because of us, all of us. Everyone who dared to dream refused to give up, even when the odds were stacked against us."

We sit in silence for a moment, lost in our thoughts, in the memories of the battles we've fought and the victories we've won.

"Do you remember," I say, my voice thick with emotion, "that day when a hot-headed teenage black boy tried to impress you with some shiny jewelry?"

Mary Jane nods, her eyes glistening with unshed tears. "I do. And I remember thinking, even then, that you were destined for great things, Turland. You had a light inside you that nothing could extinguish even as I didn't know your name, but I knew that about you."

I feel a lump forming in my throat, and I blink back my tears. "And you, Mary Jane. You've been my rock, my true guiding star, and if I never found you again, I could say I experienced something special, and I knew that. I couldn't have done any of this without you."

She squeezes my hand, her grip firm and reassuring. "We're in this together, Turland. Always. And no matter what the future holds, I know we'll face it side by side, heart to heart."

I nod, my chest swelling with a love so fierce and all-encompassing that it takes my breath away. And as we sit there, in the quiet of the night, I know that this is what it means to be truly alive, to have found one's purpose, one's reason for being.

Ultimately, it is not the accolades or recognition that matters but the lives we've touched, the hearts we've healed, and the dreams we've ignited. If there are people like Mary Jane in this world who believe in the power of redemption and second chances, then there will always be hope and the promise of a better tomorrow.

And so we sit, our hearts full and our spirits soaring, ready to face whatever the future may bring, secure in the knowledge that we are not alone, that we are part of something greater than ourselves, a tapestry woven from the threads of love, of faith, of the unbreakable human spirit.

Chapter 36: Full Circle

The phone's shrill ring pierced the morning's tranquility. I reached for it, my fingers brushing against the cool plastic. "Hello?"

"Turland, it's Denise." Her voice trembled. "It's Mr. Washington. He's not doing well."

The words hit me like a blow to the chest. I gripped the phone tighter, my heart pounding. "What happened?"

"He collapsed this morning. They've taken him to the hospital." Denise's words came in a rush. "I thought you should know."

"I'll be there as soon as I can. Thank you for calling." I hung up, my mind reeling. Mr. Washington, the pillar of our community, had believed in me when no one else would besides my Grandmother. I couldn't imagine a world without his steady presence.

I found Mary Jane and Coolidge in the kitchen, their faces etched with concern as they took in my expression. "What is it?" Mary Jane asked softly, reaching for my hand.

"It's Mr. Washington," I managed, my throat tight. "He's in the hospital. It doesn't look good."

Mary Jane's warm eyes filled with tears. She pulled me into an embrace, her arms offering solace. Coolidge's jaw clenched, his gaze distant. "He's a fighter," he said finally. "If anyone can pull through, it's him."

We stood there momentarily, united in our worry and love for the man who had been and become a father figure to us all. As the silence stretched, a thought took hold, growing stronger with each passing second.

"The neighborhood festival," I said, looking back at them both. "We have to make it happen, now more than ever. For Mr. Washington."

Mary Jane nodded, her lips curving into a sad smile. "He'd want that. He always said the community was his greatest legacy."

"Then let's make it a celebration he'd be proud of," Coolidge declared, his voice thick with emotion. "A tribute to everything he's done for us."

In that moment, our shared grief transformed into determination. We would honor Mr. Washington in how he'd taught us best—by coming together, lifting each other, and showing the world our neighborhood's resilience and beauty.

The garden had always been a place of solace for me, a sanctuary where I could escape the world's chaos and lose myself in the simple act of nurturing life. As I stepped outside, the vibrant colors and sweet scents of the blooming flowers and ripening vegetables enveloped me, a testament to the love and care poured into this once-barren patch of earth.

I knelt beside a tomato plant, its branches heavy with fruit, and began to prune away the dead leaves carefully. The repetitive motion soothed my troubled thoughts, allowing me to reflect on the journey that had brought us here.

It seemed like a lifetime ago when these streets were filled with despair and decay when hope was a foreign concept to most of us. Slowly, through the tireless efforts of people like Mr. Washington, change took root. The garden was just one manifestation of that transformation—a living, breathing symbol of what could be achieved when a community came together.

As I moved from plant to plant, tending to their needs, I couldn't help but feel a sense of pride in what we had accomplished. The neighborhood was still far from perfect, but a newfound sense of unity and purpose had been absent for so long. And I knew, deep in my heart, that I had played a role in that change.

Lost in my thoughts, I almost didn't hear the footsteps approaching behind me. I turned to see Coolidge, a clipboard in hand and a determined look on his face.

"We need to talk about the festival," he said, his tone serious but tinged with excitement. "I've been going over the plans, and I think we can make this the biggest event the West Side has ever seen."

I stood up, brushing the dirt from my hands. "I'm all ears, Coolidge. What do you have in mind?"

He flipped through the pages on his clipboard, rattling off ideas. "We'll have live music, food stalls, games for the kids... But I thought we could also showcase some of the community's talents. The dance crew, the poetry group, the artists... This could be their moment to shine."

I nodded, a smile spreading across my face. "That's a great idea. It'll be a celebration of everything that makes our neighborhood special."

We began to walk through the garden, discussing the festival's logistics. Coolidge had already started reaching out to volunteers, and the response had been overwhelming. It seemed like everyone wanted to be a part of this, to contribute in their way.

As we talked, I couldn't help but marvel at the man Coolidge had become. Gone was the angry, directionless youth I once knew, replaced by a passionate and dedicated leader. He had found his calling in mentoring the next generation, showing them that there was another path, a better way.

"You know, Coolidge," I said, touching his shoulder. Mr. Washington will be proud of you, of everything you've accomplished."

He looked down, a hint of emotion flickering across his face. "I just hope I can live up to his example. He always believed in me, even when I didn't believe in myself."

"That's what he did best," I replied, my voice soft. "He saw the potential in all of us, even when we were at our lowest. And now, it's our turn to carry on that legacy."

We stood there for a moment, surrounded by the garden's life and beauty, each lost in our memories of the man who had shaped us in many ways. Then, with renewed purpose, we turned our attention back to the festival, to the celebration of community and resilience that would honor Mr. Washington's enduring spirit.

Then, as I stepped back into Mary Jane's bakery, the sweet aroma of freshly baked treats wafted through the air. The tiny bell above the door chimed, announcing my arrival amidst the bustling activity. Mary Jane looked up from the counter, her hands dusted with flour, and a warm smile spread across her face.

"Turland! Just in time to taste my famous lunchroom cookies," she said, gesturing for me to come closer.

I navigated through the crowd of neighbors gathered in the cozy space, exchanging greetings and laughter. The bakery had become more than just a place to satisfy a sweet tooth; it was a sanctuary where the community could unite and find solace in each other's company.

"These smell heavenly, Mary Jane," I remarked, taking a bite of the offered cookie. The perfect blend of sweet and butter danced on my tongue. "You've outdone yourself this time and took me back to school for real."

She beamed with pride, her eyes crinkling at the corners. "Nothing but the best for our community. We've all been through so much; this festival is a chance to celebrate how far we've come."

As I savored the treat, I couldn't help but notice the genuine warmth that radiated from every interaction in the bakery. Neighbors shared stories and offered encouragement, their voices rising and falling in a symphony of camaraderie. At this moment, the bakery felt like the beating heart of our neighborhood, pumping life and love into every corner.

Lost in thought, I almost didn't notice Coolidge entering the bakery, a group of young men trailing behind him. They were laughing and joking, their eyes bright with excitement. Coolidge spotted me and made his way over, a grin spreading.

"Turland, you gotta see what the guys have put together for the mentorship booth," he said, his voice brimming with enthusiasm. "They've been working on it for weeks."

I followed him outside, where a colorful booth adorned with photographs and artwork stood. The young men buzzed around it, making final adjustments and proudly displaying their creations. Coolidge moved among them, offering words of encouragement and guidance.

As I watched him interact with the younger generation, I couldn't help but feel a swell of pride. Coolidge had come far from the troubled young man I had met in prison. Now, he stood as a community pillar, dedicating himself to uplifting and guiding those who needed it most.

"You're doing an amazing job with these young men, Coolidge," I said, my voice filled with admiration. "They look up to you, and it's clear that you're making a real difference in their lives."

Coolidge's eyes shone with emotion as he turned to me. "I wouldn't be here without you. You showed me that change was possible and that I could be more than my past mistakes. I want to pay that forward, to give these guys the same chance I had."

In that moment, surrounded by the vibrant energy of the festival preparations and the love that flowed through our community, I experienced a deep feeling of purpose. We were all connected, each playing a part in the tapestry of our neighborhood's story. And as I looked at Coolidge and the young men he mentored, I knew that our legacy would endure, passed down from generation to generation, a testament to the power of hope and redemption.

***

With the morning sun peeking over the neighborhood, casting a gentle light over the empty lot, I arrived at the festival site, my heart brimming with anticipation. The once desolate space had been transformed overnight, a testament to the tireless efforts of our community. Colorful streamers fluttered in the gentle breeze, their vibrant hues starkly contrasting the weathered brick buildings surrounding us. Booths lined the perimeter, each adorned with handmade signs and decorations showcasing our neighbors' unique talents and passions.

I surveyed the scene, taking in the hum of activity as volunteers bustled about, putting the finishing touches on their displays. The air was thick with freshly cut grass and the tantalizing aroma of food being prepared in the nearby stalls. It was a sensory feast, a celebration of life and resilience in adversity.

As I walked through the lot, I couldn't help but feel a sense of awe at what we had accomplished. Years ago, this space had been a symbol of neglect and despair, a reminder of the challenges that plagued our community. But now, it had been reclaimed, transformed into a beacon of hope and unity.

"Turland!" a voice called out, snapping me from my reverie. I turned to see Ms. Johnson, an elderly woman who had lived in the neighborhood for decades, waving at me from her booth. "Come and see what the children have created!"

I made my way over, a smile spreading across my face as I saw the colorful artwork that adorned the walls of her booth. "These are beautiful," I said, marveling at the intricate designs and heartfelt messages lovingly crafted by the neighborhood's youngest residents.

Ms. Johnson beamed with pride, her eyes glistening with unshed tears. "They poured their hearts into this," she said softly. "Every brushstroke and word is a testament to their love for this community."

As the festival officially began, the lot came alive with the sounds of laughter and music. Families and friends gathered, their faces alight with joy as they embraced one another, sharing stories and memories. Children darted through the crowds, laughter ringing like a symphony of innocence and wonder. The air was electric with a sense of belonging, a feeling that we were all part of something greater than ourselves.

I watched as Coolidge led that group of young men through the festival, their eyes wide with excitement as they took in the sights and sounds. They still hung on his every word, eager to learn from someone who had walked in their shoes and emerged stronger on the other side. It was a decisive moment, a testament to the impact one person could have on the lives of others.

As I walked through the throng of people, I couldn't help but feel a deep sense of fulfillment. This was what community was all about—coming together in times of joy and sorrow, supporting one another through the ups and downs of life. We had faced many challenges over the years, but through it all, we remained strong, united by our shared humanity and unwavering commitment.

As the festival's energy reached its zenith, I ascended the stage steps, my heart pounding with nervousness and profound gratitude. The crowd fell silent, their eyes fixed upon me, waiting for the words that would give voice to the emotions we all shared. I took a deep breath, steadying myself, and began to speak.

"Today, we celebrate not just the spirit of our community but also to honor a man who has been a guiding light for us all. Mr. Washington, your wisdom, your compassion, and your unwavering belief in the potential of every person here have shaped us in ways we can never fully express."

I paused, my eyes seeking out Mr. Washington in the crowd. He sat in a place of honor, his lined face etched with the weight of years and the depth of his experiences. Our eyes met, and in that moment, I saw the flicker of pride and understanding between us.

"You taught us that true strength lies not in the absence of struggle but in the resilience to overcome it. You showed us that hope is not a fleeting dream but a powerful force that can transform lives and communities. And you repeatedly reminded us that we are all bound by the threads of our shared humanity and that by lifting each other, we elevate ourselves."

As I spoke, I could feel the crowd's energy shifting, their emotions rising to the surface. Tears streamed down the faces of those who Mr. Washington's love and kindness had touched, while others nodded in solemn agreement, their hearts swelling with the truth of my words.

"Mr. Washington, we stand here today as a testament to your legacy. The seeds you have planted in each of us have taken root, and we are forever changed by your presence in our lives. We promise to carry your teachings forward, to be the light for others as you have been for us."

My voice caught in my throat as I neared the end of my tribute, the weight of the moment threatening to overwhelm me. But as I looked out at the sea of faces, I saw the strength and resilience that Mr. Washington had nurtured in each of us. We were his legacy, the living embodiment of his hopes and dreams for our community.

"Thank you, Mr. Washington. Thank you for being our mentor, friend, and guiding star. We are forever grateful for the gift of your wisdom, and we pledge to honor your legacy by continuing to build a community rooted in love, compassion, and hope."

As the final words left my lips, the crowd erupted in applause and cheers, their voices rising in a chorus of appreciation and respect. And there, amidst the sea of people, I saw

Mr. Washington, his face shining with the light of a thousand suns. He nodded to me, a small smile playing at the corners of his mouth, and at that moment, I knew that we had truly honored him in the way he deserved.

The festival continued, a whirlwind of music, laughter, and joy, but time seemed too slow for me. I moved through the crowd, my heart full and my mind at peace. We had come so far and endured so much, but in the end, we had emerged stronger, united by our shared love and respect for one another. And as I looked around at the faces of my community, I knew that Mr. Washington's legacy would endure, a shining beacon of hope and inspiration for generations to come.

As the festival continued, I found myself gravitating towards the heart of the celebration, where Mr. Washington and Coolidge stood, their faces etched with the same mixture of pride and contentment that I felt flowing through my veins. The three of us came together, a trio of generations united by a shared love for our community and a fierce determination to see it thrive.

Mr. Washington placed a weathered hand on my shoulder, his eyes sparkling with wisdom that seemed to transcend time. "You've done well, Turland," he said, his voice rich and warm. You've taken the seeds we planted together in each other all those years ago and nurtured them into something beautiful—something that will endure long after we're gone."

Coolidge nodded, his gaze fixed on the vibrant scene before us. "It's like a tapestry," he mused, his words carrying the weight of hard-earned insight. Each of us is just a single thread, but together, we create something stronger and more resilient than any of us could be alone."

I felt a lump form in my throat, overwhelmed by the depth of their words and the enormity of the moment. Here we stood, three generations of dreamers and fighters, each shaped by the struggles and triumphs of our past yet united by a shared vision for a brighter future.

As we stood there, watching the festival unfold around us, I found myself approached by countless community members, each eager to express their gratitude and appreciation for the work we had done. Their words washed over me like a balm, soothing the scars of past struggles and filling me with a renewed sense of purpose.

"Thank you, Turland," a woman said, her eyes brimming with tears of joy. My children have a safe place to play, where they can dream and grow. And that's because of you."

A young man, barely older than I had been when I first set foot on this path, gripped my hand tightly, his voice trembling with emotion. "You showed me that there's another way," he said, his gaze fierce and unwavering. "That we don't have to be defined by our circumstances, that we can rise above and create something better."

With each interaction, I felt the bonds of our community growing stronger; the sense of unity and purpose that had once seemed like an impossible dream was now a tangible reality. As the sun set over the festival, its golden light illuminated the faces of those around me, and I knew this was just the beginning.

We had weathered the past's storms and fought tooth and nail for the right to dream and hope.

The future stretched out before us, a canvas waiting to be painted in the vibrant hues of our shared dreams. Looking at Mr. Washington and Coolidge, I knew we wouldn't be the only ones to face challenges. Still, hopefully, others will have the same courage, resilience, and unbreakable spirit that had always defined our community.

I found myself drawn to the quiet sanctuary of the community garden. The scent of rich earth and vibrant blooms filled my senses as I stepped along the well-worn path, my footsteps a whisper against the soft ground.

At the garden's edge, I paused, my gaze drifting over the flourishing plots that had once been barren soil. The transformation was breathtaking, a testament to the love and dedication poured into every seed and sprout.

In this tranquil oasis, my mind wandered to the journey that had brought me to this moment. The memories of my past, once heavy and suffocating, now felt distant, like fading shadows in the brilliant light of the present.

I thought of the young man I had been, trapped in a cycle of despair and hopelessness, unable to see a future beyond the confines of my circumstances. The prison walls had held more than just my physical form; they had imprisoned my spirit, my dreams, and my sense of self.

But in the darkest times, a flicker of hope ignited within me based on God and the smile of a woman I didn't even get her name. That smile was a tiny ember that refused to be extinguished. That hope sustained me and guided me through all the trials and tribulations of my transformation.

I felt an overwhelming sense of gratitude as I stood there, surrounded by the fruits of our collective labor. I was grateful for the second chance I had been given, for the people who had believed in me when I couldn't believe in myself, and for the strength I had found within to forge a new path.

My role as a community leader, a distant and unattainable dream, was now a cherished reality. The trust and respect I had earned from those around me was a gift beyond measure, a reminder of the power of perseverance and the resilience of the human spirit.

With a deep breath, I turned back towards the festival, my heart filled with a renewed sense of purpose. As I rejoined the celebration, my neighbors' laughter and chatter enveloped me like a warm embrace.

The smiles, joy in their eyes, and unity in their voices were a powerful reminder of what we had achieved together. Once fractured and weighed down by the burdens of the past, our community had emerged stronger, more vibrant, and more connected than ever before.

And at the heart of it all, our elders' enduring wisdom and guidance shone like a beacon. Mr. Washington, Coolidge, and the countless others who paved the way for us were a testament to the unbreakable spirit that had carried our neighborhood through the darkest times.

As the festival continued into the night, the glow of string lights and the rhythm of music filling the air, I knew that this was more than a celebration. It was a declaration of hope, a promise to honor the legacy of those who had come before us and to build a brighter future for future generations.

With each passing moment, I felt the weight of my past falling away, replaced by a profound sense of belonging and purpose. The journey had been long and arduous, but every step, every struggle, and every triumph had led me to this moment.

As I looked out over the sea of faces, each reflecting the love and resilience that had brought us together, I knew this was exactly where I was meant to be. No longer a prisoner of my past, I was a leader, a dreamer, and a beacon of hope for the community I call home.

Chapter 37: New Horizons

The morning sun pours through the kitchen window, lighting up the newspaper on the aged wooden table in front of me. My eyes scan the headlines, absorbing the stories of a community that has started to shine in the eyes of many. An article about local leaders caught my attention, and I found myself lingering on the section discussing potential candidates for the upcoming election.

"You know," I say, glancing up at Mary Jane as she pours a cup of coffee, "I've been thinking about running for office."

She raises an eyebrow, a smile playing at the corners of her lips. "Oh? And what brought this on?"

I shrug, leaning back in my chair. "Just seeing all the change happening around us, the progress we've made. I want to be a part of that, to keep pushing things forward for even more people and communities."

Mary Jane sets her mug down and sits beside me, her hand finding mine. "Turland, you've already done so much for this community. Your story, your journey—it's inspired so many people."

I nod, feeling the weight of her words settles in my chest. The path that led me here, from the cold confines of a prison cell to this warm, sunlit kitchen, has been like a winding road. But every step, stumble, and triumph has brought me closer to this moment for this feeling of a deeper purpose.

The front door opens, and Coolidge enters with a wide grin. In his hand, he clutches a letter with a university logo emblazoned on the envelope.

"I got in," he announces, his voice brimming with excitement. "The social work program at the university—they accepted me!"

Mary Jane leaps to her feet, engulfing her son in a tight embrace. "Oh, Coolidge! I'm so proud of you!"

I rise from my chair, my smile mirroring theirs. As I join their hug, I feel the weight of the past lifting, replaced by a deep optimism for the future.

"Congratulations, son," I say, clasping Coolidge's shoulder. "You're going to do amazing things."

Coolidge's eyes meet mine, and in them, I see a reflection of my journey—the struggles, the doubts, and the unwavering determination to break free from the chains of the past.

"I couldn't have done it without you," he says, his voice thick with emotion. "Seeing you change, seeing the difference you've made, showed me that anything is possible."

As we stand there, basking in the glow of this shared moment, I feel a deep sense of gratitude wash over me. The road that brought us here has been paved with pain and sacrifice, but it has also been illuminated by the power of second chances, of redemption hard-fought and well-earned.

As I look out the window at the neighborhood that has become a testament to the strength of the human spirit, I know this is only the beginning. Together, we will continue to build a future filled with hope, one where every story has the chance to be rewritten and every dream has the opportunity to take flight.

Mary Jane's words echo in my mind as Coolidge and I step out into the neighborhood, the sun-dappled streets alive with the energy of change. We walk side by side, our footsteps falling into a shared rhythm, a testament to the bond that has grown between us.

"I never thought I'd see the day," Coolidge muses, his gaze sweeping over the freshly painted storefronts and the vibrant murals that adorn the walls. "This place, it's like a different world now."

I nod, a smile tugging at the corners of my lips. "It's a world we built together, brick by brick, story by story."

We pause at a corner, watching young people emerge from a newly renovated community center. Their laughter rings out like a promise of brighter days to come.

"You know," I say, turning to face Coolidge, "seeing all this, seeing the impact we've made—it makes me wonder if I could do more."

Coolidge raises an eyebrow, curiosity sparking in his eyes. "What do you mean?"

I take a deep breath, the words swirling in my mind, finally reaching the surface. "I've been thinking about running for office, about being a voice for our community on a bigger stage."

Coolidge's face turns into a grin, and he claps me. "Dad, that's incredible! You'd be amazing at it."

We resume our walk, the idea taking root, spreading its tendrils through my thoughts. "I never thought I'd be in a position even to consider something like this," I confess. "But now, after everything we've been through, I feel like I have a responsibility to keep pushing forward and fighting for what's right."

Coolidge nods, understanding etched into his features. "You've already changed so many lives, Dad. Imagine what you could do with a platform like that."

We come around the block, and the sight of our home comes back into view, where the warmth of Mary Jane's love radiates from its walls. "I wouldn't be here without you," I say softly, my voice thick with emotion. "Without both of you."

Coolidge's hand finds mine, and he squeezes it tightly. "We're a team, Dad. Always have been, always will be."

As we climb the steps to our front door, a revitalized sense of purpose ignites within me, fueled by the love and support of my family and the enduring resilience of my community, which has become my heart and soul.

Deep within my soul, I am confident this is just the start of a journey that will elevate us to unimaginable heights toward a future shaped by hope, redemption, and the unbreakable power of love.

As we step inside, the aroma of Mary Jane's freshly baked bread envelops us, a comforting embrace that whispers of home and belonging. Coolidge heads to the kitchen, eager to share more of his news with his mother, while I linger in the living room, my gaze drawn to the framed photographs that adorn the walls—snapshots of a life reclaimed, of love rediscovered.

A knock at the door pulls me from my reverie, and I open it to find Big Mike standing on the porch with a shy smile. "Hey, Mr. Deville," he says, his voice tinged with a newfound confidence. "I hope I'm not interrupting."

"Not at all, Big Mike," I reply, ushering him inside. "You're always welcome here."

We settle onto the couch, and Big Mike begins to share the latest developments in his life—a steady job at the local auto shop, a budding romance with a young woman he met at the community center, a revitalized sense of life that radiates in his eyes.

"I couldn't have done it without you," he says, his voice thick with emotion. "You believed in me when no one else did when I didn't even believe in myself."

I place a hand on his shoulder, my heart swelling with pride. "You did the hard work, Big Mike. You chose to change, to build a better life for yourself. That takes courage and strength."

Big Mike nods, his eyes glistening with unshed tears. "I just want to make you proud, Mr. Deville. To show you that your faith in me wasn't misplaced."

"You already have, Big Mike," I assure him, my voice wavering. "More than you could ever know."

We sit in comfortable silence for a moment, the weight of our shared history, of the bonds forged through struggle and triumph, hanging in the air between us.

Finally, I clear my throat, thinking about the task ahead. "I'm going back to the prison tomorrow," I say softly, my gaze fixed on the carpet at my feet. I'm going to speak to the inmates to share my story."

Big Mike's eyes widen, and understanding dawns on his face. "That's a big step," he murmurs, his voice laced with concern. Are you ready for that?"

I take a deep breath, the memories of those long, lonely years behind bars flooding my mind, the echoes of despair and hopelessness that once threatened to consume me. "I have to be," I whisper, my voice barely audible. "For them, for myself, for everyone who's ever felt like they didn't deserve a second chance."

Big Mike reaches out, his hand clasping mine in a silent gesture of support and solidarity. "You've got this, Mr. Deville," he says, conviction ringing in his tone. If anyone can make a difference, it's you."

I nod, a flicker of determination igniting in my chest, a stronger flame with each passing moment. "I just hope they'll listen," I confess, my voice raw with emotion. "They'll see that change is possible, that there's hope, even in the darkest places."

Big Mike smiles, a knowing glint in his eye. "They will," he assures me, his words infused with a wisdom beyond his years. "Because you're living proof of it, Mr. Deville. You're a testament to the power of redemption and the strength within us all."

I feel a sense of calm wash over me, a quiet strength that arises from the love and encouragement of those who have shared this journey with me.

As I prepare to face the ghosts of my past and confront the demons that once held me captive, I know that I am not alone. The seeds of love and transformation that I have sown in the lives of others will continue to flourish and bloom into a future filled with promise and possibility.

***

The towering gates of the prison loom before me, a stark reminder of the life I once led, the mistakes that defined my existence for so long. As I step out of the car, the weight of my past seems to press down upon my shoulders, a tangible presence threatening to suffocate me.

But then I feel a gentle hand on my arm, and I turn to see the warden, a man whose eyes hold a glimmer of understanding and compassion. "Welcome back, Mr. Deville," he says, his voice a soothing balm to my frayed nerves. We're honored to have you here today."

I nod, swallowing past the lump in my throat, the emotions that threaten to overwhelm me. "Thank you," I manage, my words a mere whisper in the face of the momentous task ahead.

As we walk through the narrow corridors, the echoes of my footsteps mingling with the distant murmur of voices, I am struck by the familiarity of it all, the sense of déjà vu that washes over me like a tidal wave. But there is a difference now, a shift in the air, a newfound purpose propelling me.

We enter the assembly hall, and I am greeted by a sea of faces, a tapestry of stories and struggles etched into every line, every scar. For a moment, I am transported back to my own time behind these walls, the endless days and nights spent grappling with the demons that haunted me.

But as I take my place at the podium, the weight of my past seems to lift, replaced by a sense of clarity, of purpose. I clear my throat, my voice trembling with the force of the emotions that surge through me.

"I stand before you today not as a stranger but as someone who has walked in your shoes, who has known the depths of despair and the heights of hope," I begin, my words echoing through the cavernous space. "I am here to tell you that change is possible, that redemption is within reach, no matter how far you may have fallen."

As I speak, I can see the flicker of recognition in their eyes, the dawning realization that I am one of them, that I have emerged from the same darkness that threatens to consume them. And with each word, each confession, I feel the weight of my past lifting, the shackles of shame and regret falling away.

"I was once where you are now," I continue, my voice growing stronger and more assured. "Lost, broken, convinced that I was beyond saving. But even in my darkest moments, there was a spark of hope, a glimmer of possibility that refused to be extinguished."

I tell them of my journey, the choices that led me to this moment, and the people who believed in me when I could not believe in myself. As I speak, I see the transformation before my eyes: the hardened faces softening, the guarded eyes filling with tears.

"Your past does not define you," I declare, my voice ringing out with a conviction that startles even me. "You are not the sum of your mistakes, the product of your circumstances. You are so much more than that, every one of you."

As I look out at the sea of faces, the men and women cast aside by society, forgotten and forsaken, I am driven by a profound sense of being human at this moment, a deep desire to be the source of hope I once yearned for.

And at that moment, I knew that this was my calling, my destiny, to be the voice for the voiceless, the champion for the downtrodden. To show them that there is a way out, a path to redemption, and a future worth fighting for.

As my speech comes to a close, the assembly hall erupts in applause, a thunderous ovation that shakes the very foundations of the prison. Inmates rush forward, their eyes glistening with unshed tears, their hands outstretched in gratitude.

One by one, they approach me, their stories tumbling from their lips in a cathartic release. They speak of their regrets, fears, and dreams for a better life. And as I listen, my heart swells with empathy, understanding, and a fierce determination to be the catalyst for change.

"Thank you," a young man whispers, his voice trembling with emotion. "Your words gave me hope, made me believe I could be something more than this."

I clasp his hand in mine, feeling the weight of his struggle, the burden of his past. "You can," I assure him, my eyes locked on his. "You have the power within you to rewrite your story, to create a new ending."

As the inmates file out of the assembly hall, their steps are slightly lighter, their heads held a little higher. I feel a strong sense of understanding and a revived dedication to the cause that has shaped my life work.

The drive back to the Patterson home is a blur, my mind still reeling from the intensity of the experience. As I pull in front of the house, I am greeted by a flurry of activity, laughter, and music spilling into the warm evening air.

Inside, the house is a bustling hive of preparation, family and friends scurrying about with plates of food and decorations. The atmosphere is electric, with a palpable sense of excitement and anticipation.

"Turland!" Mary Jane exclaims, her face breaking into a radiant smile as she rushes forward to embrace me. "We're so glad you're here. Coolidge will be thrilled to see you."

I return her hug, feeling the warmth of her love, the strength of her support. "I wouldn't miss it for the world," I reply, my voice thick with emotion.

As I make my way through the crowd, exchanging greetings and well-wishes, my heart swells with pride and gratitude for the incredible journey that has brought me to this moment. And as I catch sight of Coolidge, his face alight with joy and accomplishment.

Coolidge spots me from across the room, his eyes widening with surprise and delight. He makes his way through the throng of well-wishers, his gait confident and purposeful.

"Turland," he says, his voice brimming with emotion as he pulls me into a tight embrace. "I'm so glad you made it back from visiting the prison. It means the world to me to have you here."

I hold him close, my heart swelling with pride and affection. "I am so proud of you, Coolidge," I murmur, my words catching in my throat. "You've accomplished so much; this is just the beginning."

We pull apart, and Coolidge's eyes shine with unshed tears. "I couldn't have done it without you," he says softly, his voice raw and honest. "Your support, your guidance... it's made all the difference."

I shake my head, a smile tugging at the corners of my mouth. "No, Coolidge. This is all you. Your hard work, your determination. You've earned this every step of the way."

We stand there momentarily, lost in the significance of this shared experience, our bond stronger than ever. Around us, the party continues in full swing, the laughter and chatter a joyful symphony.

"I've been thinking a lot about the future," Coolidge says, his tone turning contemplative. "About the work that still needs to be done, the changes we need to make in our community."

I nod, understanding the weight of his words. "It's a long road ahead," I agree, "but I believe in the power of what we can achieve together. We must keep pushing forward and fighting for what's right."

Coolidge's eyes sparkle with determination, with a fierce commitment to making a difference. "I'm ready," he declares, his voice ringing with conviction. "I want to be a part of that change also, to use my education and experiences to help others, to give back to the community that's given me so much."

My heart swells with admiration and profound gratitude for the incredible young man standing before me. "I do not doubt you will," I say, thick with emotion. And I'll be right there with you every step of the way."

We once more embrace our connection, a palpable force, a testament to the power of love, family, and the unbreakable bonds that have carried us through the darkest times and into the light of a brighter future.

As we rejoin the celebration, mingling with the guests and basking in the warmth of this incredible community, I am filled with hope, possibility, and the limitless potential that exists ahead. I firmly believe that collectively, we can conquer any obstacle, confront any challenge, and create a world filled with deeper understanding, compassion, and justice.

I step onto the porch, the cool evening air a gentle caress against my skin. The sounds of laughter and music from the party drift into the night, a joyful symphony that fills my heart with warmth. I lean against the railing, my eyes sweeping over the gathering of community members, each face a reflection of the love and support that has carried me through this incredible journey.

In the soft glow of the porch light, I see the faces of those who have stood by me and believed in me when I couldn't believe in myself. I see the faces of those whose lives I've touched and whose stories have intertwined with mine. And I see the faces of a community transformed, a neighborhood that has risen from the ashes of despair to become a beacon of hope and possibility.

I feel a gentle hand on my shoulder as I stand there, lost in thought. I turn to see Mary Jane, her eyes shimmering with unshed tears, and Coolidge, his smile a radiant beacon of pride and love. At that moment, I feel deeply grateful for the grace I've received from this wonderful community.

"I want to thank you both," I begin, my voice trembling. Thank you for allowing me to reset my life and for allowing me to become the man I always hoped I could be. None of this would have been possible without your love, support, and unwavering belief in me."

I turn to Mary Jane, taking her hands in mine, my heart pounding with the weight of the words I'm about to speak. "Mary Jane, had it not been for the day I first laid eyes on you, none of this would be happening. I held on to your smile for thirty years, and if you would bless me by being my wife, I could hold on to you forever more."

Tears stream down Mary Jane's face, her voice a whisper of raw emotion. "I want to hold on to you forever, too. That day at the jewelry store reset our lives, and we didn't know it."

Coolidge looks at both of us, his smile reflecting the love and pride that fills his heart. "You are welcome," he says while pointing at himself, his words a testament to this unbreakable family bond.

Standing together, enveloped in the warmth of our love, I know we all feel the same profound sense of hope, renewal, and limitless opportunities. The journey ahead remains challenging, with many obstacles to face. However, I am confident that we can accomplish anything through the love of this family, the support of this fantastic community, and the strength of my beliefs.

And so, as the night sky sparkles with the promise of a brighter tomorrow, I embrace my loved ones, my heart overflowing with gratitude and hope. In this moment, I am not just a man given a second chance but a symbol of the transformative power of love, redemption, and the human spirit's unbreakable resilience.

Chapter 38: A Night of Grace

Turland sat quietly on the front porch steps, his eyes fixed on the vast sky above him. The stars twinkled like countless diamonds scattered across an endless velvet canvas, their light piercing through the darkness that had once defined his world. He breathed deeply, taking in the cool night air and savoring the silence that enveloped him—a stark contrast to the constant clamor of prison life.

Memories of the day flashed through his mind like a kaleidoscope of emotions. He saw the faces of the inmates, their eyes filled with a glimmer of hope as he spoke to them about second chances and the power of redemption. He recalled the proud smile on his son's face, a boy he had never imagined he would have the privilege to raise. And then there was Mary Jane, her gentle "yes" still echoing in his ears, a promise of a future he had once thought impossible.

Exhaustion and gratitude intertwined within him, forming a bittersweet knot in his chest. Thirty years behind bars had taught him to cherish moments like these, to hold onto them like precious jewels, knowing that they were fleeting and rare.

The soft creak of the screen door broke his reverie, and he turned to see Mary Jane stepping outside. She moved with a gentle grace, her presence a comforting warmth amidst the cool night breeze. She held two steaming mugs of tea in her hands, the wisps of steam dancing in the moonlight.

She sat beside him, her shoulder brushing against his, and handed him one of the mugs. The silence between them was warm and familiar, a language they had learned to speak without words. It was the connection forged through their time of shared struggles and unwavering faith, a bond that had survived the test of time and distance.

Turland sipped the tea, the warm liquid soothing his throat and settling in his stomach. He glanced at Mary Jane, her profile illuminated by the soft glow of the porch light. At that moment, he saw the woman he loved and the embodiment of hope.

"I never thought I'd see a night like this," he whispered, his voice barely audible above the chirping of crickets in the distance. "A night where I'm not staring at cold concrete walls, wondering if I'll ever breathe free air again."

Mary Jane reached for his hand, her fingers intertwining with his. "But you did, Turland. You made it through. And now, you're here, with me, with our son. You're home."

Turland nodded, a lump forming in his throat. Home. The word tasted foreign on his tongue, yet it filled him with a warmth he had never known before. He squeezed Mary Jane's hand, marveling at the softness of her skin against his calloused palm.

"I couldn't have done it without you," he said, his eyes meeting hers. "Your love, faith, and smile... kept me going, even in the darkest times."

Mary Jane smiled, her eyes glistening with unshed tears. "And your strength, your resilience... it inspired me, Turland. It gave me hope when I thought I had none left. I was just what I thought was a single black woman trying to keep her son out of jail."

They sat in comfortable silence, their gazes drifting back to the starry sky above. The vastness of the universe seemed to mirror the depth of their love, infinite and boundless. At that moment, Turland knew he was where God intended for him to be and ordered these steps. No matter what challenges lay ahead, God knew they could face them together, hand in hand, their hearts beating as one.

"You know," Turland began, his voice low and contemplative, "there were times in prison when I thought I'd never make it out. Days when the walls seemed to close in on me, the darkness threatened to swallow me whole, and when my grandmother passed away, realizing I would never see her again."

He paused, his gaze fixed on the distant horizon. "Still, even in those moments, I found hope. Something that kept me going, no matter how hard it got."

Mary Jane turned to him, her eyes searching his face. "What was it?" she asked softly.

Turland's lips curved into a gentle smile. "Prayer," he said. "Talking to God every single day. Pouring out my fears, regrets, and hopes... it became my lifeline."

He closed his eyes, memories flooding his mind—the solitude of his cell and the whispered words that echoed in the stillness: "I'd pray for strength, guidance, forgiveness. And somehow, amid all that darkness, I'd feel a flicker of light—a sense of peace that I couldn't explain."

Mary Jane listened intently, her hand still clasped in his. She could feel the depth of his emotions and the raw honesty of his words.

"There were times when I doubted when I questioned everything," Turland continued, his voice thick with emotion. "But even then, I could feel God's presence. Like a constant companion, walking beside me through the storm and, when needed, calming those storms."

He turned to face Mary Jane, his eyes shining with a new-found clarity. "And now, looking back, I can see how every step of that journey led me here. To this moment, with you."

Mary Jane felt a tear slip down her cheek, moved by Turland's vulnerability. "Your faith is inspiring," she whispered, her voice trembling slightly. It's a testament to your spirit and your soul's resilience."

Turland reached out, gently wiping away her tear with his thumb. "It was that faith that kept me holding on to your memory," he said softly. "The thought of your smile and laughter was a beacon of hope in the darkness, and I didn't even know your name, but God did."

Mary Jane leaned into his touch, her heart swelling with love and admiration. "And now, we have a lifetime ahead of us," she said, her eyes sparkling with promise—a future filled with love, family, and new beginnings."

Turland nodded, his gaze drifting back to the stars above. "I never thought I'd have this," he admitted quietly. "A second chance, an opportunity at redemption. But here I am, with you by my side, and I know anything is possible."

They sat silently for a moment, their hearts beating in sync, their souls intertwined. The night air whispered around them, offering a fresh beginning and a new chapter in their narrative.

As they held each other close, Turland understood that regardless of what awaited him, he would confront it with the same steadfast faith that had seen him through his darkest moments. For in Mary Jane's love, in the warmth of her embrace, he had found one of the true gifts that comes from grace. And that was a gift he would cherish for the rest of his days.

Mary Jane's gentle voice broke the silence, her words soothing my weary soul. "Your strength, your resilience... it's inspiring, Turland," she said, her fingers intertwining with mine. "You've overcome so much, and now, you're using your experiences to make a difference in the lives of others."

I nodded, feeling a wave of tranquility embrace me. "I understand that it won't be easy," I admitted, my thumb tracing gentle circles on her skin. "But I can take on the world with you."

Mary Jane leaned her head on my shoulder, her presence comforting against the cool night air. "We've both faced our share of challenges," she said softly, her words a gentle reminder of our struggles. But through it all, we've found strength in each other, in the love we share."

I felt a smile tug at the corners of my mouth, a sense of gratitude swelling within my chest. "You're right," I said, kissing her forehead tenderly. "And that love, that connection... it's what will guide us through whatever the future holds."

We sat there momentarily, lost in the night's beauty and the warmth of each other's presence. Holding Mary Jane close, I knew I had found something precious and worth fighting for.

I turned to face Mary Jane, my heart swelling with the depths of my emotions. "You know," I began, my voice soft yet filled with conviction, "I used to dream about moments like this, about a future where I could be the man I knew I was meant to be."

Mary Jane's eyes glistened in the starlight, a gentle smile gracing her lips. "And now, here you are, living that dream," she said, soothingly balm to my soul.

I reached out, cupping her face in my hands, my thumbs brushing away the stray tears that had begun to fall. "building a life with you," I whispered, my forehead resting gently against hers. "A life filled with love, laughter, and all the beautiful moments we've been dreaming of."

Mary Jane's breath hitched, her hands resting on my chest. "I want that too, Turland," she murmured, her voice a soft caress in the night. "More than anything."

We stayed like that for a moment, lost in the intimacy of our connection.

"I love you, Mary Jane," I breathed, lips brushing softly against hers. "With every fiber of my being, I love you."

She smiled, her eyes shining with the radiance of a thousand stars. "And I love you, Turland," she whispered, a sacred vow in the stillness of the night: "Always and forever."

A hush fell over us as we turned our gazes upward, the vast expanse of the night sky stretching out like an endless canvas. The stars twinkled above, their gentle light casting a soft glow upon our faces. At that moment, the rest of the world seemed to fade away, leaving only the two of us beneath the celestial tapestry.

As I stared at the heavens, my mind drifted back to the countless nights I'd spent in my cell, searching for solace in the tiny sliver of sky visible through the barred window. Back then, the stars were my only companions, the silent witnesses to my prayers and dreams. And now, here I was, standing beside the woman I loved, marveling at the beauty of the universe.

"Thank you," I whispered, my voice barely audible above the soft rustling of the leaves in the breeze.

Mary Jane squeezed my hand, her eyes still fixed on the stars above.

I nodded, my heart swelling with a profound sense of gratitude. Closing my eyes, I began to pray, the words flowing from my lips like a gentle stream.

"Dear Lord," I whispered, my voice trembling with emotion, "I come before you tonight with a heart filled with thanks. I am forever grateful for the blessings you've bestowed upon me and the love you've brought into my life."

The stars seemed to pulse in response, their light growing brighter as I continued my prayer.

"Through the trials and the darkness, you never left my side. You guided, strengthened, and showed me the power of your grace. And now, as I'm here with Mary Jane, I know that your love has been the force that has sustained me, the light that has led me home."

Tears began to stream down my face, but I made no move to wipe them away. They were tears of joy, of relief, of a love so profound that it defied words.

"Thank you for this second chance, for the opportunity to build a life filled with purpose and meaning. May our love be a testament to your goodness, a shining example of the redemption possible through your grace."

As I finished my prayer, I experienced an overwhelming peace, a tranquility I had never known. When I opened my eyes, Mary Jane gazed at me, her cheeks glistening with tears.

"Amen," she whispered, her voice raw with emotion.

I pulled her close, our bodies molding together as we stood beneath the starlit sky. And in that perfect moment, I knew we were exactly where we were both meant to be, two souls bound together by a love that had withstood the test of time and the trials of fate.

She reached out, her fingers intertwining with mine, our hands perfectly fitting. "Your journey exemplifies the strength of transformation and redemption, a reminder that no matter how far we may stray, there is always a path back to grace."

I felt my heart swell with emotion, my love for this woman growing deeper with each passing second. She had been my anchor, my guiding star, the one constant in a world that had often felt like shifting sands beneath my feet.

Her words echoed the sentiments of my own heart, a perfect reflection of the hopes and dreams we shared. I pulled her closer, our foreheads touching as we breathed in the sweet night air.

"I love you, Mary Jane," I whispered, my voice raw with emotion. "More than words could ever express. You are my home, my haven, the one person who sees me for who I truly am and loves me all the same."

She smiled, her eyes shining with a love that took my breath away. "And I love you, Turland. With every fiber of my being, with every beat of my heart. You are my soulmate, my partner in this life journey, and I will stand by your side, now and forevermore."

Our love had been forged in the fires of adversity, shaped by the challenges we faced in our pasts. But it had emerged a more substantial and purer, shining light on a hill of hope in a world that had often felt shrouded in darkness.

The stars above twinkled in silent approval, their ethereal light casting a gentle glow upon our intertwined hands. In this moment of tranquility, the world seemed to fade away, leaving only the two of us lost in our love and gratitude depths.

Her chest's gentle rise and fall against mine brought back memories of the life we tirelessly built together and the dreams we cultivated despite the challenges we faced.

"Turland," Mary Jane whispered, her voice a soothing melody amidst the crickets chirping. I never knew it was possible to love someone this deeply, to feel so complete in another's presence."

I turned to face her, my eyes locking with hers, a silent conversation passing between us. In the depths of her gaze, I saw the reflection of my soul, the missing piece I had searched for all my life.

As the night wore on, we remained there, wrapped in each other's arms, our hearts beating in perfect synchrony. And as I closed my eyes, a whispered prayer of thanks escaped my lips again, carried on the gentle breeze to the heavens above.

For in this moment, I had everything I could ever need, everything I had ever dreamed of. And with Mary Jane by my side, I knew that our journey was only beginning, a beautiful tapestry waiting to be woven, one precious thread at a time.

The End